**J. R. Ward** lives in the South with her incredibly supportive husband and her beloved golden retriever. After graduating from law school, she began working in health care in Boston and spent many years as chief of staff for one of the premier academic medical centres in the nation.

Visit J. R. Ward online:

www.jrward.com
www.facebook.com/JRWardBooks
@jrward1

*By J. R. Ward*

*The Anne Ashburn series:*

The Wedding From Hell:
The Rehearsal Dinner*
The Wedding From Hell:
The Reception*
Consumed

*The Black Dagger Brotherhood series:*

Dark Lover
Lover Eternal
Lover Revealed
Lover Awakened
Lover Unbound
Lover Enshrined
Lover Avenged
Lover Mine
Lover Unleashed
Lover Reborn
Lover at Last
The King
The Shadows
The Beast
The Chosen
Dearest Ivie*
The Thief
Prisoner of Night*
The Savior

The Black Dagger Brotherhood:
An Insider's Guide

*Black Dagger Legacy series:*

Blood Kiss
Blood Vow
Blood Fury
Blood Truth

*Fallen Angels series:*

Covet
Crave
Envy
Rapture
Possession
Immortal

*The Bourbon Kings series:*

The Bourbon Kings
The Angels' Share
Devil's Cut

*Standalone:*

An Irresistible Bachelor
An Unforgettable Lady

*ebook novella

# J.R. WARD

## THE BLACK DAGGER LEGACY

# BLOOD TRUTH

piatkus

PIATKUS

First published in the US in 2019 by Gallery Books,
an imprint of Simon & Schuster, Inc.
First published in Great Britain in 2019 by Piatkus

13 5 7 9 10 8 6 4 2

Copyright © 2019 by Love Conquers All, Inc.

Interior design by Davina Mock-Maniscalco

The moral right of the author has been asserted.

A CIP catalogue record for this book
is available from the British Library.

Hardback ISBN 978-0-349-42396-8
Trade paperback ISBN 978-0-349-42063-9

Printed and bound in Great Britain by Clays Ltd, Elcograf S.p.A.

Papers used by Piatkus are from well-managed forests
and other responsible sources.

Piatkus
An imprint of
Little, Brown Book Group
Carmelite House
50 Victoria Embankment
London EC4Y 0DZ

An Hachette UK Company
www.hachette.co.uk

www.littlebrown.co.uk

*To Jennifer Lynn Armentrout,*
*with so much love and respect.*
*"I just really like you."*

# GLOSSARY OF TERMS
# AND PROPER NOUNS

*ahstrux nohtrum* (**n.**) Private guard with license to kill who is granted his or her position by the King.

*ahvenge* (**v.**) Act of mortal retribution, carried out typically by a male loved one.

**Black Dagger Brotherhood** (**pr. n.**) Highly trained vampire warriors who protect their species against the Lessening Society. As a result of selective breeding within the race, Brothers possess immense physical and mental strength, as well as rapid healing capabilities. They are not siblings, for the most part, and are inducted into the Brotherhood upon nomination by the Brothers. Aggressive, self-reliant, and secretive by nature, they are the subjects of legend and objects of reverence within the vampire world. They may be killed only by the most serious of wounds, e.g., a gunshot or stab to the heart, etc.

**blood slave** (**n.**) Male or female vampire who has been subjugated to serve the blood needs of another. The practice of keeping blood slaves has been outlawed.

**the Chosen** (**pr. n.**) Female vampires who had been bred to serve the Scribe Virgin. In the past, they were spiritually rather than temporally focused, but that changed with the ascendance of the final Primale, who freed them from the Sanctuary. With the Scribe Virgin removing herself from her role, they are completely autonomous and learning to live on earth. They do continue to meet the blood needs of unmated members of the Brotherhood, as well as Brothers who cannot feed from their *shellans*, or injured fighters.

*chrih* (**n.**) Symbol of honorable death in the Old Language.

*cohntehst* (**n.**) Conflict between two males competing for the right to be a female's mate.

**Dhunhd** (**pr. n.**) Hell.

*doggen* (**n.**) Member of the servant class within the vampire world. *Doggen* have old, conservative traditions about service to their superiors, following a formal code of dress and behavior. They are able to go out during the day, but they age relatively quickly. Life expectancy is approximately five hundred years.

*ehros* (**n.**) A Chosen trained in the matter of sexual arts.

*exhile dhoble* (**n.**) The evil or cursed twin, the one born second.

**the Fade** (**pr. n.**) Nontemporal realm where the dead reunite with their loved ones and pass eternity.

**First Family** (**pr. n.**) The King and Queen of the vampires, and any children they may have.

*ghardian* (**n.**) Custodian of an individual. There are varying degrees of *ghardians*, with the most powerful being that of a *sehcluded* female.

*glymera* (**n.**) The social core of the aristocracy, roughly equivalent to Regency England's *ton*.

*hellren* (**n.**) Male vampire who has been mated to a female. Males may take more than one female as mate.

*hyslop* (**n. or v.**) Term referring to a lapse in judgment, typically resulting in the compromise of the mechanical operations of a vehicle or otherwise motorized conveyance of some kind. For example, leaving one's keys in one's car as it is parked outside the family home overnight, whereupon said vehicle is stolen.

*leahdyre* (**n.**) A person of power and influence.

*leelan* (**adj. or n.**) A term of endearment loosely translated as "dearest one."

**Lessening Society** (**pr. n.**) Order of slayers convened by the Omega for the purpose of eradicating the vampire species.

*lesser* (**n.**) De-souled human who targets vampires for extermination as a member of the Lessening Society. *Lessers* must be stabbed through the chest in order to be killed; otherwise they are ageless. They do not eat or drink and are impotent. Over time, their hair, skin, and irises lose pigmentation until they are blond, blushless, and pale-eyed. They smell like baby powder. Inducted into the society by the Omega, they retain a ceramic jar thereafter, into which their heart was placed after it was removed.

*lewlhen* (**n.**) Gift.

*lheage* (**n.**) A term of respect used by a sexual submissive to refer to their dominant.

*Lhenihan* (**pr. n.**) A mythic beast renowned for its sexual prowess. In modern slang, refers to a male of preternatural size and sexual stamina.

*lys* (**n.**) Torture tool used to remove the eyes.

*mahmen* (**n.**) Mother. Used both as an identifier and a term of affection.

*mhis* (**n.**) The masking of a given physical environment; the creation of a field of illusion.

*nalla* (**n., f.**) or *nallum* (**n., m.**) Beloved.

**needing period** (**n.**) Female vampire's time of fertility, generally lasting for two days and accompanied by intense sexual cravings. Occurs approximately five years after a female's transition and then once a decade thereafter. All males respond to some degree if they are around a female in her need. It can be a dangerous time, with conflicts and fights breaking out between competing males, particularly if the female is not mated.

*newling* (**n.**) A virgin.

**the Omega** (**pr. n.**) Malevolent, mystical figure who has targeted the vampires for extinction out of resentment directed toward the Scribe Virgin. Exists in a nontemporal realm and has extensive powers, though not the power of creation.

*phearsom* (**adj.**) Term referring to the potency of a male's sexual organs. Literal translation something close to "worthy of entering a female."

*Princeps* (**pr. n.**) Highest level of the vampire aristocracy, second only to members of the First Family or the Scribe Virgin's Chosen. Must be born to the title; it may not be conferred.

*pyrocant* (**n.**) Refers to a critical weakness in an individual. The weakness can be internal, such as an addiction, or external, such as a lover.

*rahlman* (**n.**) Savior.

*rythe* (**n.**) Ritual manner of asserting honor, granted by one who has offended another. If accepted, the offended chooses a weapon and strikes the offender, who presents him- or herself without defenses.

**the Scribe Virgin** (**pr. n.**) Mystical force who previously was counselor to the King as well as the keeper of vampire archives and the dispenser of privileges. Existed in a nontemporal realm and had extensive powers, but has recently stepped down and given her station to another. Capable of a single act of creation, which she expended to bring the vampires into existence.

*sehclusion* (**n.**) Status conferred by the King upon a female of the aristocracy as a result of a petition by the female's family. Places the female under the sole direction of her *ghardian,* typically the eldest male in her household. Her *ghardian* then has the legal right to determine all manner of her life, restricting at will any and all interactions she has with the world.

*shellan* (**n.**) Female vampire who has been mated to a male. Females generally do not take more than one mate due to the highly territorial nature of bonded males.

*symphath* (**n.**) Subspecies within the vampire race characterized by the ability and desire to manipulate emotions in others (for the purposes of an energy exchange), among other traits. Historically, they have been discriminated against and, during certain eras, hunted by vampires. They are near extinction.

*talhman* (**n.**) The evil side of an individual. A dark stain on the soul that requires expression if it is not properly expunged.

**the Tomb (pr. n.)** Sacred vault of the Black Dagger Brotherhood. Used as a ceremonial site as well as a storage facility for the jars of *lessers*. Ceremonies performed there include inductions, funerals, and disciplinary actions against Brothers. No one may enter except for members of the Brotherhood, the Scribe Virgin, or candidates for induction.

*trahyner* **(n.)** Word used between males of mutual respect and affection. Translated loosely as "beloved friend."

**transition (n.)** Critical moment in a vampire's life when he or she transforms into an adult. Thereafter, he or she must drink the blood of the opposite sex to survive and is unable to withstand sunlight. Occurs generally in the mid-twenties. Some vampires do not survive their transitions, males in particular. Prior to their transitions, vampires are physically weak, sexually unaware and unresponsive, and unable to dematerialize.

**vampire (n.)** Member of a species separate from that of *Homo sapiens*. Vampires must drink the blood of the opposite sex to survive. Human blood will keep them alive, though the strength does not last long. Following their transitions, which occur in their mid-twenties, they are unable to go out into sunlight and must feed from the vein regularly. Vampires cannot "convert" humans through a bite or transfer of blood, though they are in rare cases able to breed with the other species. Vampires can dematerialize at will, though they must be able to calm themselves and concentrate to do so and may not carry anything heavy with them. They are able to strip the memories of humans, provided such memories are short-term. Some vampires are able to read minds. Life expectancy is upward of a thousand years, or in some cases even longer.

*wahlker* **(n.)** An individual who has died and returned to the living from the Fade. They are accorded great respect and are revered for their travails.

*whard* **(n.)** Equivalent of a godfather or godmother to an individual.

# BLOOD TRUTH

# PROLOGUE

*One year ago . . .*

Rexboone, blooded son of Altamere, could Windsor-knot a silk tie blindfolded.

It was not a skill that he had set out to cultivate, but rather one to which he had become inured by virtue of his circumstance in life. In this regard, it was like his knowledge of Domaine Coche-Dury wine, the plays of Shakespeare, and Audemars Piguet watches. Without even being aware of exactly how or where he had picked up the particulars, he knew the difference between a John Frederick Kensett and a Frederic Edwin Church. When Rolls-Royce purchased Bentley (November 1931). When the two split again (31 December 2002). How to lead a female in a waltz. Where to get the best Savile Row suit.

Henry Poole & Co was the answer to that one.

"Damn it."

He undid the tangle at the popped collar of his monogrammed shirt and tried the knot thing again. Maybe it would go better if he were blindfolded. Clearly, his eyeballs weren't helping much.

On that note, he closed his lids.

The problem was that his palms were sweaty and he was having trouble breathing. So going choke around this throat of his, even if it was courtesy of a length of Hermès's best silk, was not making him feel any less woozy.

Emotions were the problem. And wasn't that a surprise.

As a member of the *glymera*, the vampire race's aristocracy, there were only two choices for feelings. You either sported a mild, displaced approval or a patronizing, brow-arch-based disapproval.

Helluva range there. Like choosing between a wax figurine and a plastic mannequin.

Fine, if you were *really* upset about something or someone—like your lawn man trimming the ivy beds badly or maybe a piano (Steinway, of course) getting dropped on your frickin' foot—you could, in an icy tone, offer a corrective missive that skewered said gardener or the owner of that concert grand so viciously that they felt compelled to suicide as a public service.

None of these options appealed to him at the moment. Not that he had ever wanted any of them.

With a tug to bring the knot up to his neck, and then a smooth draw down the two tails, he opened his eyes.

Well. What do you know. He'd done it.

Flipping the collar tabs down into place, he drew his bespoke suit jacket off the mahogany dressing stand, shoulder'd and arm'd the fine fabric, and finished his sartorial presentation by tucking a square of coral-and-blue silk into his breast pocket.

"Time to go," he said to his reflection.

And yet he didn't step away. Looking into the floor-length mirror, he did not recognize the dark-haired male staring back at him. Not the classic facial features so characteristic of aristocrats. Not the broad chest, which was not. Not the long legs or the veined hands.

You should be able to see yourself clearly. Especially when you were in your own walk-in closet in your own bedroom suite at your own home, with the lights on and no distractions.

Even more disturbing, he could inspect each distinct part of what he had on and recall in precise detail where he had gotten it all: who had made the shirt, jacket, and slacks, how he had chosen them, when they had been fitted. The same was true for the background behind him, the rows and rows of suits hanging from brass rods organized by season and hue, the colorful button-downs grouped together like schools of fish, the lineups of perfectly polished, handmade leather dress shoes like a marching army . . . all of it pieces he had picked out.

So where the hell was he among this enviable wardrobe?

As there would be no answer to that one coming, he strode out of his dressing room and through his bedroom and sitting area. Out in the hall, he passed by flower arrangements on demilune tables, a gallery of oil paintings, and then the closed doors of his blood *mahmen*'s former suite of rooms. From what he understood, the quarters were left as they had been when the female had died twenty years before, the lock turned one last time, ne'er to be released again.

But not, he gathered, because of his sire's mourning.

It was more a case of done and dusted. His father's next *shellan* had been installed, like a painting, a mere six months later, with all the rights and privileges accorded thereto. Including the expectation that she be referred to as Boone's *mahmen*.

The fact that the female did not play that role, even on a step level, was never taken into account, and the same was true of Boone's feelings both about the loss of who had birthed him. Then again, Altamere didn't believe in giving emotions any airtime, and he extended that dubious courtesy to his new mate. Once their mating ceremony was over, Boone never saw them together outside of social engagements.

The female didn't seem particularly bothered by the cold distance. In fact, she didn't seem any more thrilled with her *hellren* than Altamere was with her, although going by the regular deliveries from Chanel, Dior, and Hermès, the arrangement certainly suited her closet.

Her suite was the one next to Boone's blood *mahmen*'s. And if she ever was called unto the Fade? Boone was willing to bet one of the two sets of rooms would be cleaned out, redecorated, and given to someone else of female persuasion. It was rather like throwing out dead batteries and replacing them with new ones, as if some part of this mansion, this life of his father's, required the component of a *shellan* to be automated—and thank God you could get one quick on Amazon Prime when the old one ran out of juice.

As Boone thought of what was waiting for him downstairs, he decided he shouldn't be too hasty to judge.

On that note, his sire's suite was next in line.

Boone had never been allowed in there, so he couldn't comment on the decor one way or the other. But he would bet two-thirds of his liver and one whole kidney that nothing was out of order, and most of it was navy blue.

Altamere had probably come out of the womb in a navy blue sport coat, gray flannels, and a club tie.

As Boone continued on and hit the curving staircase, the subtle creaking under the plush red runner was so familiar, he could not imagine what it would be like to live anywhere else. His home—his *father's* home—had never been a place of joy, but as with an insidious expertise in all things considered to be "in good taste," as well as his relentless need to do the right thing, such constrictors were all he knew and thus a dispositive part of who he was.

Unchosen, but undeniable.

Rather like this arranged mating he found himself in.

Bottoming out on the first floor, he went over to the sitting room on the right. Where the female awaited him behind closed doors.

"Is there something with which I may assist you."

Boone halted. The words were, assuming one translated them properly, a question. The attitude and tone were an accusation.

He pivoted around. Marquist, the household's butler, was not a *doggen*, but rather a civilian vampire. Other than that non-typical, the male fit the bill of head servant of a grand estate to a T: Formally dressed in a uniform right out of Buckingham Palace, he had lacquered-back gray hair, suspicious eyes, and an upper lip so stiff you could get a paper cut from it every time he opened his mouth.

The guy also had an uncanny ability to show up where you didn't want him.

Boone checked the knot of his tie with his fingertips. "I am receiving a visitor."

"Yes. I was the one who let her in and summoned you."

Boone continued to meet the stare coming back at him. "And?"

"Your father is not here."

"I am aware of that."

"You will be alone with her, then."

"We are in a receiving parlor with security cameras. I am very sure that you will be monitoring their feeds. We are hardly by ourselves."

"I am going to call your father."

"You always do."

Boone turned his back on the male and meant to enter the parlor. But as his hands gripped the brass handles, he could not move. Meanwhile, there was a huffing sound behind him, and then Marquist snob'd off, the hard soles of those polished shoes clipping like curses as he retreated to his lair of polish cloths, table settings, and tight-assed glowering.

Boone's hesitation hadn't been about the butler, but the fact that it had gotten Marquist to leave was a bonus.

"Shit," he whispered.

His body refused to move, and it was a toss-up as to why. There was a lot to choose from. In the end, he closed his eyes to take a deep breath, and that was what did it. As with knotting the tie, provided he couldn't see, he was good to go.

As he opened the double doors, his lids flipped up.

The female was standing at one of the floor-to-ceiling windows that faced out the front of the manse, her back to him, the fall of raspberry damask drapery setting off her blond hair and her pink-and-black Chanel suit. In the glass panes, her grave reflection was like the portrait of a beautiful female from the past, the profile a remote, though faithful, representation of something no longer among the living.

Rochelle, blooded daughter of Urdeme, looked over her shoulder as he shut them in together—and the instant their eyes met, he knew.

And was relieved.

"Boone," she said roughly.

He exhaled a breath that he hadn't been aware of holding for the last month. "It's okay. I know why you came."

"You do?"

"When you called me directly, instead of going through proper channels, I knew it had to be because you wanted out of this arrangement. And as I said, it's all right."

She seemed surprised, as if she had expected to have to explain herself. As if she had anticipated a hard conversation. As if she had braced herself for anger and indignation on his part.

"No . . . it's not all right."

"Yes, it is. Come here."

As he held out his hand, she walked over to him, but their palms did not make contact. He was careful to drop his arm before she was close, and he drew her over to the sofa by indicating the way across the formal room. When they were both seated on the soft cushions, he had a thought in the back of his mind that they were cardboard cutouts of their parents. In spite of being out of their transitions some fifty years, he and Rochelle were dressing and behaving as if they were three or four hundred years old: Suits and court shoes. Discreet jewels for her, pocket squares for him. Perfect manners.

Inside, he knew it wasn't right. None of this was right, and not just the arranged mating. None of this household, this bloodline he had been born into, was as it should be, and abruptly, as he contemplated the reality that he had been prepared to follow through on a lifelong commitment he knew was wrong for him, anger took hold.

Thank the Virgin Scribe Rochelle was braver than he.

"I am so sorry," she said with a sniffle.

He shifted and took his handkerchief out of his inside pocket. "Here."

"What a mess." Taking what he offered, Rochelle dabbed carefully at her eyes. "What an . . . absolute mess I am making out of everything."

More tears came for her, and he wished he could put a friendly arm around her shoulders for comfort. But he hadn't touched her in any way yet, and now was hardly the time to start.

"We can choose not to do this."

"But I want to. I truly do." She pressed under one side of her nose and looked at him. "You're amazing. You're everything I should want, but I just don't—oh, God. I shouldn't say that."

Boone smiled. "I take it as a compliment."

"I mean it. I wish I could love you."

"I know you do."

Abruptly, she shook her head over and over again, her blond hair breaking across her shoulders in thick waves. "No, no, we have to press on. I don't know why I came here. There is no getting out of this, Boone. Arranged matings can't be broken."

"The hell they can't. Tell them all you do not find me acceptable. It's your right. That's how you—how we—take care of this."

"Except that's not fair to you." Tears glistened in her eyes. "There will be all kinds of judgment on you, and—"

"I'll handle it."

"How?"

He didn't know. But what he was sure about was that having the *glymera* believe he was undesirable as a *hellren* for a fellow member of the upper classes seemed a better lot than forcing this mating. It wasn't that he didn't like Rochelle or that he found her unattractive. She was smart and funny, and she was classically beautiful. Over time, there was a possibility of things developing between them, but they were essentially strangers.

And as they sat here alone for the first time, the question he had been asking himself since night one was finally answered: The only reason he had gone down this path of expectation was because he'd thought maybe he could make it work better than his father had. In fact, he had been determined to succeed where his sire had failed by meeting the expectations of the *glymera* and yet still living a life that was authentic.

Except winning that kind of a race would only get him a hollow trophy, wouldn't it—in the form of a mating to a female he wasn't in love with . . . just so he could prove a point to a male who would undoubtedly not notice the nuances outside of "normal."

"It's going to be all right," he repeated.

Rochelle took a deep breath. "I don't want you to think I was being hasty in calling you. Or impulsive."

Impulsive? he thought. What, like signing on for seven hundred years of mating, the possibility of young, and the certainty of death's hard stop, even though the pair of them had shared just two supervised greeting teas, the required parental dinner, and the announcement cocktail party? All told, he had spent maybe five hours in Rochelle's company, and until now, it had all been witnessed.

"Boone, I want to explain. I'm in love . . . with someone else."

As he smiled, he wondered what that kind of connection felt like. "I'm really happy for you. Love is a blessing."

Rochelle looked away, her face turning into a mask of composure. "Thank you."

Boone wanted to ask questions about the male. But again, even though they were technically engaged, as the humans would say, they were essentially strangers, and that was what made all this so crazy.

She thought it was hard breaking the engagement? Try ending a full-blown mating.

"Just tell them I am not worthy," he insisted. "And then you're free to mate the other male."

As Rochelle's eyes came back to him, he reflected that they were the same color blue as his own, and for some reason, that irritated him. Not that there was anything wrong with her; it was just . . . enough already with the proper-bloodline stuff. They were so alike in terms of coloring, save for his dark hair, that they could have been brother and sister, and how creepy was that.

Rochelle flattened the handkerchief he'd given her on her lap, smoothing the square, running her fingertip over his monogram in the center.

"So you . . . you don't want to do this, either?"

"I think it would be better if we knew each other"—at all—"and we were choosing this. I know that's not how our kind do the mating thing, but why? My sire and my birth *mahmen* were never happy with each other, and they had an arranged mating. After she died, my father went and did it all over again with the same result. A part of me thought maybe I could show him how it's properly done, but honestly? Especially if you're in love with someone else? Not only what are the chances of a happily ever after for us, but why bother."

"I can't leave you with all the social stigma. It's not fair."

"Don't kid yourself. If we end this for any reason other than me being unacceptable, the social fallout on you is going to be downright brutal. That male you love? He will not be allowed to mate you. You will be considered ruined and ineligible for a proper *hellren* for the rest of your life. On top of that, your whole bloodline will be shamed and they will blame it all on you. Are you saying you'd rather enjoy that result?"

Rochelle winced. "You're going to be shunned to some degree, though."

"It will be nothing compared to what the *glymera* will do to you. I'd rather be the talk of the party circuit for a year and get side-eye for a decade than know I ruined your life and the life of your male."

Rochelle shook her head. "You're getting the bad end of this. Why would you do this for anyone?"

"I don't know. I guess . . . love is worth sacrificing for. Even if it's not my own."

"You are such a male of worth," she whispered. "And you are so brave."

Was he really, though? Maybe in the context of the *glymera*, but the realist in him knew that true bravery was not facing the slings and arrows of haughty stares and disapproving comments. After the raids, after the Lessening Society had killed so many innocents in their homes, how could anybody suggest that arbitrary social mores were the be-all and end-all of anything worthwhile? Or that thwarting them for a good reason should get you the vampire equivalent of the Purple Heart?

Rochelle searched his face as if trying to assess whether he could handle the pressure. "You really don't care about what they think of you, do you."

Boone shrugged. "I've never been a big fan of the social scene. There are people here in Caldwell who don't have any idea that Altamere even has a son, and I'm fine with that. My father will take some heat, but I assure you, after the way he's dismissed me all my life, I'm perfectly comfortable with not worrying about his problems. And please don't feel guilty. This is the best for both of us."

Rochelle dabbed at fresh tears. "I wish I were like you. I'm a coward."

"Are you kidding me? You're being brave here. And don't make a hero out of me." He smiled bitterly. "I've got plenty of faults. Just ask my sire. He'll give you a list longer than your driveway."

As she fell silent, the sadness that came back into her eyes made him want to hold her. But Marquist was watching on the closed circuit—and more to the point, Rochelle was not his to comfort.

Calling off the arrangement was so the right thing to do—

"No," she said in a stronger voice. "I will take responsibility for this. I am not going to let you—"

"Rochelle. I don't know who your male is, but if he's in our class? You cannot be the one who breaks things off. If you refuse to perform on this arrangement, his family will *never* allow you two to be together. You know this. You will be sullied, and it will haunt you for the rest of your life. Let me take the hit."

"I still don't know why you would do this for me."

"If I had someone to love, I would want to be with her. But I don't."

He frowned and considered all of the females he knew or had met. They were all aristocrats. "And honestly, I can't see where something like true love would come from for me. So I want to help the two of you."

Rochelle dabbed her face with his handkerchief again. "I really wish I could love you. You are a male of true worth. But no, I can't let you—"

The double doors burst open, the heavy panels thrown wide by Marquist.

Boone's sire, Altamere, strode in, his wing tips clipping over the marble until they hit the carpet and were silenced. The male's dark hair was brushed back from his finely boned face, and his pale eyes were the color of steel in his anger. Absently, Boone noted that the suit his father had on was made of the exact same fine wool his own was. The slate blue color was flecked with threads of heather and pale gray, the speckling so subtle that one could not notice it without pressing a nose to the lapels.

The cut of the jacket and slacks was not the same, however. Boone had always taken after his *mahmen*'s side of things, his shoulders broad, his arms thick, his legs long and muscled. He had always been aware that his father disapproved of his physique, and could remember a hushed comment after his transition, made under his sire's breath, that Boone had the body of a laborer. As if that were a birth defect.

Or maybe something that made him doubt the fidelity of his *shellan*.

Boone had always wondered about that.

"Whate'er are you doing," Altamere demanded.

As that hard stare locked on Boone, it was not a surprise that the male ignored Rochelle. To him, females were nothing but background, something pretty on the periphery, an accessory rather than an active participant in one's life.

Boone got to his feet. "Rochelle has come to tell me I am not worthy of our arrangement. She has rejected me, and because she has honor, she wanted to do it in person. She is taking her leave the now."

He could feel Rochelle looking at him in shock, but he was prepared to shoot down any attempt she might make to deny what he'd laid out. Meanwhile, over Altamere's shoulder, Marquist was a watchful presence, a living, breathing camcorder that was taking everything in.

"You are *not* going to embarrass me like this," Altamere hissed. "I will not allow it."

As if he sensed there was a deeper story.

The anger that had curdled in Boone's chest found further purchase in his very soul. "The choice is not yours to make."

"You are my *son*. It is no one else's—"

"Bull*shit*." As his sire blanched at the curse word, Boone's voice grew deeper and louder. "We're done with me trying to please you. I was never very good at it, anyway—at least not according to you, and it is beyond time that I stand up for myself."

In the back of his mind, the tally of his sire's neglect and condescension was like an electric meter going haywire, the count spiraling up into the stratosphere: Boone's body type. Boone's desire to read rather than be social. Boone's *mahmen*'s death ignored. Boone's step*mahmen* entering the house like a cold draft. Boone's never measuring up no matter what the standard.

Altamere jabbed a finger in Boone's direction. "I'm giving you one last chance. I don't know what the two of you are doing with this nonsense, but it stops here. The mating goes forward, or you're going to find that how the *glymera* shuns you holds not a candle to what I will do to shut you out."

Rochelle burst to her feet. "It is I who is unworthy of him—"

"I'm not afraid of you," Boone interrupted with clarity. "And you're right, sire mine, things are going to change around here."

Altamere narrowed his eyes. "What's gotten into you?"

Boone slowly shook his head. "This has been a long time coming. What is that economic theory you quote so often? That which cannot continue, does not. I'm done with living lies."

As he stared into the eyes of the male who was supposedly his sire, he challenged Altamere to keep pushing him. And made it clear, at least psychically, that if that happened, he would pop the top off the great unthinkable.

Namely, the doubts around his paternity.

In front of witnesses.

You want to talk about shame? The *glymera* generally reserved its strictures and scorn for females, but a cuckolded male? Well . . . that didn't bear thinking about, did it. To the point where Altamere had never even brought up the idea of a paternity test because the ramifications were too socially dangerous. Instead, the unanswered possibility that Boone had been fathered by another had lurked around the house, a ghost of infidelity that followed the "son" wherever he went.

Condemned for a suspected sin that had not been his own.

But that ended tonight.

After a long, tense silence, Boone's sire finally looked at Rochelle. "I do not blame you for this choice."

Altamere turned around and walked out, Marquist falling in behind him, the two disappearing into the study.

In the wake of the departure, Boone reached up to the knot of his tie and pulled it loose. It felt great to breathe.

"Why did you do that!" Rochelle said.

He thought of everything his father had ever said about him. "I am unworthy. It's not a lie."

"This is all my fault," Rochelle groaned as she collapsed back onto the sofa.

As Boone dismantled the Windsor knot altogether, he thought back to the fact that he'd had to tie it with his eyes closed. Had entered this parlor with his lids down. Had lived . . . his whole life . . . in a blindness that was not just a choice, but a matter of survival.

Subconsciously, he had known that if he looked too closely—or at all—he was not going to be able to keep going. There was so much he had absorbed without realizing it, sure as if the toxic airs of the aristoc-racy had been an actual gas that he had breathed in and been poisoned by. Except that was stopping the now.

If Rochelle could stand up for her love, he could gather the reins of his own life and decide who he would like to be. Where he would like to go. What he would like to learn. Without apology.

Her courage had inspired his own.

"I am so sorry," Rochelle said with dejection.

Boone shook his head. "No matter what happens next, I am not."

# ONE

Boone's shitkickers shredded the frozen tire tracks down the middle of the alley, his powerful body churning through the dirty city snow, air sucking into his lungs cold and punching out hot as steam from a locomotive's stack. In his right hand, he had a twelve-inch serrated hunting knife. In his left, a length of chain.

Up ahead, by about thirty feet, a *lesser* was running as if its undead life depended on all the Usain Bolt the thing was pulling. The telltale sickly sweet stench of the enemy was thick in its wake, a tracker that Boone's sensitive nose had picked up on seven blocks ago. The slayer was sloppy of foot, flappy of hand, and given how saturated its smell was, Boone wondered whether it was already injured.

The Black Dagger Brotherhood's commanding officer, Tohrment, son of Hharm, set the nightly territories for the Brothers and fighters, carving up sections of downtown into quadrants that would be stalked for the enemy. Trainees such as Boone were paired with more experienced people, either Brothers or members of the Band of Bastards, in the interest of safety—especially as there was a new threat out on the streets.

Shadow entities. That were killing innocent vampire civilians.

Boone glanced over his shoulder. Tonight, he was working with Zypher. The Bastard was a great partner, a big, brutal male who nonetheless had a teacher's patience and an eye for constant improvement.

It was supposed to have been Syn. And a relief when it wasn't.

Syn was . . . different.

Boone's favorite to work with, bar none, was Rhage. But the Brotherhood was otherwise occupied tonight. Every last one of them.

And Boone was the one who had set them on a mission that he hoped and prayed didn't result in death.

His father's, specifically.

In the intervening twelve months since their blowup over the broken arrangement, he and Altamere had settled into an uneasy détente. Which was what happened when you finally called a bully on their push-and-shove. The two of them kept up appearances, something that was not hard given how starchy and superficial their relationship had always been, but Boone had drawn a line and instead of the threatened repercussions, in return he'd gotten a retreat of hostility.

He probably should have moved out, but as petty as it was, he had enjoyed getting the upper hand and keeping it. Especially after he joined the Brotherhood's training program, something he was well aware his father disapproved of. Altamere's "son" a soldier? Fighting in the war? How brutish. The move had made Boone's bookish decades seem like a fine hand of cards.

But he loved the challenge and he was damn good at the work—and a new kind of life and rhythm had started, where he and his sire rarely saw each other.

Except then came the invitation: The pleasure of his father and step*mahmen*'s company requested at an aristocrat's home this very evening. Going by the card stock alone, it was clear that other members of the *glymera* were included on the guest list.

Social gathering? Maybe. Treasonous violation of Wrath's ban on the Council coming together? More likely.

It had been the first time in a year that Boone had spoken to his sire about anything of note. Yet how could he not urge the male to stay home? That viper pit of aristocrats had already tried to take down Wrath's throne, and if they were planning another attempt?

The training center had taught him in detail all of the things the Brothers were capable of doing to someone who crossed them. And he might not like his father . . . but that was the point. With his alarm bells going off about treason, if he didn't at least try to keep the male away from that party, he would feel like he had killed Altamere himself.

And that was too close to what he had at times wanted to do, and who needed to live with that guilt?

Predictably, his father had refused the wise counsel. So Boone had gone to the Brothers directly, and that was why he was paired with a member of the Band of Bastards this fine, crystal-cold winter's evening.

Refocusing on his hunt, he threw some more speed into his legs, his thighs beginning to burn, his calves tightening, his bum ankle issuing the first of what was going to be a lot of complaints. All of that was background chatter easily ignored, utterly forgettable.

*Just breathe*, he told himself. The more oxygen he could get into his lungs, the more he got into his blood, fuel for his muscles, speed for his body.

Power.

And what do you know, he was closing the distance. The problem? He was getting farther and farther away from Zypher, who was dancing with a slayer of his own three blocks—now four blocks—back.

Time to do this.

Per protocol, he hit the locator beacon on his shoulder to notify the other squads that he was about to engage. And then he closed his eyes.

Dematerializing was something that vampires ordinarily had to concentrate and calm themselves in order to accomplish. Boone, however, had trained himself to find that place of inner equilibrium even when he was running full tilt boogie in pursuit of the enemy. And courtesy of all his practice, his physical form disintegrated into a scatter of molecules and he shot forward, passing the *lesser*.

4 J. R. WARD

He re-formed in front of the enemy, his boots planted, his knife up and his chain down, ready to party.

The slayer did what it could to slow its roll, arms pinwheeling, shoes slapping at the snow and skidding as it tried to stop on ice. Momentum was not its friend. Unlike some of the scrawny new recruits, this one had a football player's thick neck and barrel chest, and all that body weight was a boulder bouncing down the side of a mountain, all keep-going instead of back-that-ass-up.

As he had been trained to do, Boone's peripheral vision imprinted the alley's contours and possible cover opportunities. His brain also did a lightning-quick assessment of threat potential, cataloguing fire escapes, rooflines, doorways, and windows, all of his instincts feeding information into the calculation of his own safety. On the physical side, his body braced for contact.

And the length of chain began to swing.

Boone wasn't aware of giving his hand and arm that particular command, but things had started happening like that in the field over the past month. According to the Black Dagger Brother Vishous, there were four levels of skill development: unconsciously unskilled, which meant you didn't know how much you didn't know and couldn't do; consciously unskilled, which was when you began to be aware of how much you needed to develop; consciously skilled, which was the level at which you started to use what you've trained yourself to do; and, finally, unconsciously skilled.

Which was what happened when your body moved without your brain having to micromanage every molecule of the attack. When your training formed a basis of action so intrinsic to who you were and what you did in a given situation that you were unaware of any cognition occurring. When you entered "the Zone," as the Brother Rhage called it.

Boone was in that sweet spot now.

The whirring sound of the chain links circling beside him was soft yet menacing, like the easy breathing of a great beast—and Boone knew the second the slayer was going to move because one of its shoulders lifted and its hips angled ever so slightly.

The knife the *lesser* had tucked in its hand came flying out at Boone end over end—proof that Boone's subconscious hadn't considered quite everything. But his reflexes were on it, jerking his torso to one side, the surge of aggressive energy flowing through him so acute, so pleasurable, it was almost sexual.

His counterattack started with the chain. Licking the links out, he sent them around the slayer's neck, a snake of metal with a tail that swung wide and doubled up on itself. With a tight loop locked in, he yanked with his full body.

The slayer pitched forward into the snow face-first.

And that was when Boone lifted his own hunting blade over his shoulder.

◆    ◆    ◆

*Pyre's Revyval Club*
*33rd and Market Streets*

A vampire among humans pretending to be vampires.

And he was not the only one.

Among the two hundred or so bodies churning, churning, in the dim, laser-pierced cave of an old shirt factory, there were only four or five who were true biological specimens as opposed to made-up characters of a deluded mythology. But unlike the costumed and masked men and women who were desperate to appear as something other than they were, the male and his kind did not announce their DNA status in any fashion. They were just among the others, blending in, observing . . . at times participating.

The male was head and shoulders taller than the men who black-cape'd around the open belly of the abandoned building, and with the power he had in his body and the razor-sharp fangs that could drop down out of his upper jaw, he was never without violent means. Conventional weapons notwithstanding.

As he stood off to the side, he was aware that he was looking through his dark sunglasses with purpose, and that exhausted him. He was tired of his other side. But if he could not exercise his *talhman*, his evil, even a little bit, then coming here was a waste of time. Like dangling meat just outside the iron bars of a monster's cage.

And that was the point. He needed to be sure he still had control of himself. There was a long time when he had not been able to rein himself in, and a long time when the consequences of his poor impulse control had not mattered. Things had changed, however.

He was in the New World now.

He was aligned with the King now.

So he tested himself here. Because if he were to snap? If the reins on his monster slipped free the grip of his mind and . . . things . . . occurred? Then, in this club, it was only humans or random vampires at risk. Who cared if a couple of them caught the brunt of his bad side. What was more important was the self-knowledge that he could be among these easy targets and resist the thoughts that plagued him. Be stronger of mind rather than temptation. Curb the hunger to kill.

And if he wasn't able to stay in his lane? Well, sometimes pressure had to be released in one place so the rest of the whole could continue in relative peace. And again, having a problem here was better than anywhere else in Caldwell—

Over to the right, the crowd was thickening up, sure as if the bodies were cells and a tumor was spontaneously sprouting amongst otherwise healthy tissue. It was some kind of argument, the dim light and the black costumes and the pushing and shoving making it impossible to tell who the aggressor was, what the tussle was about, whether punches were being thrown or if it was just another case of humans posturing in front of a peanut gallery.

At least that was the information his brain registered. His *talhman*, on the other hand, was aroused by the physical expression of anger, tantalized by the possibility of blood welling and dripping from wounds, kindled by the prospect of stalking and taking down prey.

"Not for us," the male muttered.

Reaching up, he pulled the black skull cap he had on lower. The action was reflexive, and it was only afterward that he recognized what he'd done.

He was preparing to go in. Get something. And he didn't want his identity known.

As it turned out, his testing field found him.

From the chaotic knot of humans, a female broke free, and his first thought, as he recognized her as one of his own species, was what the hell was she doing getting involved with a bunch of rats without tails? But then nothing about her mattered at the same time all parts of her became significant.

She seemed harried as she looked around, her black hair tangled in the mask that covered her eyes and half of her face, her lipstick smudged, her bodice asymmetrical, one breast about to pop out.

The discordant scatter of her aura instantly changed as their eyes met. Her body, lost on its feet, caught itself, becoming still. Her breathing stopped and then resumed at a calmer pace. Her hands readjusted the bustier into proper position.

He was willing to bet her thoughts did the same beneath her skull, her cognition righting itself.

And focusing on him.

Leaving the melee she'd come out of in the dust, she strode up to him, kicking her bouncy hair over her shoulder, tilting her chin high.

Whether that was so she could meet his eyes from her lower height or as a show of independence and aggression, he couldn't tell. And didn't actually care.

"I am Nightingale," she announced.

*Like that is supposed to mean something to me?* he thought.

By way of responding, he let his eyes travel the curves of her body from behind his dark lenses. That black hair was long, so very long, cascading over her shoulders and falling down to her hips, a river of spiral curls that caught and held the flashing blue in the lasers. That black bustier of hers trimmed her waist and pushed up her breasts, creating creamy globes that she had powdered with something shimmery. Her lips were blood red . . . her throat pale and lovely.

"What's your name," she said on a drawl.

The male drew in through his nose, scenting her. She was turned on, her sexual stimulation obvious and directed at him, an equation she wanted him to solve, a distance she had decided he would carry her, a fantasy she had chosen him to satisfy.

His blood surged. And underneath his own arousal, his *talhman* prowled. If she knew what he was really like, she would not have picked him out of the crowd. But that was the danger and the excitement of what places like this offered, wasn't it: anonymous sex with strangers who you could wallpaper with your own fantasies, each side fulfilling needs that might or might not have been expressed outright, the reality that you didn't know what you were really getting lending an edge to it all.

An edge that patched over the lack of true attraction, a tarp of make-believe to cover the holes left by the shingles that had blown off the roof of reality.

Vengeance, he decided. As he measured the hellfire in her eyes, and the way she glared back at the crowd like someone in the club had gotten into her face, he was willing to bet she was in search of some hot and heavy in retaliation for an offense.

Talk about burning off steam.

The male extended his hand and placed the tip of his forefinger on the soft spot between her collarbones, that divot in her flesh that was undefended by her skeletal makeup, that vulnerable, soft eyelet of her throat. When he pressed in, restricting her airflow just a little, she gasped.

And then moaned like she had a delicious ache between her legs.

The male pressed in again, harder this time . . . so that he felt her throat work against the compression.

The struggle was what fully hardened him, his erection thickening behind his button fly.

The male knew what was going to happen next. They would find a darkened corner or perhaps stay here in the crush of masked people. His hands would round her waist and sink onto her ass. He would pull her in close and roll his hips so his arousal brushed against her—given her much shorter height, it would be just under those pushed-up breasts.

She would shiver and offer herself, limp and willing and open, to him.

He would tremble because of the *talhman*, but she would assume it was on account of his arousal.

And when he got up under that long skirt, his thick, hard sex pushing deep into her, she would come, and in that little death, as the French called it, she would never know how close she was to her actual demise.

He would not climax.

He never did.

And provided his self-control held, she would never know how wrong she was to choose him. If he failed to control himself, however? Well, she was going to learn an important lesson—only once, of course. Because the dead not only had no tales to tell, there was no more education for them, either.

"Tell me what your name is," she breathed.

The syllables vibrated against the pad of his finger, and his heated blood, his killing instinct, amplified the vision of her in her mask until he could see each individual hair on her head and every pump of her jugular vein.

The male focused on her lips.

Slipping his enormous palm around to the nape of her neck, he pulled her headfirst into him, her body following like water poured from a vase. But he did not kiss her. Even as she dropped her head back against his hold and leaned her lower body into his own, prepared to accept his mouth on hers, he stopped before contact was made.

With his free hand, he drew her wrist up. Maintaining eye contact with her, he hissed and bared his fangs.

The nick he gave her was a small one, but it was in the right place, blood welling up and running down the pale, soft skin of her inner arm.

Her breasts pumped in that tight bustier, that shimmery powder catching the light. "Now what will you do?" she breathed.

Shifting his grip on her hand, he extended his tongue and ran it up the flow he had created, lapping what had escaped her vein, swallowing the dark wine. Her taste was acceptable, not that his standards were high, so when he reached the knife-like incision he had made, he closed a warm seal around it with his mouth.

Sucking.

Licking.

He knew exactly when she orgasmed. Her eyes squeezed shut and she bit down on her lower lip, her hard, white canines making the soft, red-painted flesh plump in submission. Her hips pressed into him and then rotated, and he imagined the sweet stinging pulses that gripped her core were more tantalizing than satisfying.

"Take me downstairs," she groaned.

So private down there on the subterranean level. No prying eyes. Little foot traffic, and what passersby there might be would be drugged out and disinterested in anything other than themselves.

A bigger challenge.

The male picked her up, splitting her thighs around his torso, her breasts pushing against his chest. He carried her off using one arm. She didn't weigh much.

The female didn't bother looking at the crowd as they departed. He was the only thing on her mind now.

The way down to the lower level was easily located, and as he headed through the crowd in that direction, she nuzzled into his neck and worked her core against his torso. When he got to the steel door marked "EXIT," he yanked it open. The stairwell was concrete and smelled of alkaline dirt and cold mold, and the temperature dropped precipitously as they got away from the radiating bodies and whatever heat system was in force in the open area.

"What's your name?" the female said into his ear.

Down, down, down, the echoes of his heavy boots and heavier body rebounding around. At the bottom landing, he unlatched the steel door with his mind, his will opening the thing wide. The corridor beyond was strobed with old ceiling lights that flickered in their rusty, decrepit mounts, the dull illumination seizuring from above, making shadows dance in an evil waltz. The scents in the frigid, stale air suggested many others had used the corridor for the same purpose the female intended—

The male's *talhman* stretched its clawed will under his skin, fresh aggression blooming throughout his body and making him wonder whether his control on this night might not fail him—

The blackout, when it came, only announced itself with its departure, the world returning unto the male in a rush of sensation, his lapse of awareness having stolen everything from him: eyesight, hearing, touch, and taste.

But he was still with the female—and she was alive.

He had pushed her up against an inset doorway, and his hands were trying to find a way under her skirt—

Well, one of them was. The other was feeling around for the latch to open the door.

From past experience, he knew that behind each of the many old wooden portals there were storage areas filled with discarded manufacturing equipment, decaying wooden crates, and colonies of rats that made homes out of the dank, dark caves.

Inside . . . he could do even more to her.

As the thought occurred to him, he wasn't sure which part of him was talking. The sexual drive . . . or the monster. They were not one and the same, but at times, he had found it difficult to know the difference.

"Your name," she demanded as she rubbed herself against him. "What is your name . . ."

"Syn," he growled into her throat. "I am Syn."

# TWO

In the alley about fifteen blocks to the west of Pyre's Revyval, Boone led with the tip of his blade, coming down on his *lesser* with the one-two body punch of gravity and all his heavy weight. The steel dagger went into the undead's eye socket, and as it cleaved through the pupil and sclera, penetrating the brain via the pathway of the optic nerve, he took a mental note down on his cognitive ledger.

This was a violation of training.

The rule for trainees was, whether you were working in pairs or were alone—and especially if it was the latter—you were to dispatch the enemy back to the Omega the instant you got a clear chest strike. *Lessers*, these sickly sweet-smelling, de-souled humans hell-bent on eradicating vampires, were essentially immortal in a *Death Becomes Her* kind of way: No matter how much damage you did to their bodies, they were still capable of cognition and movement. You could cut their heads off, lop limbs from their torsos, disembowel, destroy, debride—and they would remain animated, like a rattlesnake.

There was only way to "kill" them: a stab through the empty heart cavity with something steel. Then it was a case of pop, pop, fizz, fizz, relief, etc.

Back they went to their evil maker.

As someone newly trained, Boone didn't have the wealth of experience that other fighters, and the Brothers themselves, possessed. So for a soldier like him, he shouldn't be taking risks. A quick COD back to the Omega was the safest way to go—and for the first couple of weeks he was out working in the field, he'd been sure to follow that instruction. After a while, however . . .

He began to draw out the killing if he had the chance.

He could still remember the first time he'd deviated from the safety protocol. He had meant to nail a slayer in the chest, but it had rolled to the side unexpectedly and he'd sliced through its pectoral. As the undead had gone to sit back up, Boone had fumbled with his blade and, panicked, just started stabbing at anything.

Black blood had speckled, splashed, flowed. Pain had caused the *lesser* to cry out. Boone's arm had become a jackhammer going up and down in a blur of movement.

It had all been such a revelation.

His brain had lit up in a strange new pattern, sectors of his mind that had been previously dark pierced with an illumination of excitement and nonsexual arousal that shocked him. The rush had been so sharp and so unexpected, he had figured it had to be an anomaly.

That assumption proved to be incorrect.

The second time he delayed the final moment, it had been just the same: A visceral experience that had turned the volume up on the whole world, every nuance of what he was doing, how the slayer reacted, what the start, middle, and end was like, engraved on his mind. The third instance? He validated the operating principle into a kind of law.

Since then, he'd sought these moments out, careful not to get caught.

All the murdered vampires who had lost their innocent lives to these soulless monsters? All the families destroyed? The suffering of his race at the hands of these killers?

Fuck the *lessers*.

Refocusing, Boone clamped a hold on the front of the undead's throat and then he stared down into the slayer's pasty white face. The dagger was still where he'd put it, sticking out of the orbital bed, the handle angled to reflect the arc of his stab. Black blood, glossy and awful-smelling, was dripping out the outer corner of the penetration like tears, sliding down the temple, pooling in the ear.

From out of nowhere, Boone remembered what it was like to be a young lying back in the bath, the water entering his ear canals, buffering things. Was that what the *lesser* was experiencing?

As the slayer's mouth gaped like a fish's, and the arms pinwheeled like it was trying to make snow angels at what could be argued was a very inopportune time, Boone squeezed even harder, crushing the windpipe.

The gurgling gasps rising up from the *lesser*'s lips made him want to do more. Drag this out for hours. Cut into the torso—

In the back of his mind, a warning bell sounded. Taking out a small portion of the race's suffering on this slayer was one thing. What Boone's brain was suggesting to him now ... was another. It was torture. Still, he ignored the inner alarm as he wondered what it would be like to use his fangs to kill one. Even though that would be harder to explain to the Brothers, he imagined how good it would feel. How satisfying. How visceral.

Temptation tickled his jaw, his mouth cranking open, his canines descending.

All he wanted to do was hurt this motherfucker. And keep hurting it.

With his free hand, he reached out to the hilt of his dagger and secured his palm to the contoured grip. Slowly, he turned the blade back and forth, feeling the grit of the bone wear away as he turned, turned, turned—

"What the hell are you doing?"

Boone looked up in shock. Zypher was standing right in front of him, the Bastard's leather fighting gear speckled with the black blood of the slayer he had engaged with, his gun down by his thigh, his silver dagger up like he was ready to use it.

"Just finishing the job," Boone said as he retracted his blade.

Shifting back on the torso, he buried his dagger in the center of that chest, and then raised his forearms up to shield his eyes from the blinding flash. The popping was like that of a gun, echoing around the alley, and as the burst of illumination faded, Boone rose to his feet. There was no looking at Zypher. He kept his eyes trained on the melted hole in the snow, the black rim around on the burn mark part due to the explosion, part from the blood of the enemy.

*Say something*, Boone told himself.

"I'll call mine in." He went for his communicator. "And then I'm ready to go back on patrol—"

"The fuck you are. You're injured."

He looked down at his body, bending at the waist. "Where—oh."

The knife that the *lesser* had thrown was still imbedded in the meat of his shoulder, the handle sticking out of him in the same way his had protruded from that eye socket. No, that wasn't quite true. This knife was embedded straight into him. The one in that eye had been angled by thirty . . . maybe forty . . . degrees.

Dimly, he decided that was a strange thing to take note of. Then again, everything felt funhouse weird. From the moment that that other fighter's presence had registered, it was as if he had split into two entities, one that had done the stabbing and was now standing upright in his boots next to the burn mark in the snow . . . and another that was observing himself from across the alley, an impartial, detached entity.

Like a reflection in a mirror, identical but not the real thing.

For some reason, he thought of Rochelle. Which was strange as it had been a long time since he had done that.

Keeping a curse to himself, he reached across and yanked out the *lesser's* knife. As the blade released from his flesh, he should have felt something. Right?

A blaze of pain. A sting. A flare of . . .

There was nothing except maybe a warm rush under his leather jacket. His blood. Running into his athletic shirt.

Zypher triggered the communicator mounted on the lapel of his leather jacket. "I need a medic. STAT."

Boone shook his head. "It's nothing. I'm ready to keep fighting—"

"Not gonna happen on my watch."

◆    ◆    ◆

*415 Summit Lane*
*Caldwell's Millionaires' Row*

Tohrment, son of Hharm, entered an elegant parlor that was trashed like it had hosted a bar fight. Antique furniture and silk sofas were tipped over, shoved out of place, torn up. Porcelain plates were shattered. Lamps were on the Oriental, shades ruined, bulbs broken, bodies cracked.

He was careful where he put his shitkickers. No reason to add to the ruin.

The scent of fresh vampire blood was thick in the air. And that wasn't all.

He stopped in front of a large oil painting of a bouquet of flowers. Dutch. Eighteenth century. The still life, with its hard-focus depiction of dew on petals, careful detailing of the mammoth vase, and colorful, head-cocked parrot off to one side, was a prime example of the famous style.

But you could not see much of the artist's expertise. There was a black splatter across the canvas, all that old paint and timeless talent covered with a substance that was viscous and glossy—but did not smell like sweaty August trash.

So it was not *lesser*-based. But they already knew that.

Shadows. And not Shadows as in Trez and iAm, but shadows with a lowercase *s*: Entities that had appeared in Caldwell from out of nowhere, did not appear to be tied to the Omega and the Lessening Society, and which, in this instance, had attacked a gathering of *glymera* types.

With deadly consequences.

The Brotherhood had tried to save the guests. But they had only mostly succeeded.

Stepping over an armchair that was riddled with bullet holes, he went to the body of a male, aged approximately three hundred years. The tuxedo jacket the deceased had on was open, the two halves falling off to the side to reveal a narrow satin waistcoat, a pleated tuxedo shirt with pearl buttons, and a bow tie that was still knotted with watchmaker-worthy precision at the front of the throat.

Blood stained the brilliant white of that shirt in a bull's-eye pattern that was no longer getting any larger in diameter. Which was what happened when the heart stopped beating and circulation ceased. No more leaking.

It was there that logic and standard operating procedures ended. In spite of the wound and its crimson signature, none of the clothes were ripped or torn: Unlike that chair, there were no bullet holes through that jacket, the waistcoat, the shirt. No tears or piercing holes from a stabbing, either.

"Makes no fucking sense," Tohr muttered.

If he were to unfasten the waistcoat, unbutton those pearls, and open that shirt up? He would see the damage that had somehow spared the clothes and wrought the flesh beneath. The brothers had no idea how it worked. This new enemy who attacked with ruthless efficiency was a mystery, possessing powers that had never been seen before, an origin that couldn't be determined, and an agenda that seemed related to the Omega's but could not be verified as such.

As Tohr sank down on his haunches, both of his knees popped.

The face of the corpse was pale gray and getting waxier by the minute. Typical of the aristocracy, the bone structure was symmetrical and refined, the features not extraordinary but certainly attractive, if only because there was nothing wrong with any one part of the whole: The nose was in proportion. The jaw was fairly firm above the slit in the throat. The arch of the brows seemed purposely engineered for hauteur.

The lips were pursed as if the male did not approve of the manner of his death.

And who could blame him on that one.

That strange chest wound was not, in fact, what had killed him.

The bullet hole in the center of the forehead was out of place on so many levels, the tidy little round penetration sporting a scorched outer rim—which was what happened with a point-blank trigger pull. Vishous had been the shooter—and it had happened after the shadows' deadly attack, after John Matthew and Murhder had blown up two of this new enemy, resulting in the Jackson Pollock overlay of that old painting and a bunch of other expensive antiques.

With all the chaos that had erupted, it had been impossible to track the details, but Tohr would be deconstructing the entire series of events as well as the crime scene over the next couple of hours.

Including the part where V'd had to cap this corpse in the frontal lobe to prevent it from reanimating and going on an attack of its own.

A side effect, they had all learned, of a mortal shadow attack.

Tohr glanced around the room again and remembered the aristocrats scattering as the shadows had entered the parlor from somewhere inside the mansion. The Brotherhood, having been tipped off that the party was going on, had broken in through windows and attempted to save the guests.

They'd been on the property to sniff out treason. But, like a lot of nights in the war and most of the dealings with the *glymera*, the door prize had been an unexpected one.

And not in a good way.

"He staying put?"

Tohr glanced over his shoulder at the dry mutter. Vishous was as he always was: dressed in black leather, draped in weapons, and sporting an expression like someone stupid had just done something ridiculous.

V's laconic puss made resting bitch face seem like something that belonged on an inspirational poster.

"Let's be respectful, okay?" Tohr said.

"Whatever, that guy's a traitor." V stroked his goatee. "I'm not sorry he's dead, and I'm glad he's staying that way. These fucking shadows and their TKO corpses."

At least they could agree on that. The only way to keep a shadow victim from waking up and attacking everything around them was to put a bullet spiked with water from the Scribe Virgin's fountain in their forehead's two-car garage.

The whole thing had so many violations of nature, it was hard to keep count.

Tohr got to his feet and looked over at the bar that had been set up off to one side. The linen-covered table was sporting a lineup of crystal glasses, rows of top-shelf liquor, ice melting in a sterling-silver bucket, and a colony of sliceable lemons and limes. Given its stage-left position, the layout had been spared the worst of the destruction, only a couple of wine stems knocked off, one bottle of chardonnay on its side, and two lemons peeking out from under the hem of the tablecloth as if they had taken cover down there.

It was highly unusual for a member of the *glymera* in a house as grand as this one to have a self-service spread like that, but given what had happened? There was so much more to worry about than social propriety. Twenty-four guests had arrived for the gathering, and all of the males were former members of the Council, the invitation proffered by an expelled lieutenant of the Band of Bastards who had aspirations to Wrath's throne.

So, yes, V was right as usual. Everyone at the party was a traitor, and the evening had not been social in nature—which was a violation of law. Further, the Brotherhood would never have known about this, would not have been on-site to save the others, could not have stepped in in a nick of time . . . if it hadn't been for one of their own. Thanks to one brave soul, they had been able to respond instantly when the shadows had streamed in.

"How's our injury count?" Tohr asked.

There was a *shhht* sound as a Bic lighter was fired up and then the scent of Turkish tobacco wafted over.

"We've got a female in surgery," V reported. "We thought we'd gotten away with only an ankle sprain, but then she collapsed. Internal bleeding. Guess she was a victim of the shadows, too."

"Who is she?"

"This guy's *shellan*, as it turns out."

"Any chance they were targeted on purpose?"

"Hard to say at this point. But everything seemed random when it was going down."

"And no one's seen hide nor hair of Throe."

"Nope. The host with the most is still missing."

Tohr shook his head. "How did the shadows know the gathering was happening?"

"Maybe they were invited." As Tohr shot a glare over, V shrugged. "Don't you think it's a little too coincidental that all these aristocrats were standing around when the attack went down? Just like it's a little too coincidental that of the civilian deaths out in field from these entities, all were connected to the *glymera?*"

The urge to argue was nearly irresistible. Except the impulse came from being hungry and tired rather than any fault in Vishous's logic. The brother was right. The shadows seemed to be targeting the aristocrats, but it was hard to say for sure because no one knew who was behind the new threat or what their goal was.

"I need to go talk to the family," Tohr said as he went back to staring at the corpse. "Do we think the female is going to survive?"

"Hard to know, but her vital signs were poor when she went into surgery." V exhaled over his shoulder, releasing a blue stream of smoke. "I'll come with you."

"Not your style, is it."

"The son of this worthless male is worth the aggro."

Tohr shook his head at the dead body. "At least we can *all* agree on that."

# THREE

Helania, blooded daughter of Eyrn, made sure the hood of her black cape stayed up as she weeded through the crowd of live-action role players. The LARPers were overwhelmingly human, although not exclusively so. There were at least three other vampires, in addition to herself, among the two or three hundred people who were dressed in Dracula, stewing in drugs of various sorts, and looking for sex from all manner of strangers under the guise of playing characters in the game *Pyre's Revyval.*

The scent of fresh blood was so faint, she was not convinced her nose was actually picking up on it.

But she had to be sure.

As she moved through the throngs of people, hands reached out and brushed her arms . . . her shoulders . . . and she hated it. Over the last few months, however, she had gotten used to the physical intrusions. The humans who were playing at being other than themselves had no boundaries to protect of their own, and from behind their masks, they assumed she was under the roof of this abandoned, drafty old shirt factory for the same reason they were.

Not the case at all.

Through the purple lasers and gyrating bodies, she focused on the sturdy exit that was her goal. And as she closed in on the steel door, dread fisted her gut. The blood smell was growing ever thicker in the air—it was not enough for any human nose to pick up on, but to her vampire senses, it was like a scream piercing through ambient noise.

Something that was undeniable. Urgent. Terrifying.

Pulling open the heavy metal panel, she winced as the rusty hinges whined in protest. The stairwell to the lower level was badly lit, its air cold and damp, tinged with mold. She ignored all that. The coppery bloom of blood, as it rode a nasty updraft from the lower level, was all that mattered.

Slipping through the doorway, she whispered down the filthy concrete stairs. The temperature dropped perceptibly as she descended, and there was a second door at the bottom. This steel panel had had a far harder life than the upper one, its rectangular body kicked in such that it hung cockeyed from its hinges and did not sit properly in its jambs.

She opened the battered weight slowly, her hot hand on the cold lever, creating a shock that went through her nervous system like a chemical fire.

Peering around, her heart skipped a beat. The corridor beyond was broad as a street, arched at the low ceiling, stained like the inside of an old sewer pipe. Sixties-era fluorescent lights flickered from fixtures set overhead, their spastic illumination animating the series of doorways that extended into what felt like perpetuity.

The blood scent was obvious now.

Under her cape, under her hood, Helania shook so badly her teeth chattered, and even as her breath came out in puffs of white, she didn't feel the cold.

Within the folds that covered her, she felt for the gun she had holstered at her waist. She had learned to shoot it about eight months ago, and she couldn't say she was at ease with having the weapon on her. She wasn't even sure she had the guts to use it, but she was trying not to be foolish. Unprotected. A victim.

Like her sister had been.

Stepping out into the corridor, she stuck to one side without brushing against the paint-flaked, mold-smudged walls. As quiet as she tried to be, her soft footfalls seemed to echo like thunder, and the fear pounding through her veins on hooves of steel was something she wondered if the others upstairs could hear over the music.

Helania's body stopped before her brain gave the command.

The doorway was just like the others, made of wood panels nailed close together on horizontal supports, the arched top echoing that of the barreled ceiling like a stab at being stylish.

She looked around. She was alone, but there was no way of knowing how long that would last. Or whether it was even true, given the number of closed doors.

Reaching forward, her hand curled around the icy latch. She expected a lock to be engaged. When things gave way under easy pressure, her breath caught. Pushing with her shoulder, she met resistance and put more strength into it, something on the floor getting moved out of the way. But then she had to stop. Through the dense darkness that was revealed, fresh blood hit her nose like a heavy curtain, brushing into her face.

All at once, she was sucked back to eight months ago, a female she didn't know at her apartment door in tears, the four words the stranger spoke to her not registering.

*Your sister is dead.*

Helania pushed harder. The interior of the storage area was pitch black, and the strobing light from the corridor behind didn't penetrate far.

She got out her phone. Her hand trembled so badly that triggering the flashlight took a couple of tries—

The moan that came out of her mouth was that of an animal, the horror before her too great for her mind to comprehend, her senses overrun such that her vision went checkerboard and the world spun around her, out of control.

◆     ◆     ◆

The Black Dagger Brotherhood had resources that put even Boone's aristocratic background in the shade. Everything those warriors did and all that they had, from their facilities to their weapons, their toys to their serious gear, was top rate and state-of-the-art.

Take this mobile surgical unit, for instance. It was very impressive how the RV had been retrofitted with an OR and kitted out with all kinds of diagnostic equipment, including a portable X-ray and an ultra-sound machine.

Too bad its considerable capabilities, as well as the time and talents of its master, were going to be wasted on him.

As Boone pulled his heavy body into the back treatment bay, he shook his head. "Dr. Manello, this is not necessary."

The man in the scrubs and the white coat smiled, revealing pearly whites that had the telltale short canines of a human. He was a handsome guy, his dark hair and mahogany-brown eyes the kind of thing you'd see on an eighties medical drama. Mated to Payne, the surgeon was highly respected, and not just because he was capable of stitching up all manner of rips and tears, inside and out: In addition to all those technical skills, you had to be impressed by anything of masculine derivation who could be that close to Vishous's sister and still retain the structural integrity of his hey-nanny-nannies.

The human closed the rear door and crossed his arms over his chest. "How about you let me decide what's going on with that wound?"

"I'm just saying that I feel fine and—"

"Hey, can I show you something?" Dr. Manello leaned forward and tapped his white coat by the lapel. "What's this?"

Boone focused on the cursive letters that were done in black. "Your name."

"No, this part."

"'M.D.'"

"Do you have any letters with periods after your name like that? No? Well, then let's allow the Medical Doctor to make this call. If you're as a-okay as you say you are, you'll be out of here in a New York minute."

Dr. Manello's wide smile was as open and nonjudgmental as ever. Then again, you had to imagine he'd heard it all because he didn't just treat the trainees. He was part of the Brotherhood's private medical team, so he had to face off at the likes of a leaking or broken Zsadist, for godsakes.

And wasn't that enough to make your blood run cold even in theory.

"It's only a puncture wound," Boone groused as he stepped over to the exam table.

Hopping up, he was surprised to find that his shoulder started talking to him as he tried to get his jacket off. Pain, a well-known houseguest, had him wincing. Which sucked on a lot of levels.

"Let me help you."

Dr. Manello was gentle and took his time with the leather-outerwear-ectomy, but Boone would rather have had the man rip the jacket off. Left without something to command his attention in a particular direction . . . the things he had sought to avoid all night came rushing into his mind, a crowd bursting through the barrier they had been up against, chaos spinning up within the confines of his skull.

"That hurt?"

Boone glanced at the doctor. "What?"

"Your breath just got tight."

Not because of the wound. "I'm okay."

With the jacket off, Boone looked down at himself. Blood had seeped into the thin weave of his black Under Armour shirt, the ruddy brown stain located at the hollow of his shoulder.

Moisture wicking, indeed.

Boone removed his chest holster of daggers with the doctor's help, and then the nylon shirt was cut off. Okay . . . see? Not so bad. Just a little hole, the penetration about an inch and a half in length and thin as a pencil line. And due to him being properly fed, his body was already healing, the skin closing itself, reknitting, sealing the wound up.

"I told you," Boone said.

When Dr. Manello didn't reply, he looked at the human. The man was leaning back against the supply shelves and staring at Boone's naked torso.

"What?" Boone asked. "It's fine."

"I agree, the wound isn't that bad."

"So with all due respect, what's the problem?"

"Where's your bulletproof vest, son?"

Boone's mouth opened to answer that one—but he stopped the words before they came out. What he had been about to say was that his vest, the Kevlar one that, as a trainee, he was required to wear out in the field, was right over there with his leather jacket. His arm, on the side of him that wasn't injured, was even raising so he could point, in a helpful way, over to where both it and that jacket of his were lying next to the small sink.

Except there was nothing over there that would stop a bullet.

In fact, he had forgotten part of his gear when he had gotten dressed at his house. And when he had attended roster call at the checkpoint, he'd had his jacket on, so neither he nor anyone else caught his mistake.

From out of nowhere, he heard the Brother Phury's voice: *Distraction during preparation is deadly.*

"Listen," Dr. Manello said, "I don't want to be a buzzkill, or a snitch. But I can't not report this."

Boone was tempted to try and argue that it was "only once" and he would "never make this mistake again." But giving airtime to that defensive edge he was suddenly sporting was just going to make him look like an unprofessional jackass.

Which, considering he'd forgotten a critical safety requirement? Well, he'd already captured the incompetent flag tonight, hadn't he— thanks to wondering what the hell his father was up to at that party.

"We've got company, hold on." Dr. Manello went to the rear door and waited. When a pound on the panels sounded out, he unlatched things and opened up. "Hello, boys. Welcome to my humble abode."

Tilting forward, Boone looked out of the bay. Standing in the red glow of the RV's rear lights, with hot exhaust billowing around them like fog on a Steven Seagal movie set, Tohrment, son of Hharm, and Vishous, son of the Bloodletter, were everything Boone wanted to be: Experts in fighting and straight-up killers when they had to be. The pair were also stand-up males who were loyal to their own and willing to sacrifice themselves for any who fought beside them.

Whether it was another Brother. Or a soldier. Or some idiot trainee who had made a mistake that could have cost him his life.

For a split second, Boone thought maybe they had been injured out in the field, too. But as they stared at him and him alone . . . he knew why they were here.

"Is he dead?" Boone heard himself say. "Is my father . . . dead."

Tohrment stepped up into the mobile surgical unit, the vehicle's suspension tilting to accommodate his formidable weight. That the Brother Vishous came inside with him made Boone want to throw up. Even the diamond-eyed warrior, best known for his ability to flay flesh from people using only words, was looking subdued.

The closing of that back panel was loud as a slam—or seemed that way. Boone was aware of his hearing sharpening to a painful degree, the rustling of sterile packages as the doctor got supplies out to clean the stab wound like gunshots in a canyon.

Tohr's hand landed on Boone's shoulder, heavy as an anvil. "I'm really sorry, son. Your father . . ."

Boone closed his eyes. He knew the Brother continued talking, but he couldn't track the words.

"So I was right, wasn't I?" he interrupted. When no one replied, he popped his lids and focused on Tohrment. "I was right, they were plotting against Wrath."

The Brother applied a little pressure to his hold. "Why don't you sit down here."

"I thought I was?" Boone glanced at the floor and was surprised to find he was on his feet. "I guess not."

Without warning, the world went on a twirl with him in the center—or maybe he was winging around the outside of the galaxy and looking in—and then everything went black and silent . . .

Things didn't stay that way, however. The next he knew, he was lying on the exam table, with the other males standing around him and talking over his body.

Huh. So now he knew what a corpse felt like.

Staring up at them as they conversed among themselves, he noted the way their mouths moved and watched as their eyes shifted positions as the conversation ebbed and flowed. There was a nod or two. A shake of a head. Meanwhile, Boone was back to hearing nothing. Then again, when you found out you'd had your father killed? Even if it was indirectly? Well, you were allowed to retreat into your head.

Especially if, from time to time, and for good reason, you had prayed for this very moment right here.

*Mission accomplished*, he thought sadly.

But what else could he have done? He had told his father not to go to that gathering at that aristocrat's house. And when his sire had refused to listen to reason—not that the male had ever much cared about Boone's opinion of so much as a dessert course, much less matters political—he'd known he had to follow through on doing the right thing. He'd had to go to the Brotherhood: As a civilian, aristocratic or not, he had a duty to report treasonous behavior to the King. Still, it had taken him three sleepless days to make the appointment because he'd had to be sure that he was doing it for the right reason, not as some retaliation against Altamere—

"How did it happen?" he blurted.

All of the males looked down at him. Then Dr. Manello and Vishous looked at Tohr, passing the buck.

So it was bad, wasn't it.

"He was attacked by a shadow." As Boone sat up, the Brother put his hand on Boone's shoulder again. "Nope, stay down, son. You're still the color of flour—"

"What happened?"

The story had to be repeated twice—and then a third time—before he came to understand that not only was his father gone, but his step-*mahmen*, too.

The latter was apparently also a surprise to Dr. Manello. Not that his patient had died in surgery from a blood clot—of course, he remembered that—but that the female in question had been related by mating to Boone.

"I am so sorry, son," the good doctor said. "Please know I did everything I could to save her."

Boone shook his head. "I'm sure you did. And we had no relationship to speak of, really. I didn't wish her ill, but . . . wait, tell me about my sire again?"

This time, the story's totality finally sank in: His father had been standing among the other aristocrats at the gathering when shadow entities had come in and ambushed the crowd. The Brothers had counterattacked, but not before Altamere had sustained mortal injuries.

Boone rubbed his face. There was a question he needed to ask, except the syllables refused to come out. All he could do was stare helplessly into Tohr's navy blue eyes.

It was a long moment before the Brother answered. "We made sure that before there was any reanimation that your father's body was properly contained."

"Thank God," Boone breathed.

When it came to his father, "close" had been a measure of physical proximity between them rather than emotional connection. "Close" was a function of the pair of them sharing a house, passing each other in the luxurious halls, occasionally sitting in the same gracious room at a meal. And yet no matter how estranged you were from your parent . . . when it came to their death, it shook the ground under your feet—even if you were lying down.

"We're going to take you back home," Tohr said. "After Manny's finished here and you feed."

Boone glanced at his shoulder and was surprised to find that the stab wound was half stitched up.

"I don't need a vein," he muttered. "I just took one last week."

"Not an option," Manny said. "And the Chosen is on her way."

As something started to ring, Vishous frowned and took out his phone to answer a call. "Yeah." The Brother frowned, the tattoos at his temple distorting. "Where?"

Vishous turned away and lowered his voice, his words coming out so softly, Boone couldn't track them.

Tohr spoke up. "Listen, son, with all this stress, and that injury, you do need to feed. And as soon as it's done, I'll take you home."

Boone stared at the Brother's somber face. "You've done this a lot, haven't you."

"Done what?"

"Broken bad news to people."

"Yeah, son, I have." The Brother exhaled long and slow. "And I've been on the receiving end of it, too."

# FOUR

All things considered, getting summoned away was probably for the best.

As V resumed his form a good ten blocks from where Boone was getting treated, he took a minute to catch his breath in the cold. Granted, he wasn't breathing hard at all. And he needed to hustle to his destination. But . . . shit. Seeing that kid find out the why and how of his father and step*mahmen* being dead? After he'd been the one who turned the gathering into the Brotherhood?

The kid felt responsible. You could see it in his face.

It was heartbreaking. Even for someone like V who prided himself on having a meat locker for a pericardium.

Taking out a hand-rolled, he lit up and strode down the snow-packed sidewalk. On the exhale, smoke wafted forward on the wind that was hitting his back, a bright white cloud in the cold. After another two draws, he was better calibrated. Good timing, too. The place he was looking for was only three hundred yards away. And given the number of humans in that wait line? Getting himself properly nicotine'd was a goddamn public service.

Still, being sent on this "errand" was so much better than taking Boone back to the kid's house. V sucked at sympathy. What was that saying? It was just a word between "shit" and "syphilis" in the dictionary.

Okay, fine, he wasn't *that* bad.

But yeah, that young male? V totally felt for him. Plus, come on, demonstration of that trainee's loyalty to Wrath aside, V knew from crap fathers. The Bloodletter, hello.

*Whatever, time to truck with the humans,* V thought as he licked the lit end of the hand-rolled and put the stump into the ass pocket of his leathers.

As he approached the line of shivering, stamping, huffing humans, the men and women milled in their places, their eyes latching on to him through their masks, the women's bodies warming with arousal, the men's retracting like they didn't want his attention. Underneath all those coats and jackets, he could see enough of their costumes. Neo-Victorian. Black, like they were allergic to color. Lots of high heels, even on the dudes.

The bouncer at the door puffed up his sizable chest like he was looking forward to telling Vishous that he wasn't allowed in the place. That he had to wait like everyone else. That he wasn't nothing special—

V reached into that pea head and tripped a bunch of wires.

Like magic, the bouncer dropped the I'm-in-charge-here-not-you act and leaned to the side to open the way in. "Right through here."

*Thank you, motherfucker.*

Striding past the guy, V entered the club's anteroom. Oh, look, they had a coat check. And what do you know, the big-breasted, puff-lip'd attendant was staring over at V like she wanted to take his pants and check them in with her hands and her tongue.

He kept right on going.

The facility was an old shirt-making factory converted into absolutely nothing at all. The space's retrofitting for the event was happy hands at home, from the sound system's cobbled-together collection of woofers and tweeters to the strung-up lights that hung from the ceiling by bungee cords and strings to the random lasers that shot through the dim space with all the coordination of free radical electrons.

After years of monitoring humans on the internet, he was well familiar with the characters the people were playing. *Pyre's Revyval* was a popular tabletop role-playing game, and the world building and vampire-based characters of it had long metastasized out of the pages of its rule book and away from those eight-sided dice that were used to determine character motivation and strength.

As he moved through the crowd, looking for some staircase that went to a lower level, he wanted to shove people out of his way. About a year ago, he had set up an emergency calling service for the vampire species, a 911-style clearinghouse for everything from crimes to medical problems. Manned by volunteers, the callers were screened and help was assigned as necessary. The incident he was currently responding to had been logged in about twenty minutes ago. A female had phoned with the report of a body on the lower level of this place. She had refused to give her name, but she had been very clear about the location within the club—

There it was. A steel door in the far corner.

He beelined for the thing and ripped it open. The stairwell beyond smelled nasty and was refrigerator-cold, and he made fast work out of the descent. The instant he broke out into a subterranean corridor, he smelled the blood. Fresh. Female.

Vampire.

"Sonofabitch."

Striding down, he used his nose to determine whether there was anyone else around. Nope, right now, although there had been plenty of traffic tonight: All kinds of faded scents, human and vampire, masculine and feminine, lingered like shadows, nothing but two-dimensional representations of the living-and-breathing who had come down here and fucked and gone back up to the party.

The female who had done the dialing had apparently not stuck around. So it was impossible to know which of the scents was hers.

But he knew where to stop.

In front of one of the many doors.

The fresh blood was loud as a scream here.

Before he opened the way in, he frowned and dropped to his haunches. A single footprint gleamed red on the concrete floor, its heel toward the door, its triangled toes pointed away. V looked up and down the corridor. Yes . . . there. Another print. Nearly invisible. And then a final one after that, so faint he only saw it because he was looking for the damn thing.

*The killer?* he wondered. *Or the caller who reported she'd found a body?*
Maybe they were one in the same.

He rose to his full height, grabbed the door handle, and opened up. The area beyond was pitch black, and the piss-poor light from the flickering fixtures in the corridor didn't illuminate shit. Didn't matter. He knew exactly where the body was, and not just because of the overwhelming scent of blood. As his eyes adjusted, he could tell there was something hanging from the ceiling directly in front of him, and like the footprint, it glistened, the spastic light from over his shoulder blinking across glossy contours.

V unsheathed his lead-lined glove, releasing the glowing palm and fingers of his curse from the confines that protected the world from immolation. The illumination that emanated from his hand was so bright, he blinked from the glare, and as he held it forward, he ground his molars.

A masked female was hanging from the ceiling, a meat hook piercing the base of her skull, its speared point protruding out of her open mouth and touching the tip of her nose. Her throat had been slashed, the veins draining their load down the front of her naked body, her blood a transparent death shroud that colored her pale flesh bright red.

Through the mask's twin holes, her eyes were open and staring straight at V.

"Motherfucker," he said.

Just like the other two.

+    +    +

Boone opened the front door to his father's house and stepped over the threshold. The familiar smells of lemon floor polish, freshly baked bread, and roses from the ladies' parlor made him feel like he was in a distorted dream.

*It should be different,* he thought as he looked around the formal foyer. *Everything should be different.*

His father was no longer alive. And that monumental change seemed like the kind of thing that should be reflected in this mansion that had always defined the male. Sure as his station in society and his money and his bloodline had made Altamere the male he was, so too had this sprawling manse determined the course of, and provided the grounding to, his life.

"The door is ajar."

At the clipped syllables, Boone looked to the left. Marquist was standing in the archway of the dining room. He had a polishing cloth in his hand, his jacket was removed and his starched white sleeves were jacked up by a pair of black elastic bands.

*The door is ajar.*

As if the butler were part of the alarm system of the house.

"My father is dead," Boone said.

Marquist blinked. And then that cloth started to tremble ever so slightly. Other than that, the male showed no reaction at all.

"Ehrmine's gone, too," Boone continued. "They're both . . . gone."

The butler blinked a number of times. And Boone knew damn well any upset was not because of the loss of the female. Ehrmine had been no more significant to Marquist's nightly existence than she had been to Altamere's.

Without another word, the butler turned on his heel and walked away. His free hand, the one without the cloth, reached out into thin air, as if, in his mind, he were steadying himself on the wall.

The flap door into the kitchen wing opened and closed as he disappeared through it.

Boone turned to the cold breeze that was funneling into the warm house. Stepping back out over the threshold, he stood on the stoop and stared past the curving drive to the lawn. In the light of the security fixtures that were tacked under the mansion's roofline, the blanket of snow that covered the grounds of the estate was pristine, its weight buffering the already subtle contours of the property all the way down to the stone pillars by the road. At irregular intervals, mature oaks and stands of birches, currently barren of leaves, filled out vacancies like polite guests at a lawn party, and there were also flower beds that would be filled with pale blooms when the warm weather came.

As the cold wind blew against his fighting gear, he thought of his blood *mahmen*.

Back when Illumina had gone unto the Fade, he'd never gotten a clear story about what had happened to her. It had been sudden and unexpected, at least from his point of view. She had been young, healthy, and relatively free of bad habits. Nonetheless, one evening, he had come down for First Meal, and his father had informed him, over the scones and the eggs Benedict, that her Fade Ceremony was being conducted on the Thursday following.

That was it.

His sire had then risen from the head of the dining room table, picked up the *Wall Street Journal*, and departed.

Boone could remember looking down at where his *mahmen* had always sat. There had been a setting of china and silverware put out for her, as if her presence had been anticipated.

Left to his own devices, he had gone up to his room and set himself down at his desk. He'd had some notion of writing Illumna a letter, putting to page the questions going through his mind. But he hadn't gotten far with it because he'd never really been able to ask her anything in life—and death, as it turned out, did not cure that.

Next thing he'd known, it was time for Last Meal. He had dressed in a different suit than he'd worn at the start of the night, as was appropriate, and joined his father at the dining table once again. Marquist had served them, as was customary when they had no guests.

There had been no setting for Boone's *mahmen* then.

His eyes had lingered on her empty chair while his father had talked to the butler about . . . the same stuff he always did: Social gossip, house issues, staffing issues. Boone had stayed silent. Then again, even when Illumna had been alive, Altamere and his butler had always done all the talking at "family" meals, the normal boundaries between master and servant disappearing in the relative privacy.

At the time, the lack of real conversation around the loss of Boone's blood *mahmen* had not struck him as weird. That was the way things were done; the more likely a subject was to upset, the less that was aired on the topic.

Or maybe it had been more a case of the death being unimportant.

Fast-forward two decades. The fact that he was standing here in the winter wind, with a shoulder that was throbbing from its stitches and a headache that was pounding from his empty stomach . . . with no one to talk to . . . was right out of the family playbook. The aristocracy had always been better at appearances, fancy velvet curtains drawn across stages that were ultimately empty—

The first of the shapes materialized out of thin air over on the right, the big body appearing in the shadows of the house's exterior lights, taking solid form.

Boone's eyes watered as he recognized who it was. And before he could offer a greeting, there was another directly on the male's heels, a female this time.

Craeg and Paradise.

In quick succession, three others arrived. Axe. Novo. Peyton.

His trainee class.

As the five of them came up the walkway, Boone felt a loosening in the center of his chest, although what was unleashed was unwelcome. The sadness seemed like a waste of time, not only because it wasn't going to do anything to fix what had happened at that *glymera* party, but because it wasn't like he wanted his father back. Or his step*mahmen*.

Craeg took off his Syracuse ball cap. "Hey, my man."

The hug that followed said more than any words could have: *We're here for you. You are not alone. Whatever you need, we got you.*

Paradise, Craeg's mate, was next. And as she wrapped her arms around Boone, he relaxed into her embrace.

"I know this is hard," she said. "I am really sorry."

As a fellow member of the *glymera* and a distant cousin, she understood exactly how it was in aristocratic families. How grief was one more thing that was swept under the Oriental, put away in the safe, tucked into the silver closet.

Axe and Novo and Peyton were up next, and then Boone just stood there like a planker.

"Let's go inside," Paradise said gently.

"Oh, right. Yes, of course. It's cold out here."

Next thing he knew, they were all in the ladies' parlor, sitting on the formal sofas, looking at each other. He expected Marquist to burst in at any moment. When that didn't happen, he took a deep breath.

"I'm glad you guys came."

"Do you want us to stay overday with you?" Paradise asked.

"I don't know what I want, to be honest." He looked at the vase of flowers set on the coffee table in front of them all. "I just . . ."

Axe spoke up. "I know, it's hard to explain—"

"My father was traitor."

As he said the words, he realized he was trying them on for size. Testing the weight of them. Strapping on the shame for the first time, and undoubtedly not the last.

"My father . . . was a traitor." He shifted his eyes to his friends. "He was directly involved in the previous plot to overthrow Wrath, and there is a good chance he was part of a revival of that treason tonight."

Craeg cursed and turned his hat around and around in his hands. Paradise put a hand on Boone's shoulder. Axe made like he was spitting on the ground.

"I tried to get him to stay home." Boone shook his head. "I told him not to go there. But he refused to listen to me."

"Your father is not you," Paradise said. "You are not him."

"I know." He cleared his throat. "Anyway, I just want to go back to work."

He studiously ignored the volley of worried looks that his friends shared. But as long as his shoulder was good to go, what was the problem?

"When will you be doing the Fade Ceremony?" Novo asked. "We want to be there."

"I haven't gotten that far." Speaking of which, where was the body? Who had his step*mahmen's*? "But I'll let you know."

He had no brothers or sisters, no grandparents, no aunts or uncles who were still alive after the raids. But he had a couple dozen cousins in the *glymera*, none of whom he knew well at all because he had kept such a low profile socially. Benign estrangement aside, however, he was willing to bet that all of them would want to show up for Altamere's ceremony.

They would surely come, if only to gawk, assuming the news of how the death had occurred would hit the gossip phone tree—and how could it not? His father had been attacked in front of over twenty other members of the aristocracy, and all of them, evidently, had survived.

And as for Boone's step*mahmen*? He had to assume that her family would take care of, and honor properly, her remains. She had, after all, come from a very good bloodline with plenty of proud heritage of their own.

As if his father would have mated anybody lesser than he.

"I'm going to keep the ceremony low-key," Boone heard himself say. "You are all welcome to attend, but I understand if—"

The gonging sound that echoed around the foyer was a surprise, and at first, his congested brain didn't know what the interruption was caused by.

"That's the front door," he mumbled.

Getting to his feet, he was aware of a tensing throughout his chest and shoulders, although that was not because of whoever might have arrived: He didn't want to go the rounds with the butler.

But Marquist didn't make an appearance.

As Boone opened the heavy panels, he exhaled in a combination of surprise and curious relief. "Oh, it's you. You didn't have to come . . . but I'm glad to see you."

"I just heard." Rochelle's pale eyes were just as lovely and warm as they had been a year before. "I am so sorry."

There was a long pause. And then they both moved at the same time.

Even though he had not seen the female since the night their arrangement had ended, and in spite of the fact that it was totally improper, Boone opened his arms wide, and in a similar breach of protocol, Rochelle stepped in against him. At first, the contact was light, but then they were holding each other tightly. Like his father's house, she smelled the same, Cristalle by Chanel perfume and the expensive French soap she had always favored. She was dressed in the same style, too, wearing an Escada suit that tastefully set off the subtle curves of her figure.

It was black. For mourning. And as most aristocratic females only wore color, he knew she had changed for him before she'd came over.

As they eased back, he noticed absently there was loose snow on the crown of her blond chignon.

"Oh," she said with a start, "you have guests."

Boone glanced over his shoulder and saw his fellow trainees leaning forward in their various seats and staring out of the archway at him—at him and Rochelle—with wide, interested eyes.

"Come meet my friends," he said. "You already know Peyton and Paradise, of course."

As he drew her in beside him, it felt natural to walk into the elegant parlor with her against his hip. But the fact that he was still armed, and so were the people on those sofas, was a reminder that his life had diverged greatly from Rochelle's since their arrangement.

She had stayed in society, yet he hadn't heard she'd been mated? Then again, he was out of everything, for the most part.

He was so glad she'd come, though.

"Everyone," he announced, "this is Rochelle."

# FIVE

"You don't have to make me tea."

As Boone spoke up, he stared across the kitchen at Rochelle. She was over at the sixteen-burner stove, putting a copper kettle on an open flame. He was over in the alcove of windows, at the table where the staff sat and took their meals. There was no one else around. Marquist had clearly announced the passing to the other staff and the *doggen* had all retired unto mourning for their master, as was proper.

Meanwhile, the butler was probably polishing Altamere's shoes with his own tears.

Man, their relationship had had some blurry lines, hadn't it.

"Boiled water is the only thing I know how to make," Rochelle said.

The other trainees had left shortly after her arrival, as if they were hoping Boone needed privacy with the female. He was going to have to take care of that after nightfall. When he went back to work.

He would set them straight that there was nothing going on.

"And even so," she murmured, "I may burn this kettle."

"Don't worry, I'm no great chef, either," he murmured as he rolled his shoulder, testing out its range of movement.

"Where is your china?" She pivoted around and measured a square mile's worth of cupboards. "So many places to choose from."

Boone shrugged. "Let me help. We should be able to find it together."

When he went to stand up, she shook her head. "You stay put. I'll do the sleuthing."

She worked her way around the cabinets, opening up the double-sided, paneled doors, inspecting all manner of spices, mixing bowls, cooking equipment. She finally found some mugs above one of the three dishwashers. They were fine porcelain and ornamented with a hand-painted gold-and-maroon pattern. They were rarely used, however. Boone's father had not approved of them, calling them unforgivably coarse.

In a tone that suggested their height and their contours were an offense against the laws of nature.

"Are these okay?" Rochelle asked. "They do not have saucers, but I can't seem to find anything else."

"They're perfect."

"And I even located the tea." She smiled as she returned to the stove. "Do you take honey or sugar?"

At least the condiments were easy to get a bead on. They were cloistered on a silver tray on the counter, ready to be portioned out in the way the master of the house had preferred things—

Wait, she had asked him something, hadn't she?

"I can't remember," he said. "It's been so long."

He had no idea what was coming out of his mouth. But she didn't press him, and the next thing Boone was aware of was a fragrant, steaming mug in front of him, with Rochelle taking a seat across the table.

"So how have you been," he said as he took a test sip. "How are things with your male?"

He was trying to make simple conversation, but the way her eyes teared up made him regret the attempt at pleasantries.

"Oh, Rochelle." He shook his head. "What happened?"

"It just didn't work out. In spite of your very valiant attempt to help us."

As she dabbed at the corners of her eyes with her pinky, careful not to smudge her makeup, he reached across and touched her arm.

"I'm so sorry," he said.

"It's all right." She took a deep breath. "It just . . . wasn't meant to be."

The pain in her face was so difficult to witness, and in that moment, he hated the aristocracy. Undoubtedly the male had heard about the broken arrangement and hadn't wanted to deal with the baggage.

"The *glymera* is a bad place," he muttered.

"I'm very sorry about your father," she said roughly.

He opened his mouth to share that sentiment out of a sense of propriety—and couldn't get the lie out. "Thank you. It was rather unexpected."

"Life is unexpected."

"Too true."

If anyone would have told him a year ago that the pair of them would be sitting here, unchaperoned, after his father's death, with him now a soldier and her unmated? He'd have you're-nuts'd the person.

As the silence stretched out, he wanted to ask her more about her male, and he had a feeling that she wanted to know more about what had happened to his sire. But they were both lost in their own mourning, grief like a third wheel who was taking up all the conversational airspace in the room.

The two of them just sat across from each other, the tea she had made them both untouched and gradually losing its warmth.

Until it was stone cold.

✦   ✦   ✦

Dawn crept up slowly on Caldwell, the sun's rays ushering in the start of the workday for the human population, the end of the work night for vampires. The fact that the glowing bastard's arrival took a while was the only thing good about winter as far as Vishous was concerned.

He got back to the Brotherhood's crib from that LARPers club downtown just in time, and as he re-formed at the mansion's cathedral-worthy front entrance, his retinas burned and his skin prickled under his leathers. Overhead, the sky was thick with clouds, but that didn't mean shit considering the stakes at play. You got caught outside? One slice of blue heaven peeking through all the overcast and you needed to get the barbecue sauce and an urn for your ashes.

Cranking open the heavy front door, he entered the vestibule and put his mug into the security camera. Fritz did the duty on the other side, the butler's wrinkly face stretching into a wide smile.

"Sire, welcome back!"

Okay, so, V hated cheerful people. Spunky people. Folks that would be described as "happy," "chirpy," "perky," and/or "peppy."

Especially those peppy fuckers.

But Fritz, the Brotherhood's head of household, was another story. The old butler was just so unreservedly delighted by all the people around him. He lived to serve the needs of his masters and mistresses, and how could anyone, even a misanthropic motherf'er like Vishous, not love the guy? After all, just because 99 percent of the mansion's occupants could not tolerate sunlight, that didn't mean the place couldn't use a little sunshine. And all Fritz had to do was walk into a room, and the *doggen* brought that kind of warmth and optimism with him.

"How you doin', my man?" V said as he shut the vestibule door behind himself.

"May I get for you some Grey Goose, sire?"

"Nah, that's okay. I'll . . ."

As the *doggen's* face drooped into total, abject sorrow, V's voice dried up. Jesus Christ, it was like he'd kicked a puppy.

"Ah, that'd be great. Thank you, I'll take a double."

Cue the return of that brilliant smile and the bounce in that step. "I shall make you the most perfect tumbler! Right away!"

Fritz took off for the billiards room like a winning lottery ticket had been left out on the bar, and V could only shake his head. He really didn't want to be waited on, but for all the S&M he had enjoyed over the course of his lifetime, he couldn't stand the pain of disappointing that *doggen*.

The butler was like kryptonite.

On the other side of the majestic, multicolored foyer, Last Meal was in full swing in the dining room, the members of the household sitting around that long-ass table, all kinds of *doggen* serving food and drink, the loud voices and raucous laughter the kind of thing that emanated outward and filled every room in the house, no matter how remote. Ordinarily, V would have headed in there, but he took out his phone and checked his texts. Yup. Jane was wrapping things up in the training center's clinic, and then they were going to have a dinner just the two of them in the Pit.

Nice and private.

Yum.

And no, he wasn't talking about the expertly prepared food or the good wine. Not even the peach cobbler he'd requested for dessert.

Nah. He was thinking of another kind of . . . peach.

Courtesy of his impatient nature—which had just had its blade sharpened with a molar-grinding dose of sexual need, fuck him very much—V turned to the ornate staircase that led to the second floor. He wanted to be on the ascent already. He wanted to be in front of his King, making his report. He wanted to be heading back to the Pit to see his *shellan* get very, very, very naked—

"Here we are, sire!"

Fritz held out a silver tray. In the center of it, a tall glass filled with ice was sporting about six inches of Grey Goose. There was also a lemon wedge broken over the rim and a monogrammed cocktail napkin underneath the production like a little area rug.

"Thanks, my man."

V took the glass and the napkin. With his gloved hand, he dropped the wedge in, took a test sip . . . and the long sigh he let out was not a lie. The shit was perfect. Just the way he liked it, and prepared with the kind of love and devotion he would never understand, but had certainly come to appreciate.

Not that he would be sharing that sappy fact with anyone anytime soon.

"This is amazing."

Fritz beamed like a kid who'd gotten a gold star for perfect attendance, and you had to admit that the reaction was a heart-warmer. But even if V had been a hugger, and he wasn't—unless it was to strangle someone from behind—you couldn't so much as shake the butler's hand. The last person who had actually embraced the *doggen*, assuming the story was true, was Beth back before they'd all moved in here, before she'd learned the protocol. Fritz had nearly needed life support from shock. Yes, he was delighted to be valued, but if you actually told him how much he meant to you or the household? Or, God forbid, showed him affection? He went fainting-goat on you.

"Thanks again," V murmured.

Fritz bowed so low it was a wonder his jowls didn't brush the carpet. "It is my most sincere pleasure to serve you."

Hitting the stairs, V finished his Goose by the time he got to the second-floor landing. The doors to the study were wide-open and the great Blind King, Wrath, son of Wrath, sire of Wrath, was sitting on his father's throne. Behind an ancient desk the size of an SUV.

"More good news, huh." The King rolled his shoulder and it cracked like a stick. "Can't wait."

Yup, even though Wrath was fully blind behind those wraparounds, there was nothing wrong with his hearing or sense of smell.

"Just keeping the trend going." Stepping into the study, V shut the double doors. "You know, 'cuz I follow fashion like that."

The room, with its pale blue walls and French furniture, was a total mismatch for the last pure-bred vampire on the planet, but it was what it was. This was where the Brotherhood and the fighters in the household met after hours, all twenty tons of male crammed in here, trying to only put one butt cheek down on the delicate Louis XIV bergère chairs and settees. At this point, though, the absurdity had worn off, habit had set in, and now it would be weird to congregate anywhere else.

"So the dead female wasn't a false report?" Wrath said as V came over and parked it by the fire.

"No." He swirled the melting ice in his glass and took another drink. "It was legit."

"Did you get an ID off her?"

"No. She was naked. Clothes were gone from the scene."

Under the desk, George, the King's golden retriever, thumped his flagged tail in greeting, but the dog didn't leave the feet of his master.

"How messy was it?" Wrath asked.

"Very. We contained things and I removed the body with the help of Zypher and Balthazar. It's at Havers's across the river. The only thing we can do is wait for a missing persons call or for someone to post something in one of the social media groups. No one at the clinic recognized her, but somebody has got to know her and be missing her."

"Such a goddamn waste. Are we looking at a human perpetrator?"

"I don't know. Lot of scents down there, of both species. In the storage room where she was hanging, too."

"This is the third body at Pyre." Wrath cracked his knuckles one by one. "The third female, right?"

"Yup, but one was a human. It's pretty much the same M.O. as far as I can tell. At that club, after sex, everything taken, body left to bleed out. I think we've got a serial predator. I also think we need to bring in a professional on this."

"Agreed. I want to find the SOB who's playing with knives. And I want you to put out a warning on social media. I'm tempted to even shut that club down the old-fashioned way."

By the term "old-fashioned way," V knew damn well the King wasn't talking about petitioning the human mayor of Caldwell to throw a padlock on the front door of that shitty old factory. It was more a case of a hundred ounces of C4, a gas tank's worth of accelerant, two matches, and some popcorn.

And you know, it might be nice to make some s'mores.

"I'll post the warnings online," V said. "And we should make sure the Audience House has flyers. The word will get out fast."

"I want someone monitoring that place. If it is a serial killer, they'll want to go back to their hunting grounds. We can catch him that way even if he's left no clues to his identity behind."

"Or hers."

"It can't be a female."

"Says who."

"Good point."

As V considered the staffing requirements, he mostly hid a curse. They were shorthanded already, and after the altercation with those shadows earlier tonight? Things were going to be extra tight as they tried to pin down exactly what had happened at that *glymera* party.

But, whatever, someone's off-rotation was just going to have to be spent rubbing elbows with fake vampires because the King was right. They needed somebody on-site to catch the motherfucker.

"We'll take care of everything," he vowed.

The King dropped his chin and stared out over the top of his wraparounds, his pale green eyes lit with an unholy light. He might have been unable to see, but he could still send a message and a half with those peepers.

"You find this murderer," Wrath said in a deep growl, "and deal with it, do you understand me."

Vishous nodded once. "I'll handle the endgame personally."

Humans had jails for this kind of thing. Vampires, on the other hand, believed in an eye for an eye. And whether the perp could handle sunlight or not, this was going to be taken care of the "old-fashioned way."

You pick off members of the race, whether or not you knew what they were? You were knocking on a door that was going to be answered.

"I'll keep you posted."

"You do that, V," Wrath growled.

# SIX

The following evening, Boone dematerialized to the rear driveway of the King's Audience House, re-forming back by the detached garage. Following a shoveled pathway, he entered through a reinforced door, and as he went through the kitchen, he raised a hand in greeting to the various *doggen* who were preparing fresh pastries for the waiting room. The scents of baking sweet dough and homemade cherry and strawberry preserves reminded him he had not had First Meal, but as soon as he was out the flap door and away from the triggers, he forgot all about his stomach.

With long strides, he headed for the front of the mansion, zeroing in on the deep voices that percolated out of the open doors of the dining room. And as he went along, he practiced his speech: 1) his shoulder had fully healed, and he was willing to let Dr. Manello examine said healing; 2) he'd had all day to process his father and step-*mahmen*'s deaths; 3) the Fade Ceremony could wait until he was off rotation in two days; 4) there was nothing in the trainee handbook that required a mourning period following the passing of any family members.

Halfway through the foyer, he paused and smoothed his hair down. Which was stupid and a hangover from his youth. Like any of the Brothers were going to care whether his cowlick was behaving?

Kicking himself in the ass, he marched up to the archway and knocked on the jamb.

Across the largely empty space where civilians had private meetings with their King, a couple of the Brothers looked over from the fireplace. It was Rhage, the biggest and blondest of the Brotherhood, and Butch, the used-to-be human with the Boston accent. The former was eating a half gallon of mint chocolate chip ice cream with a sterling silver spoon, the tub wrapped in a dish towel to keep the cold contained. The latter was reviewing what appeared to be pictures on a cell phone, swiping with his finger, his brow down low.

"Hey, Boone, what's doing?" Rhage said around a full mouth. "I'm real sorry about your dad and step*mahmen*."

Butch looked up from the phone. "Me, too, son. That is tough stuff. On so many levels."

To acknowledge the statements, Boone bowed yet did not say anything. He didn't want to be rude, but as far as he was concerned, his sire and the male's second mate never needed to be discussed at work again.

"I'm supposed to meet Tohrment?" he said.

"The brother should be here any minute." Rhage motioned with the spoon. "Come on in."

"I can wait out here?"

"Nah, it's okay," Rhage said. "You want some ice cream? I got tubs of chocolate chocolate chip and rocky road in the freezer. And you can have your own spoon."

Boone shook his head because his throat had gone tight. Words of condolence were easier to handle than gestures. The former was what he was used to in the *glymera*—although in the case of Rhage and Butch, he knew they'd meant what they'd said the moment they'd seen him. The latter, the offer of ice cream from Rhage's personal stash, he was not used to.

He had always taken care of himself because he'd had to.

"Thank you, but I ate before I came." He didn't like to lie, but it was better than tearing up over some rocky road.

"Let me know if you change your mind." Rhage refocused on Butch. "So then what did V do?"

Butch didn't answer right away. He was back at the phone, and he waited until he finished whatever series of images was on it before looking up again.

"V got the body down and packed it up." The Brother put the cell in the pocket of his Peter Millar slacks. "He van'd the remains to Havers's, and we're just hoping someone comes along to claim her because we have no ID at this time. V's asked me to take over and investigate."

"Well, it is how you used to make a living, Mr. Homicide Detective." Rhage ran the spoon around the inside of the container, gathering the gently melted part. "Where do you start?"

Boone tried to make as if he wasn't eavesdropping by going on what he hoped looked like an idle wander around the large Oriental in the center of the room. Meanwhile, his ears were buzzing—and then there was no hiding his interest. As he came up to the desk where Saxton, the King's solicitor, sat during business hours, he paused and leaned down. There was a stack of bright yellow 8.5-by-11s, and when he saw the warning printed on them, he had to pick one of the flyers up and turn toward the Brothers.

"What happened last night?" he asked.

"Another killing," Butch said. "At Pyre's Revyval."

"The role-playing club?" Boone put the flyer back on top of the stack. "Which meets in that abandoned shirt factory."

"That's the one. You know anything about it?"

"Some of my cousins used to go there. I don't know if they still do."

"Could you call them for me? I want to talk to anyone who's familiar with the scene."

"Sure." Boone took out his cell phone. "I'll hit them up right now."

Stepping away from the desk, he started texting his third cousin once removed and his second cousin on his blood *mahmen*'s side. As he was typing out the messages, he couldn't help but think that someone else had lost somebody in their family the night before.

*Were they in a conventional mourning?* he wondered. Which would be painful for sure, but also, he imagined, a kind of relief to be "normal" inside the grief.

Instead of where he was with his sire. Nowhere.

He was just hitting send on the second text when Tohrment came in the Audience House's front door. The Brother brushed snowflakes out of his black hair with its telltale white stripe in the front and then he unzipped his leather jacket. The weapons underneath gleamed in the mellow light of the foyer and made Boone more determined.

"Hey, son," Tohrment said as he entered the dining room. "What's doing?"

Boone cleared his throat and remembered his 1), 2), 3), and 4). "I was hoping to catch you for a minute—"

"No, you're not going out into the field." The Brother took off his jacket. "I know you're convinced you're going to go stir-crazy with nothing to do, but I told you what needed to happen before you're released to go back on schedule. You're going to have to go talk with Mary and get a mental health clearance from her. Then you're going to take a couple of nights off until the Fade Ceremony. After that, we'll reassess."

Boone dropped his voice because he didn't want to be overtly insubordinate. "There's nothing in the handbook that requires—"

"There doesn't have to be." Tohrment turned his back to his Brothers and likewise got quiet. "I already made one mistake with you. I'm not making another."

"What are you talking about?"

"You should never have been out in the field last night. You were distracted for good reason because of where your sire was, and I knew that, but it slipped through the cracks."

"I took down a slayer just fine."

Tohrment leaned in, his navy blue eyes nearly black. "You could have gotten killed because you forgot your vest. If you'd been stabbed in the heart and bled out, or had been mortally wounded by a bullet, it would have been on my conscience for the rest of my life—and no offense, that particular car trunk is full enough already without my trying to squeeze in baggage with your name on it."

Boone opened his mouth. Shut it. Opened it again.

But damn it, what could he argue now?

"You don't understand," Boone muttered. "I'm going to lose my mind if I have to sit in that house and stew about—"

"You can help me."

Boone glanced over at Butch. "With the death at Pyre?"

"Yeah. Bring me over to your cousins, and then we'll go check the club out." The Brother held his palm up to Tohr. "He'll be with me the whole time. I'll take care of him and accept all responsibility for his welfare."

When Tohr looked like he was going to argue, the other Brother kept talking. "Come on, man, it's not out in the field. We're not going to be looking for the enemy, and before you throw out a line about the risk of us tripping over something we might have to do something about, unless you put him on house arrest, he's liable to meet a *lesser* or shadow anywhere in the city—just like anybody else. I'll make sure nothing happens to him, and have some pity on the kid. You wouldn't want to be locked up with nothing to do under his circumstances, either."

"I won't take any chances," Boone rushed in. "I'll do whatever he tells me to."

"It's also a good opportunity to share basic investigation protocols." Butch shrugged. "It's a skill the trainees should have in case they get called in to respond to a crime. Like how not to disturb a scene. What to watch out for. How to document. There's a legitimate training benefit."

Tohr crossed his arms over his chest and cursed. And that was when Boone knew he was going to be allowed to help.

At just that moment, his phone went off with a text. Checking what had been sent, he turned the screen to face the Brothers.

"This is from my third cousin. He'll see us later tonight."

"Then let's go to Pyre first." Butch took out his phone and dialed something, then held the unit out to Boone. "Here's the call that came in last night. Listen to it, and you can try that number again while I drive. I've already left a message once and no one's gotten back to me."

Boone glanced at Tohr as he took what was being offered to him. Putting the Samsung to his ear, he offered a conciliatory smile to the Brother.

Tohr pointed a finger in Boone's face. "You get yourself killed doing this and I'm going to strangle you again even though you're already dead. Are we clear?"

"Yes, sir," Boone said as the recording kicked in. "Crystal clear—"

All at once, the world receded, his senses and awareness supplanted by the sound of a female's desperate voice.

*. . . Hello? Hello . . . I need help—oh, God, she's dead. She's . . . dead just like the other one . . .*

✦   ✦   ✦

Twenty minutes later, Butch pulled his best friend's R8 V10 Performance Plus into a parallel parking spot downtown. The car was murdered, everything blacked out, and it was sleek as a space shuttle, capable of reaching *Millennium Falcon* speeds in spite of the fact that it weighed as much as Rhage. The thing was also a dinosaur in the best sense of the word, a throwback to the big-engined cars of the past that sounded like pro wrestlers and sucked gas like a sprinter used oxygen.

In other words, it was right up V's alley.

And by "parallel park," Butch meant "really-frickin'-close to a plowed mound of snow big enough to ski down." Ah, winter in Caldwell, New York. Where that white stuff metastasized like it had learned the trick of singularity and was trying to take over the world.

You know, the weather version of AI.

"I didn't know these cars were good in the snow," Boone murmured as the trainee eyed that mini-Killington like he wasn't sure whether he was going to get his car door open.

"Just dematerialize out on my side."

"Good deal. Thank you."

Butch got out and held things open. "And as for the R8, Audi quattro works year-round. All you need are good treads. No clearance on that front air dam, though. Two inches, tops, is all we've got to work with."

Of all the trainees, Butch had always liked Boone the best. Maybe it was because the kid was the kind of stand-up, no-fuss, steady-Freddy type that tended to form the backbone of any good team. After all, Butch had always wanted to be that guy himself—and failed spectacularly when he was a human. But finally, after a good three decades of trying to drink away his emotions, he was getting to that goal. All it had taken was the female of his dreams, a jump-started transition into a whole different species, and free rein to express himself sartorially.

But there was another reason he cared about the kid after last night. He couldn't help but take an interest because he knew all too well what it was like to lose a family member in a bad way.

Boone re-formed on the outside of the R8 and looked around at the abandoned buildings with their broken windows. "Is it safe to leave V's car here? What if it gets stolen."

"Full coverage on the insurance." Butch shut the door. "But more to the point—everyone's going to assume it's a drug dealer's whip. Guaranteed it'll be right here when we get back."

Butch hit the lock, and the pair of them fell in side by side at a walk. "You can't trust anyone on the street, but you can always put your faith in how the street behaves."

With the cracked sidewalks so not an option because of the piles of snow, they proceeded down the middle of the plowed street. Even though the only going concerns in this part of the city were the drug dealers on the corners and the prostitutes on the straightaways, there was enough through traffic so that the snowpack evened out the pot-holed asphalt underneath.

"Can I ask you something?" Boone said into the cold.

"Anything."

"That voice recording. The one that was from the call-in line—was V able to trace the phone number it came in on? I mean, he's the one who's so good at that stuff, right?"

"He thinks it was a burner. And if that's true, we're not going to find anything out about who owns it or used it unless they answer the damn thing and are willing to talk."

"And she didn't leave a name." Boone laughed in a hard burst. "Okay, that's a stupid thing to say, I guess. Because I didn't hear a name on the message."

"Tell me what you did hear."

"She was scared. She was really scared."

"What else?" As Boone recited the message word for word, Butch nodded. "Yup, you got all that right. But what about the background?"

"Like when the call came in?"

"No, of the call itself." Butch glanced over. "What did you hear."

The trainee frowned. "Nothing—" Those dark brows lifted. "Ohhhh. So she didn't call from the club. If she had, we would have heard the music and the crowd around her."

"Exactly. And V told me that he had no service on the lower level of that old factory—so it's a good guess that whoever called in also didn't have a signal down there."

"She must have phoned from outside the building, then."

"Or maybe she wasn't there at all."

"What do you mean?"

Butch looked both ways as they crossed the street even though there were no cars around. "Confirmation bias is a dangerous thing when you investigate a case, especially in the beginning. The truth needs space and airtime to reveal itself. The only way to make sure that happens is to let your brain and your senses record every nuance while at the same time you resist your rational side's desire to come to any hard-and-fast conclusions. There is a solution to the whodunit out there. I promise you that. But you have to earn the right to that revelation, and the way we do that is by sacrificing our assumptions at the altar of OMG-I-know-what-happened."

"But you have to decide some things, though, right? Like who to talk to? And what to ask them?"

"The truth will tell you who you need to interview and what you need to ask and where you have to go. You don't decide a thing." Butch shook his head. "I'll say it again. You've got to watch for confirmation bias. It sneaks in and causes you to deliberately or subconsciously deny the existence of facts which do not support a given conclusion that you've pulled out of your ass. Truth is absolute, but it's like the existence of God. You don't know you've got it until you do."

"Have you ever failed to solve a case?"

"I had a ninety-two percent success rate. Which, considering how much I was drinking while I was a detective for the CPD, is a miracle."

"Wow. You must be really good at what you're doing."

Butch thought of the last image he'd had of his fifteen-year-old sister, Janie, waving at him as she had been driven off to her death in that car full of teenage boys.

He shook his head. "Nah, I just refused to quit. Even if it killed me, and it nearly did, I wasn't going to stop what I was doing until I nailed every one of my victims' killers." He looked back over at his trainee. "That's something else you should keep in mind. Your chances of finding the bad guy increase to an astronomical level if you outwork their need to stay ahead of you. Sooner or later, all killers, even the good ones, slip up. You just gotta be ready to take advantage of that version of Murphy's Law."

"I'll keep all this in mind. I promise."

Annnnnnd see, this was why he liked working with the kid, Butch thought. Boone listened, accepted advice and criticism, and always tried to do his best.

Butch reached over and gave the trainee's shoulder a squeeze. "I know you will, son."

# SEVEN

As Boone strode along next to the Brother, it was a relief to focus his mind on something other than himself. Too bad the topic was violence and death, but that was his job, wasn't it. And he was on the right side of that ledger. One of the good guys.

That mattered.

"So what else about the call?" Butch asked him.

Up ahead, now only three blocks away, it was easy to make out the club's wait line of humans, the lot of them stomping their feet in the cold, their extravagant wigs and wild makeup the only things that showed of their costumes because everything else was covered up by Joe Blow parkas and full-length coats. In the warmer months, he imagined, they would be like a stand of peacocks, flashing their particular extravagancies in a mating ritual designed to be successful according to the LARPers' value system.

*Is the killer standing there even now?* Boone thought as he remembered the choking horror and fear in that female's voice recording.

"What else did you learn on that call?" the Brother prompted.

Boone's eyes went down the lineup of humans, memorizing each face. The body types. The hairstyles.

Rage coiled in his gut. And to answer Butch's question? Well, the other thing he'd picked up on from that call was that whoever had put the terror in that female's voice, whoever had killed the most recent victim, needed to die in the same terrible way.

Somehow, that didn't seem like a good thing to throw out there—

He snapped his head toward the Brother. "'The other one.' In the call, she said 'just like the other one.'"

"Righto. So what does that tell us?"

Boone narrowed his eyes on that wait line again, his fangs descending. "There will be others unless we stop the killer."

"Yup. That is the one conclusion that I am allowing myself to draw at this point."

On that note, Butch unbuttoned his fine cashmere coat. Which was protocol for when anyone interacted with humans. You know, just in case you needed to get to your weapon. As Boone did the same to his leather jacket, he felt that anger of his shift inside of his skin. He was so hoping that they found the guy who did this tonight—

Butch stopped dead in the street. "Not 'guy.'"

Pulling up short, Boone looked around. "What?"

"You just said you hope we find the 'guy' who did it tonight." Butch shook his head. "We don't know whether the killer is a male or female. Remember, no assumptions at this point, okay? And when we're in there, just observe. I'm going to do most of the work."

Jesus, Boone thought. He wasn't even aware of having spoken out loud.

"Yes, sir."

Butch clapped Boone on the shoulder and resumed walking. "You're going to do fine."

As they closed in on the entrance to the old shirt factory, bypassing the line, the two bouncers at the door flexed up, but they ultimately didn't follow through on the my-turf posturing. Instead, the two men just nodded the way in clarity, like they'd been hit in the face with a pair of VIP passes.

You had to love mind control over humans. And it was not a surprise that Butch clearly was a master at the manipulation.

"So you've been here before?" the Brother asked as they entered and went past a coat check.

Boone made a mental note to talk to the woman on duty, except how would that go:

*Hey, have you seen any vampires go past you?*

*Oh, yeah, sure. About three hundred every night. Were you looking for one?*

He shook himself back into focus. "Ah, I've only been here once, and it was a while ago. But like I said, my cousins come a couple times a year."

"Yeah, this doesn't seem like your scene."

Boone checked out a half-naked human who was vomiting into a plastic bag in the dark corner. "No. It's not."

Inside the large open area, there was a big crowd dancing, talking, hooking up. The music was loud, so people had to get close to communicate—and the darkness reinforced the need to go clutch: With the limited faculties possessed by humans, they had to get up in each other's spaces to hear and see properly in the dim environment. And it wasn't all *Homo sapiens* LARPing it. He could sense a few vampires milling around among the men and women, but just three or four—and they stayed away. Made sense. There was an unwritten rule that you didn't fraternize with these rats without tails, so no one in the species was going to hi-how're-ya and reveal themselves in this environment unless they had to.

"Let's go down to the lower level," Butch said over the din. "V told me the stairwell's entrance is somewhere back there."

As Boone follow-the-leader'd through the gyrating bodies, he stared straight ahead and let his peripheral vision track the masks, the drapes of clothes, the heights and the weights of Pyre's patrons. Just as he had been trained to do.

The stairwell to the subterranean level turned out to be easy enough to find, and they proceeded down a dank, cold series of steps, bottoming out in a corridor that was long as a football field and strobe-lit by a series of last-legged fluorescent ceiling mounts.

"Fourth door down on the right," Butch said. "Storage area."

Boone looked at the sequence of heavy doors. "Is that what's behind all these?"

"Think so."

The sound of something snapping brought Boone's head around. Butch had taken a pair of bright blue nitrile gloves out of the pocket of his coat and was putting them on.

"It's a little late for this"—the Brother held his hands up like a surgeon—"but old habits die hard and all that shit."

"Why is it too late?"

"There is no way they got the body out without disturbing the scene. No matter how careful they were."

From out of another pocket, Butch produced a small headlamp and put it on like a crown. Triggering the beam, he stopped in front of door number four. "You stay out here, but by all means, lean in and look around. Like I said, the scene's basically ruined at this point, but there's no reason for us to add to that by both tromping around inside."

As the Brother opened the heavy panels wide, the creaking hinges were right out of a horror movie—and so was the scent that hit Boone's nose like a slap.

Blood. Not exactly fresh, no. But there was a lot that had been spilled—

*Oh, God,* Boone thought.

Down on the dirty concrete floor, directly in the path of Butch's frontal lobe beam of light, there was a congealed puddle that was shocking in size.

As Butch stepped through the jambs and looked around, the walls of the empty storage area glistened in the icy illumination of his lamp. But at least all that appeared to be groundwater seepage as opposed to plasma.

The beam rose to the ceiling and moved in a slow circle before stopping in the center of the room directly over the congealed puddle. "This was where she was hung up. On one of these."

A series of iron eyelets, thick as a male's thumb, were set in rows in the ceiling's heavy beams. It was hard to imagine what they had been used for. Maybe as part of a dyeing system for fabric?

"Was it by ropes?" Boone asked. "How she was hung up, I mean."

"A meat hook." The Brother got down onto his haunches and looked around, his lamp illuminating the Jello-like blood too many times for Boone's comfort. "Boy . . . if she wasn't dead before he hung her up, she did not last long."

"Him?" Boone tried to cough the tightness in his throat away. "I thought you said we shouldn't draw conclusions."

"Fair enough, you caught me. But statistically, the vast majority of serial killers are male. And the ritual nature of these killings, with the females strung up, throats slashed, all of them bleeding out here at the club, is a clear pattern. The killer finds what they're looking for and does what they have to with the victims out of sight down here."

Boone coughed into his fist again. "What exactly did he do to her?"

"I didn't show you the pictures, did I?" The Brother held his phone out behind him on an arm stretch. "They're in the camera section."

Boone swallowed hard as he took the unit and went into photographs. When he called up the first of . . .

"Oh . . . *fuck*," he breathed.

One terrible image, after another . . . after another. There seemed to be an endless number of them—and abruptly, the smell of the rotten, moldy earth, and the cold pool of blood, and the idea that someone had lost their life right down here where he was made him dizzy.

"Excuse me for a moment."

The polite words were spoken fast, and he didn't wait for an acknowledgment. His body moved before he was aware of his brain ordering his legs to lift his feet so he could back away. When he hit the door opposite the one that was open, he coughed a couple more times and turned the phone screen into his leg. Dropping his head, he breathed through his mouth and felt the world spin—

The smell of fresh air in the springtime, of delicate flowers, of . . . sunshine . . . had him lifting his eyes.

Down by the stairwell's door, a figure was standing still as a statue and focused on him. And in spite of the black hooded robe that covered the head and draped down to the feet, he knew it was a female.

And that *scent* of hers. It went in through his nose and didn't stop there. Somewhere along the neuropathways of his mind, or maybe it was in his very veins, what started as a thing he smelled became a full-body sensory experience.

Like touch.

Like . . . a caress.

Straightening, he took a step forward. And another. Sure as if she were calling his name and he were powerless to resist the entreaty. But before he made it very far, she disappeared back through the stairwell's door quick as a gasp.

Desperate not to lose her, he took off in her wake, his stride nothing short of a bolt. By the time he got to where she had been standing, the distorted steel panel was easing into its poor-fit position against its jambs, and he yanked the weight open. Following that springtime scent, he jumped up the steps three at a time and broke out into the club proper.

She must have been going at a dead run, he thought. To have gotten up those landings that fast.

Boone looked around to assess whether she'd gone all the way out of the building or was trying to get lost in the crowd. If the latter was her goal? Mission accomplished. There were too many people dressed in black with too many cloaks covering their heads—

There she was. Heading for the exit. Fast.

Shoving humans out of the way, Boone didn't care if he created chaos—and unlike her, his big body couldn't bob and weave through the tight squeezes between the men and women. By the time he ran through where the coat check was, she was out the door, her scent already beginning to fade.

Out in the cold, he barraged past the bouncers and looked left and right—

There, going around the far corner of the building. The tail end of her cloak billowing out behind her.

Boone closed his eyes, intending to pull his dematerialize-in-a-pinch trick—except then he realized he had a movie theater's worth of human eyeballs focusing on him. Not exactly the kind of PR stunt the vampire race needed: *Surprise! We really do exist!*

Cursing a blue streak, he took off on foot and tried to follow her prints in the snow. There was no way of isolating which were hers, however, and her scent had dissipated into the night.

The female was no doubt gunning for some privacy so she could ghost out of here. And if she did that, he was never going to catch her.

Boone rounded the corner of the building and slowed his roll to a walk . . . which then petered out to a standstill. There were no security lights on the exterior flank of the old building. None on the warehouse next door. And the illumination from the distant streetlights only carved out a narrow visual slice down the space between the structures. Even with the reflective quality of the snow cover and a set of super-charged vampire retinas, there was a lot that he couldn't see.

"Goddamn it—"

The soft click of a gun safety being taken off duty ripped his head around.

Staring into the dense shadows, his nostrils flared as he caught her scent on the cold breeze.

*Yes* . . . he thought. *There you are.*

"You can trust me," he said into the darkness. "I won't hurt you, I promise."

◆    ◆    ◆

*I'm not going to give you a chance to hurt me*, Helania thought as she kept her nine-millimeter trained on the vampire who'd tracked her outside the club.

The dark-haired male was standing in the dim glow of streetlamps that were a good block and a half away, but there was more than enough light to assess him. And damn . . . he was downright enormous, with heavy shoulders, a barrel chest, and long, powerful legs. All that so-called real estate was covered in black leather, the jacket he had on open in spite of the cold, his hands bare of gloves.

His deep-set, pale eyes were trained right where she was standing in the darkness.

*You're too good-looking to be a killer*, she thought to herself.

But come on, like only hump-ugly males killed people?

Still, she was shocked at how handsome his face was: Strong, even features, as well as a pair of lips that made her think of things that should be last on her cognitive list given the circumstances of their acquaintance, as it were.

"I just want to ask you a couple of questions." He flashed his palms at her and slowly raised them up like he was on a TV cop show. "My name's Boone. And you can lower that gun."

Maybe he could see her, although she doubted it. She was very far back from the glow he was standing in. How had he found her? Oh, wait—he'd probably heard her taking the safety off.

And was that an aristocratic infliction to his words?

"Can you tell me what you were doing down in that corridor just now?" he asked.

"It's not restricted access. Anyone can go there."

There was a pause. "It's you. You were the one who called us."

Helania felt her heart rate double. Which was saying something considering how fast her pulse had been to begin with. But yes, she had called the Brotherhood's emergency number. Yes, she had reported what she had walked in on last night. And yes, she had gone down to the lower level just now to find out what he and the other male he'd come with were doing.

Two large males enter the club and ignore all the sex opportunities? While they make a beeline for the back where the stairwell was?

Who the hell else could they be?

"You're a Brother?" she asked.

"I'm a trainee. But I came with one and I've been put on this case." He lowered his hands. "I swear, I just want to ask you about what you saw last night. That's the only reason I followed you out here. You haven't returned our calls, and I was worried I'd lose you."

Helania stared down the barrel of her gun at him. For a split second, an image of her sister came to mind and she teared up. Was this the mistake Isobel had made? Letting her guard down around a male she thought she was safe with . . . only to pay for that misstep with her life?

"You can trust me," he said softly.

No, she couldn't. But as the image of that female hanging from the ceiling came back to her, she realized she might need him. Assuming he was who he said he was.

And that was not a given.

"What do you want to ask me," she said. "I told the operator all I know."

"What's your name?"

"Helania."

"I'm Boone. And I'm sorry that we have to meet like this."

If they were not separated by twenty feet—and a gun—she had a feeling he would have offered her his hand, and she was glad he couldn't. She didn't want to touch him—although not because she was repulsed by anything about him.

It was the opposite, and that was the problem.

"So what happened last night?" he prompted.

Helania cleared her throat. Like that would pull her thinking together. "I saw a male of the species go down to the lower level with a female. They didn't come up for quite some time, and I had to check and see if she was okay."

"Do you come to the club regularly?"

"In the last few months, yes."

*Make that the last eight months*, she thought. Since Isobel had been killed.

"The female in question—you were a friend of hers, then? You knew her."

"No, I was just worried for her safety."

"Had you seen her at the club before?"

"That I don't know. She was wearing a mask, and she still had it on when I . . ." Helania swallowed hard as horrible images flooded her mind's eye. "Anyway, with all the costumes, it's impossible to say whether she'd been there before."

"Why were you concerned about her welfare?" Boone held up his hands like he was trying not to offend her and make her defensive. "I mean, people have sex at the club, and it happens down there, I'm sure. It's all part of the experience, right? I'm just wondering why you felt the need to check on her."

"Females are allowed to watch out for each other."

"No doubt. But I'm trying to figure out how you knew she was in trouble—"

"I didn't kill her."

The male—Boone—recoiled. "I didn't think you did. Why would you call the body in if you had?"

"I have to go—"

"Was the male she was with wearing a mask? Can you tell me what he looked like?"

She shook her head. And then remembered he probably couldn't see her. "No mask, but he had sunglasses on, so I couldn't see his eyes. He was also wearing a black skull cap pulled low. He was big, bigger than you." It seemed odd to use the male's body as a comparison, as if she had crossed some line of propriety. "He carried her down there while they were kissing. That's all I know."

"How long was it until you went to check on them?"

Helania was unaware of deciding to lower her gun. One moment it was still pointed at his chest; the next it was settled down by her leg.

"I should have gone sooner." She felt her shoulders slump under her cloak. "I let them go for too long."

"How long?"

"I don't know." She'd gotten distracted searching the crowd for other signs of unrest or danger. "I was people watching. I didn't . . . I should have gone sooner."

"Can you give me any idea of how long it was?"

"It might have been well over an hour, but it could have been longer. I thought I smelled the blood, you see." In her mind, Helania replayed her descent down those stairs step by step. "I caught the scent emanating from the basement and had to follow it."

"Were you here with anybody?"

"No, I only come on my own."

The male—Boone—crossed his arms over his chest, and didn't that make him look even bigger. Especially as he frowned. "Do you have any specialized training?"

"What do you mean?"

"As in self-defense? You said in the message you left that there had been another victim. And yet you went down there, away from the crowd, to track the scent of blood. Weren't you worried about your personal safety?"

She pictured Isobel clear as day. "Not at that time, no. I was only worried about her."

# EIGHT

The female was either blindly heroic . . . or utterly reckless, Boone decided as he stared into the shadows thrown by the old building.

Thanks to his eyes adjusting, he could make out her form, the black of her cloak offering a subtle contrast to the density of the rest of the darkness she had hidden herself in. She had lowered her weapon down by her side, but she seemed poised to bolt, her body weight tilted back on her feet and leaning to one side. He wanted to see her face with a desperation that was unsettling, but that hood was still up—and for no good reason at all, he wondered whether she had held it in place as she'd run off.

He wanted to catch her scent again, but the wind was being blocked by the buildings on either side of them. Given that heat rose, even from bodies that were clothed, all that wonderful natural perfume was being wasted on the heavens above—

Wow. Since when had his romantic switch gotten flipped?

Before that question could be answered, Butch came tooling around the corner of the club. He was striding fast and came to a stop as he saw Boone.

"What's doing over here," the Brother demanded. "And I'll take my phone back, thank you very much."

"This is Helania," Boone said by way of apology. "She's the one who called in the victim."

Butch's aura changed immediately, and he walked forward, halting in the snow next to Boone. As his phone was held out to him, he accepted it with a nod.

When he spoke next, his voice was soft and very grave, and he addressed Helania in the shadows. "Thank you for letting us know about her. I'm really sorry you had to see her like that, and I want to reassure you that you did the right thing. We're very grateful for your help, and we're going to find who killed her."

The female—Helania—stayed silent, but at least she seemed to nod. And that gun stayed at thigh level, Boone noted.

"We'd just like to talk to you," Butch said. "We're here to find out who hurt her, and that was the reason you called the Brotherhood, isn't it? You wanted to help her."

"I told him everything I know. I have nothing to add."

"Then maybe you could just repeat it all for me?"

There was a long silence, during which the background thumping of the music and the chatter of humans in the wait line around front seemed to get louder. If she were calming herself to dematerialize, Boone thought, they were never going to see her again. Sure, he had her name, but courtesy of having to live among humans, vampires were good at disappearing themselves—and that included from people who were of the species.

If she ghosted out, he would never see her again.

And why did that strike him as such a tragedy?

"We can go back inside where it's warm," Butch offered. "We can find a corner in the coat check area. I promise this won't take long. We're just trying to gather as much information as we can so we can help her—"

"How do I know you are who you say you are?" she said.

Butch lifted his hands slowly to the front of his cashmere coat. "Don't shoot me, please. I'm not wearing a vest."

That gun came back up in a snap, and the quick movement made Boone think the female—Helania—might have had some training and experience with the weapon. Good to know—and it offered him some reassurance given that she'd been at the club alone.

"Go ahead," she said.

Moving with care, Butch opened the two halves.

A gasp came out of the shadows. Then again, it might well have been the first time the female had seen a set of those famous black daggers, strapped handles down to the chest of a warrior: As per the Old Laws, it was a violation punishable by banishment or even death for anyone not in the Brotherhood to possess a black dagger, much less wear them in the traditional way.

That gun didn't just go down again. It got buried somewhere in her cloak. And then the female came out of the shadows. As she emerged, the first thing Boone did was try to see under her hood, but he couldn't make out anything of her face.

"You are safe with us," Butch told her.

"I don't feel safe anywhere anymore."

"Come on, let's go somewhere warmer."

Back around front, the bouncers at the door let the three of them inside, and then Butch commandeered some folding chairs in a corner of the coat area, pulling them into a little circle behind a half curtain that hung from the ceiling. There was an awkward moment as everyone stood around, and then Butch took the lead in the downward-butt pose.

As Boone sat across from the female, he tried to look like he was focusing on her in a professional, not personal, fashion. And the former was true. He was thinking of her as a witness who might well possess more information than she'd so far shared.

But there was also an undercurrent that he could not deny.

"Like I said," the Brother stated as he took out a small, spiral-bound notebook, "this will not take long. I'm Detective O'Neal—I mean, the Brother Butch. I'm Butch. And you are?"

"Helania." She shook her covered head. "But I told him everything I know, and it's not much."

Crossing his legs at the knees, Butch stared across at her with hazel eyes that were full of compassion and understanding. "I'll bet you haven't been able to sleep or eat since you found her."

There was a long pause. And then Helania shook her head again. "Not really, no."

"I'm really sorry you had to see that." Butch's eyes stayed steady on the female, even as his pen jotted something down. "I know it's been tearing you up. My victim really suffered when she died. Can you tell me what her name is?"

"I don't know her," Helania said sadly. "I just . . . I was worried because she'd been down there with that male for so long."

"Of course you were worried about her. Females have to look after each other."

The hood of the cloak nodded. "That's how I feel. It could have been me."

"I know. It's dangerous here. Dangerous everywhere." The Brother leaned forward earnestly. "I know it's hard to trust us. Even with the black daggers I'm wearing, you don't know him or me from a hole in the wall. But I just want you to know that she's my victim now. I'm going to take care of her, and the way I do that is by finding out what happened to her and making sure whoever killed her is taken care of. The way you can continue to help her is to tell me whatever you know. No matter how trivial or inconsequential you think it might be. And the sooner you do that, the better for her."

There was another long silence, and the background thumping of the music rose to fill the void. Meanwhile, Boone tried not to interrupt. Fidget. Be an ass.

"You can trust us to take care of her," Butch reiterated. "We're all on the same team."

"What will you do if you find the killer?" came the soft inquiry.

"When," Butch corrected. "It's *when* I find them. And whether they are a human or one of us, they will get what they deserve, I promise you."

After a moment, a pair of shaking hands rose to the hood that covered Helania's head. As she drew the fall of black fabric back, Boone gasped before he could hide his reaction. Her features were fine to the point of being delicate, her yellow eyes rounded, her brows arched, her bow-shaped mouth and her pinpoint nose balanced perfectly in the oval of her face. Her hair was long and wavy, streaked with blond and red, and her skin was darker than his.

She was . . . astounding.

"I can't stop seeing her," Helania whispered. "Every time I close my eyes, I . . . I see her hanging from that ceiling. That hook . . ."

"I know." Butch put a fatherly hand on her knee. "It's really terrible. But together, we can do something about it."

Those yellow eyes lifted to the Brother's. "You won't let him get away with this."

"No, I won't."

"I've been looking for him, you see." She nodded toward the open area where the club's members were. "I know he'll come back here."

"Because he's killed before."

That yellow stare went to the floor. "Yes."

"How did you know about the other deaths?"

"There was more than one?" she asked with surprise.

"Yes."

"Oh, God . . . well, I only knew about the one other." Her lids lowered. "That female's murder was all over the species' groups on social media. It made everyone uneasy."

Boone spoke up. "So that was why you were looking out for the victim last night. Even though you didn't know her."

"Everyone's nervous," Helania said. "Who's a vampire, that is."

"Which is understandable," Butch murmured. "Now, the male or man you saw with my victim. Had you seen him in the club before?"

"I think I have. I'm not sure, though. It's dark and there are so many people."

"What's he look like?"

"He's enormous. Black sunglasses. Black skull cap pulled down low. Black leather clothes—although that's not saying much."

"Could you identify him if you saw him again?"

"Maybe. But I never got a good, clear picture of his face. His hat and glasses covered a lot of his features, and again, it's difficult to see in there."

"How about his scent? Would you recognize that?"

"I don't know." Helania touched the side of her nose. "I followed the blood, not him or her."

"So you saw the male with my victim. What were they doing?"

A blush flared in her cheeks. "What people do here. Kissing. You know."

Boone's eyes focused on her mouth and refused to be redirected. In all of his life, he couldn't remember being so captivated by a member of the opposite sex. He was liable to forget why he was sitting this close to her, and that would be unacceptable.

Kicking himself in the ass, he shifted in his seat and thought of the dead body he'd seen on the Brother's phone.

Butch was nodding. "And do you remember what time it was when you noticed the female leave with him to go to the lower level?"

"Not really." Helania's stare moved over to Boone—and what do you know, he felt like he'd been put under a heat lamp. "As I told him, I saw the male take her downstairs. I stayed on the main floor until I scented the blood. It was so faint that I wasn't sure whether I was imagining it. But then I thought about that female alone with that male and I got worried so I went looking for her."

"How long was it between when you saw them leave together and when you went to check on her?"

"Like, an hour or more. But I couldn't say for sure."

Butch took down some notes, mostly without looking at his notebook. "Did you see anyone else down there? When you found her?"

"There was no one."

"And you were all alone?"

"That's right."

"Any idea about what time this was?"

"It's hard to say. I wasn't keeping track. I had already been at the club for a couple of hours when I saw him."

"Did you come to the club with anybody last night?" After she shook her head, Butch said, "Can you give us the names of some people you talked to while you were here? You know, anyone who could give us a clue about when you arrived and when you left?"

Her jawline tightened. "What exactly are you suggesting?"

"Nothing at all. I'm just wondering if someone else might have glanced at their watch or their cell phone while they were talking to you so we could get a time frame going."

"I didn't talk to anyone. I never do."

"So why do you come here?"

Helania's eyes flared with anger. "I am of age and no one's *sehcluded* female. I can go where I wish."

"I'm sorry." Butch touched the center of his chest in apology. "That came out badly on my side. And I did not mean to suggest that you were involved in hurting her."

"Are we finished?"

"Sure, we can be finished." The Brother flipped a page over and wrote something. Tearing the sheet off, he offered it to Helania. "This is my number. I'm going to stay in touch and I want you to do the same. I'm assuming that the number you called into the service from is your cell—and that we can reach you on it?"

Helania leaned forward to take the page, her narrow wrist flashing out of the voluminous sleeve of her cloak. "Yes, it is. And yes, you can."

"I called you a number of times tonight."

"I was here and I have it on mute."

Butch nodded. "If you remember anything else, you let me know."

Helania tucked the paper somewhere in her cloak. Then she got up from her chair, and Butch did the same, and some things were said.

As Boone rose to his own feet, he didn't track the conversation. He was too busy willing the female to look at him one last time.

And then she did.

Citrines. She had eyes like those sunshine gems, deep and mysterious . . . tantalizing. It was so easy to get lost in them.

"My name is Boone," he blurted. Which was stupid. Like he hadn't told her before. Twice. Or had it been three times, for godsakes.

She just nodded. Or at least he thought she did. Then she put the hood up over her spectacular hair and walked into the club, her slight body disappearing into the crowd.

*She should be leaving,* Boone thought. *Not going back in there.*

"Come on," Butch said. "We've got to drive over to Havers's next. Before we hit your cousin's just before dawn."

It was a moment longer before Boone could turn away, and as they exited the makeshift club, he felt like he had left something crucial to his well-being behind. The urge to turn around was nearly overwhelming.

He told himself that at least she knew how to point a gun at someone.

They were almost halfway back to the car—and yup, Butch had been right, the R8 was still where they'd left it—when the Brother stopped in the middle of the street. Boone went a couple of steps farther and then pivoted around in the snow, expecting the Brother to be checking his phone for a call or a text.

Wrong.

Those hazel eyes were locked on Boone. "Watch yourself, son. She could be in on this in a small way, in a big way. You don't know."

"What?" Boone frowned. "She called us about the body. And you told her she wasn't in trouble."

"Anything I said back there was to get her to talk. Don't confuse interrogation with sincerity, even if the person we're talking to takes it that way. The first rule of homicide is you don't trust any witness, person of interest, or suspect until you have corroboration or evidence that proves their story to be true. No matter what someone looks like."

"But why would she have called us if she were involved in the killing?"

"Not our problem at this point. We just need to stick to the facts." Butch motioned over his shoulder. "That female phoned the emergency line the night our victim was strung up by the back of her skull like a side of beef with what probably *was* a meat hook. That is the only thing we know for sure about anything right now—"

"She didn't do it."

Butch shot over a spare-me-grasshopper look. "How do you know that? Because of the color of her hair? Or was it those eyes you kept trying to catch."

As Boone stomped his boot in the snow and cursed, Butch shook his head. "Look, I'm not calling you out or anything. This is the first time you've been in this situation, so it's not a surprise you require training. I just need you to keep your head in the right place. I've seen a lot more than you have when it comes to this kind of shit. I strongly urge you to take my advice—and if you can't? It's no harm, no foul, but you will not be involved in this investigation. Are we clear?"

Boone opened his mouth, intending to bring up how rattled Helania was. How she was clearly traumatized. How she . . .

. . . had beautiful citrine eyes and hair he wanted to run his fingers through.

Clamping his piehole shut, he kept a string of curses to himself.

"Hey," Butch said, "losing focus happens to everyone. Especially if you've never done this before. I just need your game head on, okay?"

When Boone nodded, the two of them started walking again. And as he shoved his cold hands into the pockets of his leather jacket, he decided that he knew one other thing for certain about Helania. Aside from the fact that she was absolutely, positively, not the killer.

He was going to see her again.

One way or another.

◆    ◆    ◆

The race's medical facility was across the river, the sprawling subterranean maze of treatment units buried beneath a farmstead's flat fields and forested perimeter. There were four entrances to the place; one in the actual old farmhouse—which formed a front for the operation to the human world—and then three other kiosks scattered throughout the acreage in the pine trees.

As Boone materialized in front of the western kiosk, he had no familiarity with the medical center. As an aristocrat, prior to his joining the Brotherhood's training program, he'd been used to Havers coming to the house if anyone needed a healer. Now, as a trainee, he was treated by the Brothers' private staff in their own clinic. Plus, if memory served, this was the new, improved facility that had just been opened after the raids.

Butch re-formed next to him and entered a code on a keypad next to a solid steel door. After the lock clicked free, the two of them entered a narrow room, the focal point of which was a set of closed elevator doors.

"You ready for this?" the Brother asked.

"Yes," Boone answered, even though he wasn't sure he was.

Butch hit the single button on the wall to summon the lift. As the doors opened, the two of them got in and then it was a case of the *Jeopardy!* theme as they descended. At the end of their little trip down into the earth, he and Butch stepped out into a sparkling-clean corridor. Looking left and right, Boone saw all kinds of signage, but none of it indicated where they needed to head.

"We're going this way," Butch said grimly. "It's a haul."

Boone fell into step with the Brother, and they were silent as they went along, taking corners and cruising down straightaways. There was no reason to ask how Butch knew where the morgue was, and the fact that that particular part of the facility was out of the way seemed appropriate given that Havers and his staff were all about preserving life. It also made sense that there was no signage for it. Unlike the various directives and arrows that were posted about Radiology, Outpatient

Surgery, Emergency Services and the ilk, there was not a thing about where the dead were taken and stored.

You had to imagine that discretion was on purpose. No reason to remind patients and families that sometimes people didn't leave through the front door, so to speak.

And on that note . . . his father's remains had been taken here.

Had been cremated here. At Boone's request as next of kin.

After about five more minutes of heel-toeing it, Butch took them around a final left-hand turn, and that was when the faint, fake-sweet aroma of formaldehyde bloomed in the air. Sure enough, up ahead, a set of unmarked double doors appeared, and Boone knew they'd found their destination.

As they came up to the morgue's entrance, Butch jumped ahead and held open the way in. Boone, on the other hand, stopped short. And couldn't go any farther.

"What's up, son?" the Brother asked quietly. "You okay?"

It was hard to say the words out loud. Much less to a male he respected. "Is it . . . is it wrong that I didn't ask to see his body?"

There was no reason to specify the "he" he was talking about.

"No, Boone. It's not wrong. Some things are better if they aren't seen."

"I had him cremated here." He focused on the Brother. "I just didn't want him to come back again, you know? I didn't want . . . that. Even though I'm only being paranoid, right? I mean, no one's reanimated for a second time after . . ."

After they were popped in the frontal lobe at point-blank range by a bullet filled with water from the Scribe Virgin's sacred fountain.

Somehow, he was not capable of putting all of that into words. The good news was that the Brother didn't seem to need it spelled out for him.

"You did the right thing," Butch said quietly. "Whatever makes it easier on you is the right thing."

"None of this, as it turns out, is easy. Not while my sire was alive, and not now that he's dead. My fantasy did not pan out the way I thought when I was being young and vindictive."

"Grieving a complicated relationship can be even harder than one that worked for you. Do you want to wait out here while I—"

"No, I'm coming in with you." Boone took a deep breath and braced himself. "I'm going to be a professional about this."

Striding through the open door, he looked around at a carpeted room that was office-like rather than holy-fuck-dead-body clinical: There were desks with laptops, and floor-to-ceiling shelves of vertical, coded files, as well as a conference table that had some photographs laid out on its smooth surface. He didn't want to look too closely at them.

On the far wall, there was another set of double doors—and the fact that they had no windows in them? That had to be where the corpses were kept.

"Does he do the autopsies himself?" he asked. "Havers, I mean?"

"Yes, I do."

Boone turned around. The race's longstanding healer was entering from the corridor outside, his tortoiseshell glasses, bow tie, and white coat like something out of an Ivy League medical school. Maybe from the turn of the previous century.

"Rexboone." The male came forward and offered his palm. "My sincerest condolences with regard to your sire's passing. I knew Altamere very well and always found him to be most enjoyable company. He will be sorely missed."

Boone shook what was extended to him and made what he hoped were appropriate murmurings of thanks. The fact that Havers had a high opinion of Boone's father made sense. The race's healer was a member of the *glymera*, and right up Altamere's alley: Wealthy, well educated, from a good bloodline. No wonder they had gotten along.

"If you are prepared to accept the urn," Havers said, "I have it ready for you."

Boone blinked. "Ah . . . yes. Thank you. I'll take it."

"Very good. After we have concluded our present sad business, then."

Havers turned to Butch. There was some talk about the victim, and then Butch signed a form of some sort. Meanwhile, Boone was aware that his heart was pounding and his mouth was dry—although not about the murder.

But come on, like he expected Altamere's ghost to pop the top off his tin can, come down the hall from whichever shelf he'd been put on, and be all pissed off at the whole cremation thing?

Ashes were so much better than a corpse in a tuxedo showing up at Last Meal and asking for another round of scotch—

With a silent curse, Boone forced himself to refocus as Havers opened one half of the inner set of double doors. The formaldehyde smell quintupled. As Butch entered the examination area with the doctor, Boone made himself follow along. He didn't make it much farther than just inside the doorjamb.

There were four workstations in the floor-to-ceiling tiled room, each of them dominated by a waist-high, stainless steel slab that had a fauceted sink at one end, a drainage hole at the other, and a system of metal tubing and electrical wires underneath. Rolling tables were in place for what he guessed were instruments and tissue samples, and the hanging scales for weighing organs and wall-mounted light boxes for X-rays and imaging test results meant you could do everything in one place.

No expense had been spared. No efficiency underutilized.

No bodies out on the slabs, either. Thank God.

"She is over here," Havers murmured.

"Over here" turned out to be a wall-sized refrigerator unit with two dozen three-by-four-foot doors stacked two high across its stainless steel face. And as Butch went forward, Boone hung waaaaay back while Havers unlatched a compartment on the top tier.

The physician pulled out a stainless steel slide, and Boone stopped breathing.

The naked female was lying on her back, her head propped up on a block positioned at her nape, her arms tucked into her sides, her legs stretched out with her feet lolling to the left and right. She had dark hair that was matted flat to her skull, and her skin was a mottled gray with bruising in places. Blood, dried and caked, covered a lot of her torso, and the meat hook that had made him so nauseous when he'd been looking at the pictures on Butch's phone was still in place, supported by that block.

As if it had been something intrinsic to her skull all along.

Boone dropped his eyes out of respect. And also because his gag reflex was beginning to do push-ups in the back of his throat.

"We have the wig and the mask she was wearing," Havers said softly.

"Yes, we saw the pictures of her at the scene." Butch made a *hmmm* sound as he bent in closer. "Come over here, Boone. You can see here where her throat was sliced. Bilateral cuts on her wrists, too. She must have been still alive when she was hung up, given the amount of blood loss on the concrete floor below her."

"I would have to agree with that assessment," Havers said. "I have not done an extensive examination of her remains, but the entry of the hook is very clean—which suggests she was likely not conscious or in shock when that was done to her. She did not fight back. But you are correct. For the volume of blood displaced, her heart was still pumping for a while after she was hung."

"Down this side," Butch commented as he shifted position, "you can see where she was dragged across a rough floor." The Brother straightened. "So he cuts her. Drags her. Inserts the hook and grips her here . . . and here . . ." Butch made like he was putting his hands on her upper arms—exactly where there was a series of bilateral, fingerprint-like bruises. "To lift her up. After which she continues to bleed out."

As Boone focused on those clusters of black-and-blues, that rage he had felt when he had first heard Helania's recorded call came back to him. The idea that someone had done this to this female . . . had hurt her like this . . . *killed* her like this . . . made him positively furious.

"Do you know if she'd had sexual intercourse?" Butch asked.

Havers inclined his head. "I believe she had, but I don't know at this point whether it was before or after her death. As I said, I've only performed a cursory examination of her."

"I need you to answer that question for me."

"I'm afraid that until we find the family, I do not feel comfortable performing an autopsy."

"You may have to get over that." Butch looked across the body at the doctor. "We can't wait long because the trail of her killer is growing cold as we speak."

Boone had coughed at the mention of sex . . . but as the doctor and the Brother continued to talk, he began to look at the body differently, seeing the marks on her skin, the wounds, the swollen places, as sources of information, rather than—

"What's that under her skin?" he asked as he pointed.

On the female's upper arm, there appeared to be a splinter of something dark beneath the gray of her skin. It was only a half inch long at the most and thin as the lead of a pencil—and it seemed to be angled into the flesh.

"I don't know," Butch said as he leaned down. "Havers, can we get whatever this is out of her?"

"But of course. One moment."

Butch took out his phone and snapped a series of photographs, not just of that discrete spot but of others like the meat hook, the bruises on her upper arms, the abrasions on her side, knees, and shins. Meanwhile, Havers returned gloved up with a scalpel and a tissue-collection jar. After cutting into the skin, he teased the object out with the tip of the blade.

"It appears to be a tiny nail," he remarked as he put whatever it was into the plastic container.

The thing made a soft impact sound, a *plunk*, as it landed.

"Looks like it," Butch said as he stared inside the jar. "Maybe it was from the scene, as he dragged her over to where he was hanging her up. There was a lot of debris in that storage room."

"Would you prefer to keep this?" Havers asked as he screwed a blue top on. "I need to label it first, but you are collecting all the evidence, aren't you?"

"I am. And I'll take it, yes. I'm going to set up a de facto investigation room for the case at the training center."

"Very good."

After Havers put the scalpel down and marked a label up with a gold pen, the container changed hands and Boone was aware of an awkward silence.

"However is my sister?" Havers inquired softly.

"She's perfect in every way."

"Good. That is . . . very good."

The Brother nodded at the body as if he wanted to redirect the conversation. "You'll let us know if anybody shows up to ID her."

"Yes, I will."

"If no one comes forward in the next twenty-four hours, I'm going to order you to do the autopsy. And even if someone does, we're going to get that done with or without family consent."

"I shall request the King's signature. On either account."

"I will make sure you have it."

"Thank you." Havers looked at Boone. "And now, would you care to sign for your father's urn?"

Boone swallowed his honest answer—because he'd rather just leave the remains here. Forever. Accepting them meant he couldn't avoid the Fade Ceremony, and the last thing he wanted to do was get social with a bunch of *glymera* gawkers. Or, to use another term, his extended family.

Undoubtedly, they all knew how his father had passed by now. And every one of them was going to want to warm their cold hearts before a crackling blaze of gossip.

"Yes," he forced himself to reply. "I'll take the urn home with me."

# NINE

As sunlight threatened in the east, Boone walked through the front door of his sire's house and closed the heavy weight behind himself. All around, the blackout shutters on the insides of the windows were coming down, the subtle whirring in the formal rooms a familiar sound, the soft clicking as they locked in place barely audible over the heat that whistled up through the old grates set into the floor.

The fact that he had a brass urn with his father's ashes in it under his arm—like the thing was a newspaper he'd picked up in the front yard—was yet another bizarro-world distortion of the way his life should have been going.

Not that coming through this door after a long night in the field to face his sire had ever been a party. But familiarity didn't just breed contempt. Sometimes it formed the bookends of your life, buttressing your novels and nonfictions alike so that they stood up straight and didn't fall off the shelves.

When those confines were suddenly and unexpectedly removed, even if they had been unpleasant, you ended up with a case of out-of-order that made you rattled.

On that note, he braced himself and looked across the foyer. The doors to his father's study were open, and the walnut walls glowed in the buttery light of the fire that glowed in the marble hearth. Heading over, he leaned against the entrance's doorjamb, his eyes traveling across the leather books that filled shelves. And the oil paintings of horses that Altamere had owned in the Old Country. And the brass sconces and the two brass chandeliers that threw illumination in a complementary fashion to that which emanated from the fireplace.

"Did you require something."

The words were technically a question. The tone was a suspicious demand.

Boone looked over his shoulder. Marquist had materialized from out of nowhere, although given the fact that there were security cameras throughout the house, his perfectly rotten timing was not a surprise. The male was also back to SOP. In contrast to the night before, when he had been clearly shocked by the news, the butler was in proper form, his pressed suit buttoned up, his starched shirt white as fresh snow, his tie knotted so tightly at his throat, it was a wonder he could breathe.

No more shaking hands. This time, the perennial polishing cloth was as steady as ever.

"No," Boone said. "I do not require anything."

Entering his father's study, he pulled the doors shut on the other male, very aware that it was tantamount to a declaration of war. But like the pair of them hadn't always locked horns? Some things, death did not change.

Some things, death made worse.

Crossing the Persian rug, Boone placed the urn on the corner of the Jacobean desk, right beside a Tiffany dragonfly lamp and a rock crystal sculpture of a rearing stallion. Maybe the ashes could just sit here for a while, like any other vase-ish thing in the room. It wasn't like there was anything to rot inside the container.

Unlike the refrigerated corpse of that female.

With a heavy feeling in his bones, Boone went around behind the desk and sat in his father's leather chair. Placing his hands palm down on the blotter, he stared out into space.

Where was the will?

The question had been brewing in his mind for the last twenty-four hours—no, wait. Longer than that. He had been wondering, for at least the last decade, but especially the previous twelve months since he'd made that paternity threat, whether his father was going to cut him out of things. Leave the money and the house and the personal effects to someone else.

Or a cat. Not that they had any pets.

But Altamere always had been a huge Karl Lagerfeld fan.

Tilting to the side, Boone tried to pull out the top drawer on the left. Locked. Same with the rest of them. As he straightened, he wondered what was more important to his sire, his supposed posthumous propriety or revenge for his first *shellan's* possible mistake with another male—

The knock on the door was sharp.

Speak of the devil.

And Boone debated not answering it just to see how far Marquist would push things. But goddamn, he was tired. "Come in."

The butler yanked the doors apart, and as the male saw Boone sitting at his sire's desk, the anger that flared in that face could not be hidden.

"Tell me something," Boone said as he took care to settle back into his father's chair and cross his legs comfortably at the knee. "Where are the keys to this desk?"

A mask of professionalism slammed down on the butler's hostility, closing off the emotion. "I do not know."

"You've been in charge of this entire house for how long? You were my father's right-hand male—and you don't know where the keys are?" Boone indicated over his shoulder, to a painting entitled *Grand Champion Altamere's Bespoke Beauty.* "How about the safe that's behind here."

As the butler registered surprise, Boone smiled coldly. "Yes, I know it's there. Are you going to tell me you don't know the combination?"

"These are private areas of your father's—"

"My father is dead. They are mine now. Everything under this roof is mine."

There was a possibility that that was a lie. It was a good idea to test the butler to see if he knew anything, however.

Marquist's eyes narrowed. "This is still my master's house."

Boone gripped the arms of the chair, ready to get to his feet and throw the butler out. But he stopped. Until he found that will, he needed to keep the male around—and there was a larger reason to lull Marquist into a false sense of security: Boone had never understood the relationship between his sire and this butler. The two had been closer than master and servant should ever have been. With Altamere gone, there was finally an opportunity to get to the bottom of it all. And if there had been any improper transfers in favor of Marquist? Gifts? Benefits?

Then Boone was in a position to find that out and get the shit back. Not because he cared about the monetary value, but as a matter of principle.

There was also a part of him that hoped the butler did something really stupid.

Easing back again, he drummed the blotter with his fingertips. "I'm doing the Fade Ceremony two hours before sunrise tomorrow."

Marquist's brows flared. "However is that possible? The post does not work that fast and the guests will not—"

"Email invites are instantaneous. One click and they land in people's inboxes. Just like magic."

The butler's evident horror made Boone think of being in the morgue and standing over the dead female's battered body. Now *that* was horrific. How invitations to a party went out to a bunch of people? Even if it was for a Fade Ceremony? Not even close.

But try telling that to someone who enjoyed using social propriety as a cudgel.

"You cannot be serious," Marquist stammered.

"There's no reason to wait on the ceremony."

"Where is the body now—"

"Ashes."

"What?"

"I had the remains cremated and the ashes are right here." He leaned across the desk and plinked the urn with his forefinger, a little tinny sound rising up. "This is what we're going to do the ceremony with."

Marquist stared at the container in disbelief. And when his eyes finally returned to Boone, the vile rage in them was a shock. Who knew the male had it in him?

"Your father *never* approved of you."

Boone gasped and put his hand over his sternum. "No . . . *really?* Oh, God, I'm heartbroken. All these years I thought I was his model son." Dropping the act, he leveled his stare across the desk. "Do you think his opinion matters anymore?"

"He did not deserve you."

"Nor I him. We were a curse to each other, but that's over now." Boone made a dismissive motion with his hand. "Go. I'm done with this conversation—"

"You are *not* your father."

"And you can leave this house anytime. Aaaaanytime. Matter of fact, keep this attitude up, and I'll lock you out of this place so fast, it'll make your goddamn head spin."

◆　　◆　　◆

Across town, in a suburban neighborhood of seventies-era apartment buildings, Helania sat in her two-bedroom, basement-level flat by herself. Overhead, the humans who lived above her were starting their day, the muffled footfalls making a circuit between what she imagined was their bathroom, their bedroom and their kitchen.

Same layout she had. Except one of her bedrooms hadn't been used in eight months.

The sofa she was parked on was old and worn, and to mask the age, she and Isobel had put a king-sized duvet cover over the cushions and the arms. Homemade needlepoint pillows of flowers and plants crowded where you could sit, but none of that was permanent. Her Etsy store did fairly brisk business, so there was always turnover here in her own apartment. Always bolts of velvet and boxes of batting and bowls of tassels, too.

But the side hustle to her main online editing gig wasn't just a nice supplemental income. It had kept her sane after her sister's killing.

Sometimes, the only thing that kept her in her skin during the daylight hours was filling in blocks of color with wool yarn, the repetitive nature of her box stitch forcing her mind to focus on something other than the murder of her blooded next of kin, her roommate, her best friend.

Her only friend.

Twisting around, she looked at the closed door to the left of the bathroom. On the far side of it, there were twelve cardboard boxes of various sizes, all of which were filled with Isobel's clothes, and toiletries, and mementos, and books, and . . .

Helania had taken Isobel's things off the walls in there, off the shelves, off the bureau, too. She had emptied the closet, emptied the drawers, emptied the blanket chest at the foot of the bed. She had stripped the bed, packed up the sheets, folded up the blankets. But that was as far as she had gone. She had intended to give it all to charity. She still did.

Not yet, though.

Maybe . . . not ever.

It was hard to part with the inanimate objects her sister had chosen and worn, collected and kept. As much as Helania told herself that none of it was Isobel, and as much as her logical side believed that, her heart would not budge.

She might as well have been giving away parts of the body.

Rubbing tired eyes, she leaned back into the sofa cushions and closed her lids. It didn't take her long to picture that male, the one with the dark hair and the black clothes and the aristocratic inflection to his voice.

The image that persistently invaded her thoughts was of him standing in that cut of illumination between the two buildings, his breath leaving him in puffs of white, his big body poised, his eyes staring into the darkness.

Directly at her.

When they had gone back into the club and sat on those folding chairs with the Brother, he had looked at her the whole time. Part of her wanted to believe—needed to believe—that it was just part of the questioning, the investigation, the job he had been sent by the Brotherhood to do.

A professional obligation.

But another, deeper, more worrisome side of her . . . wondered about things that should not have been on her mind at all.

Things like maybe he had stared for another reason.

"You have *got* to stop this," she said out loud.

Upstairs, there was a resounding *thump!*, which was good news. That was the outer door to the humans' apartment shutting. Things would quiet down now.

Another image of that male popped into her head. It was of when she had first seen him down in that basement corridor. He had been backing away from the open door to the storage room where that female had been killed, his head turned away from the cell phone in his palm, his eyes squeezed shut as if he were trying to wipe something out of his mind.

Perhaps a picture of that murdered female.

*You can trust me. I won't hurt you—*

As her phone went off with a text, she frowned and glanced over at her cloak. The black folds were hanging on a peg by the door, next to her parka and her yellow rain slicker. Getting to her feet, she wondered who the wrong number was looking for.

It was not someone reaching out for her.

Both parents gone. Sister . . . gone. No extended relations. And as for friends? Isobel had been the social one, and after her death, all those people who had orbited her sister's charismatic center had spiraled off in search of another sun around which to circle.

Maybe it was the Brotherhood.

Helania dug into the cloak and took the burner phone she used out of the hidden inner pocket. It was a text from an unknown number:

> I just wanted to apologize if I didn't handle things as well as I could have tonight. I'm worried I made you feel uncomfortable by racing after you. I am very sorry. Please do not be deterred from sharing things with Butch or anyone else. All that matters is that we find out who is hurting these females. Thank you for reading this, Boone

Helania froze where she stood.

Then she looked over to where she'd been sitting and wondered if he'd somehow picked up on the fact that she'd been thinking about him.

Back on the couch, she read the message through two more times, noting that unlike the texts she'd used to get from Isobel, there were no abbreviations. No emojis. No text grammar. It was more like an email. Or a handwritten letter.

Abruptly, she realized she was sitting forward with her phone cupped in her hands.

Like she might do something with it.

Like she might reply to him.

Her heart rate jumped into a higher gear, and she felt a flush hit her face. As her fingertip floated across the phone's screen, she watched from a distance.

No text. Nope.

Things were ringing.

She slapped the phone up to her ear, shocked that she had put a call through. She had no idea what she was going to say or why she was calling him. Especially as she was just a civilian, and he was not only clearly an aristocrat, but also someone who was affiliated with the Black Dagger Brotherhood—

"Hello?" a male voice said on the other end. ". . . hello?"

Helania cleared her throat. "Hi."

There was a sharp intake. "Helania?"

"I got your text." Like he didn't know that? "And I, ah..." She looked around her apartment as if the cheap furniture and galley kitchen could throw some syllabic suggestions her way. "I just wanted to reassure you that I—look, it's an awkward situation. You didn't do anything wrong. I was . . . it's just hard. This whole thing is hard."

"Of course it is." There was a rustling like he was sitting up against some pillows—and she had to wonder if he was in his bed. "I only figured that I didn't help things and I wanted to make it right somehow."

More rustling. He was definitely in bed—and damn it, she was suddenly wondering what he looked like without all that outerwear on. Not *naked*, of course. Just street clothes. Jeans . . . t-shirt—

Oh, horseshit. She was wondering what he slept in. And whether it was a birthday suit.

"Hello?" he said.

"Sorry." Helania shook her head. "It's okay. Everything is okay."

*Yeah, right*, she thought. Nothing was okay. Not why they had met or what she had noticed about him when they had . . . or what she was thinking about now.

"I've never done anything like this before," he murmured.

*Well, what do you know. I've never called a male out of the blue and talked to them, either. Especially not after I met them at a murder scene.*

"How are you tied to the Brotherhood?" she blurted. "I think you said something about it, but I can't remember."

"I'm in their training program."

"For the war?"

"Yes, I'm a soldier."

"So you fight?" Okay, that was a stupid thing to say. But wow. "Against the *lessers*?"

"Among other things," he said dryly. "I'm off rotation at the moment."

"Because you're injured?" For some reason, that spiked her anxiety. Which was nuts given that they were strangers. Why did it matter to her if he was hurt? "Sorry, that's none of my business—"

"No, I'm not wounded." There was a pause. "My sire died recently."

"Oh, no." Helania forgot all about beds and birthday suits. "I am *so* sorry."

Closing her eyes, she wanted to know the why of the death with the same urgency that she didn't want him to be hurt by the enemy.

*What is happening to me?* she wondered.

And jeez, it was like three people were on this phone call: him, her, and this inner-voice thing that kept speaking up in her head.

"He was killed last night, actually." Boone exhaled. "So it's pretty new."

Helania sat back against a sea of needlepoint pillows. "That is no time at all."

"You are so right."

It was hard to believe he was functioning as well as he seemed to be. The first two nights after Isobel had gone unto the Fade? There had been no way she could handle anything. Hell, that had been the whole first week or so. Maybe month.

"What happened?" she heard herself ask.

# TEN

Boone's suite was in the front of his father's house, and the combination of rooms took up a good quarter of the mansion's grand expanse. He had a sitting room, an inner sanctum with no windows for sleeping, a walk-in closet, and an agate bathroom that had always been one of his favorite places in the world. There was also a *petit déjeuner* with a small fridge, microwave, coffeepot and the like.

It was a world unto itself within the larger universe of the household, and as he extended his legs under his covers and stared across at his shelves full of the works of Nietzsche, Hegel, Sartre and the Greek greats, he realized he had never brought anyone else up here.

Well . . . until now.

Yes, he realized Helania wasn't actually with him. But as he held his phone tight to his ear, he felt like that lonely track record he'd been rocking was being broken.

She might as well have been with him in the flesh . . . and he liked it.

But on that note.

"Will you excuse me for a moment?" he said.

"If this is a bad time—"

"No!" He sat up so fast, he knocked a pillow onto the side table and had to catch the lamp with his free hand. "I mean, no, not at all. Just give me one sec."

He went to put the cell phone facedown on the bedside table, but then changed his mind and stuffed it under the remaining pillows. Then he moved the covers aside and leaped buck-ass naked out of bed. His body did not appreciate the chill, but that was not the reason he hightailed it into his closet. He felt like he was streaking in front of the female, his hey-nannies out on display, his cheeks flashing, everything he'd come into this world with on parade.

In his closet, he flipped on the overhead lights—and looked at his collection of tailor-made suits with serious consideration. But come on, they weren't on a date. It was a damn phone call, for godsakes. Not even FaceTime.

He pivoted to the casual section and snagged out of a built-in set of drawers a pair of nylon warm-up pants and the Syracuse sweatshirt Craeg had lent to him a month ago. Back in the bedroom, he jumped into bed and shoved his hand under the pillows. After some hunt and peck with his palm, he grabbed that cell like it was going to self-destruct if he didn't get a hold of the thing.

"Helania? Hello?"

"Hi. I'm still here."

Boone felt a blush hit his face and was so glad she couldn't see him. And then he went to get back under the sheets—only to decide that that was inappropriate. Jumping out of bed again, he landed on the fallen soldier pillow, lost his balance, threw out an arm—and caught himself on the wall while he banged the side of his foot into that side table.

"Boone? Are you okay?"

"Fine—yup, fine, just great." *FUCK. Fuck. Fuckfuckfuck.* "Just stubbed my . . ." *Right side of my entire body, goddamn it.* "Toe."

Screw making hospital corners on the fucking bedsheets, he decided. At this rate, if he didn't sit his ass down, he was going to end up on life support with a concussion and a broken hip.

"I didn't mean to get too personal," she said.

"No, it's fine."

Stretching out on top of the duvet, he brought his foot up and inspected the damage. Nice work. A crowbar couldn't have done it better.

Clearing his throat, he said, "I'm just not used to talking about my sire's death, you know? The whole thing seems surreal. I came home tonight and sat at his desk for the first time in my whole life. I keep expecting to wake up and find him here."

"You must miss him terribly."

Opening his mouth to answer that truthfully, he decided to leave that one where it was. Somehow, he didn't think *Hell, no, I'm glad he's pushing up daisies—oops, filling out an urn, I mean* was going to help him make a good first impression.

Second impression, that was. His first being chasing after her into the dark like a stalker.

He really needed to ask the guys in the training program for some help with this dating stuff.

Boone refocused. "I was told it happened quickly. He didn't suffer. And that is a consolation."

"So you weren't . . . there."

"Not when he passed, no."

"Can I ask you something?"

"Anything."

"Do you feel responsible? Because you weren't with him, I mean? Even if . . . there was maybe nothing you could have done?"

Boone rubbed the center of his chest as a dull ache abruptly flared into something he was becoming familiar with—and probably needed to get used to. Guilt, it turned out, had a half-life like something that was radioactive.

And a sting that was just the same as being stabbed.

"I am completely responsible," he said roughly.

"I know what that feels like."

"Who did you lose?"

When she didn't immediately reply, he had a thought that he would wait forever for her answer. And the moment that realization hit him, he reminded himself of Butch's warning: The truth was, he did not know this female at all and they had met under unusual and traumatic circumstances. A combination of male lust and high drama was probably making him feel a connection that was deeper than it actually was.

Take out the "probably."

After a very long time, she whispered, "My sister."

Boone sat forward, the math adding up. "Tell me."

Even though he knew. He *knew*—and it was a relief, in a tragic way. It would explain why she was in that club, watching after other females so closely.

"She was killed eight months ago," Helania whispered.

"At Pyre," he insisted, even as he resolved to let her go at her own pace. "She was killed at the club, too, wasn't she."

There was another long silence. "Yes."

Boone closed his eyes and gripped his cell phone hard.

"That is just terrible," he said. "I can't even imagine what you've been through. What your family has—"

"It's just me. Isobel was all I had. Our parents died in the fifties."

"Can you tell me what happened to her? And I'm asking you as a friend, not as part of any investigation, I promise—"

"I have to go."

Boone cursed internally—and had to fight not to press her. "I understand. Just . . . if you ever want to talk, you know where to find me?"

When there was no reply, he realized that she had hung up already.

◆    ◆    ◆

The thing Butch liked most about the Pit was the people in it.

As he sat down on his black leather sofa, with a bottle of Lagavulin on the coffee table in front of him and a rocks glass with ice-and-a-splash against his palm, he smiled over at his roommate. Vishous was behind his Four Toys, the bank of computers and monitors, the kind of thing that could be used to land the space station on the head of a pin in the middle of a hurricane.

Ya know, if you were wicked bored or some shit. And had nothing better to do than save humanity.

He and V had moved into this carriage house when the Brotherhood had taken residence in the great gray mansion across the courtyard. And then, after he had mated Marissa and V had settled down with Doc Jane, its two bedrooms had managed to accommodate everyone.

Plus Butch's wardrobe.

Okay, fine, the carbon-based life-forms were good to go in their allotted four-wall-configurations. His clothes, on the other hand, had kind of metastasized from his closet out into the hallway. But no one was complaining about the extremely expensive and very classy fire hazard. Yet.

"What's that grin about," came a mutter from behind all that computer equipment.

"I'm just in a good mood." Butch swirled the Lag in his glass. "You know, I'm sure you had one once. It probably scared you, though."

"Nah, I gave it up for Lent."

"You're not Catholic."

"You infected me." V leaned back and looked around the monitors. "Gave me a case of mono-Pope-leosis."

"That joke is blasphemous, but worse, it's not that funny."

"Well, at least I can guess why you're full of the joys of spring, tra-la. Marissa still recovering in your bed?"

"Wait, wait, I can't talk right now." Butch took his heavy gold Jesus piece out of his silk shirt and squeezed his eyes shut. "I'm praying for your eternal soul."

"Don't bother."

"Come on, don't you want to go to Heaven?"

"I wouldn't know anyone up there. And don't get too prissy with that religious bullshit, true? I don't want to spend eternity without you, so you need to come to *Dhunhd* with me."

"Will they have Milk Duds there?"

"Yes, but they'll all be melted together. And we'll be surrounded by Yankees fans, televangelists, and no booze."

"We'll think of some way to pass the time."

"We always do."

Butch took another long draw off the rim of his glass and let his happy glow bloom all over his shit. And yes indeedy, doody, his beautiful *shellan* was in fact sleeping off a marathon session that had taken them through Last Meal and left Marissa too satisfied to need food. And didn't that make him feel like he'd been a good husband. Or *hellren*, to use the vampire word.

Grabbing the remote, he angled the whacker over the foosball table and turned on the flat-screen. No reason to change the channel. ESPN was on so much, it was like it had punched out all the other networks in a bar fight.

V cleared his throat from behind the monitors. "So I made a mistake."

Cue the sound of tires screeching.

Butch tilted forward so he could see the guy. "What did you say?"

"You heard me."

"Throwing around the m-word, huh. It must be serious. What happened? Did you try to solve *pi* to twelve thousand digits and get number eleven thousand nine hundred ninety-nine wrong?"

Those diamond eyes shot over. "I'm being real."

Butch dropped the bullshit. "Talk to me."

V typed some things on his keyboard, that diamond stare of his going back and forth as if he were reading something on one of the screens. And as silence grew between them, Butch was content to wait the guy out. The brother was not a big talker to begin with unless he was exercising his constitutional right to be sarcastic. And then he could be downright chatty. But when it came to anything remotely emotional? It was hard for him.

"I ruined that scene down in the club's storage room," V muttered. "Didn't I."

Butch blinked. "You took all those pictures first."

"But I wasn't careful after that." Before Butch could respond, V continued, "I was so focused on getting the body out of there and over to Havers's before dawn came that I just wrecked the goddamn place. It wasn't until you went there tonight that I realized what I'd done . . . tromping all over the floor, shoving things out of the way, calling in Zypher and Balthazar with their size fourteens."

"It was an evolving situation. A lot of things were happening."

"No excuse." Those eyes looked over. "I made things harder on you with the investigation. I might even have fucked you for finding out who did it. It was inexcusable."

Thinking back to that storage room, Butch couldn't deny that there had been substantial displacement of the scene due to the body being removed. But as much as he would have liked to do a proper quarantine and search, they had never discussed what the protocol for responding to a murder would be. Further, there were extenuating circumstances.

"Here's the thing," he said, "there are priorities for us that didn't exist when I was on the human side of things. Getting that body out of there was the prime directive. Could you have disturbed things less? I don't know. Most of the club had emptied out, from what you told me, but there were still humans on-site. It was not a secure retrieval of the remains by a long shot. You did what you had to. I can deal with the rest."

"Next time, if there is one, I call you in first. Everybody calls you in first."

"Good deal." Butch frowned as he thought about the case. "You know, I got a bad feeling about it all."

"Why?"

He threw back what was left in his glass and gave the ice a ride, circling, circling, circling. "I don't know, maybe I'm just out of shape with this kind of work."

"I spilled my beans. You spill yours."

Butch smiled a little, thinking that was fair enough. "Well, I do think the killer is one of us. Female vampires are strong. It would take one hell of a human to overpower one."

"Wait, I thought you said that the female who'd found the body already told you the victim was with a vampire that night."

"I'm trying not to jump to any conclusions."

"Smart. Okay, so what if the victim was drugged? A human man could get uphill of that."

"It's a possibility. Havers will run a toxicology on her tissue when we get the autopsy done. But even still, that meat hook? It requires a lot of strength to impale that through the base of someone's skull."

"Maybe they had help. What if there were two killers?"

"That's a possibility." Butch shrugged. "There wasn't a lot of struggle, I can tell you that. My victim didn't fight her attacker. So she knew her killer—or was compromised. I looked at her nails and her hands, nothing much there. And there were no defensive wounds on the outsides of her forearms or her knuckles."

"What if she wanted him and then the sex got out of hand."

"Could have defo happened that way."

"You think we've got a serial killer?" V murmured as he typed some more and looked at his screen.

"Three victims dead in the same place within the last year and a half. I'd say that raises a red flag. Do you remember what happened with our first or second victims?"

"I know about the second one. We got a call in the following night and I went down there. The body had already been removed by someone, the scene was cold, the phone call to the service made from a burner we couldn't trace. There was no body, no name on the caller, and no one reported a missing person thereafter."

"Cold trail."

"I even wondered if it was a hoax. Now I'm thinking it wasn't."

"What about victim number one?"

"It was a human. Found the article in the *CCJ* about an hour ago. I'll send the coverage to you when I'm finished here."

Butch stared at the coffee table without seeing the laptop, the *SI* magazine, the bag of Doritos he'd brought in along with the scotch from the galley kitchen. If there had been three bodies down there, then yes, they were probably dealing with a serial killer, but again, he was mindful of the lecture he'd given Boone. No jumping to conclusions. Keep everything on the table at this early stage.

"Just because one human woman and two of our females died at that club," he said out loud, "doesn't mean they were killed by the same person. Could be or could not. What I need is information on those other two deaths—"

"Got it."

Butch leaned forward to pour himself more Lag. "Got what?"

"The recording that came in about the death that happened eight months ago."

Butch paused in mid-refill. "Wait, you found that call in?"

Without taking his stare off his monitor, V cocked the eyebrow by the tattoos at his temple. "Gimme a sec to finish buffering things."

Butch whistled under his breath. "You are a genius."

"I know."

A moment later, Butch's phone vibrated on the coffee table. Putting the bottle down, he snagged the cell and looked at the notification on the screen.

An email from Vishous with an audio attachment.

"You are totally forgiven for disrupting my scene," Butch murmured to his roommate.

V lit a fresh hand-rolled, that huge body leaning back in his padded leather chair. "If there's a next time, it will be handled differently. You have my word."

"I hope there won't be, but I have a feeling we are not going to be that lucky." Butch fired up the voicemail on the speaker, entering numerical codes to get access and waiting through a preamble. "I don't know how you waded through those hundreds of recordings."

"Next up, I do more digging on that first human victim. The killer could have started with them and shifted over to us."

Butch opened his mouth to say something further, but a female's voice came out of his phone: *I—I want to report a death. A murder . . . a killing. At Pyre's Revyval downtown. It happened the night before last. A female. She—she was found on the lower level by friends. She was taken . . . out of the club by them . . . she was dead . . .*

"Sonofabitch," Butch muttered.

"What?" V said.

"It's the same female. It's the same one who reported the death last night."

# ≫ ELEVEN ≪

The following evening, Boone left the house at nine p.m. He had a good seven hours before his father's Fade Ceremony, and there was one and only one place he was going to go. Dematerializing downtown, he re-formed by the parking spot where he and Butch had left the R8 the night before. With a limping stride, his shitkickers ate up the distance toward the front door of Pyre's Revyval, the steel-reinforced treads of his boots punching a pattern in the fresh snow that had fallen during the day.

He would have broken out in a run. Except that would have meant he was desperate.

Actually, he already *knew* he was desperate—but that was the kind of thing he was more than happy to keep to himself, thank you very much.

Well, and then there was his ankle. Turned out he'd done more than stub his toe when he'd jumped out of bed and landed wrong on that pillow. But he was not going to let a little pain slow him down.

As he closed in on the club's front entrance, he eyed the length of the wait line and thought of how many people were no doubt already inside. In costumes and masks. Milling around in the dark. At least he could try to locate Helania by scent. Although the larger question was whether she was going to want to see him. Still, there was an official reason for him to be in res, so to speak—and he'd told Butch he was heading over to monitor things.

He couldn't live with himself if that female was the next victim.

God, he couldn't get Helania out of his mind. Over the course of the day, as he had lain in his bed not being able to sleep—and refusing to jerk himself off, because that just seemed frickin' skeevy—he had run their conversation on the phone back and forth, over and over again. As he'd replayed the I-saids and she-saids, he realized that her loss of her sister and his loss of his father made them a kind of kin: He and this stranger were united by the fact that they were both chained by grief. Self-doubt. Regret.

Even though his fellow trainees and the Brothers and fighters had all reached out to him, he experienced their support as an echo from sources far away, something on the other side of the valley, the mountain range, the Grand Canyon. And it wasn't that he didn't appreciate the texts, the voicemails . . . the RSVPs to the Fade Ceremony later this evening.

Which, P.S., had come in via email.

*Because goddamn Paperless Post had worked just fine for the invites, Marquist, you tool.*

But yes, Boone was truly grateful for all the kind words and show of love from everyone involved with the training program. It was just . . . when he'd been on the phone with Helania, he hadn't felt like he'd had to translate anything about where he was. She'd just seemed to be there with him. And he needed that kind of intuitive connection right now because there was so much he didn't understand about where he was at.

When it came to Altamere, this sad, hollow feeling he got whenever he thought about his sire was nothing he could properly frame—and maybe Helania could shed some light on it. Even if she'd been close to her sister, perhaps she had a few discordant sectors in her own grief, too. They could talk about it. Over coffee. Over the phone. Over emails, letters . . . smoke signals or homing pigeons.

He didn't care.

And if she didn't want to have anything further to do with him? Well, in that case, he would just hang in the shadows and make sure she didn't get killed.

Ah . . . the romance.

As he came up to the head of the wait line, he prepared to break into the bouncer's brain so he didn't have to break into the club, but messing with the human's neurons turned out not to be necessary.

"Hey, you're back." The man opened things wide. "Go right in."

*You've got to love mind control,* Boone thought. Especially when it sticks.

Striding through the coat check area, he entered the club proper and scanned the crowd. As he was looking for Helania, he filtered out the men, skipped over the human women, and tried to zero in on anything vampire.

So many bodies. So many scents: The club's vast open area, coupled with the darkness, the colognes, the costumes, and the masks, was going to make things harder than he'd thought . . .

It was difficult to say when exactly his instincts pricked with recognition, and given the overwhelming visual and olfactory stimuli, it was impossible to isolate exactly who had gotten his attention. Not Helania, no.

But someone here was sparking a reaction in him.

Boone gave his eyes free rein to go wherever they wanted. And as he was trying to pinpoint whoever it was who had hit his radar, his phone went off in his chest pocket. The first round of vibrating he ignored as he pressed forward through the tightly packed bodies. When the thing went still and then immediately started shimmying again, he cursed and took the Samsung out.

Butch was calling. Shit.

"Hello?" Boone said.

The Brother was short and to the point.

So was Boone: "*Fuck.*"

✦    ✦    ✦

Helania materialized on the sidewalk in front of a lovely antique house. The neighborhood was fancy, the other sprawling homes likewise set far back from the narrow road, the rolling snow-covered lawns marked with big trees that were no doubt magnificent in the warmer months.

Jeez, the garages around here were bigger than anything she had ever lived in.

As she squared off at the walkway that led to a fancy, imposing entrance, she missed her cloak. One advantage to going to Pyre was that she could shelter herself under all those black folds. Now, in street clothes of jeans, a sweater, and a parka, she felt exposed.

The broad, glossy black door opened and she jumped back.

"Come on in," the Brother Butch called out in his Boston accent. "It's wicked cold tonight."

The male was dressed in a deep blue sport coat and an open-collared pink shirt, his slacks sporting some kind of subtle pattern. He looked like the owner of the house instead of a warrior for the species, but she wasn't fooled. She had stared into those eyes of his.

Beneath the wardrobe of a gentlemale, he had the soul of vengeance and not just a little street in him.

Burrowing into her puffy jacket, she came up the cleared path. Even though things had been shoveled and salted, she focused on precisely where she put her running shoes, sure as if she were on uneven ground.

It was easier than meeting the eyes of the male who waited for her.

The steps of the mansion creaked as she mounted them, and then she was inside and standing in a lovely foyer, the glow of the lights, the warmth of the interior, the scents of fresh baked goods a homey embrace.

Funny, the things that made you realize you lived alone.

"So thanks for coming." The Brother indicated over his shoulder. "I thought we could talk in this sitting room back here. Or whatever they call it. Can I get you anything to eat or drink? Coffee? We've got fresh danish—the cherry ones will reaffirm your belief in God, I swear."

Anxiety tickled the back of Helania's neck and tightened the center of her chest. "I ate before I came. But thank you."

It was a lie, and for a split second, she glanced at the Brother, thinking maybe he had second sight and was going to know she'd fibbed about the food. But there was no eating or drinking for her at the moment. Her stomach was churning like a cement mixer, all kinds of proverbial stones and gravel going round and round and round in her midsection.

On that note, she shrugged out of her puffy parka before no-thank-you on the danish turned into I'm-going-to-be-sick-all-over-this-nice-rug.

"Okay, let me know if you change your mind."

The Brother led the way past what appeared to be a waiting room on one side and something bigger with closed panel doors on the other.

"So this is the Audience House," she murmured.

"Sure is. I figured you'd feel safe here."

On the far side of the closed doors, she could hear deep male voices, and she had to wonder if they were from other members of the Black Dagger Brotherhood. The idea that she was under the same roof as even one of the great males made her awestruck. Growing up, there had been tales in the species about the famous warriors who protected the vampire race and the King, but no one she knew had ever met any of them.

Butch was right. She did feel safe here and that did matter.

"Here we are."

The Brother indicated the way into a room that was like a museum, a massive oil painting of some kind of aristocrat hanging on the opposite wall, the furniture old and beautiful, the fireplace made of spectacularly veined marble. She was not surprised at the wealth. Ever since Wrath, son of Wrath, sire of Wrath, had started seeing civilians and sorting out their problems, stories of this home's grandeur had filtered through the civilian population.

Where else would the King spend his time?

"Would you like to sit here?" the Brother said as he pointed to a silk-covered chair.

Helania eyed the banked fire that was throwing off not just cheery crackles and shifting light but heat. So much heat. Which was not great for an uneasy stomach.

She brushed a hand across her damp forehead. "May I sit a little farther back from the hearth?"

"Of course."

As she parked it in an armchair angled in at the far end of the sofa, a cool draft wafted over her and it was perfect. "Thank you."

As Butch settled onto the sofa, she surreptitiously checked out how many ways she could get out of the room. There was a pair of closed panels over there . . . the door they'd come in across the way . . . and two French sets behind her, which were her best bet for dematerialization—or, in a pinch, some good old-fashioned Hollywood stuntwoman stuff.

After Isobel's violent killing, she had gotten used to looking for escapes.

"So I'm just going to close this door so we're not disturbed." The Brother shut them in together. "And I want you to be aware that there are cameras here . . . here . . . and over there. So we're recording everything—not because I think you're guilty of any wrongdoing, but just because it's part of the security system of this house."

*Where is Boone*, she wondered.

Although, considering the reason she was here to speak with the Brother, it seemed ridiculous to worry about anyone else. Yet she had spent a lot of time thinking about that other male. What his voice sounded like in her ear. What he had looked like the night before.

Whether she would see him again.

She couldn't believe she had all but hung up on the guy. It had been incredibly rude, but she'd gotten flustered. She hadn't spoken of her sister's death since it happened because she didn't have anyone to speak of it to. Her emotions had gotten the best of her, the top popped off a maelstrom of feelings.

None of which were pleasant.

"So are you okay speaking to me on camera?" the Brother prompted.

"Oh, sorry. Yes, I am." She cleared her throat. "Did you find out something?"

The Brother leaned forward on the luxurious cushions, his elbows planting on his knees. His hazel stare was direct, but his expression was relaxed—and she wondered whether the latter was on purpose to put her at ease.

Fat chance of that.

"Actually," he said, "I have a couple of follow-up questions—"

The sound of pounding footfalls cut the Brother off, and those penetrating eyes shifted over to the door he'd closed.

The heavy wooden panel was thrown open and Boone burst into the room like he was prepared to give someone CPR, deliver a baby, and save a litter of puppies. With his face flushed and his body still in rush mode even though he'd arrived at his destination, he took a deep breath. And another.

"SorryImlate." All one word. And then he inhaled again. "Traffic was hell."

Helania didn't mean to laugh. But the giggle came up her throat and flew out of her mouth before she could throw a leash on it. Dollars to donuts, he'd dematerialized from wherever he'd been and the idea he had been in such a fluster-rush to get over here?

Maybe ending their call so abruptly hadn't offended him too much—

Okay, wow. He was smiling at her.

Dropping her head, she tried not to look like she was blushing. And then she checked him out in her peripheral vision. Well . . . what do you know. The dark hair, the blacked-out clothes, the height and breadth of him . . . were exactly as she remembered. Maybe even better. Maybe . . . even more attractive.

Oh, who was she trying to fool. Everything was definitely better than her memory had painted.

And it wasn't like she'd pictured him hunchbacked and dragging a foot.

Speaking of which, was he—

"Are you limping?" the Brother demanded.

"Nope." Boone shut the door. "Not at all."

As he hobbled forward, she became obsessed with the fact that he clearly had hurt something—and she went so far as to fish into her parka for her phone. Which made no sense. The only number she could call for help was the Brotherhood's and they were here *with* a Brother.

Besides, Boone's health and well-being were not her problem.

On that note, she tried to remind herself that her preoccupation with the male was a symptom of her loneliness—and a red flag. With the number of times she'd replayed their phone call word for word, she was fairly sure she had worn out the grooves in her recollection and that her brain was obligingly filling in the parts that had eroded, the composite of him morphing more into what she wanted to believe of him instead of what was really there. Which was the nature of initial attraction, wasn't it. That sizzle and shock of awareness tended to be more about what you were seeking than what you actually found.

Except . . . now that he was in the same room with her? Instead of being let down by what he looked like—some off-center part of his nose ruining what she'd assumed was aquiline perfection, a bad cowlick in a weird place making the shape of his head wonky, his shoulders less wide, his chest flatter than her fantasies had projected—she had to force herself not to stare with fixation.

Fortunately, he was talking to the Brother now, apologizing for being late. And the Brother was forgiving him, albeit with a stern tone.

*Girl, you need to get yourself together*, she thought. *Right now.*

Focusing on the low-slung table in front of her, she discovered there was a collection of crystal animals on it, the bears and the bunnies and the deer and the squirrels all fat-bodied and round-faced, the firelight coalescing inside the perfectly smooth globes of their bodies and features, making that which was glass seem to be made of water.

Boone's reflection was in every one, like a kaleidoscope of the male, but it was all a distortion of the real thing, parts of him expanded and compressed by turns.

Was she just lonely and turning him into a fantasy? Although, if you had to ask that question . . .

Helania didn't want to look at him again.

But she couldn't fight the impulse.

And wondered what else she would not be able to deny him.

# TWELVE

Amazing how knowing someone meant you could read their vibe so well.

For example, as Boone glanced at Butch, he could tell the Brother was annoyed. It was less the expression and more the aura of the male, a bad smell that emanated from him as he sat on the sofa. Was it because of the whole being-late thing? Or the number of texts and calls that had been unanswered as Boone had gone over to the club?

Whatever, it couldn't possibly be because he was excited to be breathing the same air as Helania and the Brother had picked up on it.

Nah. Boone was super cool. Super chill.

He coughed a little.

"Do you want to take a load off," Butch said dryly. "Over here with me. On the sofa."

This was not a suggestion. A hey-wouldja. A how-'bout. It was more do-what-I-say-or-I'll-break-both-your-legs.

But at least the Brother wasn't kicking him out. So bonus.

Boone scrambled across the room and threw himself down on the cushions like his ass was putting a brushfire out. He crossed his legs.

Uncrossed them. Then played I'm-looking, I'm-not-looking with Helania. He was pretty sure she'd glanced at him when he'd come in, although if she had, she hadn't stared at him for long.

But what she *had* done? Smiled at his stupid joke. She had actually laughed a little, too.

In the back of his mind, because he was insane, he decided this meant they were totally compatible and destined to be together forever.

Yup, one lift to her lips and an awkward giggle were totally signs of eternal passion and happiness.

Annnnnnnnd on that note, he had to ease back on his fantasy life.

As she sat in that armchair, wearing normal street clothes, her hair pulled back into a braid, her citrine eyes down on some Baccarat crystal figurines, he had no clue whether she cared he was there. If she had even thought twice about their conversation early that morning. If that smile had been nervousness or actually about him. He couldn't read her at all.

It was good to remind himself that just because the four minutes they'd had on the phone together had been a game changer for him did not mean that those two hundred and forty seconds had registered in the same way for the other party to the call.

"So the reason we're here," Butch said to her in that even tone of his, "is because I'd like you to listen to a previous call into the emergency dispatch number. Will you let me play it for you?"

Helania shifted in the armchair she was sitting in, repositioning the parka in her lap. "All right."

The Brother pushed a crystal bunny back and put his cell phone face-up by its front paws. A moment later, a voice Boone recognized instantly came out of the speaker.

*I—I want to report a death. A murder . . . a killing. At Pyre's Revyval downtown. It happened the night before last. A female. She—she was found on the lower level by friends. She was taken . . . out of the club by them . . . she was dead . . . Indecipherable sounds. She had been . . . she had been hung by the neck in a storage room and—*

Boone's hand shot out and cut the recording off. "That's enough."

As the Brother's eyes whipped toward him, he shook his head. "She knows what the message said. She doesn't need to hear it again."

Over on the armchair, Helania wrapped her arms around herself and squeezed her lids closed, the color in her face draining away until she was pasty white.

Butch took out his spiral notebook. "Was that you?"

Boone had to stop himself from snapping at the Brother. Of course it was her, damn it—and Butch knew that.

"Yes," she whispered. "It was me."

As Butch's phone chimed with a call coming through, the Brother silenced it and made a note for himself. "Can you tell us about what happened that night?"

When Helania did not respond, Butch said, "You're the only thing we have to go on at this point. In two out of the three deaths down at that club."

She opened her eyes. "So there were a total of three?"

"Yes. The first was a human, about a year and a half ago. We're doing what we can to track that down." Butch's phone rang again, and he silenced it a second time, slipping the thing into the breast pocket of his sport coat. "I know this is hard, Helania. I know—"

"No," she said roughly. "You do not know."

"Then explain it to me." Butch put his hands together as if he were praying. "Please."

The quiet that stretched out seemed to last forever. But then Helania opened her mouth—

The knock on the parlor door was loud, a demand.

Butch cursed and got to his feet. "Will you excuse me? I'm going to make this go away."

As the Brother strode over, you had to pity whoever was outside the room. But that drama wasn't what Boone was interested in.

Left alone with Helania, he focused on her. "I'm sorry you had to listen to that recording."

He wanted to take her into his arms. Protect her from anything and everything. But they were strangers.

Butch ducked back into the parlor. "Boone? Could you come over here?"

With a nod, he got to his feet and went across. "What's up?"

The Brother dropped his voice. "Havers wants me to go to the clinic. A family has come forward with a missing persons on a female fitting the description of our victim. He wants me to handle the possible ID of the remains. We're going to have to reschedule with Helania—"

"I can talk to her." He hurried on before the Brother could hell-no him. "I'll even record the session on my phone. Listen, she's been through enough. She doesn't need to come back here just because you don't trust me to remain professional."

Butch glanced around Boone's shoulder. "Okay. But stick to the facts."

"I promise. I won't let you down."

Butch nodded and went across to Helania to take his leave. And then Boone was closing the door behind the other male.

Taking a deep breath, he sat on the sofa where the Brother had been. "Are you okay talking to me about this?"

It was a while before she answered, and in the silence, he turned things into a multiple choice situation: A) *Fuck no, I don't want to be alone with you;* B) *Are you insane, I have to go;* C) *Do you have any idea what you're doing, or are you just winging this?;* and D)—

"Actually, I'd rather do this with you."

Okay. Wow. His D) had been more along the lines of *I'm not a celebrity, get me outta here.*

"With your permission, I'll start recording on my phone?" See, he could be professional. "It's just so Butch can listen, and this way, maybe you can be all done with this."

"I thought the room was recording it?"

Boone looked around and saw security stuff everywhere. Duh. "Well, this is just an extra belt and suspenders thing, then."

"All right."

Boone put his phone on the coffee table, and when he was sure it was working, he sat back. "Can you tell me what happened? And take your time. I have all night."

◆    ◆    ◆

Helania stared at the phone because it was easier. She could tell the thing was recording because a little counter at the top of the screen was marking passing seconds that would turn into minutes.

*This may well be a waste of time*, she thought, given that her voice seemed to have left her. She really did not want to talk about the nightmare that had unfolded eight months ago and was still very much with her. But she had called the Brotherhood for help. What had she thought was going to happen?

More to the point, if she wanted to stop whoever was killing females . . .

"My sister, Isobel . . ."

As that name left her lips, she was suffused in sadness, and found herself falling silent again as memories came to her.

She cleared her throat. "Isobel was not like me. She was outgoing— she liked to be with people, and people liked being with her. She had a boyfriend, and she went to Pyre with him a lot."

Boone frowned. "Tell me about the male."

"She was happier with him than I had ever seen her before. She had had boyfriends from time to time, but he was different. Her eyes sparkled whenever she talked about him."

"What was his name?"

"I don't know." Helania shrugged. "I never met him."

As Boone's face settled into a mask, she shook her head. "It wasn't him who killed her. I know Isobel, and she never would have been with someone who was abusive. Besides, she was giddy whenever she spoke about him. She couldn't wait to see him."

"Was he of the species?"

"Yes, he was."

"How long were they together?"

"She first told me about him a couple of months prior to her death, but I had the sense she had been seeing him for a little while before then."

"How long is 'a little while'?"

Helania took her parka off her lap and put it on the floor beside the chair. "Let me think . . . she mentioned him sometime in February last year. But her mood picked up around the human holidays before then? So I think they first started seeing each other maybe in December. But it's hard for me to say for sure. She was always really social and out most nights with her friends anyway. Again, though, something changed around the holidays last year. She was different. In a good way."

"Are you close to any of her friends?"

"Not really." Helania shook her head. "I usually stayed home."

And didn't that sound lame to her own ears.

"Do you think any of Isobel's friends might be willing to talk to me? About the boyfriend?"

"Again, I didn't spend a lot of time with them, but her social media is still live because I haven't had the heart to delete her Instagram or Facebook. Some of them have to be on there and I could contact them."

"That'd be great."

Boone smiled a little, and the subtle movement made her focus on his lips. He had a really nice mouth, she decided, a full bottom, a peaked top. It looked soft—

"So, Isobel had this boyfriend," he said, "and as far as you knew, they had a good relationship."

Okay, she totally and completely needed to stop with the mouth thing. "Yes."

"And she would meet him at Pyre. Was there anywhere else they would go? Would she stay over at his place?"

"No, not really. Not often, I mean. Mostly she was at our apartment during the days." Helania looked down at her hands. "I think she felt as though she had to look after me. It was a throwback to when we were younger."

Back in the era when Helania had been different and at a disadvantage. And Isobel her champion.

"Your sister sounds like a female of worth," Boone said softly.

"She was the very best person I've ever known."

As she said the words, she realized something. For Isobel to be dead and her to be the one who lived? It seemed like a waste, and that was part of her guilt.

"Tell me about the night she died—"

"Killed," Helania corrected. "The night she was killed."

Boone nodded gravely. "Tell me what happened. And as I said, take your time. I don't care how long you need. I will sit with you until dawn if we have to."

"It brings it all back, you know." Abruptly, Helania felt like she couldn't breathe, and she sat up straight, as if that would give her lungs a little more space to expand into. "It brings back . . . everything."

While she struggled with her emotions, Boone just sat on the sofa beside her chair, his eyes steady, his body still. And in the end, his calm presence was the only thing that made it possible for her to go on.

Inhaling deeply, she sighed out the words. "It was four in the morning when I found out. But at least I still had time to get to her."

"At Pyre?"

"No, at the house where they brought her. After she was found at Pyre." Helania tangled her fingers, knotting them and then forcing them to release. "She had these two friends who she saw all the time. One she met in nursing school. Another was somebody she'd crossed paths with out in the scene. They were the females who went looking for her that night—and one of them found her."

As Helania teared up, Boone held something out. A handkerchief. And of course it was monogrammed, as befitting his station. She wanted to tell him no-thank-you, but she couldn't stand the crying. For godsakes, if she couldn't handle speaking about Isobel's death without losing it, how in the hell was she going to be strong enough to find the killer?

Accepting what he offered, she put the soft folds to her cheeks. "Thank you."

"Would you like some water?"

"No, I just want to get through this." She took another deep breath and backtracked, names and faces jamming in her head, syllables getting twisted in her throat. "That night, Isobel . . . Isobel and her two friends went to Pyre. From what I was told, her friends lost track of her in the crowd at the club. When it was time to go, they couldn't find her and tried her phone. They told me they even went down to the lower level, but they didn't see anything or scent anything out of the ordinary. They went home, thinking she'd gone to their place, and they were worried when she wasn't there."

"So how did they find her?"

"One of them went back. She broke into each of the storage areas, and that was where . . ." Helania pressed the handkerchief into her stinging eyes. "That was where the female found Isobel hanging from a hook on the ceiling. Her throat had been . . . cut. She was stiff, I was told. Cold. The—ah, the one who found her called the other friend. To-gether, they removed her from the scene. There are so many humans at that club, as you know. They couldn't leave her, especially with the dawn coming."

"Of course they couldn't."

Helania glanced down at his phone and watched the numbers go up for a little bit. "I will never forget what the knock on our apartment door sounded like. Four a.m. Knocking. I knew something bad had happened because no one ever came to see us. Isobel always went out. Anyway, I went to check the peephole . . . there was a female on the other side and she was crying. I opened the door, and she all but col-lapsed into me. It took her three tries to get it all out, and I don't know whether that was because I couldn't hear right or because she couldn't speak right. The next thing I knew, we were driving across town. I don't even remember what kind of car it was, but good thing she had it, as we were both too upset to dematerialize."

Glancing up from the phone's counter, she focused on Boone's face. "I could smell my sister's blood in that car. It was what they had used to move her."

Boone squeezed his eyes shut and cursed. "I can't even imagine."

"I just kept thinking, she can't be dead. She can't be dead . . . she can't be dead. It just seemed—I mean, Isobel was the most alive person I knew. How could anyone like her not be breathing?"

Helania folded the handkerchief and dabbed at her face. As she breathed in, she caught the whiff of a delicate smell, as if the square of fine cotton had been handwashed in something as gentle as it was expensive.

She continued, "It was a proper house that we went to. A nice house, not as fancy as this by far, but set back from the road with lots of bushes and an attached garage." She blinked and saw the place clear as moonlight in her mind. "It was clean inside, and the furnishings were all new and fresh. Isobel . . . she was on the floor in the living room, wrapped in white. A sheet, it was. Like a mummy. They had laid her out on the hardwood floor. The scent of her blood was more intense, and even wrapped up like that, I could see a red stain spreading on the back of where her neck was.

"Her friend, the one who found her, and I washed her for the Fade Ceremony. The other friend hung back and watched. At nightfall, the three of us took her out to a state park that has a lot of very hidden places in the woods. It was early June, so the ground was soft. The friend who found her and I had shovels. We dug down ten feet. It took us hours. We put her there. I don't know who cried more." Helania held up her palms. "I tore my hands apart."

Boone leaned in. "You have scars."

"I wanted to remember Isobel." Helania drew in a long and slow breath, and stared at her right palm. "When I got home, I put my hand in salt water. As a tribute."

She traced the network of ridges that crossed where her lifeline was, running her fingertip over the remnants of all those blisters. As a vampire, any wounded skin on her body didn't merely repair itself but regenerated, so that ordinarily, she could never find any traces of any injury.

If you were to bring a wound or broken area of flesh into contact with salt, however? You had those scars for life.

"I just wanted to honor her in some way."

"Of course you did. How could you not?"

Helania looked him. "That's the reason I've been going to that club. Why I watched that female the night before yesterday. Why I checked on her. I need to find out who did this to Isobel, and I don't want them doing it to anyone else—and I've already failed once, or you and I wouldn't be talking."

Boone frowned. "Listen, Helania. I'm not saying you can't handle yourself—I stared down the barrel of your gun, remember? Just please don't be a hero at the expense of your own safety."

"I'm not going to stop going to Pyre," she said sharply.

"I'm not asking you to. Just call me. Anytime. If you see something, if you think you're in danger, don't hesitate to call me. I'll be there in a heartbeat."

A strange feeling came over her, and it took a moment to figure out what it was. With Isobel there to look after her, even after Helania had gone through her transition, she had always had a protector. Now, Boone seemed to want to step into that tragically vacated role, and the idea that she might have someone to turn to again eased her on deep levels.

"Promise me," he said. "That you'll call."

"I promise," she heard herself reply. "Is that all? For this interview?"

Rubbing his eyes as if he were tired, Boone seemed to have to refocus. "Actually, about the boyfriend. Did you ever hear from him after the death? Did he try to contact her phone, her social media, you or any of her friends?"

"I don't know about her friends. And I'm assuming he tried her on her phone, but I don't know where it is."

"You don't have her phone?"

"It was lost that night." When Boone frowned and sat back, she knew exactly where he went in his head. "It was not the boyfriend, I'm telling you. She was thrilled whenever she spoke about him. I'd never seen her so happy, those last couple of months."

"I believe you. It's just . . . you don't know his name, you never met him, and he didn't show up looking for her after she was gone. Doesn't that strike you as odd?"

Helania wanted to argue the point, but the truth was, she had sometimes wondered about the very same things. Yet calling into question Isobel's true love had seemed disloyal.

"I was not part of her scene." Helania took a deep breath. "And if he was trying to find her by calling that phone, I would never know, would I."

"What about the clothes she was wearing? Did any of those get saved?"

"Her friend told me they threw them out because they were ruined."

"We really need to speak with those two females. What are their names?"

"I don't know what their given names are. But I can find them on social media. I cannot forget either of their faces."

"That would be really helpful."

Helania let herself fall back into the armchair. Closing her eyes was a bad idea. The world got to spinning.

"Are you all right?" Boone asked.

"Just a little woozy."

"When was the last time you ate?"

Helania forced her lids to open as she started to do that math. When the hours added up—and kept adding—she frowned.

"You need to eat." Boone reached out and turned off the phone. "And so do I. Let's take a break and have First Meal together."

Her knee-jerk reaction was to say no, conclude the meeting, and go back home to change. She could still make it over to Pyre and have plenty of time there before dawn. Except . . . just as all that stick-to-the-plan, find-the-killer, keep-your-distance occurred to her, from out of nowhere, she pictured her sister.

Isobel had always worn her hair short and spiky, the red color even louder and brighter that way, untempered with the blond that marked Helania's far longer waves. And she had had bright blue eyes. Brilliantly blue, like a robin's egg. And a super-white, ultrawide smile.

Even her coloring had been vivid.

Add to all that her laugh? Isobel had been captivating to people. The few times Helania had gone out and watched on the sidelines as her sister had charmed friends and strangers alike, she had been astounded by the presence of the female. Just like everyone else.

There had been so many times over the last eight months that Helania had regretted the fact that she had been the survivor. Isobel had always been better at living. Why had the recluse been the one to stay on the planet? And to that point, if her sister had been offered a nice meal with a nice male when she was starving? She wouldn't have said yes. She would have hell-yeah'd that idea—and then made sure that the conversation was even better than the food.

Helania looked into Boone's eyes. They were . . . beautiful eyes. Thickly lashed. Deeply set.

She thought of the dead body she had found the night before last. If that female had known that she was going to die that evening, if she had had the date of her demise given to her, what would she have done differently?

*I am alive,* Helania thought to herself. *Right now, I am not dead.*

So it was about time she started living, wasn't it.

"Yes," she heard herself say. "I would like to eat with you. Where, though? Here?"

Boone's eyebrows popped, as if her acceptance of the invite had surprised him. Except then he rushed on. "The *doggen* are busy in the kitchen serving the folks here. But I know a great place to take you. You're going to love it."

# THIRTEEN

The Remington Hotel was a Caldwell fixture, a throwback to the Roaring Twenties that had somehow survived the modernization of downtown. Surrounded by skyscrapers, the thirty-floor, bi-winged building was a gracious grande dame in the company of robots, its courtyard the kind of thing that was in every tourism ad for the city. It was the sort of place where people had Sunday tea in their dress clothes, and couples got engaged in the formal dining room, and there were suites with plaques on the doors pointing out that President Taft had stayed there in 1911 and Hemingway in 1956 and President Clinton in 1994.

Boone rematerialized in the alley beside the hotel, and for a split second, as he stood in the cold alone, he wondered whether Helania was going to change her mind and reroute in her molecular form to somewhere else.

But then she was beside him. In the flesh.

"I'm dressed casually," she said as she indicated her parka and jeans.

He nodded down at his set of leathers. "As I am. That's why we're going to Remi's."

As he motioned to the head of the alley, they walked together toward the cars that were passing by on East Main Street.

*Say something*, he thought. *Say . . . anything—*

"You mean the movie?"

Boone shook his head. "What?"

"*Say Anything.* You know, with John Cusack?" When he gave Helania a blank look, she said, "It has that classic scene with him holding the boom box over his head and Peter Gabriel playing. What made you think of it?"

Okaaaaaaaaaaaay, he must have spoken that out loud. "Ah, sure . . . it's one of my favorites."

"Mine, too." She laughed a little. "Cameron Crowe's best, in my opinion. I also like all the John Hughes movies from the eighties. I had a crush on Jake Ryan forever—you're really limping, by the way."

Was he? He couldn't feel his face, much less his legs—and talk about pop culture refs. Thank you, the Weeknd.

"How were you hurt?" she asked. "Were you fighting?"

"Yes." With a down pillow that had had a helluva ground game, as it turned out. "The enemy nearly got the best of me."

Helania stopped dead. "Oh, my God. Are you serious? Did you see a doctor—"

"I'm sorry, no." He held up a hand. "Look, I want to impress you. And if I tell you how it actually happened, you're going to think I'm the biggest planker on the planet."

"I don't even know what a planker is."

As she stared up him, with those big yellow eyes filling her heart-shaped face and the wisps of her red and blond hair teased on the wind and that bright flush on her cheeks from the cold . . . she was the most beautiful thing he'd ever seen.

All of the aristocratic females in all of the ball gowns in the world couldn't hold a candle to her.

"Do you mean 'dweeb'?" she prompted.

"I haven't heard that word in a million years."

"Well, to be fair, you brought the eighties into this first." That slight smile, the one he loved so much, tilted her mouth again. "Tell me how you got hurt. I promise I won't judge. I mean, come on, I am the most socially inept person you will ever meet. I have lived a whole life through movies that I watched at home. I can quote you a hundred thousand lines from a thousand rom-coms, but you ask me to talk to someone I don't know? I freeze solid. So I am in no position to judge."

*I want to kiss you*, he thought. *Right now.*

"WhenyoucalledlastnightIwasnakedandIdidn'tthinkthatwasappropriatesoIrantomyclosetandgotdressedandwhenIcamebackIendeduptrippingonapillowdon'taskhowandIstubbedmytoeandsprainedmyankle."

Helania blinked. And then laughed out loud. "I'm sorry, can you try that again?"

"Naked when you called. Ran to get dressed. Back by the bed, tripped on a pillow. Stubbed toe, sprained ankle. Man-card revoked. Tragedy ensues."

As she laughed again, he decided he was going to take classes in stand-up. Just so that he could hear that sound.

"So you were naked?" she said.

"Yeah." Okay, now he was doing the blush thing. "I didn't want to disrespect you."

"We weren't FaceTiming. I couldn't see anything."

"But I knew I had no clothes on."

He meant to keep the tone light and funny. But something in his voice changed, and she picked up on it instantly—because that lovely little smile drifted away from her expression.

"I don't know how to do this," she said roughly.

"Walk down this alley, you mean?" He tried to bring the mood back around. "I think you're better suited to the job than I am—"

"No." She motioned between them. "This."

Instantly, Boone got serious. "So you feel it, too."

Her eyes went to the open end of the alley, where the traffic was stop-and-go, bumper-to-bumper. There must have been a basketball game that had just gotten out, he thought. Or a concert. A show.

Maybe this had been a mistake to drag her into the human world.

"I don't want to misrepresent myself." She shook her head. "Isobel would do something like this. Not me—"

"You're the one I want to share a meal with. Not anyone else."

"I just don't want you to have high expectations. A lot of the time— even before I lost Isobel—I didn't feel right with other people. It's like a gear that can't quite engage. It's always been that way and I don't want you to think it's you. I'm a little off—"

Boone reached out and took her hand. The instant the contact was made, Helania fell silent.

"I'm not expecting anything more than dinner," he said. "On my honor."

There was a pause. Then that smile came back even wider, and what do you know—it brought a friend. A dimple popped up, sweet as could be, on one of her cheeks.

Crocking his elbow, he grinned. "May I have your arm?"

Ducking her head, she put her hand through the space he made for her, and then they were walking down the alley together once again.

"You tripped on a pillow?" she murmured.

"At least it was after I'd gotten dressed or God only knows what else I could have hurt on that bedside table."

Her laugh made him feel taller and stronger, even as his physical dimensions did not change.

And what do you know, Helania was still smiling as they got out onto Main Street proper and entered the Remington's famous courtyard. Courtesy of the hotel's two wings, there was a vast open mall created by the embrace of its stone extensions, the main entrance a majestic anchor with its hanging flags and Art Deco details. Illuminated by old-fashioned gas lanterns and marked by rows of trees wound with thousands upon thousands of Christmas lights, it was a fairy tale in the heart of downtown's steel-and-asphalt anonymity.

"This is so beautiful," she said as she looked around.

"Yes," he murmured as he focused on her face. "You are."

She was so taken by the spectacle that it appeared she didn't hear him. Probably just as well. Right under his surface was an intensity that he didn't want to reveal to her. Yet.

"It's magical." She reached out a hand and stopped just short of touching one of the lit-up branches. "Something out of a book."

"The hotel's famous for this courtyard."

"I've only seen pictures of it before," She paused and then turned in a slow circle. "The glow reminds me of sunlight back before my transition."

She was right, he thought as he followed her lead and glanced around. All the little bulbs threw off a mellow, banked illumination similar to a summer sunset's.

"Did you sneak out of your parents' house to look at the sun, too?" he asked.

"Isobel told me I had to do it." Helania smiled. "She said I absolutely had to see the sun before my change. As the older of the pair of us, she'd been through the change already. She showed me where to go through the basement of our family's house, how to follow the crawl space and get out through an old storm door."

"I always thought that humans smoking cigarettes behind their parents' backs was like us with sneaking out to see the sun."

"Exactly." Helania shook her head. "I didn't stay long. It was July when I did it and . . . yes, that's what the color of this light reminds me of. It was right at sunset when I went out. My parents were making First Meal, and Isobel distracted them in the kitchen. I'll never forget the feel of the warmth on my face."

Boone thought back to when he and his cousins would duck out and watch the sun set and rise. They had done it so many times. Right up until their transitions. After that, everything had been different. No more sun.

"Isobel was so proud of me. She hugged me and told me I had to do it again and again. But that was her. I never went out another time."

"You miss her."

"Every night." Helania glanced at him. "You must feel the same way about your father."

Boone shrugged. "I have certainly noticed his absence, that's for sure."

They started walking again, heading for the formal entrance with its bank of glass doors and silver and brass flourishes. Hanging above it all, there was the American flag as well as the ones for the State of New York, the United Kingdom, and Spain.

"Welcome to the Remington," a uniformed doorman said with a brief bow.

"Thank you," Boone answered as the human gave the revolving door a shove and Helania went through first.

Inside, the cavernous lobby was all black marble, gold and silver carpeting, and burnished metal fixtures. Seating areas clustered around the bases of broad square columns were like presents under human Christmas trees, and discreetly dressed staff whispered by as they attended to the hotel's guests.

"Oh . . . wow." Helania slowed again, her eyes lighting up. "It's a palace."

"This way." As he took her hand, he felt the network of scars and wished he could have helped her bury her dead. "Remi's is down here."

Over in the far corner, there was a theater-worthy heavy velvet curtain with gold tassels, and as he drew her behind it, the first strains of jazz could be heard faintly. The staircase that was revealed was cramped, the marble steps worn in places where a century's worth of feet had trod. On the glossy black walls, hundreds of framed, vintage photographs of flappers and dandies from the twenties and thirties were hung so closely together, they formed a mosaic of black and white tiles.

Down at the bottom, the mellow music was louder, and at the maître d' stand, Boone slipped the gentleman a hundred-dollar bill and was rewarded with one of the best tables in the house, right in front of the small stage. He sat with his back to the trio who were playing so Helania could have the better view.

As she stared up in wonder at the piano player, the clarinetist, the guy on the bass, he felt something warm bloom in the center of his chest.

There was nowhere else on the planet he wanted to be. And the happiness he felt, the sense of connection and communion, was a shock that illuminated how lonely he had been.

For such a very long time.

◆　　◆　　◆

Helania felt like she was under a heat lamp. And not in a bad way.

As she took off her parka and sat across from Boone, the sensual music wrapped them in an embrace, bringing them closer together than they actually were. The dim lighting and thoughtful staff offered little to no interruption, and even the small table, as well as the chairs that were tilted in, seemed to encourage the intimacy.

Before she knew it, plates of cheese with fruit appeared, and then heartier fare, a stew with meat and vegetables, which quite possibly could have been the best thing she'd ever eaten. Or maybe the company was the spice that turned a humble dish into a gourmet masterpiece: In spite of the fact that she often felt tongue-tied with other people, that was not the case with Boone. There seemed to be an endless array of topics for discussion, everything from favorite books and music, to current affairs, to happy childhood memories, shared along with the common bread basket.

It was all quite remarkable. And then even the dishes of dessert had been cleared, and they were still talking.

Running her fingertips over the belly of her wineglass, she stared into the chardonnay she'd been nursing . . . and wondered how the night was going to end.

"What are you thinking about?" Boone murmured.

Shaking her head, she was curious if he'd guessed that she'd been with a male before—and whether or not that was going to be a problem. He was obviously from the aristocracy, and there were a lot of rules for them. Well, there were rules for civilians, too. But Isobel had urged her to break out of her shell and get herself a male, and so she had done that about a decade ago. The relationship had lasted about a year and then fizzled, a social experiment that had failed in the lab.

"Talk to me," he murmured. "Whatever it is, just talk to me."

It was a shock to realize she actually wanted to tell him everything. But she couldn't exactly find the right words.

Deliberately, she pictured Isobel's face, and took a deep breath.

"I was born hearing-impaired." She touched one of her ears. "I wasn't completely deaf, but I couldn't hear much more than low sounds. Speech was difficult for me, and that was why communicating with other people was so hard. I learned sign language back in the sixties, and I'm still very good at reading lips, but you know . . . things were different back then. Physical problems in young were not as well accepted. So it was hard for me. Hard for my whole family."

She glanced up at him and was relieved to find that he hadn't recoiled with disgust—which was not only something that people had done to her in the past, but the kind of thing the aristocracy was known for.

Boone, contrary to his station, was leaning in even closer, his expression open . . . accepting.

Taking another long inhale, she said, "Other young were downright cruel, but Isobel was there for me. I can remember the first fistfight she got into over my disability." Helania had to smile. "She pounded the crap out of this little boy who had been making fun of me. I was too busy trying to get along in the world to worry about what people thought of my deafness, but she cared and she was fierce about it."

"Is that why you think you can't get along with people?"

"It's a hangover from all those years, you know?" She touched her ear again. "Anyway, I had been told that there was a possibility that my transition would fix the problem with my ear canals, but I never believed it. When I came through the change, I was shocked to hear everything so clearly. I hated it at first. Everything was so loud, especially the high notes of things like hinges on doors, phones ringing, whistling. It was a difficult adjustment."

"It must have been a different world to you," he said.

"Totally different. I mean, I had kept to myself before then. After my hearing worked? I shut down for about a year. That was when Isobel insisted that we move out and start living on our own. She seemed to understand that I needed space to myself, and my parents were—they were very concerned and very well intended. But they were relentless in trying to draw me out, and all that pushing was having the opposite effect. Things got better after Isobel and I began living together. Movies were what saved me. While Isobel was out with her friends, I played them on the TV. First with those record-like discs, remember the ones that came like big albums in those plastic sleeves?"

Boone laughed. "Yes, God . . . I haven't thought of them in years."

"Right? Then Beta and VHS. Then DVDs. Now we have Netflix and Hulu." She took a sip of her wine. "So when Isobel was out in the world, I would sit alone and watch movies, first with the sound turned way down and then gradually . . ." She shrugged. "I got used to it. Now, I can even be in crowds and not get overwhelmed by the all the layers of sound. But it took years. I read an article once that said the adjustment to a sense was all about neuropathways being developed. My brain has had to rewire itself, in other words."

"But you're still not completely at ease with people."

"No, I'm not. Is it nature in the form of innate introversion? Or nurture from those two and a half decades of being deaf and getting ridiculed by kids my own age as well as some of their parents? I'm not sure. And I suppose it doesn't matter. I am what I am."

There was a note of apology in her tone, but then she had long felt that she had things to make up for, damages to explain, limitations to excuse—

Boone reached across the table and took her hand, the one with the scars on the palm. "I wouldn't change a thing about you."

"Well, that's lucky for me," she whispered, "as I've not had a lot of luck being anything different."

As the jazz trio's tempo changed, his thumb stroked over her flesh. "Dance with me?"

A spike of warmth flared in the center of her chest, right where her heart was. The glow was a surprise, and akin to a fire being lit in a cold, drafty room: A shocking, very pleasant change.

*Isobel would approve of this*, she thought abruptly. *All of it.*

Boone. The jazz music. The cozy pub-like atmosphere. Helania . . . taking a chance on someone.

And in this moment, it felt like the dice she was rolling were not so much on Boone, but . . . on herself.

"Yes," she said with a slow smile. "I would like that."

They got to their feet at the same time, and given that their table was right in front by the stage, it was just two steps over and she was up against his body.

Dearest Virgin Scribe, he was big. Her head only came up to his pecs and his arms seemed enormous as they wrapped around her. But he held her gently, letting her decide how close to get, and what do you know . . .

She wanted close.

It was a tough goal to accomplish, however. He had never taken his leather jacket off, and it wasn't until she snuck a hand underneath it and ran into a holstered gun that she realized why.

"Sorry," he said tightly.

"It's okay." She looked up into his eyes. "At least I know I'm safe."

His face got deadly serious. "Always. I'm never going to let anything happen to you."

As tears pricked the corners of her eyes, she laid her head on his leather-covered chest. She didn't want to ruin the mood, but the truth was, that vow was hard to hear.

Too much like the past. Too much like Isobel.

Dragging herself back to the present, she concentrated on the way he moved, the subtle swaying of all that muscle, the promise of things left as yet unexplored.

Naked things. Pleasurable things.

God, he smelled good. Leather, a slight whiff of gunmetal . . . but mostly the clean male underneath.

Helania thought once again that she had no idea where this was going or what exactly was happening between them. But she wanted things to end up in a bed.

Soon—

One of Boone's hands stroked over her shoulder and down her back, following the contours of her curves. The warmth, the subtle pressure of the caress, the span of his large palm and deft fingers . . . all of it reverberated throughout her whole body, making her feel like she was a tuning fork calibrated for him and him alone. Tilting her head, she looked up at him again.

His face was a stark mask of hunger and his eyes burned as he stared down at her.

Except she didn't need to see his tight expression to know how badly he wanted her.

She could feel his arousal.

# FOURTEEN

"No, I'm going to do it."

The dead tone cut through the anxious talk in the clinic's private meeting room, a bomb blowing a hole in the conversational landscape. In the silent aftermath, Butch focused on the female who had spoken up through the tense gathering. Sitting in a chair off to the side, she was well into middle age, which for a vampire didn't mean much in terms of physical changes—as per the species' typical lifespan, she still looked like the twenty-five-year-old she had been after she'd gone through her change three hundred or so years before.

But the centuries she had been through showed in those eyes of hers.

And that tone.

Clearly, she had seen many bad things over the course of her life. This, however . . . this coming to see if a dead body was that of her daughter was undoubtedly the very worst. And these males around her, the *hellren*, the son, the uncle and the grandfather? They all fell quiet and dropped their stares to the floor in deference to her.

No doubt part of it was because no one could argue her right, but more than that? Butch had the sense that nobody except her had the strength for the grim task.

And he was not surprised that the *mahmen* was the one who'd woman'd up. After however many years in homicide, he had learned about the differences between the sexes. Men were physically stronger, true. But the women? They were the warriors. As much as those males who had come with her would have run into a burning building to save her, not one of them was strong enough to take her place for this heart-breaking duty.

Because they couldn't handle it.

"All right," Butch said. "Let me know when you're—"

The female got to her feet. "I am ready now."

The private meeting room they were in was next to the morgue's viewing suite, and as Butch held the door open for her, she didn't look back at her family. She walked out into the hall with her head up and both hands on her purse. She still had her coat on, the brown wool three-quarter simply cut and simply made.

He had a thought that he should suggest she take it off. But she didn't look like the type who was going to faint.

No, she was steady as bedrock even though he could feel the fear boiling out of her very pores.

Butch held another door open for her, and they stepped inside a small tiled room that had three chairs off to one side and a watercooler. Across the way, a horizontal, six-foot-by-four-foot glass pane was displaying the pulled curtain on its other side.

"No," she said as she eyed the window. "Not like this."

"It will be easier for you to—"

"If that is my daughter, I'm not going to identify her body through a piece of glass."

Butch could only nod. "Give me a second."

Going over to the narrow door by the window, he knocked once. When Havers opened up, Butch kept his voice low.

"We're coming in."

"But that is not the way—"

"That is absolutely the way we're going to do this," Butch whispered. "At her request."

Havers glanced over Butch's shoulder and then bowed. "Of course. We will accommodate her wishes."

As the race's physician stood to the side, Butch looked at the female. "We're ready when you are."

The female took several deep breaths, and that purse she had a death grip on started to shake.

"Ma'am," he said, "I'm going to suggest you take your coat off and leave your purse here."

She looked over at where he pointed as if she had never seen a chair before. Then she went across and set her bag down. Removing her coat, she was careful as she folded the wool up and placed it on the seat, and when she straightened, she tucked her blouse into her slacks. Her clothes were not fancy, but neither were they casual; they were the kind of thing an executive assistant would wear to work.

And he totally understood her need to prepare herself. Sometimes, composure on the surface was all a person could ask for.

When she came over to him, he offered her his hand. He just wanted her to know she wasn't alone. "I'm going in with you."

The female stared at what he held out to her. "It's not your family."

"She became my family the moment I took this case on."

"You've done this before?"

"A hundred times."

After a moment, she nodded. And then she put her palm against his own, her cold, clammy skin making him incalculably sad.

"What's that smell?" she said before she stepped through the jambs.

"It's the disinfectant they use to clean the rooms."

"Okay."

As Butch drew her inside, her eyes flashed to the body that was lying face-up on the gurney. A white sheet covered the remains from head to toe, the ends hanging freely on all four sides.

The female blanched and weaved on her feet. When Butch caught her, Havers seemed to recognize that his presence was extraneous and the healer had the good sense to step all the way back against the wall.

"Help me over there," the female said softly. "I can't seem to walk."

"Lean on me." Butch tightened his hold on her waist. "I won't let you fall."

"Thank you."

Escorting her over to the head, he could feel the pressure on his arm where she was relying on him, and he pictured his Marissa in her place, standing over a slab, on the verge of seeing if their dead daughter was in front of them.

"Take your time," he choked out as they stopped together.

The female took a deep breath, but then grimaced and rubbed her nose as if she didn't like the astringent smell in the room.

He'd been mostly truthful about the disinfectant. It was used to clean, yes. But also, no one wanted the family to smell any blood or any decomposition, and in the case of these particular remains, though they had been kept in cold storage for the majority of the time, there had been stretches when they had not been exposed to the required temperature.

"Okay," she said roughly. "Let me see."

Butch reached out with his free hand and drew the sheet back from the face, folding it down high on the neck so that none of the wounds showed.

The female clamped a hand on her mouth as all the color drained out of her face.

Butch closed his eyes briefly and cursed. "I'm so sorry. But I have to ask you. Is this your—"

"Yes, this is my daughter," the female said hoarsely. "She is . . . ours."

When Butch went to re-cover the face, the female shook her head. "No. Not yet."

She leaned down, and as her hair swung free, she had to tuck the loose part behind her ear. With a shaking hand, she reached out and touched the short, dyed black hair at the temple. Then she stroked the cold, gray cheek.

Tears fell from her eyes, landing on the sheet at the arm. The first two slid off the dry cotton. The others that followed were absorbed.

"What happened to her?" The female looked up in desperation. "Who did this to my Mai?"

◆    ◆    ◆

On the other side of the Hudson River, deep in the field of conflict in downtown, Syn stalked through an alley in search of the enemy, his instincts way out in front of him, then to the side, now to the back . . . and again trained on what was before him. It was another cold, clear night, no wind to ruffle the loose flakes of snow that had fallen during the day, nothing to disturb the dense, dry, deep freeze that had stalled over Caldwell.

"—down at that club. Vishous got the body over to Havers's and now they're trying to figure out who she is and who killed—"

Ordinarily, Syn didn't mind being paired with Balthazar. The Bastard was a vicious killer and rarely said much, two of the highest compliments Syn could pay any living thing.

Unfortunately, that blessed silent streak was being cut short tonight. Apparently, all it took to end Balthazar's winning-personality batting average was a dead female down at that human club.

Although, to be fair, it wasn't just the chatter that was doing Syn's nut in.

Beneath his skin, his *talhman* was surging, prowling . . . triggered by the conversation about the female who had been found, strung up on the lower level of Pyre, naked.

Unbidden, one of his hands went to the steel daggers that were mounted, handles down, on his chest. Was it possible, he wondered, that those cuts to that female's throat, the slices to her wrists, the other damage to her body . . . had been made by his knives? His hands? He had a distinct memory of going down those damp, cold stairs with a

female's legs wrapped around his hips. And he could remember vividly
the pair of them up against one of those doors down there, hasty, rough
sex taking them into a storage area. Had he shut them in together after
its lock had sprung open?

Had he done other things to her besides penetrate her core?

He couldn't recall. And for the first time in a long time, warnings
prickled up the back of his neck.

In fact, he could not remember when the sex had ended. He knew
he hadn't orgasmed, of course. And he was sure she had, a number of
times. But other than that? The next thing he'd been aware of was de-
parting the club. Alone.

Syn glanced down at his hands and tried to force his brain to recall
if they'd had blood on them when he'd taken his leave of Pyre. The fact
that he pulled yet another blank made him curse under his breath.
Where had he been headed after he'd left? Home, he thought. To the
Brotherhood mansion, where he and the Band of Bastards now lived—

No, that wasn't right. Just as he'd been about to dematerialize, he'd
scented a *lesser*. Following the sweet stench, he'd tracked his prey a couple of blocks away from the club.

So, yes, when he had finally gotten back to the Brotherhood mansion, he'd been covered with the black, oily mess that had flowed
through that slayer's veins: His hands and forearms. His clothes. His
shitkickers. And he could remember checking in at the vestibule's security camera, one of the *doggen* letting him in. He hadn't paid much attention to which it had been. Had anyone else seen him come in?

Even with the stench of the enemy all over him, surely someone
would have commented on the fact that he'd had a female's blood on
him, too. Right?

"—surprised you weren't at the meeting."

Syn glanced over. "What?"

"The meeting Wrath called tonight. About the dead female at that
club."

"I was busy."

Balthazar stopped in the middle of the alley. "Doing what?"

Syn narrowed his eyes. "The same thing I do every night. Stare at my reflection and rue the day I was born."

"Seriously."

"Fine, let's go with something cheerful. How about yoga. Pilates. No, wait, I was ordering shit I do not need off of Amazon—"

"What were you doing when you should have been at the meeting, Syn?"

The question was put out there calmly and evenly. Which was also characteristic of Balthazar. The guy was a straight shooter—and to be fair, he had reason to be suspicious. He knew about . . . things . . . that had happened back in the Old Country. Things that had involved females and blood and bodies being found.

"It wasn't me," Syn said dryly. "I didn't kill whoever it was."

The lie sounded convincing, at least to his own ears. Unfortunately, that was a table, party of one.

"Syn, I don't judge you." Balthazar shook his head. "You know I never have."

"Oh, fuck this, I'm not wasting time—"

"I have *always* left you to your business. No questions asked. I know that things are . . . different . . . for you." Balthazar shook his head again. "But let me be very clear. You *cannot* be doing that shit over here. We're in the New World now. It's going to get noticed, and then we've got problems because we're not just on our own anymore. We're aligned with the King, and Wrath is not going to stand for anybody in his household doing what you do. People miss their dead over here."

"Don't worry about it. I've got it under control."

As Syn started walking again, Balthazar didn't budge. "I don't think you do."

Syn stopped and refused to turn back around. Addressing the empty alley in front of him, he said, "In the Old World, I did what I did for a good goddamn purpose. I channeled it properly."

"True enough, but there are rules on this side of the ocean."

Staring straight ahead, Syn saw trash cans that were knocked over and a stray cat pawing through a torn-open Hefty bag. As he watched the animal search for dinner, he thought about the female from the other night. There had been no justification that he was aware of for him killing her. Even if she had been a criminal, a murderer, a thief— which were his targeted prey—he hadn't known it when he'd taken her down into that lower level. Where she had been found not just dead, but defiled as well.

So maybe she was an innocent. And he had done a very, very bad thing.

He didn't want to hear what Balthazar was saying.

He didn't want the holes in his memory.

He didn't want . . . to be dealing with this bullshit any longer.

"Do me a favor," he said softly.

"No," Balthazar shot back. "I'm not going there. Don't you fucking ask me to."

Syn twisted around. As his eyes changed color, the alley was flooded with a red glow, his cousin spotlit by the color of blood. Behind him, the cat screeched and tore off, sending a glass bottle rolling.

His voice was warped as he spoke. "Then you need to stop talking to me about dead females."

Balthazar cursed under his breath. "There has to be another way."

"I told you a century ago. Sooner or later, you're going to have to put a bullet through my head. Or find someone who will."

It would be a public service, at this point. And a relief to him.

God knew he would have done it himself years ago, if suicide didn't mean you were locked out of the Fade. Although given what he had gotten up to over the years?

He was going to end up in *Dhunhd* anyway.

"You know there's only one way to stop me," he said with a growl. "And if you don't do it, the blood of the females I hurt is on your hands, too."

## FIFTEEN

Boone made it back to his father's house with about two hours to go before the Fade ceremony he'd convened. As he entered through the front door, he was rank pissed. Leaving Helania had been the last thing he wanted to do, and the fact that he'd had to go because of something connected to Altamere?

He wasn't happy about sacrificing even a second of his life to memorialize the male, much less anything as important as spending time with his female.

Not that she was technically his. She just felt that way.

Closing out the cold, he put his hands on his hips and glared at the marble floor. Which, granted, hadn't done anything wrong. It was just there to be walked on, like it had been for his whole life.

"I have got to relax," he muttered.

Of course, that would be easier if he didn't have the biggest set of blue balls this side of a hot air balloon convention. Fuuuuuuuuuuck. And he thought his bad ankle was making him walk with a limp? Every step he took, he felt like someone had tied kettlebells to his groin.

Looking around the staircase, he eyed the door to the males' guest bathroom. He could go in there, unbutton his fly and palm things up.

At the rate he was going, it would take him two strokes and he would come all over the place.

But he still couldn't shake the idea that he was being somehow disrespectful to Helania. She was so much more than YouPorn. Than some random female body to jerk off to. Than a two-dimensional fantasy tailor-made to his tastes just so he could rub one out.

She was a living, breathing, incredibly beautiful and smart young female who—

He had not kissed goodbye.

God, he had wanted to. On the dance floor. Back at their table. When they were walking out through the Remington's courtyard and then after they'd snuck around to the shadows next to the hotel's tall side so they could ghost out.

The feel of her body moving against his own as they'd danced close and slow had flipped all of his levers to the Hell-Yeah position. The Right-Fucking-NOW. The OMG-I-Will-Beg. He wanted her to distraction, his blood running hot and thick with a lust that he'd never come close to feeling before. And she had been right there with him. He had scented her arousal and stared down into her glowing eyes and known that she wanted him, too.

What had stopped him? Two things. He wasn't going to stop things with just a single kiss . . . and neither was she. Unless he was grossly misreading her—and he did not think he was—lip-to-lip would be but a beginning for them, a precursor to bare skin and a whole lot more, and he wanted the space and time to take the "yes" on both sides to its natural conclusion.

And what do you know, *Oh, hey, sorry, I've got to go Fade my father* was a total buzzkill.

The other set of brakes on the situation had been the fact that he didn't want her to think it was just sex on his end. It had been a relief to find they had so much in common other than grief, and he wanted the chance to be around her again as much as he wanted all the horizontal stuff. But he knew his aristocratic station spoke for itself: Males of his class had a tendency to use civilian females for casual sex, taking them to bed and tossing them aside. The last thing he ever wanted was for Helania to think he was disrespecting her like that. And though they had never outright discussed his lineage, he hadn't exactly tried to hide his accent or his background.

So he had gentlemale'd it in that alley: Hugging her. Kissing her chastely on the cheek. Making sure she dematerialized out safely first.

And now he was here. In this damn house. Waiting for people he didn't really care about to arrive for a ceremony that felt like a lie so he could close the door on a death that had rocked him and yet didn't matter much at all.

On that note, he should probably go check on preparations.

At least duking it out with Marquist would allow him to channel some of this going-nowhere frustration.

As Boone strode down to the dining room, and then pushed his way through the flap door that the staff used, the idea he was behaving as his father would have rankled. God, Altamere and Marquist had been consumed by proper preparations and accommodations for guests of the house, whether they were people coming for a cocktail party, a dinner party, an event, or an overday.

Those two would spend hours in Marquist's office, poring over seating charts, menus, wine and liquor orders.

Crazy.

On the far side of that flap door, there was the staging area for meal service, the silver polishing room, and then the enormous pantry. Also the closed door to Marquist's office and private accommodations— which, as it turned out, did not have an I-quit letter taped to its jamb. Or U-Haul moving boxes stacked beside it. Or a gun target with Boone's photograph in the center and bullet holes in a smiley face on his forehead anywhere in its vicinity.

Guess the male hadn't resigned yet. And it was hard to know whether that was a good or a bad thing.

The answer to the question "Where's Marquist?" was sorted in the kitchen proper: The butler was at the counter in front of the stove, his pressed jacket removed and his sleeves rolled up. His attention was focused on trimming the fat off a roast beef the size of a golf cart, that Henckels knife flying around the piece of meat, expert hands doing an expert job.

The butler did not look up. "Yes."

"Are we ready?"

"Yes." The knife flashed as Marquist changed the angle of the slice. "Everything is in hand."

"Where are the other *doggen?*"

"I am completing the preparations myself. It is the last thing I shall do in service unto my master, and no one is welcome into this sacred space."

"The others will want to participate. My sire was their master as well."

"Not as he was mine."

Boone frowned. "So how long were you two sleeping together anyway. Did it start right after he brought you here, or did he hire you because it was already happening."

Marquist hissed and looked up. And what do you know, a knife unattended was a lot like a pot on the stove—it did its job even better without being watched.

Of course, the caveat was that the blade sliced into the butler rather than the fat layer on all that beef.

The butler dropped the Henckels and raced for the sink. And as Boone watched the hot water rinsing and the wrap-up with the dish towel, he couldn't decide whether his dislike for the male was what precluded him from apologizing . . . or the fact that after all these years of monitoring his own social manners, he had totally ceased to give a shit.

He did not care that the butler was hurt. And he was not going to pretend he did.

Marquist squared his shoulders before turning back around, and as he pivoted, Boone met the male's eyes straight on.

"Don't bother denying it," Boone said. "And FYI, it doesn't matter to me one way or the other. Just like it apparently wasn't an issue for my step*mahmen*. Maybe she felt like you were doing her a favor."

As the butler's eyes narrowed like he was mulling over his responses, Boone considered what it would be like to get left out of the will in favor of the other male. Well . . . what do you know. The idea of letting this unhappy house, and all its boatload of crap, go seemed like a liberating event as opposed to an alienating one.

Marquist's expression turned haughty, like he was above any accusations. Especially those of a poke-and-tickle variety—even though they both knew what had gone on with Altamere behind closed doors.

"I would do anything in service to your father. Anything."

"I'm thinking that was very true," Boone muttered.

"*Is* true. I have served him in ways you cannot fathom, protecting him and his household, ensuring all is well. And death has not changed my devotion to him."

*You want an obelisk?* Boone thought. *A commemorative stamp. No, wait, a billboard in Times Square to all the blow jobs.*

Okay, that was crass. But come on.

"I will not dignify this with a response to anything further." Marquist's eyes narrowed again. "Except to say that your sire and I were excellent partners. In the running of this house."

Boone crossed his arms over his chest and leaned back against one of the counters. "Kind of convenient my blood *mahmen* died so soon after you came under this roof."

"What exactly are you suggesting."

It was not a question. And not for the first time, Boone wondered exactly what Marquist's background was. His motives, on the other hand, seemed clear. Ordinarily, no male civilian would choose to be a kept servant in the household of their lover. Talk about demeaning. But there were perks to being with a member of the *glymera*—and God knew the only way Marquist could ever have nightly contact with someone of Altamere's stature was if he moved in under the guise of employment.

In the aristocracy? There was no tolerance for overt male homosexuality. Social propriety dictated that no matter how miserable it made you, you were to mate a member of the opposite sex and procreate at least once—preferably twice if your lawful *shellan* survived the first birthing bed. If you were, as they called it, of a "secondary persuasion," you could take male lovers discreetly. But the relationships were never to interfere with your mate, your family, or your bloodline—and the Scribe Virgin save you if anyone ever found out about your extracurricular activities.

Oh, and as for females in the aristocracy? They weren't allowed lesbian lovers. Ever. Under any circumstances.

Just one more example of the patriarchy of the *glymera*. The intolerance. The injustice. All of it was so unfair.

"My parents were never happy together," Boone stated. "But neither of them had been brought up to expect anything more or anything less. That being said, I always wondered if my *mahmen* committed suicide, or whether it was something else, something sinister that killed her. Exactly how did she die? No one ever told me because no one ever talked about it."

"That is because the veil of privacy continues to be appropriate after death. Your *mahmen* was a fine female of worth who did her duty as was appropriate."

"Wow. You used 'appropriate' twice there. Good work. No wonder my father trusted you to plan his parties." Boone nodded at the butler's feet. "Watch it. You're dripping. Better go to Havers's and get that stitched up."

The butler glanced at the roast beef as if he were contemplating going back to his work.

"Oh, no, you don't." Boone shook his head. "You're not bleeding all over the food, even if that hunk of meat is about to go into the oven. I'll go get the other *doggen*, and they will handle everything—as they should have from the very beginning for the ceremony. It was very *inappropriate* of you to exclude them."

Marquist's smile was slow as his eyes grew calculating. "Be of care, young master Boone. I would hate for your bloodline to be sullied by anything untoward. The *glymera* is slow to forgive even minor slips. A poorly cooked *hors d'oeuvre* or badly prepared *foie gras* can be devastating to a household's reputation. Much less something of far graver import."

"You're assuming I give two shits about what any of them think." Boone dropped his chin and glared from beneath his brows. "And let me point out the obvious—you'll never get another job on an estate of this caliber if you pull any stunts of indiscretion like talking about your affair with my father. The aristocrats won't let you so much as wash their cars or clean their gutters if you spread rumors about my sire."

"This from a male who claims he does not care what people think."

"I'm just trying to help you out in case you haven't considered your next job."

"You're assuming I haven't been well taken care of. Which happens to be something I know for a fact I do not have to worry about."

Marquist did not bow as he went to leave. But considering the breach of protocol he had just confirmed—as well as the one he had threatened—who was counting?

Right before the butler walked out into the staging area, Boone said over his shoulder, "Do not use the front door. You're just staff here, not family."

Marquist paused and tightened the bloody dish towel on his sliced hand. "I'm better than family. And as soon as that Fade Ceremony is over, you're going to learn exactly how much better."

"I'm not leaving this house," Boone gritted out.

"Neither am I."

◆     ◆     ◆

As Butch re-formed on the side lawn of Boone's family's mansion, he was so not surprised by the old school money routine. The place was big as an embassy and lit up like a ball park. Through the old wavy glass of the windows, he could see antiques and oil paintings, sculptures and vases of flowers. It was exactly the kind of anonymous, venerable luxury that he'd seen in every *glymera* household he had ever been in, proof positive that intrinsic worth didn't make shit homey, and when there was only a single standard of acceptability for decorations, all you got was a reductive one-note.

He would take his Pit with his *shellan* and his two roommates over this showboat every day of the week and twice on Sunday.

"Poor kid," Rhage said as the brother arrived.

"Not hardly," V muttered as he appeared. "Boone's better off this way, true? That sire of his was a motherfucker."

Butch shot a look at his roomie. "Will you please try to not bring that up at the goddamn ceremony? It's tacky."

"I hate protocol."

"No, really?" Rhage cut in. "Wait, let me get my shocked face on."

The brother turned away—and then whipped back around with his handsome puss all wall-eyed and O-mouthed.

As he gasped and fluttered both hands by his head, V glared. "Come over here."

"Why?"

"So I can knee you in the nuts. I'd close the distance myself, but your church bells aren't worth my two steps to the left—"

"Will you guys *quit* it," Butch hissed. "This is a solemn occasion. I need you both to pull your shit together and pretend you can be appropriate for ten minutes."

V rolled his eyes. "This coming from a male who has a potato gun."

Rhage put his arm around Butch's shoulders and leaned in. "Please tell me you're not trying to reason with the Hunchback of I-don't-give-a-damn over there?"

As Butch considered doing a gonad workout of his own on Frick and Frack, the Smack-It Brothers, Tohr rematerialized and changed the vibe with his presence. With the levity draining out of the group, the bunch of them walked around to the front of the house. Up at the entrance, they stomped snow off their treads on the woven mat and put the brass knocker to good use. A properly dressed *doggen* in all black—per protocol, natch—answered and then they were inside and checking things out away from the cold.

In a predictably fancy foyer, a good fifty or sixty people were milling about, and as Butch glanced through the crowd, he caught sight of Phury and Z with John Matthew, Qhuinn, and Blay. The group of home-teamers were hanging together just outside the parlor and dagger palms were raised in greeting.

Rhage took out a cherry Tootsie Pop and unwrapped it. "Where's our boy?"

Butch nodded past the parlor's archway. Boone was over by the fireplace, looking like he was on autopilot as he talked to a well-heeled couple standing with him. When he glanced across the coiffed heads, he did a double take as he saw members of the Brotherhood, and he excused himself, weeding through the aristocratic females and males.

"You all are here," he said softly.

Butch pulled the kid into a hard hug. "Wrath wanted to come as well, but it's too much of a security risk. And the Band of Bastards also wish they could attend, but they're guarding the King at home."

Talk about your knock-down, drag-out fights. With Wrath, that was. The stay-home-sonny discussion had not gone well. After reasonable arguments to the King about being safe from assassination attempts failed, Vishous had threatened to duct-tape the last pure-bred vampire to his throne. Wrath had really lost his shit then—at which point V had mentioned that the sticky stuff worked really well on pieholes, too.

KA-BOOM.

Beth, a.k.a. the Big Gun, had eventually talked some sense into her *hellren*. Thank God.

"But Wrath's here in spirit," Rhage said as more hugs were exchanged.

Besides, apart from the security issues, Wrath's presence would have been too much of a distraction. Instantly, the gathering would have become all about the King—and given what had happened at Throe's party with that shadow attack? The last thing anybody needed was a bunch of aristocrats demanding to know what was being done to protect the species against this new enemy.

Especially because no one on the Brotherhood side knew much.

Across the way, the front door opened again, and as the trainees came in with their SOs, Boone took his leave and went to get some support from his contemporaries.

"They're a good group of kids," Tohr commented.

"The best," Butch agreed.

Paradise, Craeg, Axe, Novo, and Peyton—along with Boone—had proven to be so much more than anybody could have hoped for. They were a tough lot, smart and resourceful, too, and they had been really handy as the war with the Lessening Society wound down, and this fresh crop of bad news appeared.

Butch shook his head as he made his way over to where the other brothers were. They had to find out more about those shadow entities—as well as what exactly had gone down at Throe's house. Altamere's death had been a line in the sand, a very visible, very widely reported event that had raised the profile of the shadow threat. Previously, the attacks had been one-offs. Boone's sire's slaying, on the other hand, had been in front of twenty-three other aristocrats in a private home. And then there had been the secondary death of Altamere's *shellan*.

Talk about pieholes getting to work. Undoubtedly, phone lines had been burning up, and sooner or later, Wrath was going to have to say something about the situation.

But here was not the place and now was not the time.

On that note, Butch catalogued the aristocrats he was surrounded by. The fancy-dancy types were taking notice that brothers were in the house, all kinds of discreet pointing and commenting going on, a buzz rippling its way through the parlor. Except it was funny—or maybe not so surprising: Not one person who had been at that ill-fated party where Altamere had been killed was in attendance. Sure, there had been a small number of injuries during the shadow attack, but they had been relatively minor in nature, and with the way the species healed? All of those dandies would be back on their loafer'd and stiletto'd feet by now.

"Not a one of them showed up," Rhage remarked around his Toot-sie Pop.

"You read my mind," Butch murmured.

"The aristocracy only likes scandal from a distance."

"Pussies," V announced. "Every one of them."

As the trainees came over and greeted the Brotherhood, Butch couldn't help noticing the two worlds that Boone straddled, his blood-line's and his working life's. And given the kid's tight-lipped affect as he turned back to the aristocrats in that drawing room, it was pretty damn clear which one he preferred. Still, he was a good son for doing this—

When a blast of cold air announced a late-arriving attendee, Butch glanced over. A slender blond female with Jackie O sunglasses was com-ing in, her fine cashmere coat in its tasteful shade of coffee setting off a spectacular pair of legs and brand-new Louboutins. As she closed things behind herself, Butch could smell her tears.

Single female. Fantastic style. Obviously upset?

Sure enough, Boone was on it, immediately going back over and greeting her with a formal bow that she returned with a gracious nod. And then there was an awkward stillness between them, as if in their heads, they were hugging each other.

Well, well, well . . . didn't this make a guy feel better about all the attention Boone had been paying to that female who was connected to the club deaths. Maybe he was merely being a concerned citizen with her. Clearly, the male had deep history with this lovely lady who had just come in—and he really cared about her, too. He seemed upset that she was obviously shaken by his father's death.

Rhage leaned in and whispered, "Do I see love in the air over there?"

"They'd make a wicked good couple," Butch said.

"True that," V agreed. "I totally see the connection."

Rhage rolled his eyes. "He writes one Agony Aunt column with my Mary, and he's an expert on relationships."

"I still think we should have used the barbecue sauce."

"Mmmm, barbecue," Rhage said with a sigh as he crunched into the chocolaty center of his lollipop. "I'm hungry."

Butch had to laugh to himself. One good thing about his closest friends? You could depend on Rhage always wanting something to eat and V suggesting bodily harm as a conflict resolution and Tohr telling everyone to calm down.

It was good to know where things stood in this dangerous and confusing world they were all in.

# ⪼ SIXTEEN ⪻

*I must have gotten through the Fade Ceremony.*

This was the thought that went through Boone's mind as he signaled to the *doggen* on the periphery of the parlor that it was time for the food to be brought in and served. Yes, indeed . . . somehow it was apparently appropriate for the *hors d'oeuvres* to come out and the drinks to be offered and the conversational hour to commence.

As the *doggen* bowed and retreated to the kitchen, people stepped out of the horseshoe that had formed around the urn—and Boone found it impossible to remember what prayers he had said in the Old Language, what recitations had been repeated in a chorus by the assembled, what words of honor he, as the only son and next of kin, had paid to the now late, great Altamere.

"That was a marvelous service. You were most appropriate."

He glanced down at the older female who addressed him. Whoever it was had on a black cocktail dress, three strands of pearls, and white kid gloves. Which meant she was pretty much interchangeable with all the other females of her generation in the room.

*Who is she*, he thought with panic.

Something came out of his mouth in response, some string of syllables, and hey, they must have made sense to her because the female said something back. And then she launched into a story, her carefully painted lips enunciating her words with deliberation as if she were used to, and expected, people to hang on her every sentence.

Meanwhile, Boone couldn't translate a damn thing in any language he knew. Couldn't feel his legs, either. Couldn't feel . . . any part of his body.

In the back of his mind, as the parlor and its crowd of people seemed to retreat even further from his senses, he wondered if he'd had a psychotic breakdown. Maybe none of this was real? What if he were actually alone in this room and his brain had just sketched these people in from memory, figments of a hallucination that was even more frightening because none of it was under his control: He couldn't stop this female from talking, and he couldn't make them all leave rightthisminute—

Oh, God, now his mouth was moving again. What was he saying?

It must have been "appropriate" because she reached out and gave his forearm a squeeze before taking her leave. There was no time to catch his breath. A male stepped up and offered his hand for a shake— and Boone was amazed that he could actually clasp that palm.

Considering the pair of them were standing seven thousand feet away from each other.

Cartoon characters. Everyone around him was not just two-dimensional; they were drawn rather than photographed, outlined in a simple fashion and filled in with primary colors so as to appeal to a young's undiscriminating eye. They had no scents, no perfume or cologne, and their choice of cocktail, of wine, of seltzer . . . of caviar or canapé . . . of cigar or cigarette . . . was like a whisper at a concert, something that barely carried over the din from the main stage.

Beneath his suit, he perspired under his arms, and the collar and tie that had fit him just fine up on the second floor, before things had gotten underway, became now tight as a piano wire in a murderer's hand.

He couldn't breathe.

"—yes, but of course," he heard himself say. Because you could use that phrase as a response to almost anything in the *glymera*.

Do you miss your father? *Yes, but of course.*

Are you keeping this house? *Yes, but of course.*

Is the will settled yet? *Yes, but of course.*

Whether he was answering truthfully didn't matter. In fact, he could barely tell who he was speaking with, much less what they were inquiring of him—and that included when what appeared to be his fellow trainees and the Brothers and the other fighters came over to pay their respects and say goodbye.

As they left, he knew he couldn't stand this one more goddamn minute—

"Boone. Look at me."

He blinked . . . and finally saw someone properly. Rochelle was standing in front of him, and she was tugging at his sleeve with her gloved hand as if she had been attempting to get his attention for a moment.

Focusing on her face, he heard himself say, "I need to get these people out of the house."

Rochelle removed her dark sunglasses. Her eyes were bloodshot from crying, and he was touched that she cared so much about his father's passing.

"Come with me," she said. "You need a break from all this."

She grabbed onto his suit's sleeve and pulled him through the thinning crowd. As they left, everyone stared at them—yes, but of course—because of their history. And if he'd been in his right mind, he would have told his friend not to expose herself to the gossip.

Especially given that she led him right into the males' room out in the foyer.

Unchaperoned.

Rochelle shut them both in the onyx expanse and eased him down into the leather settee by the marble hand sink. Putting her Longchamp bag aside, she pulled a monogrammed towel from a hanging rod and waved it in front of his face, the breeze she created cooling his flushed cheeks.

Absently, he noted that Rochelle had no mascara on and her eye shadow was smudged.

*You are so kind*, he thought.

"Do you want to loosen your tie?" she asked him.

"It's not appropriate," he mumbled. "We come out of this bathroom with my tie off? They'll assume we had sex."

Shit, that was blunt.

"Sorry," he said. "I don't mean to be crude."

"Well, I don't care what they think," Rochelle said sharply. "And if you do, you can always re-knot it."

Boone shook his head, even though he didn't know what exactly he was responding to. He didn't know anything. The good news, however, was that he gradually came to feel like Rochelle was actually standing in front of him. And soon on the heels of that revelation, he started to feel his feet and legs again: The numbness that had taken him over receded from the bottom up, his torso eventually reawakening, too, his shoulders coming back online, his head returning to regularly scheduled programming.

As he exhaled long and slow, Rochelle eased off with the fanning. "Your color is more normal now."

"I don't know what happened in there."

"Panic attack." She sat down next to him. "It happens."

"Not very manly."

"It's not a question of strength. Anyone can feel stress." Moving her purse into her lap, she took out a pack of Dunhill cigarettes and a gold lighter. "Do you mind?"

"I didn't know you smoked."

"If you'd rather I didn't—"

"No, no. It's fine. I don't care."

As she went to light up, her gloved hand trembled. "The aristocracy frowns on females who smoke."

Boone propped his elbows on his knees and rubbed his face. "It was really good of you to come."

"I wouldn't have missed this."

"You really are a female of—" Boone frowned. "You're crying."

Stupid comment to make. Like she didn't know? And yet she seemed surprised.

"Sorry." She took the hand towel she'd used on him and put it on her eyes. "And you keep your handkerchief. I'll use this."

As he stared at her, he thought about that male of hers. The one who hadn't stuck around. Who had failed her.

Who needed a good beating for deserting someone as worthy as she.

"It's a Fade Ceremony," she said as she took a deep breath. "I'm supposed to tear up."

Getting to her feet, she walked into the toilet room and bent down to tap her ash into the bowl. As she straightened, she flipped a switch to activate the fan overhead and smoked with her head tilted back, her exhales directed toward the ceiling above her.

They stayed there, him on the settee, her in the doorway by the toilet, until she finished the cigarette and flicked the filter into the loo.

Flushing things, she said, "Shall we return to the fray—"

"I met someone," he blurted.

Rochelle's brows lifted. "You did?"

"Yes."

As he measured the even cast to her voice and the open expression on her face, he realized he'd brought the subject up because he hadn't wanted to mislead her. He was glad to see Rochelle and touched that she cared so much about his sire's death—and maybe if he hadn't met Helania, he might have tried to start something with her.

But Helania had changed everything.

"That's wonderful." Rochelle came back over and reached into her purse. Taking out a roll of Certs, she offered him one first. "When did this happen?"

He took the mint because it gave his hands something to do. And actually, as wintergreen filled his mouth, it woke him up some.

"Very recently." He purposely did not count the matter of hours, versus nights or months, it had been. "I feel . . . I think I'm in love with her. It sounds crazy, but it's where I'm at. I'm in love."

"You are?" Rochelle smiled. "Do I know her?"

"No, you don't."

Boone hesitated. He was so not ready to see the discrimination their class was so well known for in Rochelle's face or attitude. He didn't want to be disappointed by her.

Except he wasn't about to hide anything about the one he wanted. "She's a civilian."

"Really?" Surprise flared in Rochelle's eyes. "Not one of us?"

"No," he said. "She's not an aristocrat."

Rochelle's stare dropped to the floor, and he braced himself for her response. Damn it, he thought his friend was better than that. More decent than—

"I fell in love with a civilian, too," she said in a tight voice.

As Boone inhaled sharply, she nodded and smiled sadly. "Yes. Not one of us, either."

"Why didn't you say?" he asked.

"How could I have?" She took another deep breath. "Although if I'd known you were this open-minded . . . I might have spoken more about things to you."

"Did it not work out because of the class difference?"

Rochelle closed her eyes. And then she started to weep openly, an emotion wracking her slim body so hard he worried it would tear her in half.

# SEVENTEEN

When Helania's phone went off with a text about twenty minutes before sunrise, she tossed her needlepoint to the side and grabbed the thing off the sofa before the *bing!* even faded. When she saw who it was, she smiled—until she opened the message. She read the words twice. And then again.

Putting the iPhone aside, she stared straight ahead. For like, two seconds.

Her hand slapped back on the cell, and she typed out a quick response. Hitting Send, she bolted up off the couch and ran to the bathroom. Flipping on the light, she brushed her teeth, and before she could think better of it, she freed her hair from its band, spreading the red and gold waves over her shoulders.

And then she fluffed them.

She actually . . . fluffed . . . her hair. But it did look even better, framing her small face, giving her character she felt she otherwise lacked.

Staring at her reflection in the mirror, she remembered all the nights Isobel had stood in this exact spot and scrubbed her short hair until it had spiked up. In the background, there had always been Beatles songs playing. Maybe some Bob Dylan. Sometimes Bob Marley.

Isobel had joked when Justin Bieber had come out and she'd liked one of his releases that clearly there had to be a *B* involved for her to get on board with the downloads.

Frowning, Helania lowered her hands, resting them on the sink's edge. For no good reason, she considered the amount of time she spent thinking about her sister: What Isobel had done. What she had thought. What she had liked and disliked.

Remembering the dead probably wasn't a bad thing, especially when you were in the early stages of grief. The problem was ... she had always done that. Even before Isobel's untimely, violent death, she had felt more comfortable sitting on the sidelines of life and experiencing things in a filtered fashion, her sister living on the outside and bringing stories home.

Movies, in effect. Except the events and the people actually existed.

That one boyfriend Helania had had? Their relationship had been her sole foray into a life of her own away from this apartment. And even then, if she were honest, she had only been with him because Isobel had told her she really should try to find someone—

The knock on the door was soft, and Helania ripped around, heart pounding.

Although not with fear.

No, definitely not with fear.

She quickly turned the bathroom light off in an attempt to deny that she had spent any time on her appearance. And yet as she all but skipped to the door, she was pulling her jeans up into place and tugging her fleece down so that the soft fabric didn't have any bunches in it. When she checked the peephole, she inhaled quick.

Opening things, she didn't bother hiding the smile that hit her face. "Hi."

Boone looked exhausted. Still, his eyes lit up. "Hi."

The pair of them stood there stupidly. And then she shook herself and stepped back. "Please, come in. But as I texted, it's not fancy."

"It's perfect," he said, even though he was still staring at her and not looking around at where she lived.

As Boone came over the threshold and shut the door behind himself, she decided he had a point about the perfection. Because what do you know, with him in her little apartment? The place suddenly felt exciting and fresh. Decorated by a designer. Kitted out with windows that had nice views instead of solid concrete walls that were land-locked.

He was transformative. And not just when it came to her walls and ceiling.

He was also, she realized, the first visitor she had ever had in.

"May I get you a drink? I have milk." What, like he was a five-year-old? "And, um, I also think there's some orange juice in the fridge—"

"I'm fine."

"I can take your coat?" She shook her head. "I mean, would you like me to? Take your coat, that is."

"Oh, right. Yes."

He shrugged out of his leather jacket, revealing a fine cashmere sweater, and she noted that he was wearing slacks, not leathers. As he passed the heavy bundle over to her, she breathed deeply, catching his scent in the folds.

"I wish I had thought to buy food," she said as she put the thing on the back of a chair. "I would have—"

The weight of the coat was so great, it pulled the chair over, the whole shebang landing with a thud.

"Sorry," Boone said. "I . . . ah, I have things in the pockets."

She got to the jacket before he did, and this time, she laid it out on the table.

A gun? she thought. Or *guns*, plural. Ammo, too?

It was a reminder of what he did during the nights, and made her wonder, given that he was on a kind of compassionate leave for his father's death, exactly how long he was going to be off.

As she turned back to him, he was staring at her with an intensity that was not hard to interpret. And as she met his eyes, she was aware that she was saying yes to a question he had not yet voiced.

The silence between them became charged with sexual tension, and Helania knew he was waiting for some signal from her. She was also aware of a reckless buzzing in her head, a surging energy that was as vivid as it was foreign to her. This was all moving very fast. Boone had been a stranger that she didn't dare trust just a night ago. And now she had invited him here to her apartment, where they were all alone.

For the day.

Unless he left in the next five minutes.

"Daylight is coming," she said in a husky voice.

"Yes."

"You're welcome to stay."

Boone closed his eyes and exhaled. "Thank God. Thank . . . you. I can't be trapped in that house today. I just can't fucking do it."

"Which house?"

"My own." He shook his head. "I don't want to think about any of it right now."

Helania approached him slowly, conscious of every movement of her body, from her feet hitting the floor, to her hips shifting, to her shoulders finding the balance of her deliberate steps. When she was in front of him, she looked up into his eyes and put her palms on his pecs.

"Then let's not talk."

As the words came out, she had no idea who she was. This was not how she normally acted. Or spoke. Or thought. And yet with Boone, everything felt natural.

"Kiss me," she said.

Boone closed his eyes reverently, as if he were acknowledging that a prayer of his had been answered. And then he was pulling her into him, his big body fitting perfectly against her much smaller one in spite of the difference in their heights. Tilting her head, she parted her lips, and not just because she was ready for his mouth. Her chest was tight with excitement and need, her heart beating fast, her breath short.

His hands came up the sides of her throat, and then he cradled her jawline with his thumbs. As he dropped down, he eased his head to the side . . . and then he was doing what she'd asked. He was kissing her, soft and slow, the warm, velvet pressure rocketing through her veins and thickening her blood with a sexual drive that was a revelation.

*This*, she thought, was how it was supposed to feel. Electric and desperate, but nothing that you wanted over anytime too soon.

Arching into his chest, she reached up, way up, and linked her hands at his nape, her fingertips playing in the smooth silk of his hair as their tongues met. When her breasts brushed against his chest, he groaned and tightened his hold on her waist, his delicious scent flaring, those dark spices magnifying the heat they generated together.

Too many clothes. There were way too many barriers between their skin.

Between her core and his arousal—

When he abruptly broke off the contact of their mouths, she was surprised and wondered if she'd done something wrong. But as he tucked back her hair, his smile told her that she was more than okay for him.

"I didn't come here only for this," he said gravely. "I need you to know that."

"I know you didn't." *But for godsakes, do not stop.* "Or I wouldn't have let you through my door. But I appreciate you telling me that."

"I just needed to see you."

Helania stroked his face, feeling his smooth cheeks. She had some thought that he must have shaved again before he came over.

"It seems like I left you nights and nights ago," she whispered. "But it was only hours."

"I feel the same way."

So they were both drunk on each other, she thought. Good to know she wasn't alone in the crazy.

◆    ◆    ◆

Inside Boone's body, a roar of lust was threatening to override all of his higher reasoning. His arousal was pounding in his pants, his blood rushing through his veins, his hunger for Helania like a knife in his gut.

Putting his hand on her lower back, he rolled his hips into her and brought his lips down to hers again. As his tongue entered her mouth, he tightened his hold on the nape of her neck and kissed her deeper, penetrating her and retreating, penetrating her . . . and retreating. She must have liked the slick, hot rhythm as much as he did because she was suddenly holding on to him, her weight hanging off his body.

"Where can I lay you down?" he said roughly.

"Come. This way."

When she took his hand, he had to ignore the feel of the scars on her palm. He didn't want to be reminded of everything she had been through—at least not at this moment. If he thought about her situation too much, he was liable to stop, and he knew if he did, he was never going to have another chance with her. She would pull away. Disappear.

Or maybe that was his fear talking.

Whatever it was, now was not the time for the mind. This was about their bodies.

The bedroom she took him into was painfully simple. Nothing on the walls, nothing much on the bed but a single pillow and a handmade quilt. When she closed the door, the light from the other room was cut off, and in the utter darkness, he lost his bearings.

Yet as she stepped into him once again, he didn't care where they were. All he needed—all he wanted—was her. She was the gravity that kept him on the earth and the oxygen in his lungs and the blood that filled his veins.

"Just so you know," she said in a husky voice, "I don't usually do this.

I'm not exactly sure what's gotten into me, but what I know for sure is that . . . I don't want to stop with you."

Boone had to close his eyes as an electric shot bolted through his body. But it was easy to gather himself back so he could reassure her of something she evidently wasn't worried about: "And just so you know, I will stop if you want. At any time, and no matter how far we've gone."

When she pulled him back down to her mouth again, Boone shuffled them to the side until the mattress hit his leg, and then he picked her up by the waist, moving her off her feet and onto that quilt. As he stretched out beside her on the small bed, he scented her everywhere on the pillow and the covers.

As they kept kissing, his hand traveled up from where he'd held on to her, skating the side of her breast, moving onto her shoulder. Their noses bumped as they repositioned the mouth-to-mouth, but then they found each other properly once more. Going slowly, he eased part of his weight onto her, feeling her body sink into the mattress. He kept his hips back, though.

For godsakes, he didn't want to come too soon, and he was on the verge already.

With his eyes unable to see, every other sense of his was cranked up, and he wanted the clothes off their bodies so he could feel even more of her—and she must have read his mind. Her hands went to his cashmere sweater and pulled the hem up his torso. Backing off from her lips, he sat up and swept the fine weave over his head.

"Your shirt, too," she said roughly.

"Yes, ma'am."

Freeing his cuffs, Boone ripped that button-down over his head without bothering with the buttons—and when something tore in the process, he didn't care in the slightest. He tossed away the pressed and starched cotton with the same concern he had the sweater: none.

As he lowered himself down her again, her hands drifted over his ribs and he froze as his cock throbbed behind his fly.

"Is this okay?" she whispered into the dark.

"Touch me anywhere."

Rolling to the side, he let himself fall back on the mattress and extended his arms up and over his head, the sense that he was giving himself, his body, to her both exciting and a little frightening. He preferred control, but for her? He was more than willing to give some of it up.

Give all of it up.

The first thing that hit his bare chest was the ends of her hair, the soft brushes a tickle that went right to the thick head of his erection. Biting his lower lip, he hissed through his front teeth and arched until his spine cracked. And then her fingertips found his skin, traveling over the pads of muscle on his chest and going onto his abs. As she explored his torso, his breath got tighter and faster, and a separate heartbeat started up in his arousal, hardening him even further.

Goddamn . . . the more she touched him, the more he wanted to be doing the same to her, hovering over her naked breasts—only in his case, it would be his mouth on her skin, not her hair or his hands. As the urge to get all over her hit, he nearly gave in . . . yet he had the sense she was more comfortable learning his body first, before she became vulnerable herself—

When those fingers of hers brushed over his belly button, right above his fly, the sound that came out of him was of an animal in need.

"May I?"

Helania's voice coming through the pitch dark was like a siren calling him and he was powerless not to acquiesce. Not that he would ever have told her no.

"Please . . ." His voice cracked. "Oh, God . . . *please.*"

He felt everything. The tug of the top button. The release of the waistband. The zipper going down. His erection, which had gotten crammed off to the side and was being squeezed by the bones of his pelvis, was a barometer for it all, the licks of pleasure traveling down the shaft and nailing him in the sac—

The release, when it came, was of the constriction variety, not an orgasmic one, and thank the Virgin Scribe for that: As he lifted his hips,

Helania pulled his slacks down his thighs and his arousal punched out of its tight squeeze, slapping onto his lower belly. To help with the evac, and to distract himself from all the sensations rocketing through him, he kicked off both his loafers—and when the pants hit the floor at the end of the bed, he toe-peeled his socks off . . .

Finally, he was where he wanted to be.

Okay, that wasn't entirely true, but him being naked was a step in the right direction.

Her being naked was the rest—

When the bed wiggled and he heard shifting clothes, his heart pounded on his sternum like the thing was a door his cardiac muscle needed to get through.

"Let me help you with that." He reached out blindly. "I can—"

He stopped talking as Helania lay on top of him, her nude body the best blanket on the planet, her hips compressing his erection, her breasts oh, so soft against all his muscle. With gnawing hunger, he found her lips again, and their bodies moved together in the darkness, the friction erotic and primal, the anticipation growing.

Moving her up higher on his chest, he nuzzled into her throat and ran a fang over her jugular—and as she stiffened, he said, "No, I won't. I promise."

"I want you to."

His whole body stilled at that. But he knew things were already too hot for any kind of feeding. He was liable to drain her dry even though he'd taken a vein only forty-eight hours before. So instead of piercing her with his canines, he nipped at her collarbone and shifted her farther upward, her thighs splitting so that she straddled his torso. And then he had his prize. As he sucked one of her nipples into his mouth, she gasped into the darkness and he heard a smack on the wall, like she had planted a hand for balance. Running his palms up and down her ribs, he worshipped her with his mouth, lolling his tongue around her tender points, sucking them in and then kissing the undersides.

As she rode him, her hips rubbed her sex back and forth on his abs, her arousal driving him wild, her springtime scent filling the room.

He meant to take it slow. He really did.

But when she straightened from his mouth and set herself back on his hips, he barked a curse and arched so hard, his head hit that wall and shoved the bed out of place.

All he could feel was her slick, hot core on the hard ridge of his sex, and it was too much.

The orgasm started before he could rein the release in, hot jets exploding out of him, blowing the top of his cock off. Gritting his teeth, now he cursed for a different reason—

Helania's low laugh was all satisfaction. And she didn't hesitate.

She lifted off his pelvis, took his hypersensitive, spasming erection in her hand, and stood him up.

The next thing he felt was the incredible, tight, slick hold of her sex, the glorious pressure ramping up his pleasure and making him come even harder.

Except goddamn it, he hated how out of control he was; he was letting her down with all of this premature shit. He should be coaxing a sensual response out of her, mounting her with care, riding her nice and slow until she found the first orgasm.

He'd totally blown their first time.

Totally.

## EIGHTEEN

Given how big Boone was, it was not a surprise that his overall size was reflected in every one of his body parts.

Particularly the part that defined him as a male.

As Helania sat herself down on his hard erection, he filled her up and stretched her wide. And that first one was literal, too. He was orgasming in a wild frenzy, and as she started to ride him, she loved everything about the sex they were having: that she was on top, that he had lost control, that he wanted her this much. Rolling her hips on top of him, her thighs lifting her up and down on his head and shaft, she arched and ran her hands through her hair, lifting the weight up over her shoulders and letting her breasts swing freely.

That was when she willed the light on.

The illumination chased the darkness away, the glow from the bedside table bathing her in a soft light.

Closing her eyes as her retinas stung, she kept up what she was doing, pumping on his pelvis, his sex going in and out of her, her breasts swaying. It seemed bizarre that she could be so uninhibited with someone she didn't know well, but Boone made her feel beautiful, and besides, she wanted this.

She wanted *him*.

When she opened her lids, he was staring up at her with rapture, his eyes bouncing around between her tight, pink nipples, her mouth . . . and where they were joined.

"Oh, God . . . *Helania*." His large hands reached forward and captured her breasts, his thumbs stroking over the supersensitive tips. "Don't ever stop."

"I'm not going to."

Dropping her arms, she leaned over him and braced her weight on either side of him for better range of movement, her breasts swinging even more, brushing back and forth against his fingertips, bringing her ever closer to the pleasure he had already found.

She didn't want to let herself go. She didn't want this to be over.

She could spend an eternity joined with him.

Her body had different ideas. Within moments, rhythmic contractions started in her core and carried her over the brink, her orgasm so sharp it was almost painful, the pleasure flooding through her.

"That's right," he groaned, "come for me."

The world went on a spin at that point, but not because she was losing consciousness—although with all the sensations coursing through her, it was a wonder she didn't pass out. But no, she wasn't fainting; Boone was sweeping her off of him and rolling her to the side. With her bed only a modest twin, they had to shuffle arms and legs around so no one ended up on the floor, and then she wasn't thinking about gravity.

He was on top of her, her thighs parting to accommodate his heavy body, his sex slipping back inside of her core like it was meant to be there and nowhere else. They stared at each other for a moment, and then he kissed her softly.

"Is this okay?" he said hoarsely.

"Oh, yes," she breathed.

"You are so much more than I ever expected."

Reaching up, she stroked his face. "And I would say the same back to you."

Boone moved slowly at first, but that did not last. Before long, he was pumping into her hard, the bed banging against the wall, his pelvis slapping into the cradle of her own. Grabbing onto his shoulders, she tried not to score his skin with her nails and failed.

Helania had to hold on for dear life, and wasn't that incredible.

Raw. Powerful. Dominating.

He was everything a warrior was supposed to be, shattering her previous awkward, largely unsatisfying, sexual experiences, blowing everything, even her fantasies, out of the water. And as her body absorbed his penetrations, her head went back and forth on the pillow, her view of the ceiling vacillating as he advanced and retreated with all the strength in his rugged body.

Even though it was not over yet, she couldn't wait to be with him again.

◆    ◆    ◆

No clue how long it lasted.

When Boone's hips finally locked into Helania's, and his sex kicked out one last ejaculation, he was utterly and completely spent. And as his arms abruptly lost their strength, he barely managed to twist to the side to avoid crushing her.

They both were breathing hard, their sexes still joined thanks to the torque of his spine, their skin covered in a sheen of sweat.

He had made a mess all over her. And given that sensuous smile on her face? She didn't mind one bit.

Opening his mouth, he wanted to say the perfect thing. Express the awe and joy that was in his heart. Put together a combination of words that made her know how much all of this had meant to him.

Nothing came out.

There was just too much to be said, and he was too satiated to do anything other than mumble.

So he let his fingers do the walking.

Stroking her hair back from her face, he caressed her throat, her collarbone . . . her sternum. With a gentle touch, he drew circles around one of her breasts and then a line down her belly. Her body was as finely built as her facial features were, her curves and her straightaways subtle and perfect, and he took his time with his lazy, loving, exploration.

In response, she did some exploring of her own, running her hand up and down his arm, lingering over the bulge of his biceps and the slice of his triceps.

As their bodies cooled, they communicated by contact, everything shared and accepted, all thoughts and feelings out on the table, the experience they'd had memorized by the quiet, peaceful aftermath—

The banging sound had him jacking upright and reaching for a gun he did not have holstered on him—because, hello, he was frickin' naked. When the banging happened again, he looked to the ceiling.

Helania laughed. "It's the humans overhead."

*Creeeeeak. Boom, boom, boom.*

"They're getting in the shower."

Boone glared at the sounds. "The hell they are. They're square-dancing with concrete shoes."

"We're going to get about eight minutes of quiet next."

Boone glanced at the digital clock. "You've timed it?"

"With the amount of noise they make every weekday morning, I've had to adapt and it helps to know the different stages. You can get through almost anything as long as you know it won't last forever."

Resettling beside her, he folded her in against him and stroked the outside of her arm. "Eight minutes?"

"Soap, shampoo and conditioner."

"Is it a man or a woman up there?"

"One of each."

"Oh, God, they could breed. And then there would be more of them."

"I can always move out."

Boone opened his mouth, but then slapped it shut when he realized he was about to suggest that she could come stay with him. Talk about moving fast—it was way, way too early for that.

Next week he could bring it up. Or maybe tomorrow night.

*J/k*, he thought.

In all seriousness, he had often overheard Craeg, Peyton, and Axe talk about their females at the training center or after hours when they were all chilling on the bus. It was like a constant, low-level preoccupation for his buddies: when they were seeing their mates, where they were going to go with them, how they were going to enjoy the time they had. He'd never understood it before. Sure, he'd appreciated a fine-looking female on occasion; take Rochelle, for example—even though he'd had his reservations about committing to a lifetime with her, he had not been blind to her obvious beauty and poise.

But he'd never come anywhere close to what he'd seen from his friends.

Now? He so fucking got that drill. And like his buddies, it wasn't just about sex for him. He wanted to tell Helania about the Fade Ceremony. Find out how she was feeling about the investigation. Ask her advice about things pertaining to Marquist and his father's household and the goddamn will.

This connection he had with a relative stranger was just like what the other three males had likewise been shocked by: Instead of time and experiences revealing a compatibility that led to a relationship, with Helania, it had been less a gradual evolution of feeling for him and more like a bank vault being opened by the correct combination.

An unlocking that was an instantaneous—

*Boom! Ba-boom, ba-boom, ba-boom.*

Boone glanced at the clock. "Oh, my God, eight minutes. You're right."

"I've had some experience with them." She pressed a kiss to his chest. "Next is dressing. It's going to get louder because they're right above us."

Man, she did not underestimate the floor show. The banging and crashing, creaking and bouncing, made him doubt that clothes were the only thing involved.

"Are you sure they're not playing *jai alai* up there?" As she giggled, he looked over at her. "Listen, I can take care of this for you. I can make this go away."

"By doing what?"

"Breaking both their legs." He winked at her. "Or if there are more than two, all of the legs that are up there. It'll cut down on the noise huge."

Helania smiled. "You're joking, right?"

"Yes." He got serious. "I'm not into hurting things unnecessarily."

The instant he said it, he knew that wasn't exactly true. But *lessers* did not count. They weren't even living, for godsakes.

"Can I ask you something?" she whispered.

"Please." He tucked some of her hair behind her ear. "What do you want to know?"

"When you came here and I opened that door . . ." Her voice drifted. "You looked worn-out. Is everything okay?"

Boone twisted a lock of her red and blond hair around his finger. "I feel like I should choose my words carefully here."

"Why?"

"My sire died, as you know. But I'm not . . . I'm not mourning him like you do your sister. He and I didn't have a good relationship. I was an embarrassment to him, pretty much since birth, because I didn't look like the proper aristocrat he was. I was always bigger, more muscled, not the whip-thin body type the *glymera* prefers." He hesitated to share that he might have been the product of an affair. "Then, after my blood *mahmen* passed unto the Fade, he just moved another female in without talking about it. Like she was a sofa replacing a couch that had been stained. I couldn't take all his superficial bullcrap anymore after that. I had tried to live up to his expectations, but you can only take so much of that kind of censure before you either separate your-self or . . ."

"Or what?"

"Kill yourself." He shrugged as if it was no big deal. Even though it had been. "My final straw with him was the step*mahmen* thing. His final straw with me was a broken arrangement that brought shame on the bloodline. And then me joining the Brotherhood's training program, of course. So, anyway, when he died . . . it was a relief for me on many levels."

"I am so sorry you had such a difficult time with your sire."

"It happens. Particularly in the *glymera*, I think."

"I'm not sure what is worse. Missing someone who I loved as much as I loved Isobel . . . or suffering through the relationship you had with your father."

"Sad toss-up." And probably one of the roots of their connection. "Suffering has many vocabulary words, doesn't it."

There was a period of silence. "You were arranged?" she asked.

"I was. She ended it, and the truth was, I was more than fine with it. I was prepared to go through with things to save face for her and every-one else in my family. But the true love wasn't there for me, and it wasn't there for her, either."

Helania took a deep breath. "I'm sorry that I asked about the mat-ing thing. And just so you know, I've never been even remotely close to something like that."

Boone smiled slowly. "You can ask me anything. And if I'd known that you'd had a broken arrangement, that would have been something I'd focus on, too."

"Your father must have hurt you very deeply over the years."

"It's okay. It's just the way things were."

Helania tucked her arm under her head and played with his hand. "Tell me more about what it was like for you growing up. And the train-ing program. And . . . what happened with your father when he went unto the Fade."

Instead of feeling burdened or obligated, it was a relief to open up to someone. To her, specifically. "Where do you want me to start?"

Helania's smile was full of compassion, and so were her beautiful yellow eyes. "Wherever you want. We have all day long."

*Yes*, he thought to himself. *We do.*

And wasn't that a great thing.

# NINETEEN

Butch silenced the recording that was playing out of his cell phone's little speaker and turned his head on his pillow toward his *shellan*. Marissa was curled up under the covers beside him, her blond hair fanned over her naked shoulders, her pale blue eyes somber.

"He did a great job," Butch murmured. "Boone's a natural at interrogation. I was prepared to have to talk to her again, but he covered everything I would have asked."

"That poor female." Marissa shook her head. "I wonder if you should ask her if she'd like to talk to Mary? That's a lot of trauma to go through right there. Her sister first and then finding that body."

Butch put the phone down on the comforter between them. "I will suggest that."

"But . . . what."

Glancing at his female, he shrugged. "Nothing." When Marissa just kept staring at him, he cursed and looked at the ceiling of their bedroom. "God, you know me so well."

Which in moments like this was the good news and the bad news.

"You think she had something to do with the deaths?" Marissa said.

Butch shrugged and rubbed the heavy gold cross that hung around his neck. "I don't trust anybody. Not at this stage of things. Although putting that into words after listening to a recording like that makes me feel like an asshole."

"You have a job to do. You're being professional." She frowned. "So there were two deaths?"

"Three." He turned to face Marissa again. "Vishous looked into the first one. It was a human. There were various reports in the *Caldwell Courier Journal* about it. She was found in a storage room at the club, just like the two females, and she was killed by a knife. There was no hanging her up, however. According to the latest update from the CPD, it's still an open case. Homicide hasn't found the killer, but that doesn't mean it was a vampire, so it's hard to know how that victim fits in. We either have a serial killer who is refining his technique, or there is a coincidence with that one."

"The third female who was killed . . . her family has her remains now?"

"No." He shook his head. "Havers is doing an autopsy on her. With their permission, thank God. When they came forward and confirmed her identity, I really didn't want to put them through the hell of forcing that kind of thing. But they want to know who did this."

As things got quiet, he reflected that it did not seem strange at all to refer to his *shellan*'s blooded brother as if the male were an unrelated third party. Havers was exceedingly competent at his job, taking such very good care of his patients and staff. But as a sibling? To Marissa?

Butch was never going to forgive that guy for turning her out when she had nowhere to go. Just before dawn.

The thing with true family, from everything he'd learned? Sometimes they shared DNA with you. Sometimes they didn't. And given that the blood connection only went so far, the friends you chose were what made up the slack when your relatives sucked.

"Havers will do a very thorough job." Marissa looked away. "That is one thing you can always depend on him for. He is a superior physician."

After everything she had been through with her only sibling, she still had the class to shine some light on the positive traits the male had. But that was his *shellan*. She was way too good for Butch. And for that brother of hers.

Butch moved the phone out of the way and pulled her into him. "You are a female of worth, you know that?"

"You're biased," she whispered as she kissed his mouth.

"Are you kidding me?" He stroked her lower lip with his thumb. "I'm a facts-only kind of man. I speak the truth and only the truth, so help me God."

"The truth, hmm. Well, tell me something, Mr. Veracity. How does this feel?"

As her hand wrapped around a very personal and private place on his body, he closed his eyes and moaned.

Gritting his molars, he said, "I don't know. I can't tell. Maybe you should squeeze it a little or move things around down—oh . . . *yeah* . . . more of that. I think something's coming to me."

Marissa laughed low in her throat and nipped his lower lip with her fang. "More like coming for *me*, isn't it?"

"Yes. Definitely. Always—what was the question?"

◆　　◆　　◆

The daylight hours came and went with depressing alacrity.

At least that was what Boone thought when he glanced at the digital clock on Helania's bedside table and saw that it was a little past six p.m.

*Shit*, he thought. He felt like he'd just walked through her door.

"Where has the time gone," he muttered.

Helania yawned. "We've talked all day."

And yet there hadn't been one moment that he had struggled to find something to tell her or been less than totally interested in everything she had to say. Well . . . and they had also done some things that hadn't been exactly conversational.

"Eight minutes," he murmured.

"Hmm?"

"I feel like all these hours lasted no longer than the eight minutes those humans spent in the shower—"

*Boom! Ba-boom, ba-boom, ba-boom . . .*

"Speak of the devil," she said with a laugh as they looked at the ceiling.

"They're back already?" Boone groused. "Did I invoke them like an evil spell?"

"The human workday is over and their commute is short."

The sound of a distant ringing brought his head up. It was his phone. Out on her kitchen table in his jacket. "And our work night is just beginning. That's me. Will you excuse me?"

"Sure."

As he got out of bed, he stretched and felt his spine crack back into place. Crossing over to the door, he opened things, strode out to his leather jacket and palmed his phone.

"Hello?" he said. "Yes. Okay, sure. Yup. Ah . . . give me twenty minutes? Okay, thanks. Bye."

Ending the call, he stared at the Samsung for a moment. Then he pivoted around. Helania was in the doorway to her bedroom, her spectacularly naked body such a sight, he lost his train of thought.

"You don't have to explain yourself," she said gently. "You have a life to get back to, and I am not asking for an accounting—"

"It's about my father."

She frowned. "Is there anything I can do?"

"I just have to go deal with some unpleasantness, but I've known it was coming. One way or the other, it's all going to be okay."

Walking over to his female, he took her face in his hands and let his eyes roam around her features, his mind memorizing each one of them sure as if he were never going to be with her again.

"When can I see you?" he whispered.

Helania's smile was so beautiful, he felt like his heart expanded to fill his entire body.

"Whenever you want." She lifted up onto her tiptoes and kissed his mouth. "I'm just here."

"Well, my friends Craeg and Paradise asked me to a late First Meal tonight. Would you like to join us?"

"Really?" The shy happiness that came over her made her glow. "I would love to."

"It's a date. I'll text you the where and when ASAP."

"Okay. I'll meet you wherever."

Boone pulled her into his chest and just held her against his naked body. The contact was instantly electric, but he couldn't give in to temptation. He was liable to not resurface until the dawn.

Days and days from now.

And given where he was headed, he had to be good right now so he wasn't late. Besides, if the Scribe Virgin so provided, this would be far from the last time he had a chance to be with Helania.

"I can't wait to see you again," he said as he put his chin on the top of her head. "And I'll be counting down the eight minutes until I do."

As she laughed, he felt the reverberation in his own flesh.

"Good deal," she said as she looked up at him. "I'll be doing the same."

# TWENTY

As Boone rematerialized on the front stoop of his house, he was distracted by the slideshow of Helania that was playing on the backs of his eyelids. And what do you know, he especially liked the image of her as the bedroom light had come on when they'd first been making love, her body arched as she rode him, her hands capturing her hair and holding it up, her breasts spectacular as they swayed to the undulations of her hips—

Wait, what he was doing?

Oh, right. The door. He was trying to open the front door to the house, but the thing wasn't budging.

Frowning, he looked around—just to make sure he had the right mansion. Yup. Those were his bedroom windows.

He tried the brass latch again with his hand and then made an attempt with his mind—but obviously things were copper, so he was unable to will the lock to release. As a last resort, he put his shoulder into the heavy panels—which was stupid because it wasn't a case of the door being jammed. All he got was a sore spot.

Backing up into the snowy yard, he checked out all the windows. The daylight shutters had risen and he could see all the familiar things he'd grown up with through the panes of old-fashioned glass. Then he glanced over the grounds. Nothing particularly out of place. No tire tracks that were fresh. No strange scents.

So it wasn't as if Marquist had packed up his crap, moved out, and locked things behind himself.

Refocusing, Boone was not about to use the knocker on his own goddamn house.

Looking around again, he marched over to the hedges that anchored the front flower beds. Behind one of them, there was a garden hose that was wound about a heavy metal holder. The hose was not attached to the spigot because of the cold, and the whole setup probably should have been put away for the winter. But hey, it was his lucky night.

With a grunt, he picked the reel up and hefted it out of the bushes. Making sure he had a good grip on the thing, he went on a discus-thrower spin and let the fifty-pound holder with its green hose go flying—

Through the air with the greatest of ease.

Or . . . not really. It was as aerodynamic as an armchair, but it got the job done, crashing through the lead-lined glass windows of his father's study, shattering things, creating a jagged hole about four feet in diameter.

Looked kind of like a shark's mouth, with all the sharp parts in a bad circle. But at least he didn't have to climb through the mansion's new entry. Dematerializing into the house through the doorway he'd created, he re-formed just as Marquist came tooling in from some back room, obviously called by the sound of breaking glass.

The male was out of uniform. And dressed in one of Altamere's handmade suits.

He was also wearing one of Boone's father's formal dress coats.

"Nice outfit," Boone remarked as he stalked off for the stairs.

As he passed the butler, he made sure he clipped Marquist with the same shoulder he'd tried on the door.

"I'll see you in about ten minutes," he said as the other male scrambled to keep his balance, all bowling pin and then some. "And I know you'll get that hole fixed, given the liberties you've taken with the front door."

Hitting the carpeted steps two at a time, Boone's rage grew inside his chest and threw out tentacles, the toxic nastiness ushering away the peaceful glow he'd found with Helania. And courtesy of the anger, a part of him wanted to go down to the Audience House right now, just so he could beat the bastard butler there. But he was not going to walk in smelling like his female.

What he and Helania had done had been private—and that would have been true whether or not he was involved in that investigation of Butch's.

When he got to his suite, he wondered whether he was going to have to bust open his own door, but things unlatched easy-peasy.

Inside, he didn't waste time. Shower. Shave. Teeth brushing.

He considered putting on a suit. But in the end, he yanked on the leathers and the weapons he wore out into the field.

Made sense. Given that he was going to war.

◆    ◆    ◆

Helania took a long, leisurely shower, lingering over her shampoo-and-conditioner routine, taking her time with her soap, even sitting down in the tub and leaning back to let the warm rain fall on her body.

She was impossibly relaxed, her muscles and her bones limp, her skin glowing, her blood lazy in her veins. Which was not to say she didn't have some aches and pains. The insides of her thighs twinged depending on her leg position; her core was a little raw; her lower back stiff.

All of it just made her smile.

So well earned, and what exercise. She looked forward to more of those kinds of workouts.

When the hot water finally ran out and things went from toasty to room temperature, she had no choice but to get out and towel off.

Winding herself up in terry cloth, she glanced through the open door of the bathroom and eyed the cloak that she wore to Pyre.

On any other night, she would have gotten dressed in her black clothes, covered herself with those heavy folds, and headed downtown to watch the crowd. But she only had four hours until she was supposed to meet Boone and his friends at that all-night diner and she had work she had to do for her freelance editing job.

Trading the damp towel for a thick blue bathrobe, she went into her bedroom and stared down at the bare mattress. She'd thrown the quilt and the sheets in the washer, and as she'd stuffed the load in and hit things with some Tide, she had taken a subtle pride in the fact that she and her lover had messed things up.

She had a *lover*.

Not a boyfriend she'd talked herself into taking on, like a piece of luggage on a walking trip, but a full-fledged sexual relationship that was not a one-night stand.

Isobel would be so proud of her.

Frowning, Helania went back out to the little table by her galley kitchen. Sitting in the chair she'd tried to drape Boone's jacket over, she pulled her laptop in front of her and opened the screen. Turning things on, she was aware of a pit forming in her stomach as she went on to Facebook.

Signing in as Isobel, she accessed her sister's page with the password they had created together: Isolania101.

Her eyes watered as she stared at the banner's image. It was a close-up of her sister, that smile so bright and happy, that telltale spiky red hair something that Helania felt as though she hadn't seen in a decade.

She had taken the picture. Isobel had been sitting over there on the sofa, imminently on her way out, of course, her coat in her lap. The shirt she had on was one Helania remembered putting in those cardboard boxes: Blue-and-white-checked with a short little collar that stood up off the neck. Casual but classy—and that had been Isobel.

Even though they'd never had a lot of money, she had always looked put together because she was an expert shopper. During the darker months of the fall and the winter, she had always gone to the human mall and scoured sales before closing time. They had joked that with twenty dollars and the right stack of rebates and coupons, she could put together something worthy of Fifth Avenue down in NYC.

Taking a deep breath, Helania scrolled down the page. Everything hurt to look at, especially the part in the bio where Isobel had chosen "in a relationship."

It made sense that Boone was suspicious of the male that had been in Isobel's life, but Helania knew her sister. The kind of happiness Isobel had shown was legitimate.

Wasn't it?

Going further down, Helania read through the things that people had put on the wall after Isobel had been killed. Seeing the dates end so abruptly eight months ago was hard, the car-crash nature of the death—one night there, the next gone—represented baldly. And there were a lot of people who missed her.

So many tribute posts, although it was hard to determine who the folks really were. As usual, members of the species fudged their actual identities on social media, the extra precaution taken as a security measure both from a Lessening Society point of view, but also from a human one—

Helania stopped. Leaned closer to the screen.

One of the posts had only five words: *I love you, Issie. Forever.* No images were included, but Helania wasn't focused on that. She was looking at the avatar, the little circle with part of a face in it.

She double-clicked on the name and was taken to another page.

"It's you," she whispered.

Sitting back in her chair, she stared at the partially obscured photograph of a female's jawline and cheekbone and lips. It wasn't the complete profile, but a telltale mole beneath the ear was what secured the identification: This was the female who had knocked on Helania's door that horrible night. The one who had helped prepare Isobel's body for the Fade Ceremony. The one who had had the other shovel out in those woods.

Some people you just did not forget.

Rubbing her face, she felt her body break out in a cold sweat. But then she forced herself to gather her racing thoughts.

The name was an odd one: Rocky B. Winkle.

Helania thought about things for a while. And then she went into direct messaging and constructed what she hoped did not sound like a crazy, desperate request to the female.

As she typed, she couldn't avoid the shift that was occurring in her mind.

That boyfriend. Who was he?

And where was he?

# TWENTY-ONE

As Boone was shown into the dining room of Wrath's Audience House by Rhage and Tohr, it was impossible not to remember coming to see the King just nights before to talk about that gathering his sire had been invited to.

Stopping on the Oriental rug under the great chandelier, Boone realized he had been terrified his father would be killed because of the intel he himself was sharing with the King. And his fear had come true, just not for the reason he'd assumed . . . not because his father had been a traitor. Although perhaps, if the evening had continued on uninterrupted, treason would have come to pass. Altamere had certainly had no love for the King.

"How you doing, Boone?"

Shaking himself to attention, he focused on Wrath. The great male was sitting in one of the armchairs by the fireplace, that huge body eased back to accommodate all the blond dog in his lap. George offered Boone a wag, but there would be no in-person greeting. Not tonight.

This was business and somehow the golden knew it.

"I'm all right, my Lord." Boone bowed even though the King wouldn't know it. "Thank you for seeing us."

In a lower voice, Wrath said, "Where's the other half of this?"

Rhage spoke up from by the door. "Out in the waiting room. I think he was talking to Saxton."

Boone hadn't paid any attention to Marquist when he'd arrived, and he'd been very aware of being shuffled in here quick, as if the Brothers on duty were worried shit might go down.

Then again, Boone was packing three auto-loaders, several extra clips of ammunition—and he'd even wrapped his length of steel chain around his shoulder. You know, just in case he felt like strangling something.

"You really okay, son?" Wrath pressed. "And answer me honestly."

Boone dropped his stare. Even though those wraparounds weren't covering a set of working eyes, he couldn't look the King in the face as he fibbed.

"Oh, yeah. I'm good. It's all good."

"You sure about that."

There was a knock on the doorjamb, and Boone glanced over. Saxton, the King's solicitor, was hovering in the open archway.

"My Lord, may we enter?" the solicitor asked.

"Yeah. Let's get this over with."

Saxton came in with a thick document in his arms, and after nodding hello to Boone, he settled behind his desk. With his tweed suit, contrasting shirt and tie, and jaunty pocket square, he looked like the aristocrat he had been born and bred to be. But his gray eyes were sharp—and grew sharper as Marquist entered and the doors were shut.

Boone took a couple of steps over so he wasn't too close to the butler, because guess what? The sight of that fucking male in his father's clothes made him want to empty a clip into Marquist's frontal lobe.

"*My Lord,*" Marquist said to Wrath in the Old Language, "*it is my supreme honor to be in your presence. Allow me to pledge my fealty unto*—"

As the butler took a couple steps forward, Wrath shot a look at

Rhage, and the Brother was on it, jumping over and clapping a hold on Marquist's shoulder.

"You're good," Rhage gritted out. "You stay back here."

Marquist seemed honestly affronted. "As a civilian, I am entitled to pay respect unto my King."

Rhage took the male by the upper arms, picked him up like he was a toaster, and carried him back to where he'd been standing, setting him down on a pair of loafers that Boone remembered his father buying about six months ago.

In a bored voice, Rhage said, "Consider your respects paid. Moving on."

Marquist blinked, his brain clearly having to recalibrate the way he had expected all of this to go. And Boone was not surprised. The male was behaving as if he had social station. In reality, he had a borrowed suit and an attitude, at best.

Well . . . probably also had an inheritance.

Saxton cleared his throat. "We are here to settle the estate of Altamere, son of Himish. As you will recall"—the solicitor glanced at Boone and bowed his head—"the gentlemale passed unto the Fade two nights before last, and this previous night, as per standard custom, a Fade Ceremony was properly performed with witnesses. With that formality having been met, it is now appropriate for the last will and testament to be read and certified. A copy of what is purported to be said document was provided unto me by Marquist, son of Merihew, and I am holding it in mine hands at this time."

Boone stared at the solicitor, aware that his breathing was shallow.

"What does it say," the King demanded.

There was an awkward pause, and Saxton looked down at the inch-thick bundle of pages that were held together on the left side by a binding cord. Down the front of the book-worthy construction, satin ribbons in orange and brilliant blue denoted Boone's bloodline.

Boone spoke up. "My sire cut me out of the will. Didn't he."

Saxton's eyes were sad as he cleared his throat. "Yes, it appears as if that is the case. The codicil was added approximately a year ago."

"And he left everything to Marquist."

"Yes."

The butler did a double take. "I'm sorry . . . forgive me, but what exactly was I left?"

"Everything," Saxton replied. "If this document is indeed the final version of the will, it provides that you are to receive all of Altamere's property, tangible and intangible. Further, all trusts are updated to reflect you as beneficiary as well."

Marquist's shock was slowly superseded by a satisfied smile. "My master was more generous than I thought."

"Was it forged," Wrath demanded. As the butler opened his mouth and started to reply, the King snapped, "Do yourself a favor and shut the hell up. I'm not in a good mood right now, and if for some reason you didn't pull a fast one, you are going to want me to rule in your favor rather than order someone to turn you into an organ donor."

Marquist followed that order so quick, his molars clapped together.

Saxton made a slight cough into his hand. "Boone, whether or not you are in the will, you are legally Altamere's next of kin, given that his second *shellan* is also deceased. As such, I would like you to come over and verify your father's signature."

As the solicitor started flipping through to get to the end of things, Boone spoke up. "When was the codicil signed?"

Saxton finished turning the pages and flattened the last couple against the binding. "It appears . . . the signature here is dated February the seventeenth of last year."

Boone shook his head. "Marquist didn't fake it. The signature is legitimate."

"It's true," the butler said in a rush. "I did no such thing. Altamere alluded to the fact that he had made certain changes, and I suspected that some were to my benefit, but I wasn't sure. And I most certainly did not think it was . . . everything."

"What's up with that date?" Wrath asked Boone. "Why is it relevant?"

Boone crossed his arms over his chest, and as he felt the blades that were strapped, handles down, across his sternum, he started to get antsy.

"That's twenty-four hours after my arrangement was broken," he said without emotion. "That's how I know. My father was furious that the female had found me unworthy, so the timing makes sense."

Okay, so that wasn't entirely false. But it wasn't entirely the truth, either. Dollars to donuts—and it looked like Boone had neither at the moment, har, har—the threat about his paternity had been more of a motivator than the arrangement having failed with Rochelle.

But at this point, water under the bridge, right?

As Wrath's black brows lifted up over his wraparounds, Saxton cleared his throat. "Well . . . be that as it may, perhaps you will come over here and look at the ink nonetheless?"

Boone stalked across the carpet and approached the desk. As Saxton spun the will around, he leaned down. His sire's familiar series of slashes and flourishes was spot-on—and not something that was easy to duplicate.

"That is legitimate."

Saxton looked like he wanted to offer his condolences. "Will you be willing to sign an affidavit to this effect?"

"Yup. Just get me the papers and I'll do it—"

Wrath's voice cut right through. "Just so you're clear on it, you sign a document like that and you're letting it all go. You say you know the John Hancock is real and not falsified because of a broken arranged mating, but even if that is your belief, you could still bring a cause of action as the next of kin. You have standing. During fact-finding, something may come out that you're not aware of at this moment. Undue influence, for example."

Read: The King didn't trust Marquist's intentions much.

Boone shook his head. "I'm not going to challenge it."

Wrath's voice dropped low. "That's your bloodline's heritage, son. If your family's like any other in the *glymera*, we're talking centuries and centuries of art and antiques. And then there's the money, the stocks. Don't be foolish just because you're mad."

"I'm not mad." He glanced at Tohr and Rhage because they knew him and could read him well. "I don't feel anything at all. Marquist can have the whole lot of it. Do what he wants with it. Spend it all, save it all, sell the shit, give it away. I really don't care. After all this time . . . I'd rather be free than financially secure."

There was a long silence at that announcement, and he was willing to bet at least one of the Brothers, and probably Wrath, too, was thinking he needed a psych eval.

Marquist, on the other hand, was starting to look like he'd won the lottery.

Which, hello, he had.

Wrath stroked his dog's boxy head. "I'm going to give you two weeks to think about it."

"I don't need them—"

"You're getting them anyway." The King glared in Marquist's direction—and what do you know, getting hit by that hard stare, even though it recorded no details from an ocular point of view, slapped the happy right off the butler's face. "And listen up, you're going to allow him to stay in that house for the next fourteen nights. If I hear of any bullshit, from anyone, I'm going to rip up that will and give everything to the charity of Boone's choice."

"Y-you can't do that," Marquist stammered.

Wrath smiled, revealing enormous fangs. "This ain't the human world, motherfucker. I'm the King and I can do anything the fuck I want, including send someone to visit you in your sleep and make it so you don't come down for First Meal. You do what I say and you're probably going to walk away with tens of millions of dollars and a nice crib. Sit tight and shut the fuck up or I'll put you under the ground."

*Well. There was that,* Boone thought.

Except he just shook his head again at his King. "It's all good. But if you want us to wait two weeks, that's fine." He looked at Marquist. "You can have the money and the stuff, but if you think you're stepping into my father's shoes just because you fit into his clothes, you're in for one hell of a rude awakening. The *glymera* doesn't even accept their own. You will never have anything but a vacant house to walk around in and shit that isn't yours to stare at. Rich only looks good from the outside, trust me."

With that, he walked toward the double doors to go out.

As he came up to Tohr and Rhage, he expected some kind of conversation about how he shouldn't go into the field tonight. That he was still off rotation. That he needed more time, especially in light of this fresh piece of just wonderful news.

But the Brothers simply opened the way out for him and stepped aside.

Whether it was because they knew they couldn't stop him or on account of them not knowing where he was headed, he wasn't sure.

And it didn't matter.

Just like so much in his life.

# TWENTY-TWO

As Boone crunched through the frozen slush of an alley off God-only-knew-what street downtown, the cold wind burned his face and his ears. Also his hands. In his rush to leave the house for the show-down with Marquist, he'd forgotten his gloves, but he didn't care about frostbite. Or what had been revealed about the will. Or the fact that he was essentially homeless.

Or that his father had seen fit to all but erase him from the blood-line. In favor of a civilian stranger who had come into their lives on a whim and changed the path of the family's history. Likely in more ways than one.

Except again, none of that was on his radar.

At least not consciously.

Although his mind was utterly blank, there were great waves of ag-gression going through his body, the engine that fueled his state of fighting readiness like a nuclear reactor that was threatening to melt down the core of him.

But he wasn't pissed off at his father. Nah. He was Just Fucking Fine.

He only wanted to kill every single *lesser* that had ever existed in the history of the war. And after that was done? He was going to have to find something else to engage because at this moment, in this frame of mind, he was insatiable on an epic scale.

Coming to the end of the alley, he didn't pause before walking out into a four-lane byway, sparing not even a glance at the cars that sounded their horns and hit their brakes to avoid hitting him. In his wake, he heard crunching metal and cursing voices, and soon there would be sirens. But he would be long gone by that time.

Boone kept on going, progressing down the alley, barreling through other intersections in the grid of decaying buildings. About a half mile later, an opportunity finally presented itself. But it was a case of beggars and choosers' luck.

Rather than the *lessers* he was looking for.

The human female who ran out in his path was half dressed, bare-foot and bleeding from a number of places. And like all the Hondas and Nissans he had surprised at those intersections, he was forced to hit his brakes without warning—although the treads of his boots were much better than any set of Michelins on the snowy cover. His heavy weight stopped short on demand.

The woman craned around, took one look at him and screamed her head off. Then again, he had bared his fangs twelve blocks ago. And he was easily three times the size of her.

Slipping and skidding, she tore off down the alley away from him, leaving a bloody trail behind her as she ran.

Boone just stood there and panted, great puffs of white leaving his open mouth. Oh, for fuck's sake. The last thing he wanted was to get roped into a shit ton of human drama. But it was kind of like being in a car, heading for Starbucks for a venti latte—and having a dog run out in front of your bumper.

Sure, you could keep going and get your fucking coffee.

But you were going to waste the rest of the night wondering what the hell happened to that goddamn dog.

And no amount of milk foam was going to make you feel any better.

"Oh, come *on*," he muttered as visions of slaughtering a slayer got replaced with the hassle of stripping memories and calling 9-1-1.

Except as she continued to run, he realized she was naked from the waist down . . . and there was blood on the inside of her thighs—

A door was thrown open about fifteen feet in front of him, the shitty panel smacking into the flank of its building with the crisp, clear exclamation point of an axe going into hardwood.

The human male who came out was pulling his pants up and had a knife between his teeth. Unlike the woman, he didn't even notice Boone. He was too busy tracking the bloody footprints in the snow with his eyes—and when he saw the human female, the laugh that left his lips was pure evil.

He didn't pursue her at a run. He walked, in boots, after her, his naked torso marked with tattoos in black, his muscles covered with a healthy layer of fat.

"It's a dead end, bitch," he called out. "And ain't no one gonna save you."

◆   ◆   ◆

Syn got the message about the trainee going AWOL at the beginning of his shift. He didn't say anything about it to Balthazar because there was no need to. For one, the other male had gotten the text alert, too. But more to the point, although the Bastards helped out with the training program from time to time if the Brotherhood was short-staffed, for the most part, Syn and his boys did not truck with the young soldiers.

So really, the fact that one of those kids was out in the streets, heavily armed and without a partner, wasn't the kind of problem that anyone would expect him to solve.

So Syn blew the shit off as he and Balthazar covered the western quadrant of the city. The collection of abandoned walk-ups and filled-up crack dens happened to be his favorite assignment because the humans who were in these neighborhoods stuck to themselves. No matter how many gunshots or screams or strange smells percolated up into the night air? You could be guaranteed some privacy to work in.

Naturally, the Lessening Society knew this, too, and as a result, this stretch of ten or fifteen blocks was the best hunting in the city. And what do you know, two slayers appeared about an hour and a half into their sweeps. Syn killed his quickly—a disappointment, but that was what happened when you got sloppy with your knife and hit the jugular too soon: He'd been aiming for a shoulder stab so he could draw out the death, but the fucker had zigged when it should have zagged.

And then it was a case of Old Faithful, a goddamn geyser of foul-scented black oil.

The fucking asshat bled out so quick, Syn decided the Omega must be putting his new recruits on Coumadin.

Meanwhile, Balthazar, the lucky shit, had gotten a live one with good fighting skills. The two of them were going hand-to-hand in the alley even though there were plenty of guns available, at least on the Bastard's side. But hunting had been slow of late, and that meant, if you got the chance to hone your skills, you took advantage of it.

Who knew that the end of the war would be so boring?

After Syn stabbed his pathetic leaker back to its boss, he got out of the way, even though he was dying to "help" Balthazar out. And by "help," he meant jump in and stab the enemy. A couple hundred times.

Give or take.

The trouble was, it was early in the night, and a move like that would get his partner for the shift cranky as shit and thus guarantee a long grind of no fun—

As the wind changed direction, the scent of red blood that reached his nose was faint and kind of distant. But the copper perfume made his fangs drop down and his mouth salivate. Both of which were sure signs he had not fed in way too long—especially as the plasma that had gotten his attention was human in derivation, not vampire, and usually that watered-down stuff failed to interest him.

Lifting his chin, he sniffed at the air. Very fresh. Like . . . really fucking fresh.

Whistling loud through his front teeth, he waited for his comrade to respond—and the Bastard didn't waste time. Balthazar threw a vicious right hook that sent his slayer careening into a dumpster, and then he looked over.

Syn tapped his nose and then pointed farther down the alley.

Balthazar nodded once and got back in his fight, jumping on his *lesser*, grabbing the back of its hair and playing Hopper Ball with its face and the side of a brick building, *bangada-bangada-bangada*—

Jesus, that black splatter stain was an urban Rorschach test if Syn had ever seen one.

Turning away, he knew that Balthazar had things well in hand, and if there were any slayer backups that rode up on the scene? Then Syn wasn't going to be far at all.

Following the scent, he went farther into the alley, and some three hundred yards later, he found bloody footprints in the snow—and two other pairs of tracks with them. And just as he was starting to follow the road show, he heard a male voice farther down, the deep tones ricocheting around like whoever it was was at a dead end.

Something was flashing, something pale, in the shadows far ahead.

Syn fell into a jog, and when he entered the darkest part of the alley, his eyes adjusted quick: A woman was running for her life in the snow, some portion of her clothes hanging off her, blood streaming down her legs, her movements uncoordinated as if she were in great pain or had been drugged. Closing the distance, a man stalked after her, his slow, even steps a metronome of death that was imminent—

A third figure appeared without warning, a great dark shape materializing from out of thin air directly between the man and the woman.

Like only a vampire can.

Syn recognized the black leather jacket and the stance instantly. The face took a second longer to come online.

Well, what do you know. He'd found the missing trainee. And Boone was a mountain of muscle blocking the path of the man, protecting the injured woman.

Gallant move, even if the victim was a human. Too bad the Good Samaritan routine broke a shit ton of the Brotherhood's rules, starting with the Do Not Get Involved in Business That Is Not Ours. Which was pretty much the first no-no on the list.

Fortunately for the kid, however, his kind of freethinking was, along with his location and the load of shit he was no doubt about to throw down, not a problem Syn was looking to solve.

At the end of the night, who was he to rain on a parade like this?

# TWENTY-THREE

As Boone reassumed his corporeal form between the man and the woman, his sudden appearance caused a big reaction on both their parts: The victim behind him screamed and her assailant with that knife in his hand jumped back and fell right on his ass.

And a partridge in a pear tree, to go with the winter theme of the alley.

Boone glanced over his shoulder at the woman. "Close your eyes."

Her pale face was bruised badly, her hair matted with blood. She wasn't shivering in the cold temperatures, either, which was not a good sign.

"Sweetheart," he said softly, "put your hands over your eyes. I'll tell you when you can look again. Trust me. I'm not going to let anything happen to you, but you do not need to see this."

Her chest was heaving, her stare peeled wide. But something about him got through to her. Nodding in a series of head jerks, she lifted her blood-soaked hands to her face and caved in on herself, squatting down and ducking into a tight ball.

Like maybe she was used to protecting herself from blows.

Boone refocused on the man and bared his fangs.

Her assailant was pushing his heels into the snowpack as he tried to crab-walk backward, that knife in his hand hindering his process. Gone was the manly bluster, the aggression, the all-powerful sense of I-gotcha.

He'd even wet his fucking pants.

As Boone walked toward the man, he knew which weapon he was going to use to kill the guy.

"She's just a whore," the human said. "For fuck's sake."

There was another bunch of words spoken, but Boone was done with that shit.

Lunging into the air, he attacked full frontal, one hand zeroing in on the front of the man's throat, the other making sure to lock on the wrist that controlled that knife. There was no struggle to speak of. Humans, even the males, were no match for vampire strength, and it was the work of a moment for Boone to twist that arm out of its socket so that the blade was dropped.

The raw sound of pain coming out of the assailant was music to Boone's ears, but he couldn't let that go on for long.

Forcing his fingers into the man's open mouth, he yanked the head up by the lower jaw with such force, most of the torso came up, too. And then he slammed the back of the skull into the snowpack, ringing the fucker's bell. The impact got him the stunned immobility he was looking for: The man was still alive—his chest rising and falling, the veins up his throat continuing to pump with a pulse—but cognition was dimmed.

That would come back soon enough.

Not that there was any way out of this for the assailant—

From out of the corner of Boone's eye, he caught sight of the knife the man had used on the woman. The weapon was lying on its side, the stained blade glinting dully.

*Oh, good,* Boone thought. This was going to be more fun if things weren't sharp.

Palming the hilt, he sat back on his heels and waited for those bloodshot eyes to start to focus again. It didn't take that long at all, a testament to both the man's relative youth and the cushioning properties of snow.

When Boone was sure the assailant was ready, he leaned down and put the knife right in that face.

Mumbling. Lot of mumbling. Followed by some desperate begging.

"I want you to watch me," Boone drawled. "Okay? You with me? Don't piss me off, that's a bad idea. You ready? Answer me."

When the head nodded, Boone pointed to the tip with his forefinger. Then he moved down to the man's waist and pointed at the crotch area.

Lots of moaning, and the arm that still worked slapped a hand across that sensitive place.

"Yeah, no," Boone said softly. "Not going to go like that."

Fishing into one of the pockets of his jacket, Boone found the bandana he always kept on him in case he needed to apply pressure to a wound. Then, in a quick strike, he drove the knife into the back of the assailant's protective hand.

When the man opened his mouth to scream, Boone shoved the folds of cotton in between all those teeth.

After which he made a fist and punched the guy in the shoulder socket so hard, something cracked in there. It was a good test of the silencer—and one that was passed. The scream was muffled sure as if he had a burlap sack over that head. The pinwheeling legs, however, were a pain in the ass, kicking up snow, moving the torso around—and Boone would have taken care of that problem except he was worried about the human female losing much more blood and body heat.

Pulling the knife out of the back of the hand, he waited until the human could focus once more. Then he grabbed onto the front of the guy's pants and inserted the tip of the blade. The urine-soaked fabric was relatively hardy, the navy blue weave the kind of thing that janitors wore to work, but it was no match for even a dull blade.

Commando. Go figure.

Positioning himself between the man's legs, Boone pinned those twitching thighs open with his knees. Just as he was about to put the blade in place, he paused and thought that he was taking things too far.

But then he thought of the woman behind him.

"This is for her," he said in a growl.

◆    ◆    ◆

Helania arrived at the twenty-four-hour diner a little before midnight. As she re-formed in the shadows of its back parking lot, she had to smile. The place was literally called The 24 Hr. Diner.

Talk about clarity of mission.

Stepping onto the sidewalk that ran around to its front entrance, she liked the stainless-steel-looking outer panels and the curved windows and the fact that there were a surprisingly large number of humans taking up space inside in booths by the windows and on stools at the counter.

Entering, she hesitated next to the cash register by the door. The decor was what you'd expect from something out of the fifties: red-and-white color scheme, gingham napkins and drapes, waitresses in skirts with ruffled shirts and aprons. The menu was posted above the counter, individual jukeboxes were at every seat, and there were glass compartments full of pie slices on plates by the soda fountain.

Boone wasn't anywhere to be seen, and she didn't recognize anyone as being from the species.

The sense that she was out of place on a lot of levels created an irrational panic in the center of her chest, and she considered turning around and walking back out. But then she squared her shoulders and told herself she was staying, even if it meant she got stood up and had to have a piece of pie by herself.

It was beyond time for her to stretch her horizons. Even if it was only so far as a booth at The 24 Hr. Diner.

An older woman with a name tag that had "Ruth" on it walked over. "Mornin', darlin', you ready to sit?"

The Southern accent was a surprise. But then again, Helania had never heard one in person before.

"Um, I'm supposed to meet some friends here?"

"They come in yet?"

Helania looked around again. You know, just in case she'd missed three vampires sitting in and among the humans. "Ah, no. I don't think so."

"How many you be?"

At least that was what she thought the woman said. "I'm sorry, what?"

Falling back on old habits, she lip-read the answer that was given to her: *How many do you be?*

"Three?" Okay, so this whole question-as-answer thing she was rocking was annoying. As if the woman was in a position to confirm the number psychically in the event Helania had it wrong? "I mean, four. In total. Three plus me."

The smile that came back at her was so unexpected and so . . . kind . . . that Helania nearly teared up.

"You're nervous," the woman said. "You meetin' a man?"

"Um . . . well, yes. Yes, I've just started . . . um . . . seeing someone. And he and his friends are meeting me here—a couple. I mean, there's another couple coming. With him."

"Oh, a double date! Come on, y'all can sit over here where it's quiet."

Helania followed the waitress down to a booth at the end of the lineup opposite the counter. As she skootched in so she was facing the door, "Ruth" brought over four glasses of water and leaned a hip against the free side of the padded bench.

"So, tell me about your beau," the human said.

*Well, he's a vampire and he kills the undead for a living. He's also a great kisser.*

"We're just getting to know each other." Inside and out, in her case, she thought with a blush. "And he's a really nice guy."

"Honey, you're makin' sense then. I was married to my Merv for fifty years and I liked him just as much when I buried him as when I walked down that aisle to him." The woman leaned in and dropped her voice. "Mark my words, the nice guys are the ones you want to take home and keep. Bad boys just break your heart, and that's a rite of passage a smart woman only goes through once. The nice guys? Those are who you settle down with."

Ruth gave Helania a wink as she straightened. "You want coffee?"

*Do I?* Helania wondered.

"Yes, please?" God, again with the frickin' question mark. "I mean, yes. Please."

"Cream and sugar? And listen, we don't do none of that almond milk or soy silliness, so don't even ask. Our cream is from cows. The rest of that crap just ruins perfectly good coffee."

As Helania didn't know how she wanted anything at this point, she just said she'd take it black. And while Ruth went off to rustle up the caffeine, Helania rubbed sweaty palms on her jeans. Figuring that her parka wasn't helping the hot waves going through her, and knowing she was going to have to shake hands pretty soon, she stripped out of her jacket and crammed the down folds in between her thigh and the wall of the booth.

Just as she was checking out the table-sized jukebox, her senses fired and she looked up.

A very nice-looking couple were coming through the door. The female was blond and truly striking, possessing the kind of double take attractiveness that turned her casual jeans and wool coat into formal wear. The male beside her was very tall and wearing a Syracuse baseball cap, his big body at ease—even as his eyes made the rounds of the diner like he was expecting to maybe, possibly, only-if-it-was-necessary attack an aggressor.

As they both focused on her, Helania's first thought was *What would Isobel do?* And the answer to that was obvious: Her sister would have jumped out of the booth, rushed up to them, hugged them even though they were strangers, and brought them back so she could commence becoming their best friend and confidante.

Okay, right . . . when Helania considered pulling off that dance card, she had to go hell-no on all of those moves. For godsakes, she was so nervous, she would probably trip and fall on her face if she tried to slide out of this seat. And then before she could think of a B plan, the couple waved and started to head down the way.

Swallowing hard, Helania eyed the glass window next to her. She could always just dematerialize out. Leave them to clean up the human memories. Go back to her apartment and never try this kind of thing again.

Ever.

Except then she realized something. It wasn't about what Isobel would do.

It was a question of what Helania would do. And just because she couldn't come on strong and be insta-buddies with two people she didn't yet know, this did not mean she had failed some kind of test. It was also not a moral condemnation of her shy nature.

When the couple arrived at the table, she took a deep breath. And then, in a surprisingly calm and level voice, she said, "Hi, I think we're having a meal together? I'm Helania."

With a feeling of dread, she waited to see what they would do—

The female smiled and scooted into the booth on the other side. "We are so happy to meet you! I'm Paradise, and this is my *hellren*, Craeg. Boone's had the best things to say about you."

"Yup," the male agreed. "He's wild about you."

Paradise gave her male a look. "Let's not make her feel weird—"

"I'm just saying." Craeg shrugged. "Come on, *leelan*, he's like I was with you. And there's nothing wrong with her knowing it, either."

Paradise looked across the table and smiled. "Listen, if we just blew Boone's cover, we'll apologize to him later. But it's true. He seemed really excited when he texted us you were coming."

"Lots of emojis." Craeg took a drink of his water. "And he never does emojis."

As Ruth arrived with the coffee and some menus, Helania felt her eyes sting with tears again. Blinking quickly, she exhaled in relief . . . and happiness.

Check her out. Meeting people. Making friends, possibly.

And waiting for a guy who was "wild" about her.

All in all, the night couldn't be going better.

# TWENTY-FOUR

As dull knives went, the assailant's weapon of choice did a bang-up job. Well, slice-up job was more like it. Not to put too fine a point on things.

Har-har, hardy har-har.

And what do you know, Boone figured he must be feeling a little better if he were able to make bad jokes to himself. The human male, on the other hand, was feeling so much worse, for so many different reasons. Although, given the way that his chest was no longer going up and down, one could assume that he wasn't feeling anything anymore.

Over so soon, Boone thought as he eased back from his kill. But he'd had to work fast—and now there was a lot of mess to clean up. So much red in the snow, so much red on the man's skin, so much red—

Boone looked up. The entire dead end of the alley was bathed in a red glow, the strange light illuminating the wall, the backs of the buildings, the trash that had accumulated and been snowed upon . . . as well as the woman who was where Boone had left her, crouched down, tucked in, holding her palms against both her eyes.

Jumping to his feet, he switched the crappy knife into his other hand and unsheathed one of his guns with his fighting palm. The eerie illumination was radiating out of the depths of the shadows about thirty feet away, from two laser points—

The scent of a male vampire came to him on the cold breeze, and Boone frowned. "Who goes there. Identify yourself or I'll give you a name you won't like—"

"Tough talk from a trainee."

Boone lowered his gun. He recognized that voice. Recognized the scent, too. And more than both of those, something was triggered in his mind, something . . . that he couldn't quite place.

"Show yourself," he said.

The tremendous figure that stepped out was dressed in the same kind of black leather Boone had on. But with the red light coming from what appeared to be his eyes, there was no seeing the face.

"Nice work," the male drawled. "You could be a surgeon. Cleanup, however, is gonna be a bitch."

Boone recoiled. "Syn?"

A high, keening whistle pierced the night, the sound coming from a number of blocks down the alley in the opposite direction.

Instantly, the red glow drained away, and that was when Boone saw the male properly: His Mohawk, his hard, harsh face, his broad shoulders.

"Give me the knife." The Bastard came forward. "Quick."

"What? Why?"

"Because I fucking say so." When Boone didn't comply, Syn cursed and spoke more slowly. Like he figured Boone's hearing was broken. "Give me the human's knife and go tend to her. Unless you think she'd rather it be me?"

Oh, yeah . . . that would be a hell-no. No offense to the Bastard, but anybody who'd just run for their lives did not need Syn in on their rescue.

Tossing the knife at the Bastard, Boone went over and knelt down by the woman. She still had her hands covering her eyes, and God . . . there was a lot of blood under where she was squatting.

"It's okay, you're safe now." He holstered his gun and went into his pockets. "We're going to get you some help."

Taking out a folded square, he ripped off its plastic wrap and flapped the Mylar blanket free of its folds. When he went to put it around the victim, she cried out and tried to shrink away from him. Without her hands for balance, she fell over into the dirty snow.

"No, no, you're safe now." He put the silver sheeting around her shoulders and gently righted her. "Here. This will help conserve your body heat."

Boone held the blanket in place and glanced in Syn's direction.

Someone was coming down the alley, and with the way Syn was standing over that bloody body with a knife in his hand? You could only pray it was another vampire—

"Jesus Christ," came the annoyed voice. "What the *hell* did you do now?"

"Shit happens," Syn replied.

"You know, it actually doesn't when you're not involved."

As Boone frowned, he recognized Balthazar, another one of the Bastards. But what he didn't understand was the conversation.

"You made a fucking mess." Balthazar stopped at the foot of the human. "And now we gotta deal with it."

Boone opened his mouth to cop to the sieve-like condition of the body, but Syn beat him to the punch.

"Look, the fucker deserved it. And do not pretend that you didn't take your time with that slayer back there. Unless, of course, you think that cranial damage is the way to get *lessers* back to the Omega? Otherwise, it looked to me like you were having a nice time at that concussion party you were throwing—"

"Do not turn this back on me—"

"You could have just stabbed your prey, too. So try not to bitch at me for doing exactly the same thing you did."

Boone opened his mouth to set the record straight, but both of them ignored him.

"That"—Balthazar pointed at the dead body—"is a human. No *pop!* and *fizz!* bye-bye . . ."

"Who are you?"

As the argument over the dead guy continued on, the question was posed softly, and Boone looked back at his victim. The woman had lowered her hands some and was staring out at him through two black eyes.

"I'm just here to help you." He made sure he positioned his body so there was no way she could see what was lying in the middle of the alley. "We need to get you treated by a medical—"

"No," she whispered.

"You're bleeding. Internally."

"Where did you come from? Is this a dream?"

Boone took his phone out and put a code into the group text of people on duty for the night. "I'm going to have someone come here—"

"No!" She jerked away. "I don't want to go to the hospital—"

"It's not a human ambulance. Don't worry."

"Human . . . ? "

*Fuck,* Boone thought.

"Listen, just stay with me," he said as he repositioned the Mylar blanket. "You need to stay conscious."

◆    ◆    ◆

"He hasn't gotten back to me."

As the male half of the couple across from Helania put his cell face-down on the booth's table, she was feeling the need to bolt again. Twelve-thirty, almost—and Boone was nowhere to be found.

The only thing that made this even remotely bearable was that it appeared he'd also stood up his friends. By thirty minutes. And counting.

"Well," Paradise said as she sat back in her bench seat. "I'm starved. How about we order and hope he shows up?"

"Works for me." Craeg opened a menu. "The cold makes me hungry. Plus, is anyone else smelling the cheeseburgers?"

As the female stared expectantly across the table, Helania wasn't sure what to do. "Is there any chance Boone could be hurt?"

Although given that he'd told her he was off rotation? He was probably not seeking medical attention for a war wound.

"You mean hurt from being out in the field?" Craeg said from behind the laminated picture of a Reuben sandwich and a piece of pie, the front page of the menu. "You don't have to worry about that. We're all equipped with locators when we're out engaging. But he's off rotation. He'll be here any second. I know it."

Well, at least she knew he hadn't lied to her about that.

Paradise nodded. "I think Craeg's right. Let's order and go about our business. He will show up. What do you say, Helania? Eat with us?"

The sense that she couldn't breathe came over her, and she looked out the window again. Except just as she opened her mouth to no-thank-you things, Ruth approached them.

"Still waiting for one more?" the waitress said. "Want some coffee to pass the time? You turned me down last time, but I'm feeling lucky tonight."

"Actually, I'm ready to order." Craeg put his menu down. "But females first."

"Well, now, there's a gentleman." Ruth winked at him and took out her order pad. "Who wants what?"

Everyone looked at Helania.

She took a deep breath and pictured herself going back to her apartment alone. To sit and wait. And see what had happened with Boone.

Clearing her throat, she pushed the mug of untouched coffee to the center of the table. "I'd actually prefer some hot chocolate. I guess I should have thought of that before the coffee came. And I'd like two eggs over easy with white toast and bacon—a double order of bacon."

"I'll take that java off your hands," Craeg said.

"It's cold," Helania warned.

"Caffeine is caffeine."

Helania smiled weakly and pushed the mug farther in his direction. "They have cream and sugar, if you like."

"But none of that weird stuff," Ruth interjected.

As the waitress went through her spiel about the evils of lactoid alternatives, Helania wondered what she was going to talk to Boone's friends about. And as another couple settled into the next booth and laughed loudly, her old fear of not being able to hear properly came back.

*Lips*, she told herself. She could always read their lips.

While Paradise and Craeg ordered, she resisted the urge to wipe her brow. Under the table, her heel started bouncing and her palms sweated—

"So, tell us how you two met," Paradise said. "Boone's always so quiet, and we want details."

Helania blinked and shook herself back to attention. Ruth was gone, the menus cleared, and Craeg was halfway done with the mug of cold black coffee.

"Ah . . ." The idea of going through everything about her sister and the slain female made her upset stomach worse. "At Pyre's Revyval."

"Oh, that club." Paradise linked an arm through her *hellren's*. "I didn't know Boone was into that kind of stuff. He mostly stays to his own, but you'd think it would come up. Then again, even though it turns out we're distantly related, I never knew him before now. He stayed away from society."

"You're an aristocrat, too?" Helania blurted.

The female laughed and popped the collar on her plain fleece. "Hard to believe, right?"

*Not if you go by those cheekbones*, Helania thought.

"Boone and I are like fourth cousins or something." The female shrugged. "But then everyone's related to each other, aren't they."

"I'm quiet, too." Helania flushed, and wondered why she felt the need to bring that up. "In case you haven't noticed."

Craeg spoke up. "Nothing wrong with that."

"I agree," Paradise tacked on.

Helania looked across at their relaxed shoulders and their open, welcoming faces. "How did you two meet?"

"We both joined the training program," Paradise said. "But even before we did, as soon as he came through the door . . . I knew he was the one for me."

"Same over here," Craeg agreed. "And listen, don't worry about this late thing. Boone is a stand-up guy. He always does the right thing, shows up when he says he's going to, takes responsibility and commitments seriously."

Paradise nodded. "That's right. He's one of the most dependable males I know."

# TWENTY-FIVE

Standing in the glow of the surgical van's red taillights, Boone stared at the closed doors of the RV's back end like they had the answer to the universe on them. Dr. Manello had readily agreed to treat the human woman, and to keep too much attention from being drawn to the big-ass bloodstains in that alley, Boone had picked her up and carried her four blocks over to be examined.

Whereupon the good doctor had helped her into the treatment bay and shut things up tight.

Watching the exhaust rise up through the red glow reminded him of when Syn's little ocular trick had turned everything Freddy Krueger. Who knew that vampire eyes could do that? Then again, there were all kinds of subspecies in the world.

Maybe the male had a little something else mixed in his veins. Who knew. But there was a more pressing issue with that Bastard—and not just the fact that, for some inexplicable reason, Syn had decided to take the blame for the dead human male back there in the snow.

Which was something Boone had tried to rectify in the alley. Syn had just talked over him, however, and then things had had to be sorted with the victim. But that misattribution of castration and other fun and games was going to be dealt with.

Back to Syn. When the Bastard had appeared in the alley, Boone's memory had fired off with a connection made, but there had been no piecing together the mental triggers. Now he remembered. Last night, when he'd gone to Pyre to search for—read: look after—Helania, he had sensed a presence in the crowd that he recognized, but couldn't immediately identify.

It had been Syn. He was absolutely certain of it.

And ordinarily, that wouldn't have been any big deal. The Bastard might have been a full-blooded warrior, but that didn't mean he couldn't blow off steam around some humans. Other members of the species did go there. It was just . . . why hadn't he mentioned it to Butch in the group text that included everybody? The Brother had been updating everyone on the investigation, and had specifically asked whether anyone had been to Pyre's Revyval.

Maybe Syn hadn't seen the message, though. Or had had a conversation in private?

The surgical RV's back doors opened, and Dr. Manello stepped down into the snow. After closing things back up, he shook his head at Boone.

"Can I ask you something?" the man asked.

"Yes?"

"Did you catch the bastard who did that to her?"

"I did. And I took care of things."

"Thank fuck. Because that poor girl . . ." The physician shook his head. "She's in rough shape. I'm giving her an IV right now to replace fluids and get some antibiotics into her. I stitched her up where necessary, but she's going to need follow-up with a doctor to get them all removed. And more immediately, I don't think she has anywhere safe to go and we can't just leave her here."

"What are you suggesting?"

"I don't know." The doctor stared at the closed doors. "I'm going back in. I'll let you know when she can have a visitor—and you, or someone else, is going to have to wipe her memories."

*How far back to go*, Boone wondered as the physician reentered the RV.

Boone was still standing in the taillights when heavy footfalls brought his head around. Syn was striding toward him, the warrior's heavy legs eating up the distance.

"The mess is gone," he announced.

"What did you do with the body?"

"We wrapped it up and hauled it out of there. Started a trash fire on the blood in the snow. But no one's going to give a shit—"

"Why did you cover for me?" Boone demanded. "And then not let me talk."

Syn crossed his arms over his chest and there was a period of silence. Just as Boone was about to ask again, the Bastard nodded over his shoulder in the direction of where things had gone down.

"How often do you do that."

Not a question. And even though Boone knew what the male was asking about, he said, "Do what?"

"Sing Christmas carols at the top of your lungs," Syn snapped "What the fuck do you think I'm talking about?"

Boone looked away. In truth, he recognized that what he'd done with that assailant went way too far—and that was only part of the problem. The reality that he could not have stopped himself was the even bigger issue.

He was not about to talk about all that, however. "I killed him. I saved her life and I took her assailant's—"

"You disabled the fucker and then castrated him while he was still alive. And then you started cutting pieces of him off until he died."

"Balthazar did the same thing. You said so yourself."

"Not even close. He toyed with a slayer. You, on the other hand, inflicted pain in a deliberate manner."

"Splitting hairs."

"You think? You had a victim waiting for aid, and you still had to get the suffering in, right? Even though she needed medical attention, you just had to get that release or the roar inside your body was going to destroy you. Am I right."

Again, not a question. And Boone became acutely aware that any of the Brothers could show up out of thin air at any moment.

Boone cursed at himself. At what he had done. At the fact that the Bastard seemed to be walking around in Boone's own skull.

Syn's voice dropped in volume, the deep tones nearly seductive. "When you came out into the field tonight, even though you're not supposed to be here, you would have kept going until you found something to play with. Until you got the poison out of you. Until you slaked your thirst for bloodshed."

With a slow pivot, Boone turned to Syn. "How do you know so much about . . ."

The change in the Bastard was instantaneous. Gone was the snake-like knowing stare, as if it had never existed.

"I'm just giving you feedback on your performance," Syn said dryly. "Isn't that what we're supposed to do with you trainees."

*Bullshit*, Boone thought. *You know exactly what I was doing in that alley. And your eyes lit up because you know how good it feels to have something at your mercy.*

A sudden feeling of dread washed over Boone. "Have you ever been to Pyre's Revyval?"

The warrior's expression didn't change. And his body didn't shift. And his eyes didn't flicker in the slightest.

"No," he said evenly. "I haven't."

◆    ◆    ◆

Helania was back at her apartment, sitting at her little kitchen table in her P.J.s, her laptop open and hard copies of work fanned out in front of her. Not that she was getting much editing done. She had been in this chair, staring into space, for how long now?

Two hours. It was a little after four a.m.

After a nice-enough meal at The 24 Hr. Diner, she had left Paradise and Craeg in the back parking lot around one-thirty. Dematerializing home, she had taken a load off on her sofa and cradled her phone in her palms like it was a crystal ball, soon to tell her what the future held.

Following about a half hour of that nonsense, she had forced herself to get up, get changed and move over here. Like this was so much more productive, her papers lying untouched on the table, her screen saver spitting bubbles out over the Word document she should have been typing into, her butt going numb.

With a stretch, she looked toward her door as if that would send vibes out into the universe that someone needed to be coming through it. And no, she wasn't talking about old school Avon.

That black cloak hanging with her other jackets by the exit was a re-minder of the distraction from her true purpose. The time wasted. The neutral that she had allowed herself to fall into.

All because of Boone. And still, she had heard nothing from him.

Pushing her chair back, she put her hands on her stomach. She'd eaten way too much at the diner, but given that she couldn't remember when her last meal before that had been, she probably didn't need to worry about the calories. Furthermore, it did not appear that anybody was seeing her naked tonight.

Dearest Virgin Scribe, where was Boone? What had happened to him—

Her phone started ringing, the vibration sending it on a little wan-der next to her laptop, and instantly, her hand snapped out to grab the thing. As she saw who it was, she exhaled a soft curse.

"Boone—"

"Helania, I am *so* sorry." His voice over the connection was the best thing she had ever heard. "I didn't mean to miss the diner—"

"Are you okay—"

"—but I had to deal with an emergency—"

"—all I care about is—"

"—I'm fine."

"—that you're all right."

They both ended there and took a deep breath at the same time. The relief was stunning as it flooded through Helania's body, her muscles loosening, her head swimming such that she became lightheaded: She had had him dead. Maybe it was at the side of a slippery, winter road. Or downtown in an alley. Or on his bathroom floor, head struck on the edge of a porcelain tub.

Death came in so many forms, and after Isobel's loss, Helania was worried that destiny was going to put a curse on anyone she loved—

*Cared about*, she amended. She couldn't possibly love him this fast . . . right?

"Thank you so much for calling me." She rubbed her aching head. "I was just really concerned about you."

"May I come see you?" he asked. "I don't have to stay the day, I just—"

"Yes, please. I would love to see—" The knock on her door was a surprise, and she turned around. "Is that you?"

"It is," he said, his voice coming through both the phone connection and the thin panel.

Helania tossed her phone down, rushed over, and whipped things open. She didn't even bother looking at him. She just went right against his body, and he was the same, his arms shooting around and holding her tight.

He smelled freshly showered, and his clothes were casual, as they had been the night before—not that she cared in the slightest about his wardrobe. The only thing that mattered was the way his heart beat evenly in his broad chest, his pulse strong. Healthy. Alive.

"Here, let's go in," he said as he moved them into her apartment.

As Boone closed the door and locked things up behind them, she put her hands to her cheeks. The flush that went through her made her dizzy, and she went over and sat on the sofa. Lowering her head between her knees, his loafers entered her field of vision as he came across to her.

"Are you okay?" he asked.

"Please don't take this the wrong way, but I was worried you were dead." She shook her head. "Yes, I realize that sounds crazy—"

"I'm so sorry." His knees popped as he got down on his haunches. "I got caught up in something out in the field that I needed to see through. I called as soon as I could."

Helania lifted her eyes and then brushed his face with her hand. "What happened?"

"It was awful." He shifted over so he sat beside her among all the needlepoint pillows. "Human female. Badly hurt. I was downtown and she crossed right into my path. I didn't want to get involved, I really didn't, but then this guy came out behind her, chasing her with a knife. I couldn't let that go."

"Did you save her?"

"I did. And after I . . . resolved . . . things with the human male, I got her treated by the Brotherhood's surgeon. They ended up taking her back to the training center, but she can't stay there for long. I believe they're exploring options in the human world for her, and hopefully, they'll get her into a halfway house. As long as her memories are properly scrubbed, she won't have any recollections of the species—and at least part of the trauma she went through."

Helania reached for his hand. "She's so lucky she ran into you. What did you do with the man? Did you turn him over to the police?"

"He won't be a problem for her anymore. That's all that matters."

Helania blinked as his meaning sunk in. "Well . . . I guess it would be hard to report the crime."

"It does get complicated and there are rules against interacting with humans. But I couldn't let it go. Someone needed to help her."

Helania thought of what Craeg and Paradise had said about him, that he always did the right thing.

"I'm glad you stepped up." She smiled. "We missed you at the meal, but you were where you needed to be."

"I didn't mean to disappoint you," he said gravely. "Or make you worry."

"Everything is better now. As long as you're okay."

As they stared at each other, Helania was aware of a deepening of their connection, a strengthening of the tie that had been instantaneous and was somewhat inexplicable. And yet neither of them acknowledged the profound moment.

It was too soon for words to be spoken. Too scary. And yet what was happening was very real—and maybe that was why they both stayed silent. If you found a treasure, you didn't want to shine too bright a light on it until you were sure that you weren't going to get mugged.

Self-protection, after all, took many forms, and not all of them were cowardly.

With a murmur of something sweet and soft, Boone pulled her against his chest, and his heavy arms were so good wrapped around her shoulders and waist. "Did you enjoy yourself with Craeg and Paradise? They're really good people."

"You know, I actually did. I mean, I'm rusty at making conversation, but even for me, they were really easy to open up to."

"What did you talk about?"

Tilting her head back, she looked into his eyes. "Craeg says you're wild for me."

The sensual smile that stretched Boone's mouth had Big Plans written all over it. And not in a conversational sense. "Did he."

"Are you?"

"Well, if you remember yesterday . . ." His broad hand stroked down to the curve of her waist. "I think 'wild' seems pretty accurate."

"Mmmm . . ." She focused on his mouth. "Yes, if memory serves, I think that covers it, but you may need to remind me."

"My pleasure."

As he dropped his mouth to hers and kissed her, he tasted like toothpaste and she breathed in deep so she could smell his aftershave. The idea that he had taken care to get himself clean before coming over made her smile.

"Would you mind if we went somewhere flatter," he said with that sexy smile of his. "And naked'er?"

Getting to her feet, she was struck by a desperate need to be with him and she pulled him off the couch with a yank. "Let's hurry."

"I like your attitude."

In her bedroom, she hustled over to sit on the foot of her mattress, and then she ripped off her T-shirt. Before she could work on her boxer shorts, Boone knelt between her knees and slowed her down.

"Allow me to help you."

As he moved up to kiss her, she wrapped her arms around his big shoulders and lifted her hips. "I just want to be naked with you."

The growl that percolated up out of his throat was oh, so satisfying, and he wasted no time in pulling those boxers down her legs and off her feet. Then his big, callused hands were stroking up her thighs as he continued to kiss her, his tongue teasing and retreating, getting her hotter. In fact, everything seemed heightened, every shift of his body, every point of contact—and certainly each lick of that tongue of his.

Lying back on the mattress, she expected him to come with her so they could get down to business. He didn't. Looming above her, his hands drifted over her breasts, squeezing them together and holding them in place so that the tips almost met. His mouth alternated between her hypersensitive, swollen nipples, sucking, licking, and—

The release that lightning'd through her was a shock, and she jerked her head up even as she moaned.

Meanwhile, Boone stared at her over the swell of her breasts, lids low, fangs descended, massive shoulders blocking out the view of the outer room behind him.

"That's right," he said in a husky voice, "come for me."

The sight of his pink tongue extending down and running a circle around her tight, bright pink nipple was enough to leave her in thrall again. God, she had no idea where her response was coming from and she really didn't care. Maybe it was because they had already done this a few times the day before and her inhibitions were down. Maybe because it was because he had awakened her as a female.

Maybe it was just because he was hot as hell and he wanted her as much she wanted him.

When Boone finally released her breasts, she was sure he was going to mount her—and she was so ready. As incredible as her releases had been, she wanted him inside her with a greed that was as shocking as that first rogue orgasm had been.

Except . . . no.

He didn't come up higher on her. He went lower.

Much lower.

His hands locked on her hips as his lips kissed a path down onto her ribs . . . her belly . . . her belly button . . .

As she figured out where he was headed, her legs sawed with impatience, and she arched back into the mattress, her head turning to the side so she could watch. But damn, there were times to tease, cajole, sensually build up the anticipation. This was not one of them. And she prayed he somehow knew it.

Tonight, she was not playing. Her hunger was just too strong.

Boone caressed down one of her legs and then moved it to the side, opening her up. "Helania . . ."

No preamble. Thank the Virgin Scribe. He went right in, worshipping her core with his mouth, sucking in her sex and licking deeply into her core. She came again immediately, shouting his name, fisting the quilt beneath her, contorting her body from the pleasure. And as she writhed against his face, he took everything she had to give, the slick feel of his tongue, his hot breath, his relentless attention, rocking her world.

Closing her eyes, Helania panted and groaned. Then she had to open her lids and watch him again.

As if he knew she was looking at him with wonder and heat, he deliberately licked up the center of her as he held her stare, his pink tongue and bright white descended fangs the kind of thing she was never going to forget.

But what about him? He needed—

All thought left her mind as another release rocketed through her, her undulating pelvis creating friction against his mouth, and magnifying everything.

Boone might not have been into teasing, but he sure took his time with it all. He seemed content to spend what was left of the night and all of the coming day right where he was, the purring sound he was making deep in his throat suggesting he was enjoying this as much as she was.

But eventually he straightened, his hands going to his fly.

"Oh, God . . . yes . . ." she said. And she would have sat up to help him, but she was utterly boneless, her body at once totally satiated and ready for more.

The next thing she felt was his hard, hot length penetrating her. And there was nothing else she needed in order to go over the edge again. Even as he started moving, she was already there: The sensations plowed through her and then were cranked up even higher as he began to pump—and she got a hell of a show as he swept his sweater and shirt up over his head, his chest and heavy arms on display as the last of his clothes disappeared.

Now he was holding her by the hips again, pulling her into him, pushing her away in a rhythm to his thrusts. The pounding increased until her breasts were jerking back and forth, their ultrasensitive tips carrying echoes of the sex they were having sure as if he were touching her all over through that connection down below.

Boone's eyes were on fire, and his fangs flashed as he suddenly reared back and locked into her. The force of his orgasm was so great, the cords of muscles that ran up his shoulders into his neck stood out in stark relief, the thick veins popping, the power in his body activated in service to her.

Boone was utterly magnificent.

And he did not stop filling her up.

For a very, very long time.

# TWENTY-SIX

"I have to say," Helania murmured, "that the night ended even better than I imagined it would."

As Boone's female cuddled in closer to him, he smiled. They were lying naked on her little bed, her sprawled over his chest, their bodies throwing off so much heat that covers were unthinkable—in spite of the fact that they had finally collapsed from the sex well over an hour ago.

The scent of dark spices was thick in the air, and he wondered if she'd noticed.

Male bonding was not a subtle thing. Yet he was aware that there were a lot of things unsaid between them—nothing bad; on the contrary, just stuff that seemed too good to be true.

"You know," he murmured, "I have to agree with you. There were many finishes on both sides . . ."

They had made love for God only knew how long, and talk about hot and heavy. For some reason—maybe it was the stress they had been under and the release of all that pent-up energy—the session had been a marathon one. To the point where he was worried he'd chafed her.

And then there was another issue. Cleanup.

"Should we . . ." He cleared his throat. "I've made a mess all over you."

Helania's low, sexy chuckle made him feel like he was Male of the Year. "It's not a mess. And most of it is inside me—where it can stay."

He smiled so broadly that his cheeks hurt. "You are amazing. I know . . . I know that sounds like a line, but it's not. You bring me to my knees and lift me up at the same time. It's the definition of magic."

"I'd say we're good together." She yawned so wide, her jaw cracked. "Very good."

Boone kissed the top of her head as they both fell silent. A moment later, she groaned and rolled away from him, lying flat on the mattress beside him.

"Do you need more room?" he asked as he moved over.

"I think I left the heat on too high. Hold on."

As she got to her feet and walked over to the thermostat on the wall, he admired the view of her shoulders, her waist . . . her beautiful lower half . . . and thought back to when he'd been kneeling between her legs, making love to her sex with his mouth. He had taken his time—and he couldn't wait to go back there. To give her pleasure, to hear her say his name in that hoarse way, to feel her most intimate place against his lips . . .

All he wanted was to return to that experience.

"It's just on seventy," she said with confusion in her voice. "Guess we create our own heat."

"You can say that again."

When she turned back around, his eyes went to her breasts. Her nipples were a deep rose color and very pronounced, the tips protruding out of their creamy swells, the swaying of her body as she walked toward him causing them to move.

Desire licked at his pelvis again, his cock jumping in response. But as much as he wanted to be with her again, the rest of his body was spent.

Helania stopped at the side of the bed and looked down at his arousal. "Don't take this in the wrong way, but how are you still . . ."

"Hard?" he drawled. "It's just what you do to me."

Although actually, he couldn't believe he was erect again, either. And then suddenly, he wasn't worried about his stamina anymore: Helania got up on him, those soft thighs of hers spreading wide over his hips, that core of hers hovering just above his arousal.

"Be honest," she said as she put her hands on either side of his torso. "And you can totally tell me no if you don't want to—"

"I will never not want to be with you," he groaned, his pelvis rolling, his well-used cock begging for more attention.

"If I do the work—"

"Please, fuck me." He bit his lower lip with one of his fangs and arched up. "I will beg for it. I will beg you for—"

Leaning down to him, she kissed his mouth. "No need for that."

Her hands went to his arousal and she stood him up. As she lowered her body down onto him, they started moving together, the sex resuming as if they hadn't just been at it for two hours straight. And for some crazy reason, he didn't last long. Neither did she.

It was the best kind of madness, wasn't it.

After she collapsed on his chest again, they breathed together for a little bit and then she slid off of him, rolling onto her back once more. Skootching over, he made sure she had room both on the mattress and the pillow, and when her hand gripped his, he squeezed her palm in return.

And things were peaceful . . . for a little while. Blissful . . . for a time.

But the wolves that nipped at his heels eventually returned to him, reality intruding on the sacred space with Helania in a rush, as if it had resented being locked out by the passion: His father's death. His father's lover. His father's will. And so many other things.

Closing his eyes, he resolved not to think about what had happened at the Audience House. Or about that woman he had saved in that alley. Or what he had done to that man—which he acknowledged had been wholly inappropriate, and which he would never do the likes of again.

And then there was Syn—

Resolutions to the contrary, Boone quickly became a live wire under his skin, the stress of it all spiking his adrenaline in a fresh surge, as if the quiet and peacefulness of Helania's bedroom were top soil that helped a poisonous plant to grow.

But FFS, you'd think all those orgasms would have drained the energy out of him completely. Then again, he had had blood from that Chosen's vein when he'd been injured out in the field. That was known to give a male superstrength—

"So I reached out to Isobel's friends," Helania murmured.

Boone's lids popped back open, and he turned his head on the pillow. "You did?"

"On Facebook. I found the page of the female who came here to tell me about Isobel—the one who I . . . buried my sister with. Anyway, I private-messaged her. And then I decided, why stop there? I hit up everyone who left a tribute for my sister."

"Did any of them get back to you?"

"Some did." There was a pause. "I asked them all about the boyfriend. A name. Contact info. Possible location."

Boone forced his voice to stay level. "Did any of them know him?"

"No. They'd heard about him, but no one knew him or had met him." There was a pause. "And no one has seen or heard from him since, either."

Boone tried to keep his curse to himself. "Maybe there's a reasonable explanation."

"I really used to think there was." She sighed. "But if he'd been abusive . . . I just don't know why Isobel would have lied to me? And I know what I saw here in this apartment. I lived with her my whole life, I could read her better than anyone could. She was happy."

All Boone could do was shake his head. He wanted to step carefully around the subject of that boyfriend out of respect for her and her Isobel, but damn, his warning bells were ringing: Even if her sister had been happy, males sometimes snapped. Hello . . . he himself had tonight in that alley.

"We need to keep digging," he said. "What about the female who came to see you? Did she answer?"

"No. Not yet. And as with a lot of people in the species, she's clearly using a pseudonym. So I don't know what her real name is."

As a shiver went through her, he lifted his head and eyed the quilt that had been pushed off onto the floor. "You cold?"

"I don't know what I am," she said with exhaustion. "What I do know for sure is that I'm glad you're here."

Boone stroked her arm. "Me, too. I'm glad I'm here, too."

They were quiet for a while, and Boone passed the time attempting to control the twitching of his thigh muscles. And his legs weren't the only thing wide-awake. He was totally erect again, his arousal straining, his blood thickening in his veins. But whatever, Mr. Happy down there could fuck right off with the bright ideas. Sex was the last thing on Boone's mind, even if it was the first thing on his libido's agenda. He had worn his female out enough, and hopefully, with the Virgin Scribe's blessings, they would have so many more days and nights together to look forward to.

"Your friends really like you a lot," she said.

"I like them a lot, too." He tried to get his mind focused on something . . . anything. "You should meet everyone else in my trainee class. At least twice a month we all go out together. I'll find out when the next time is and let you know—and I'll make sure that I don't miss it."

"It makes me happy when you talk about the future."

On that note, there was a temptation to ask if he could move in, given that he wouldn't have a place to live in fourteen days—and then maybe he could make a joke about how's that for the future. But he stayed quiet on his drama. She had enough going on—

"Would you care if I were poor?" he blurted.

As Helania looked over at him and they were face-to-face, he figured this was the very definition of pillow talk.

"I didn't know you were rich," she said. "I mean, I'd guessed you were a member of the aristocracy by your accent, but I hadn't really considered the financial repercussions."

He squeezed her hand again. "Would you, though? Care if I didn't have money?"

"Not in the slightest. I've never known what it's like to be wealthy. So if you are not, it doesn't change my situation in the slightest, and I'm happy where I am now."

As Boone exhaled in relief, he was not surprised that her answer meant that much to him. "I'm so glad. Most of the females in the *glymera* are more interested in expense accounts and credit cards."

"Your arranged mating." She hesitated. "Why exactly did the female break it off?"

As Helania seemed embarrassed to have asked, Boone smiled in hopes of reassuring her that no subject was off-limits. "It wasn't an issue of money. She was in love with someone else. That's why. And guess what, he was a civilian, too. You'll meet Rochelle someday. She's remarkably down-to-earth considering where she comes from, and she was braver than I was when it really counted. She did us both a favor."

"You would have mated her, then?" Helania paused. "And listen, if I'm getting too personal—"

"I have nothing to hide from you."

As Boone felt the bed begin to shake, he looked down his naked body and half expected to find that a dog had snuck in and was wagging its tail against something—but nope. His foot was going back and forth incessantly, sure as if it were attached to someone else's body.

By force of will, he made the thing stop and then focused on what she'd asked him. "As for my following through on the mating, I guess the way I felt was . . . I knew I didn't love her, but given how the aristocracy is, if I'd pulled out of the arrangement, the shame falling on her would have been intense and lifelong. She never would have been considered by any other male for a mating, and her family would never have forgiven her for the social embarrassment. It would have ruined her life."

"Just over a broken arrangement?" When he nodded, she seemed horrified. "That is cruel."

"True enough. But the good news was, I got her out of it. I told my father, and through my sire, the rest of society, that she didn't find me worthy. It was the way to keep the fallout from landing on her."

"But what then happened to you?"

"Well, I'm a male." He rolled his eyes. "So the rules are different. Sure, I took some shit—'scuse my French—except it was not anything compared to what Rochelle would have had to deal with. It's not fair, but there are double standards all over the place in the *glymera*, and they usually undercut the freedom and roles of females."

"She must have been very grateful for what you did."

"I think she was—and still is. But I mean, it was not her fault that we were put together, and it wasn't mine, either. It was just the situation, and for the reality we were in, I would rather have sacrificed my reputation so she could be free to be with the one she loved than have her condemned to spinsterhood and ridiculed at every turn."

Helania smiled. "That's what your friends said about you."

"What?"

"Paradise and Craeg said you always do the right thing."

As an image of that human male's bloodied and sliced-open body came to mind, Boone thought, *Not all the time . . .*

"But after the arrangement was broken," Helania prompted, "your father wasn't pleased, right? You already told me there were issues in your relationship with him and I would assume . . ."

"He was absolutely furious at me. And that's why I bring up the money thing. In two weeks, I won't have a place to live and will be pretty close to penniless. My sire cut me out of his will. I just found out."

Helania lifted her head again, and he had to admire the bright flush on her cheeks. Her high coloring, coupled with her red and blond hair, was so beautiful, he was in awe of her. And the longer he stared at her, the more lust surged under his skin, prowling, looking for a way out.

Meanwhile, all he could think of was . . . males really were pigs, weren't they.

"I just don't understand," she said. "How could a father disinherit his own son over a situation like that."

"That is the *glymera* for you. And there were some other things, too."

Like him maybe, possibly, not having a blood relationship to Altamere. And he would have given that whole sordid story airtime, but he suddenly was tired of talking about his father. It felt as though the male had already taken up way too much space, and besides, with his sire being dead and the will's amendment being what it was? Boone wasn't inclined to expend a whole lot of energy on what was now an in-the-past kind of thing.

Helania lifted her head up and looked over at him. "Was that why you went downtown tonight? To clear your head?"

Boone thought about Syn's red eyes glowing in that alley. As well as what he himself had done to that human.

"Yes," he said. "I'm still off rotation, but I needed . . . I just had to go out and be by myself for a little while. Walk the streets. Get some cold, clear air. After I left the King's Audience House, I had to get everything out of my head, even if it was only for a little bit."

Of course, the mechanism that had worked best was killing that woman's assailant. And Syn was all too correct. Boone had needed that release before he could trust himself to be around anyone. Including, if not especially, his Helania.

"And again," he murmured, "it was when I was walking the streets that I ran into that human woman."

Helania laid her head back down on their pillow. "As I said before, she's lucky she found you. And so am I."

Boone kissed the top of Helania's head and smiled up at the ceiling of her bedroom.

They were quiet for a time, and yet neither of them was still. Helania's body kept shifting against his own, as if she were in search of a comfortable position and being denied that prize, and he was the same, fidgeting this way, that way.

It seemed ironic that in the midst of their mutual discomfort, he decided that he really did love her.

He *loved* Helania.

Yes, the timing was not the best. Yes, it had happened quickly. But when you knew ... you knew. And the next step was to tell the person—

Helania let out a soft snore, and when a second one came, Boone closed his eyes again and told himself to follow suit. There would be time for revelations later. And maybe something downright romantic, with roses and candlelight.

Or maybe he'd chill and keep it to himself for a little while. Like a week. Tops.

Assuming he could keep his happiness to himself.

A short time later, exhaustion claimed him, his consciousness draining out and being replaced with a dense void of thought, emotion, and dreams. But as he fell off that cliff, there was a smile on his face.

He couldn't wait to tell her he loved her. And do it properly.

# TWENTY-SEVEN

At first, Boone didn't know what woke him up. He wasn't even sure if he had roused from sleep. He felt as though he were floating, everything fuzzy and far away, both his body and wherever he was more ether than substance in the manner of a dreamscape. And yet something was very, very real in the midst of the haze . . .

His name. Across a vague and shifting awareness, he could sense his name being called from far away.

Something . . . was calling him home.

Someone.

A sense of needing to rush sharpened his thoughts, the urgency making him try to run—except he didn't seem to be connected to any corporeal form: He had no limbs to command into action, no feet to pick up, no arms to pump. Further, there was no solid ground upon which to ambulate.

Had he died and gone unto the Fade?

Who was calling for him?

Desperation made his heart pound, and it was then that he felt the heat. There was a fire somewhere close by, the burning so intense, surely it would melt the skin from his bones—

Boone shot up right, a great breath exploding out of his mouth as he ripped free of the dream—or had it been a nightmare?

Looking around frantically, he saw a dim bedroom that was mostly empty. Barren walls. Sheets tangled around his calves.

It was a split second before he recognized where he was, and as soon as he did, the last dregs of his confusion washed away and he reached for his female . . .

He was alone on the bed.

"Helania?"

A tortured moan answered him from somewhere else in the apartment, and stark terror had him leaping all the way across to the open doorway, his feet not touching the floor at all. Except Helania was nowhere to be seen in the living area or the kitchen, the couch and the chairs around the little table empty—

Abruptly, he looked down at the front of his hips and recoiled. He was painfully aroused, his erection jutting from his hips with such force, it stuck straight out.

He was on the verge of an orgasm even now.

A feeling of dissociated dread came over him as he realized he was panting and flushed. Lifting his hands, he noted the sheen of sweat that was all over his skin, and as he inhaled through his nose, the scent in the air caused his alarm bells to go off even more loudly.

In slow motion, he turned to the open doorway of the bathroom. Helania was lying on the tile floor, her naked body facedown and spread out, the bath mat shoved aside as if she were seeking to cool as much of herself as she could.

Even from across the way, he could see her sex gleaming—and the wave of lust that came over him was so great, it brought him to his knees.

As he hit the floor hard, she tried to shut the door and mumbled something.

"Oh . . . God," he said under his breath. "The needing."

Driven by an instinct to protect her, even though there was nothing he could do to stop the surging hormones of her fertile time, Boone dragged himself back to his feet and stumbled toward her, his legs sloppy and uncoordinated, as if he were drunk. Bumping into the couch, he threw out a hand to a wall, to a table, to the doorjamb, to whatever he could find—until he fell again and had to crawl on all fours.

"Helania—"

"Shut me in . . . shut me inside . . . leave if you can . . . I didn't know, I swear to it . . ."

Putting out his arm, he stopped the door from hitting one of her legs, the position of which seemed to be unknown to her. Then he flopped back against the doorjamb and tried to connect to his rational side through his own nearly overpowering hormonal response.

Vampire females were only fertile about every ten years or so, and that was a blessing. When their needing hit, as Helania's clearly had, they suffered terrible sexual cravings, the torture so great that most, if they were not trying to become pregnant, asked to be drugged. The only other solution, outside of being put out of their misery medically? A male had to service them by easing their cravings in the carnal way.

Filling them up over and over again.

"Go . . ." she mumbled through her tangled hair. "I'm so sorry, go . . ."

"I'm not leaving you." And not just because it was daylight. "Do you want me to call the doctors?"

As a human, Manny could drive over. Bring drugs. Ease her suffering—

No, wait. Doc Jane. Yes, a female would be better.

When Boone went to get up, he didn't have enough coordination to make it to the vertical, so he crawled back into the bedroom. Finding his slacks, he fished through the pockets. No phone. Where was his fucking phone? He'd had it when he'd come in the apartment because he'd been talking to her on it, for fuck's sake.

On all fours, he went back out into the living area, shuffling along the floor, bunching up the throw rugs, trying to ignore the way his cock bobbed while gritting his molars against his own sexual need. He went back to the sofa. Patting around, he searched through the needlepoint cushions—

When he finally found the goddamn thing, his hands were shaking so badly, he struggled to pick it up and hold it. And then he realized he didn't have the number to the clinic.

"Mother*fucker!*"

◆    ◆    ◆

It was strange how you could miss the living sure as if they were dead.

As Butch sat by himself in one of the training center's interrogation rooms, he was at a table that had been screwed down to the floor. The chair he'd parked his butt in, on the other hand, was moveable—although only because he'd released it from its own four-point tether with a Phillips head. There were three other ass palaces, and he was prepared to offer a similar liberation as a courtesy to anybody who came down here to join him.

The fact that he was alone in this makeshift think tank was what made him think about his former partner, José de la Cruz.

Or, like, *miss* his former partner. Or, fine, maybe the word was more "mourn."

"You should be here, José," he said out loud.

Refocusing on the opposite wall, he let his eyes wander around the gruesome display he'd made on each of the killings at Pyre. Going from left to right, he'd started with killing number one. Under that roman numeral, he'd Scotch-taped the articles that had been in the *CCJ* sequentially, with the most recent one at the top. No photos. No real notes.

See, if he'd still been with the Caldwell Police Department, he would have the incident report and all the attendant documentation to work with. The crime scene photographs. Evidence taken in. Names of witnesses, suspects, etc.

Hell, maybe he'd have been the one assigned to the case.

But nope.

Under roman number II, he had some details about the second killing listed: "Female, Isobel, blooded daughter of Eyrn, found by ???, in storage room ???. Removed by unknown female(s). Body buried ??? (public land). Call to dispatch logged following night from Helania, other blooded daughter of Eyrn."

The question was whether they needed to go so far as to request permission from Helania, as next of kin, for an exhumation. The problem with that, assuming a typical civilian Fade Ceremony had been performed, and the body wrapped only in layers of cloth, was that the remains would be severely degraded by now. There wouldn't be much more than bones left.

The other problem with that idea was that he had to weigh any potential for evidence against the trauma on Helania. If there was a chance of finding out anything material from whatever was left of the remains, he would do it in a heartbeat—and go so far as to force the issue with a decree from Wrath if he had to. But he didn't know what the hell he was looking for or could hope to find, and the ground was frozen. So it just seemed cruel.

Roman numeral III was the column with the glossy, gruesome photographs. Starting at the top, he had the same kind of basics: "Female, Mai, blooded daughter of Roane, found by Helania, blooded daughter of Eyrn, January 23. Fourth storage unit on the right. Remains removed by V."

The black-and-white images that Butch had put up included some of the ones taken by Vishous at the scene: The facial close-up that showed the hook. The full-length of the hanging body. The storage room through the open door. And then there were ones Butch himself had taken in Havers's morgue: The slices in the throat and cuts to the wrists. The bruises. The abrasions from her having been dragged. That little nail Boone had noticed.

As he'd told his *shellan*, Mai's family had agreed to an autopsy and Havers was going to do it at nightfall once he worked his way through his surgical schedule.

So right now, it was just a waiting game.

Balancing his chair on its back legs, Butch crossed his arms over his chest and stared at the board he'd created.

He had done exactly this with José countless times: Put everything they knew about a case up on a wall so they could stare at the shit until something clicked. God . . . there had been so many deaths that they'd investigated together. So many lives lost that they'd tried to redeem in some small way. So many family members that they'd had to deliver bad news to.

Mothers, fathers, sisters, brothers. Grandparents. Aunts and uncles and cousins.

And meanwhile, he'd been busy trying to kill himself with the drinking.

José, on the other hand, had been a family man. A good Catholic who loved his wife and his children.

"Wonder if you could see what I'm missing, José," he said into the still air.

There was so little to go on, and the familiar churn of his brain as it chewed over what he had and what was not yet found, what he knew and what he wondered about, was a gateway to a ten-year span of his former life. As a human.

The great shift in his existence, in his very identity, did not seem weird anymore. Probably because he liked everything about being a vampire: His *shellan*. His friends. His work, his purpose, his lifestyle.

Contrary to the fables about those with fangs, he was one of the very rare half-breeds who had been "turned" from what was essentially human into something that was wholly not. In the real world, a bite from the "undead" didn't condemn a pious virgin to an eternity of bloodthirsty stalking. You were either born of the species or you weren't. Except in his case, and that of a mere handful of others.

And just as that species divide was a hard line not crossed, so, too, were the two worlds that separated *Homo sapiens* from vampires. So . . . when he came over to this side, he hadn't been able to take José with him. And he hadn't been able to say goodbye. Or explain where he had gone or what had happened to him.

One of his biggest regrets in life was the fact that he had disappeared on his former partner. He had always imagined that José hadn't been surprised, though. Given the way Butch had been living? Only an idiot wouldn't have seen the coffin headed his way.

Butch stared at the photograph of Mai's remains and felt guilty. As horrible as a dead body was, as soul-shattering and terrible as it was for a loved one to see that or hear about that from an officer of the law, the only thing that was worse was nothing. No answer to the "where." No clue as to the "how" or the "why." No opportunity to begin the mourning process and therefore no way of ever working through their grief to some kind of peace.

He hated the fact that undoubtedly José would have showed up at that shitty apartment Butch had been living in—just like the guy had always done when Butch had been too hungover to get out of bed—and found absolutely nothing. No partner smelling like scotch, passed out on the bed. No cranky bastard in the shower who was cutting himself while shaving because of the DTs. No off-balance asshat trying to put his pants on one leg at a time.

Nothing.

No body. No note. No answers.

And the thing was, José had been the kind of guy who would have been eaten alive by that. God knew, Butch had seen the man's commitment to strangers. For his own partner? Who he had, for some unknown reason, cared about for years?

José would have searched for answers.

Seriously. For quite a while.

On occasion, even though it was a bad idea, Butch went out at night and put himself in the position of almost running into the guy. There was even one evening when he and Marissa had gone to a fancy restaurant and José had been there, across the way.

Butch had gone over. And spoken to the man.

Then reworked some of José's memories.

But it didn't feel like enough. And it wasn't enough when it came to moments like this, when he wished he could call the guy and work through an issue or . . . in this case, a murder. Or two—assuming the first hadn't been part of it all.

See? Exactly what he wanted to talk over with José.

Thinking back to his former partner, Butch tried to imagine what the man would say—and he could almost hear José's voice: *When you can't connect the dots, get more dots.*

Maybe what Butch needed to do was reach out to the race and appeal for help through social media. He could just open up the phone lines and the confidential email box and see what came back to him. He'd have to give Mai's family a heads-up about it at nightfall, but then he could drop a post in the closed Facebook group for the race and send out an email blast to everyone who'd been by the Audience House.

And then what, he wondered—

When his cell phone went off, he nearly fell backward. And as he hung in the balance between landing on four legs and falling on his head, he had a crazy thought that José had psychically picked up on the vibe that he was needed and had mysteriously dialed the seven numbers that were connected with Butch's new phone.

The chair hit the stone floor properly and Butch snapped up the Samsung. Turning the screen over, he—

Oh.

Accepting the call, he said, "Hey, Boone, what's doing—"

The barrage of words coming at him was so jumbled and frantic, all he could think of was, *Fuck.* For the most part, Boone was sensible, a measured and balanced kind of guy. Like, in that alley tonight: When Syn had been going nuts on some human, Boone had had the presence of mind to take care of an injured woman.

So whatever this was? Was serious shit.

"Slow down, son," Butch interrupted sharply. "You gotta speak more clearly."

It took a couple of tries—but then the message got through, and all Butch could do was close his eyes and curse. This was bad. Really fucking bad. And P.S., what the fuck was that kid doing at Helania's apartment overday—

Oh, who the hell was he kidding? He knew *exactly* why Boone had gone over there. And now the worst complication that could happen between members of the opposite sex had come home to roost.

'Urprise!

Popping his lids, he checked his watch. And of course it was one in the afternoon.

"Okay, Boone, here's what I want you do—no, I'm going to take care of everything. But unless you want her to get pregnant, you need to lock yourself in a room—what? Yes, I know she's suffering, but if you get in there with her, you're going to end up with a young in about eighteen months. You need to lock yourself away from her *now*. Things are only going to get worse. In the meantime, I'll get Doc Jane and she'll be to you ASAP."

There were some more jumbled syllables, and Butch cut them right off. "Get yourself locked in. I'll handle the rest."

As he hung up and dialed the Pit, he had to shake his head. See . . . *this* was why you did not get involved with witnesses.

Things could go from sucky to totally tits up in the matter of hours. Although he had to admit, the needing thing?

Even with all his homicide experience, he would never have seen this one coming.

# TWENTY-EIGHT

Boone wanted to think the Brother Butch was wrong. He wanted to believe the best of himself, that he was a gentlemale first and foremost, that he had self-control and restraint—that he could therefore take care of Helania as she twisted and contorted on that cold tile in the bathroom. He wanted to confidently expect that he could rise above her needing, and cover her with a light sheet, and stand over her with a bath-sized towel, fanning her to cool her down.

With everything that Helania meant to him, he truly wanted to believe that he could put her needs before his own as they waited for help to come.

In the end, however, as the hormone surges she was wracked with got more and more intense, he had no choice but to do what the Brother instructed. And it even got so bad that he not only put himself in the bedroom and closed the door, but also pushed the mattress against the panels to try to keep things shut.

Which, when he thought about it, was stupid. If he was strong enough to move the bed over there, he was strong enough to shift it back.

But that was beside the point.

As he curled up on the floor in the bedroom, his knees all the way against his chest, his arms locked around them, his body shivering not from being cold, but from the paralyzing sexual need that crushed him . . . he squeezed his eyes shut and prayed that he didn't go to her.

Not because he didn't want to get her pregnant.

But because he did.

The idea that he could be free from his family's legacy . . . and start his own, with Helania? It was the kind of destiny he hadn't even known he could pray for. And now, with the possibility right in front of him?

Well . . . in the room next door?

A happy family was the only thing he could picture. The only thing he wanted. The only way he could keep going in what had been feeling like an empty void of late. Mated to Helania, with young . . . he would have purpose. Grounding. A place and a bloodline that he had created with love, not been born into.

Except . . . he didn't know what Helania wanted. And in the absence of being sure where she stood, he couldn't take a chance. When females went through their needing, all males in the vicinity were affected to some degree—but a male who was emotionally tied to the female to begin with? Who had clearly bonded to her? Boone's sexual urges were nearly as bad as her own—

The *bing!* that went off beside him brought his head up and he looked at his phone.

It was Jane, texting him that she was just outside the door to the apartment.

Groaning, Boone went to stand up, and he nearly orgasmed as his cock bounced around, brushing his leg, knocking against the floor.

Fucking hell, he was still naked. Willing the light on, he located his slacks and managed to get his seesawing legs into them. Yanking on his shirt, there was no tucking it in. His hands were shaking too badly.

Moving the bed out of the way, he stumbled from the bedroom, training his eyes on the door Doc Jane was standing on the far side of. He did not allow himself to look toward the bathroom. He did not take any breaths in through his nose. He refused to permit his feet to turn his sorry ass around and propel his body into that bathroom and down onto that floor and in between his female's legs.

He didn't so much walk over to the apartment's door as run head-first into it, his loose inability to control his legs making proper balance impossible. Fumble . . . fumble . . . fumble with the doorknob. When that didn't go well, he yanked at the damn thing—

It was locked. Dead bolted.

Somehow he sprang things and then—

"Oh, thank God," he mumbled as he saw V's mate standing in the basement hallway.

As Doc Jane entered and closed things behind herself, he backed up—or rather tripped over his bare feet and fell on his ass. Landing in a heap, he knew he was a total mess.

And going by the expression on the doctor's face, she rather agreed.

"Knock me out," he mumbled. "Do it first so you won't have to deal with me. I'm worried I'm dangerous. I can't . . . think . . ."

Doc Jane's mouth started to move, and Boone was instantly transported back to his sire's Fade Ceremony, someone standing in front of him, communicating in what was theoretically English, but which made no sense to him whatsoever.

What did make sense?

The fact that V's female put her old-fashioned doctor's bag down. Retrieved from it a syringe and a small clear bottle with a rubber top. And then promptly loaded some kind of drug into the belly of the needle.

As she knelt beside him, she said, "Roll up your sleeve for me?"

Roll. Up. Sleeve.

*Got it*, he thought.

He tore the thing off from the shoulder and threw it somewhere.

Holding out his bare arm, he watched as she rubbed an alcohol square in a circle on his bicep and then poked him a good one.

Boone opened up his mouth to thank her.

But the shit was fast-acting. For real.

◆    ◆    ◆

Helania's body was a rope and the hormones flooding her system were angry hands on either end, twisting, twisting . . . pulling . . . until surely the fibers that made up her corporeal form would snap. Facedown on the tile, she was on fire from the inside out, nothing relieving her of the agony, the sawing need, the clawing, useless desire.

She had no idea where Boone was. But he had left her as she'd told him to.

At this point, she wasn't even sure where she was.

Forcing her lids open, everything was blurry, so she blinked until a small sink became semi-apparent. Bathroom. She was in the bathroom.

Rolling onto her back, she felt a draft as her belly was exposed to the air. There was no corresponding cool place for her shoulders, though. The furnace inside her body had heated the tiles on the floor.

Relief, there had to be . . . some relief.

Again on her stomach. Now on her side. Legs straight. Legs up. One leg down and the other up. Shoulders flat, shoulders curved.

Nothing helped. But that was the nature of the needing.

How could she possibly have missed the signs? Restlessness. Being too hot. Bacon and chocolate at that diner, both of which she ordinarily never had an interest in.

The fact that, for the first time in her life, she'd had sex without really knowing the other person for very long. Her uncharacteristic boldness now made so much sense. It had been a prodromal to this fertile time.

When had her last needing been? She could not recall.

Oh, God, Boone. She would have warned him to stay away if she'd been thinking more clearly, if she had caught the signs—

The cool breeze came from out of nowhere, as if someone had opened a window and let some of the outdoor air in. Except she had no windows to open—

Lifting her head, she looked up and did not understand what she was seeing. But it appeared as though a female angel had come and covered her in a white cloud. Wait . . . unless it was just a sheet?

"Hi," the angel said. "I'm Doc Jane. I'm here to help you."

Helania blinked a couple of times to see if the vision before her changed. Nope. Still a female angel with short blond hair, dark green eyes, and . . . a pair of blue doctor's scrubs for clothes?

Giving up on trying to make sense of it all, she let her head fall back down to the tile. "Help . . . me . . ."

"I'm going to check your vitals, and then we'll see about taking care of you with some meds, is this okay with you?"

Meds? And what kind of angel talked about vital signs? Besides, if she'd gone unto the Fade, she was now dead for an eternity, so all that was a moot point.

As another blast of heat churned through her, Helania moaned and abruptly didn't care what the plan was. Anything was better than this terrible grinding need.

"Yes, please. Thank you."

She had no clue what she was saying.

Things happened at that point. Something was put on her arm . . . after which there was a slow constriction and a release. Then a cold disk that was heaven pressed into the front of her chest. After that, there was a beep next to her ear—no, wait, that was inside her ear.

"Helania? I'm going to give you a shot of morphine, with your permission. It will ease you and make this so much more bearable. Is that okay?"

The angel's voice was closer now and Helania tried to open her eyes. "Yes. Anything . . ."

At this point, if she had to get in a bath of dry ice, she'd jump in—

Another surge owned her, and as she cried out, she was aware that the spikes of hormones were still getting stronger. As impossible as that seemed, she could feel the intensification—

The easing came on in a wave and flooded through her body, calming down the boil sure as if she were a pot taken off an open flame. But she did not trust the relief, and for a time, she braced herself and waited for the suffering to come back.

"It's all right," that female voice said. "Just let yourself relax. I'm going to stay here and monitor you. I won't let it get away from us."

The tears came hard and heavy, Helania weeping for no cogent reason and every variation of an exhausted one.

"Mother Nature can be so cruel to females," said the voice.

Wiping her eyes with her forearm, Helania craned around. As the details of the mystical female came through with greater clarity, she frowned. No wings. No aura. No preternatural presence. Instead . . .

"You're not an angel."

The female laughed, her forest green eyes flashing. "Oh, trust me, I'm *so* not. Just ask my *hellren*."

Helania glanced down at herself. What she had assumed was a fluffy white cloud covering her tortured body turned out to be one of her own sheets. She recognized the faded pattern of little pink and yellow flowers.

"How are you feeling now?" the doctor asked.

"Where's Boone?"

"He's out cold by the sofa. I've given him some help as well."

Helania closed her eyes. "I swear, I didn't know it was coming. The needing."

Was she making any sense at all? She felt like she was babbling.

"From what I understand," the doctor said, "it is not always possible for you all to guess the timing of it. And Butch tells me that you've been dealing with a lot of stress. That can throw things off as well."

"You're not a vampire?"

"No, I'm not."

Oh, of course. How else could the female have come here during the day. Wait . . . it was daytime, wasn't it?

Whatever. It did not matter.

"I should have been smarter." Helania closed her eyes. "I should have . . ."

"How about we get you to your bed? It's cold in here and that floor has to be very hard."

Was it? Given the morphine, the tiles felt as soft as feathers. Still, when the doctor offered a hand, Helania put her own into it and did her best to participate in the effort of getting her body to the vertical.

With that goal accomplished, the doctor hitched a hold around Helania's waist and supported more than half her weight as they hobbled out into the living area, the tails of the sheet dragging behind.

As they rounded the corner to enter the bedroom, she finally saw Boone. He was on the floor in front of the sofa, his arms and legs flopped in a disjointed series of angles, his torso twisted so he was half on his back, half facedown. He looked like he'd been sucker punched and had gone down hard.

"He's fine," the doctor said. "I gave him a lighter dose and he's slipped into sleep. And before you ask, I checked his vitals. He is just exhausted."

"Are you sure?"

"Yes. He fed from a Chosen just three nights ago."

*A Chosen*, Helania thought.

"It was a medical-need feed," the doctor said gently. "Not to worry. There is nothing there."

"It's not my business."

"That's for you and him to decide." The doctor smiled. "Come on, let's get you to lie down. If you faint on me, I may not be able to keep you from crashing to the floor."

Helania allowed herself to be drawn over to her mattress—which, for some reason, had been moved out of place. But what did she care. As she lay down, she knew the doctor was right to get her back on the horizontal. A wave of dizziness made the room spin, and then her body got so weak, she wondered if she'd had a stroke or something.

Staring at the wall, she thought of Boone, there on the floor, stuck with her indoors for what was no doubt going to be the longest day of their lives. Even with the doctor's kind ministrations.

At least she wasn't pregnant. As far as she knew, they hadn't had sex after the fertile time had come.

Otherwise, she would have felt even worse than she already did.

Still . . . what a mess this all was.

# TWENTY-NINE

Boone regained consciousness and was surprised to find himself on the sofa. But at least he knew where he was—Helania's apartment while she was going through her needing . . . although he did not remember getting up off the floor. Maybe he'd done it when Doc Jane had given him the second shot. Or the third.

What time was it—

"It's after midnight."

He jerked his head up. Doc Jane was sitting at Helania's kitchen table, a tablet propped open in front of her, some kind of movie playing on its little screen.

"Did I say that out loud or do you read minds?" he asked as he struggled to sit up.

Man, his shirt was more wrinkled than a map at the end of a long trip.

The doctor smiled and turned off whatever was playing. "You spoke the words."

Boone stretched and cracked his shoulder. Then he looked toward the bedroom. The door was open, but the lights were off inside so he couldn't see Helania.

"Don't worry, she's fine. I just checked on her twenty minutes ago."

With a groan, he leaned forward and plugged his elbows into his knees. "I feel like I've been hit by a truck."

"You have been. The hormone load you've been under with the opiates chaser? You're going to feel logy for a while."

"I didn't expect this."

"Neither did she." Doc Jane shook her head. "Female bodies of any species are a thing, but vampire ones? It's so unfair."

"Is it over? For her?"

"Hard to say. From what I understand, she's been under a lot of stress, and that could shorten or lengthen the course of the needing. Or she could follow the typical timeline. I will say, in the last hour there's been an improvement compared to how she was. I think the worst of it is behind her, and she'll feel a lot better in another six hours."

"Thank God."

"She will need to feed. And she has to come in for a checkup tomorrow night."

"For what?"

"To see if she's pregnant."

Boone went very, very still. "But we didn't have sex."

Doc Jane's face became professionally composed. "During the needing or at all in the last twenty-four hours?"

"Ah . . ." As he blushed, he cleared his throat. "During the needing."

"When was the last time you were with her."

He closed his eyes and reminded himself that to Doc Jane, the sexual act was part of the medical record, a biological event. But damn, he felt a little like he was confessing to a *mahmen*.

"Boone," she said quietly, "it matters. For her health and well-being, it's better that we know—although if you'd prefer that I ask her personally, I'm happy to wait until she's better able to talk to me—"

"Maybe six hours before the needing hit. At least four."

Doc Jane nodded. "Okay, then she should be checked out. If she is pregnant, she is going to need prenatal care immediately."

Boone blinked. Then blurted, "I'm going to mate her if she is."

Doc Jane's smile was steady. "Let's take this situation one step at a time. You can cross that bridge if you get to it."

◆　　◆　　◆

Helania woke up slowly. Her first thought was that the morphine must still be heavily in her system: She couldn't feel her arms or her legs, and the buoyancy of the bed was overexaggerated, as if she were in a canoe in a still body of water rather than lying on a mattress.

Turning on her side, she looked toward the open doorway of her bedroom and wondered what time it was. Whether the doctor was still in the apartment. If Boone had—

Sure as if she'd called his name, he appeared in between the jambs. He looked as wiped-out as she felt, his hair sticking up at bad angles, his shirt wrinkled to the point of ruin, his slacks hanging low on his hips as if he had lost ten pounds of water weight.

"Are you okay?" he said.

His voice was rough, and as he came in the room, she braced herself for an onslaught of painful desire.

"I think so." When her body didn't grind in on itself, she exhaled. "I'm a lot better. Where is . . ."

"Doc Jane? She had to go to the clinic. But I told her I'd call her back immediately if you needed anything."

Helania tried to sit up, and when the world spun, she debated letting that idea go. But as her equilibrium returned, she tucked the sheets around her naked body and shoved her hair out of her face.

"What time is it?" she asked.

"Four o'clock."

"In the afternoon? It only lasted three hours?"

"In the morning."

"Oh."

Boone sat on the bed carefully, as if he were trying not to put all his weight on the mattress. As they stared at each other, she felt the opposite from what the previous night at Remi's had been like with him: Instead of him being unusually easy to talk to, now she was tongue-tied worse than ever.

But she had to speak. "I'm so sorry."

He recoiled. "For what? You didn't have any control over any part of it."

Okay, so that was technically true. But as soon as she thought of what Boone had looked like, drugged on the floor in front of her sofa, she still felt responsible.

Helania stared him right in the eye. "It is important for me to say this and for you to hear it. I did not know my needing was coming. If I had, I would have sent you away or not even let you in. You need to believe me."

"Helania, I totally believe you—"

"Do you?"

Boone shook his head in confusion. "Where is this coming from? I've never doubted you about anything."

Exhaustion made her more candid than she would have been otherwise. "I just want to make sure you know I'm not trying to force you into a mating or anything."

"Whoa . . ." He leaned forward, as if he might be able to understand her better if they were closer together physically. "Why would I ever think that?"

"You're a member of the *glymera* and have money. I don't want you to think I'm looking for a free ride."

"Are you—do you remember the conversation we had last night? About how I might be poor and I asked you whether that would be a problem?"

God, he was right, she thought. Her brain . . . nothing was working right up there. And yet it was still a good point to be clear on.

"I just think things need to be said out loud."

Boone steepled his hands and rested his chin on the tips of his fingers. "Fair enough."

They sat in awkward silence for a time, and all she could think about was how she wished the night before had ended differently. If only his emergency with that human woman had lasted a little longer, daylight would have kept them apart, and then none of this would have happened.

"Doc Jane would like you to come into our clinic," he said.

Helania shook her head. "There's no need to. This isn't the first time for me. I've always been fine afterward."

"You need to be checked out."

"Why?" As he just stared at her, her thought process slowly came around. "I'm not pregnant."

"We had sex right before it hit."

"I'm not pregnant."

"You may be."

"I'm not."

As they got quiet again, she realized she was being unreasonable, but she couldn't back down. The idea that she might be responsible for another living thing? She refused to contemplate the possibility—and she felt like as long as she didn't open that door mentally, then that outcome would not be part of her destiny.

She was a hermit who could barely take care of herself. How in the world . . .

"Do you need to feed?" he asked.

Helania looked up at him. "Feed?"

As he popped his brows—like he was wondering if her mental lapse was something medically significant—she shook her head. "No, I don't have to take a vein."

"When was the last time you did?"

"Before Isobel died. She had a friend who let us take his vein, but I haven't been in touch with him since she passed."

"Eight months?"

"I don't need to more than once a year, really." God, if that wasn't shining down on how infrequently she left the damn house, she didn't know what a bright light was. "I'm fine—"

"Helania, you need to be—"

"I'm not pregnant."

"I'm not debating this with you." Boone surged to his feet. "Tomorrow at midnight, you are going to be out in front of this apartment building, where I will pick you up so we can go into the training center together."

"I don't have to be checked out—"

"You do. Because if you are pregnant, then it's my young and I am going to make sure that the both of you are taken care of on every level there is."

As he stalked out of her bedroom, Helania stared after him. She wanted to call him back, but to what end? So they could argue over something that wasn't happening? They had both just been through a version of hell, and what they needed was food, sleep, and a break. More talking was not the answer.

Besides, there was nothing to talk about.

She wasn't pregnant.

# THIRTY

Boone arrived back at his father's house—wait, it would be Marquist's house now, and he needed to remember that—in a foul mood. He hated conflict to begin with, and it turned out that that non-affinity was even more intense when it had to do with Helania.

Everything had gone badly around his departure from her.

But damn. She was so determined not to have his young that she wasn't willing to take care of herself. What the hell?

As he came stomping up through the snow, he was hoping the front door was locked again. He wanted to take his entire body and break something down with it, leaving bloodstains on the wood and bruises on his flesh.

Unfortunately, the frickin' thing opened right up.

Inside, he went straight back to the kitchen, following the dense, floury aroma of baking bread that permeated that whole wing of the house. As he passed through the polishing room and the pantry, he stopped in front of the butler's suite of rooms. Everything was open, for once, and he walked into the sitting room/office area.

Well . . . look who had moved out.

Several discarded cardboard boxes and a roll of tape were in the center of the faded Oriental rug, and a stack of leather-bound books was sitting on the armchair by the fireplace, ready for relocation. The ledgers for the household accounts were still open on the serviceable desk, the ink pot and old-fashioned pen that the head of staff had always used in their ready position on the blotter. But the sepia photographs of what he had always assumed were Marquist's sire and *mahmen* were gone. And so, too, were his personal effects from the side tables.

Going deeper inside, Boone entered the bedroom. Although he had been in the front office area before—back on the nights when he'd had to go to the butler for spending money—he had never proceeded any farther. Private space was private space. He had been taught that since birth. But given that the butler clearly was no longer butle'ing for the household, so to speak?

No reason not to look around.

The bedroom had a twin mattress on a nineteen fifties wooden frame against the far wall. The matelassé quilt was precisely arranged and folded up over the pillow. The night stand on the right had a single lamp on it, a coaster for a glass of water, and a charging stand that Boone was willing to bet had been forgotten in the rush to move up a floor and down many, many rooms to the best suite in the house.

Heading over to the bureau, he opened the top drawer. Well, what do you know. Rows of boxer shorts and undershirts. Next one was full of starched button-downs. On the bottom were a hundred pairs of bundled black socks.

Marquist had left his butler uniform behind.

To confirm this, even though it didn't really matter to Boone and he already was sure of the answer, he crossed the bare wooden floorboards and opened the narrow closet door. Sure enough, there were about ten different black suits. Some overcoats. A heavy black robe.

Probably leaving it all for the next hire. And what a line in the sand, huh.

Once the staff, now on the hiring side of things as the estate's owner.

Boone stood there, staring into the closet, for a long while, and he supposed he was waiting for some kind of anger to take over. It really seemed like he should care more about this extraordinary turn of events.

Especially given the fact that he might just have the next generation of his bloodline to think about.

The longer he considered everything, however, the more he questioned what he had ever gotten out of this august background of his. Sure, the money had been nice, but none of it had been his. And the house was fine, if you liked museums and stage sets that were designed to impress. But he couldn't say that there had been many other benefits.

Cursing, he left the set of rooms and went out to the kitchen. As he entered, the *doggen* who were busy preparing Last Meal stopped everything they were doing, each one of them freezing in mid-chop, mid-stir, mid-mix.

That was when the sadness hit him. He had known these wonderful, loyal males and females all of his life. Some had been hired by his *mahmen*. A couple had been inherited from his grandparents. And they were staring at him in a combination of panic and mourning.

"It's all right." He smiled at them in turn. "It's all going to be fine. He's going to have to keep you on, so nothing will change for you."

Thomat, the chef, lowered his blade. "May we prepare something for you, my Lord."

*My Lord.* The nomenclature that referred to the head male of the house.

"Thomat, it's not like that." Boone walked forward and stopped opposite the *doggen,* the counter that separated them a metaphor for their different stations. "But I thank you for the honor. You have been . . . all of you have been so wonderful to me."

"This is your house, my Lord." Thomat shook his head. "No one else's. Now, it would be our pleasure to serve you."

"I'm not even a guest here. I've been ordered by the King to stay under this roof for the next thirteen nights. So I will serve myself."

When he offered his palm as a measure of respect, the *doggen* stared at it. Then Thomat stepped back from his side of the counter . . . and bowed so low, his toque nearly brushed the lamb he'd been trimming.

As Boone looked around, he noticed several other members of the staff had come in. And every single *doggen* was bowing to him as well.

Closing his eyes, he wanted to tell them they were going to have to move on. But he didn't have the strength. Still, he was surprised by how touched he was by the show of loyalty and respect.

It warmed the heart, it truly did.

◆    ◆    ◆

Helania passed the night hours cleaning everything she could get her hands on. She started with her bed and her towels, stripping everything and filling her washing machine with a big load. Then she hit the bathroom with the Scrubbing Bubbles, getting down on her hands and knees and all but rubbing through the layers of tile to the frame of the building. Next on the elbow grease docket was her kitchen. She emptied out her refrigerator, took the shelves to the sink, and sponged them with soap and hot water until they gleamed. She also handwashed the floor, the fronts of the cabinets, and all the drawers.

She even took out the tray the silverware was in and vacuumed what was underneath. When that didn't go far enough, she put the forks and the knives and the spoons on the counter and wiped out the tray itself.

In the sitting area, she pulled the duvet cover off the sofa. Threw that in the wash. She vacuumed the rug and then went around and reorganized her needlepoint pillow supplies. When she got out the step stool and Swiffer'd a cobweb from the corner up at the ceiling, she was ashamed of how long it had been since she had really paid attention to the place.

It had been well before Isobel had passed.

Had been *killed*, she corrected herself. As she had Boone.

Sometime around dawn, she ran out of steam. Sitting on the bare sofa and listening to the dryer do its business on the duvet, she fought against emotions that were just below the surface.

Isobel would know how to handle this, she thought as she put her hand on her flat stomach.

If her sister were alive . . . Isobel would know what to do. About the possibility of pregnancy. About the situation with Boone. About these tears that seemed determined to break through her self-control.

"Why did you have to go?" she said hoarsely.

The instant the words left her, her eyes shot to the cloak she wore to hide herself at Pyre. And it was then that anger simmered as she realized she should have been out looking for her sister's killer.

Who had not been found yet.

Helania looked around at her sparkling-clean apartment. One night of losing focus was allowable, but no more than that. She was not pregnant, and no matter how protective Boone was feeling, she was going back to work down at that club tomorrow evening.

She had her dead to *ahvenge*. And sitting around and being weepy and ridiculous was not going to serve that larger purpose.

Reaching into the pocket of her sweatshirt, she took out her phone. She had silenced the ringer because she'd needed time to get her head straight—which had evidently translated into her getting her living quarters straight.

As she turned the unit over, she braced herself to see a bunch of notifications that Boone had called or texted, and she wasn't sure how she felt about that. Part of her wanted to talk to him. Part of her didn't—

No calls from him. No texts, either.

Staring at the blank screen, she was struck by a hollow ache in her chest. But what could she expect? She'd wanted space.

He was giving it to her.

# THIRTY-ONE

The following evening, Helania leveled the muzzle of her nine-millimeter at a target far down the gun range. She was in shooting dock 4, ear protection on, an open box of bullets on the counter in front of her, an empty one on the concrete ground by her feet.

Focusing on the center of the bull's-eye—which radiated out from the outline of a torso—she steadied her arms in front of her and squeezed off one . . . two . . . three . . . fourfivesix—

"—closing in fifteen minutes. We are closing in fifteen minutes. Please begin to pack up now."

Lowering the gun, she hit the switch on the cubicle's wall, and the target rushed to her like a dog called home, its bottom bending back against the draft created by the speed. When the heavy paper was in front of her, she unclipped it and stared at the holes she had made.

All of them were concentrated in the center of the concentric circles, off by only one ring . . . two at the most.

"You're damn good with a gun."

As she looked over at the attendant who'd approached her, she marveled once again at how the mufflers on her ears managed to dim the gunshots while allowing voices to come through.

Stripping off her ear protection, she said, "I'm okay."

"Better than most."

She smiled because she felt like she had to, and actually, she had nothing against the guy. He was the nice older one who wore a US Veteran hat and always had on some kind of concert T-shirt from the eighties. With baggy blue jeans and a weathered face that had her thinking he was in his late sixties, early seventies, he looked like he was well familiar with manual labor, long hours, and AC/DC.

"You want me to walk you to your car?" he said. "It's late."

"I'll be all right, but thank you."

"Keep your gun loaded and out. I'll watch you on the monitor like I always do. Nice girl like you, I'm glad you know how to shoot."

With a curt nod, he limped back down the lineup of vacant docks. She was pretty sure he was missing one leg and had a prosthetic, but she hadn't asked. And she did appreciate his concern for her. Usually.

Tonight, it made her uncomfortable, although not because she was threatened by him in any way. She just wondered why she got special attention. Was it because he sensed a weakness in her?

Somehow, she didn't want that question to be answered. Inner strength was very important to her all of a sudden.

Holstering her gun at her hip, she packed up the unused shot in her nylon bag, threw out the empty box of bullets, and pulled her parka on. On her way to the exit, she went by the glassed-in kiosk where the attendant sat and waved at him. He pointed to a grainy black-and-white TV that sported an image of the parking lot and gave her a thumbs-up. She nodded in return.

Outside, she walked over to a ten-year-old Toyota truck. She and Isobel had bought the thing new by pooling their savings. Though they could always dematerialize places, vehicles—especially those with a flatbed—were really handy for big shops, when you were moving, and on those rare occasions when you simply felt like driving somewhere.

As she got behind the wheel, she hit the clutch, put the gearshift in neutral, and started the engine. Out on the road, she headed for home . . . and wondered whether she was going to end up there. So many detours: She could go to the grocery. She could hit the twenty-four-hour Target for cleaning supplies. She could just drive around until she needed gas.

At which point, she could get some gas and keep driving around.

Yet she knew Boone was waiting for her and wouldn't leave until she showed up at her apartment. Even though he still hadn't reached out, he was indeed the kind of male who, if he made an appointment with someone, always showed up. Well, except for that diner thing, and he'd certainly had a valid reason for missing that meal.

He would be in front of her building, just as he'd said.

God . . . she really wanted to drive away, drive far, far away. The idea of going to some clinic to be poked and prodded at had no appeal whatsoever, and she was struggling with the balance of interests. It was her body, but Boone wasn't wrong. If she were pregnant, half of what was inside of her was his.

Part of him.

So he had some rights in all this.

Not that she was pregnant, of course. What were the chances, really. Sure, they had had sex beforehand, but it had been hours before.

At least four. Maybe six.

Shit.

Ten minutes later, Helania pulled into the parking lot around the back of her building. Getting out, she shouldered her nylon bag and walked through the packed snow to the rear entrance. She used her key to get in, and then took a right and went down the stairwell to the basement floor.

As she bottomed out on the lower level, she opened the steel door—

Boone was standing beside her apartment's unimpressive, nothing-special entrance: His big body was leaning against the wall, his hands in the pockets of his leathers, his dark head lowered. He came to attention the split second he noticed her, and given the way he straightened his leather jacket, it was obvious he was feeling as awkward as she was.

"Hi," she said as she came forward.

"I didn't know if you were . . ." He cleared his throat. "Hi."

"You didn't know if I was going to show up?"

"The car is waiting for us outside."

"I'd like to drop my stuff off."

His nostrils flared. "You were shooting."

"Yes." She frowned. "It's important to keep my skills up."

"I'm not suggesting it isn't. I'm in a training program, remember. The Brothers stress all the time how critical practice is."

As they stared at each other, she remembered sitting across from him at Remi's, the conversation flowing so smoothly that it had been like air in her lungs: easy and life-sustaining. And yet now they were here, with nothing but jagged syllables and ragged silences between them.

Helania dropped her shoulder bag and crossed her arms over her chest. It was a while before she could find the right words.

"I don't know . . ." She took a deep breath and looked into his eyes. "I don't know how to get back to where we were. I've lost us. And even as I say that, I know it's ridiculous because it's not like we've been together for long at all. So what exactly am I not getting back to? Still . . . I miss where we were and I hate where we are."

Things got wavy as the tears came, and she cursed, thinking of the target range attendant. No wonder people assumed she needed to be taken care of left and right. She was a goddamn mess—

"Helania. Come here."

She put her hand out. "No. No, I don't want to lean on you. I don't want . . . I need to stand on my own. For the first time in my life, I want to be strong."

"It's not an either/or, you know. You can be strong *and* rely on your friends and family."

"I'm not so sure about that. And even more to the point, I'm done with ruining other people's lives. Isobel watched over me for decades, and you know what? I've been thinking a lot today, and I've been wondering what else she could have accomplished in her too-short life if she'd freed up all those hours. Would she have moved in with her lover? Mated him and had young of her own? Would she have not even met him because ten years ago, instead of buying a truck with me, she'd bought a house with another male, a different one, and forged a future with him? There were a lot of paths she could have taken, but instead, she wasted years on me, years that, as it turned out, she did not have to spare."

"You can't blame yourself for what happened to her," Boone said. "And you have no idea what the future would have held one way or the other."

"It was my fault. Those wasted years were my fault."

Boone frowned. "No offense, but what does this have to do with you and me?"

"If I'm with young, you're going to want to get mated."

"Of course I will. How could I not?"

Helania shook her head. "But I don't want that. I don't want you falling on another sword of duty."

"It's not like that."

"Really? You think? How is my being pregnant any different from an arranged mating?" As he gritted his teeth, she could tell by the set of his chin that he knew she was right. "You always do the proper thing. I get it. But here's the issue. If I ever get mated, I'd like to think . . ." Pain lanced through her chest. "I'd like to be chosen out of love, not obligation—and please do not say 'I love you' right now. Those three words are sacred, not a panacea because you don't want to hurt someone's feelings or ignore the reality that you and I find ourselves in. We are essentially strangers, and you know this. And yet we're facing something that could change both of our lives forever."

He shook his head and cursed. "You make it sound like a car accident."

"It is one."

Abruptly, he rubbed his face. "Well, then, let's go to the fucking clinic. Because isn't that what one does when one is in a goddamn car accident?"

Helania looked away sharply. And then the words she'd been holding in broke out of her. "I don't want to be pregnant."

"Yes," Boone muttered, "I believe you've made it very clear that you do not want my young. But be that as it may, Doc Jane is going to check you out and we are going to do whatever else she says because we're adults in an adult situation of our own creation."

"You didn't know I was going to go through my needing. So this is on me."

"Like you could control when it came? And besides, you did go through it, and I was with you right beforehand. And I'm not arguing about that or anything else about going to the clinic anymore."

The bitterness in his voice brought her eyes back to him. Boone's face was taut, his brows down, his unfocused stare trained somewhere in front of him.

The sight of him looking so unhappy made her feel even worse, and she knew, if she kept this attitude up, she was just going to destroy them both. Maybe right here and now.

Besides . . . perhaps it was all over nothing.

"Fine," she said, "gimme a minute and we'll go."

Boone just nodded without looking at her. "I'll meet you in the car. It's out front."

◆    ◆    ◆

Boone went out the back way of the apartment building so he could get some fresh air. As he walked around to where Fritz was waiting in the Brotherhood's black Mercedes, his chest hurt so badly, he wondered whether emotional pain could cause a heart attack—and then didn't particularly care about the answer.

Because hey, if he dropped dead in a snowbank, at least he wouldn't feel this shitty anymore.

As he rounded the corner and saw the car, he was tempted to tell Fritz to drive away and then text Helania that he wasn't going to make her do anything she didn't want. After which he would go jump off a bridge and take a nice long swim in the Hudson.

And following that, maybe he'd find some alcohol.

What he was *not* going to do was take out his frustrations by mutilating a slayer or a human. While he'd been tossing and turning all day, determined not to call or text Helania because it was clear she wanted space, he'd been haunted by his own actions in that alley. The fact that that particular man, that assailant, had more than deserved what had come his way was beside the point—and the terrifying thing was the question that Boone had refused to voice to himself.

But God, what if the man had *not* deserved it? What if Boone had crossed paths with an innocent human who just happened to be out walking the streets?

He liked to believe he wouldn't have done anything. He *wanted* to believe he would have kept going until he found a *lesser* or a shadow.

Except he didn't really trust himself on any of that, and it made him wonder if maybe Helania knew something about him that he didn't. Maybe that was why she didn't want his young.

Approaching the Mercedes, he shook his head as Fritz got out from behind the wheel. "No, I've got my door. Thank you."

The butler's face fell, sure as if Boone had called into question his *mahmen's* worth.

"Oh . . ." Boone rubbed his aching head. " Oh, okay. Sure."

"Right away, sire!"

For an older male, the butler could move quick—then again, he seemed to do a lot of things fast. On the way over here, he drove as if traffic laws and speed limits were so other people were less in his way.

"Where is your female?" the butler inquired politely as he held open the rear door.

*I don't know where she's gone,* Boone thought to himself. *Even when she's right in front of me.*

"She's coming."

Hopefully.

A moment later, she did. Just as he settled in the far seat, Helania walked out the building's front door. She hesitated when she saw the uniformed butler and the S 65, but then she squared her shoulders and walked over on the shoveled paths. She was in jeans and the parka she'd worn the night they went to Remi's, and her boots were ankle-high and well-used. With her hair pulled back and no makeup on, she seemed fresh and natural.

As well as someone he needed to protect—and he knew that she didn't want that from him.

"Greetings, mistress," the butler said with a wide smile. Then he bowed lower. "It is my pleasure to be of service. I am Fritz Perlmutter."

"Um . . . thank you?" she murmured.

"Please," Fritz said cheerfully, "take a seat and we shall proceed with alacrity."

As Helania got in, Boone looked away. "This won't take long."

Fritz jumped in behind the wheel and turned around to them. "I shall put the partition up now! Please attach your seat belts and let us go."

While the black glass lifted, panels also came up on all the windows, blocking the views outside the car. Great. He couldn't pretend to be look-ing at the snowy landscape. But this was part of the security around the Brotherhood's training center. Someday, maybe he and the other trainees would get unfettered access. It hadn't happened yet, however, and even if it had, Helania was not cleared to know where the facility was.

Trying to do something with his hands—other than compulsively crack his knuckles—Boone pulled his belt around his chest, and as he clicked it into place, there was a lurch and the subtle roar of a very pow-erful engine.

So, how about those Mets, he thought to himself.

"By the way," he said, "Butch has set up an evidence room at the training center. After you're finished at the clinic, he'd like you to stop by and see him."

"Okay."

As his phone vibrated in his leather jacket, he wanted to thank the Scribe Virgin for the valid distraction, but as he took it out, he frowned. Rochelle had texted him, but he'd have to look at the message later. He couldn't focus on anything right now.

"Were you able to stay at your house during the day?" Helania said.

Boone's heart pounded at the unexpected sound of her voice, and he glanced at her reflection in the divider's pane of smooth glass. "Yes. I slept there. The King gave me a total of fourteen nights before I can go elsewhere."

"Where will you stay after that?"

"Craeg and Paradise offered me their spare bedroom. But I'll find something on my own."

There was a time, little more than twenty-four hours before, when he would have wondered if he could stay with her. That window of opportunity had closed, however. And as she herself had said, he didn't know how to get back to that space.

"I'm really sorry about your sire—"

Boone jacked around and raised his voice. "Okay. We need to stop with the bullshit here. You and I have waaaay too much going on between us for you to be making any comments about my living situation or my goddamn dead father. I realize I am not handling this well, but to be honest with you, I don't understand what's wrong. I honestly don't. I don't get this mood you're in, but frankly, that fact that I do not understand it is just a reminder that I really don't know you. We had fantastic chemistry, and I was really looking forward to exploring that with you for like . . . well, for however long it lasted. But I don't get this and I don't get you, and it's doing my fucking nut in. So excuse me if I can't make small talk right now, especially about big things in my life."

He expected her to yell back at him. Accuse him of being some kind of emotional thug. Rail against the fact that she could be pregnant—again.

Instead, she just nodded. "That's fair. You're right."

Boone looked away to the blacked-out window next to him. As he felt the car make a wide turn, and sunk into the bucket seat from acceleration to a fast speed, he knew they were getting on the Northway.

"I was hoping you'd yell back," he heard himself say.

"I'm sorry to disappoint you."

After a moment, he felt a soft touch on his arm and glanced over at her. "What."

"If I can't take care of myself, how can I take care of a young."

Boone blinked. "What?"

Helania retracted her hand and tucked it into her thigh. "I don't want to go get checked out at the clinic because I don't want to find out I'm pregnant. And I don't want to be pregnant because I'm terrified of being responsible for a young."

Opening his mouth to say something, he shut himself up as she started talking in a rush.

"I don't have the skills necessary to cultivate friendships. I get scared to go out by myself to the supermarket. I live in terror of the humans upstairs lighting the building on fire during the day and me not knowing what to do to avoid the sunlight. I haven't slept well for eight months because the truth is, I hate living alone. And I worry all the time about the fact that there's no one for me to call if I need something." She shook her head and looked down at her hands. "That is *not* the kind of parent a young needs. That is *not* the kind of person who is strong enough to be a *mahmen*."

Helania's eyes swung back to his own. "And you're right. I am in a ridiculous mood. Maybe it's the hormones still working their way out of my system, but even if that's a part of it, the needing stuff doesn't change the reality I'm in. I mean, God, I still don't know who killed my sister— all I have on that front is that whoever it was might have done it to another female. I am just . . . I've fucking had it, Boone, with everything—including myself. This is supposed to be the era of girl power, but you know what? I'm the opposite of a strong, resilient female, and I hate it. I *hate* it and I cannot get away from that reality because everywhere I go, there I am."

Boone blinked again. Then he cleared his throat. "I think you give yourself a helluva lot less credit than you deserve. There aren't many people, male or female, who would go to Pyre every night and do what you've been doing."

"I wasn't in time to save that other female's life."

"But you didn't get yourself killed in the process, either. And you brought the Brothers into it. You went where you had to go."

"It's not enough," she said, her voice cracking. "I couldn't save that female. I couldn't save Isobel."

Reaching out, he brushed a tear from her cheek and wanted to pull her into his arms. "You're doing what you can. You're helping with the investigation."

"I'm going back there. To the club. You need to know that."

Boone inclined his head. "I know. I never thought you wouldn't."

"Even if I'm pregnant."

As his gut twisted in a knot, he refused to let his fear show—or allow the wave of protective aggression he felt to get any airtime. He was all too familiar with what it was like to live under the overhang of someone who thought they knew better than you did when it came to your own damn life. He was not going to share that wealth with Helania just because he was a male and physically stronger than her.

"As long as it's medically safe," he said, "I wouldn't try to stop you."

"You mean that?"

"Yes, I do." He leaned in toward her and wished he could take her hand. But he did not want to crowd her. "That's how much I trust you. That's how much I believe in you. You are braver than you realize and stronger than you know, and I support you."

As he spoke the words, he realized they were the dead honest truth. And sometimes, to have faith in yourself, you had to have someone light that path for you. He'd learned that from the Brothers. From his fellow trainees.

"I thought you were going to want to me to stay home," she whispered.

"And then you would fail your sister, right?"

Her eyes shimmered with tears. "I'm already having so much trouble with living with guilt. Adding to what I'm carrying right now by giving up on finding Isobel's killer? I can't fathom it."

"Makes sense to me." Boone shook his head as he considered his own past. "Look, I've seen what the *glymera* turns females into. I've lived in that nightmare. I wouldn't want someone lording over me—why would I think you'd want that? As I said, provided it's medically safe, I have no right to turn you into a piece of furniture just because you're pregnant—nor would I want to."

The softening started in her eyes, the hostile, separating light dimming. Then her features relaxed, followed by her shoulders and the arms she'd crossed over her chest.

"Thank you," she said.

"I'm just speaking the truth as I know it." He *so* wanted to pull her into his arms, but stayed where he was. "And I request only one thing."

"What's that?"

"Next time, just ask me what I think instead of dub my opinion in with what you hope isn't true. I promise, I will always be honest, and maybe you won't like some of my positions on things, but at least we'll be arguing over real differences instead of hypothetical ones."

Helania took a deep breath. "Do you remember when you took me to Remi's?"

"That was like, three nights ago," he said with a short laugh. "So yes, I do. Although even if it were three years prior, I can assure you I would remember every second of being with you."

Helania flushed, and the color was lovely on her face.

"When I told you I'm not good at this"—she motioned between them—"I really was being truthful. I can't relate well to people."

Boone shrugged. "Is anyone good at it, though? Especially if attraction's involved."

"I don't know. Craeg and Paradise seemed totally in lockstep."

"Oh, my God, see, you're catching them now. They had a huge amount of conflict in the beginning."

"Really?"

"Yup. And hey, you could ask them about it, but they probably wouldn't get the story right. True love, when it clicks, is the great eraser. All the conflict and work to get a relationship up off the ground just disappears when people hit smooth sailing." Boone shrugged again. "But what do I know."

Falling quiet, he let his head ease back on the rest and closed his eyes. He was nowhere close to drifting off, but maybe she'd figure he was sleeping—

Helania's hand snuck into his own.

And the instant she made the contact, he looked over at her. She, too, had laid her head back, and her breathing was even and slow. But she wasn't asleep, either.

He knew this because as he squeezed her palm . . . she moved her head over in his direction and then leaned against the outside of his shoulder.

"Helania?" he said softly.

"Hmm?"

"Just so you know, you don't have to be good at relationships with me. Be yourself. I'll be myself, and as long as we keep talking? We should be okay."

Her lids opened, her lashes raising up to reveal a light in her eyes that he had never seen before. "I would really like us to do that."

"Talk some more?" he murmured as he brushed a stray hair out of her face.

"Be okay," she said softly. "I would really like us . . . to be okay."

# THIRTY-TWO

Helania dozed as they traveled, going in and out of a light sleep. It was a relief to have no dreams. She was frightened of what might come out of her subconscious. But at least she felt as though the air had been cleared to some degree with Boone.

When a series of stops and goes began, she sat up from where she'd leaned against him.

"Are we getting close?" she said.

Boone shifted around in his seat. "Yes."

Helania cracked her neck and stretched her arms. "So this is where you go for training."

"Yes, it is. The facility is pretty hardcore. They have everything."

"Well, it is the Brotherhood's."

She was aware that they were chitchatting, avoiding a relapse into any emotional depths. Still, she felt a lot better after having spoken her worst fear out loud, and she marveled at how much vocalizing it to someone who she knew cared about her helped.

And now she was able to reconnect with Boone so much better. Especially given that she knew he wasn't going to stop her down at Pyre.

Provided the doctors didn't have a big opinion about things. Dearest Virgin Scribe . . . what if she were pregnant?

"Thank you," she said, "for letting me get all that out."

As he looked over at her, she drank in the handsome planes of his face . . . and wondered how they would appear on a little boy with her coloring and his body type.

"I will always make time for you."

Putting her hand on her belly under her parka, she thought . . . well, that statement was kind of an I-love-you, wasn't it.

The Mercedes bumped to a stop and stayed in place, the engine sounds cutting off sharply. And then the butler with the hangdog face and the California-sunshine smile opened her door.

"Mistress, we have arrived!" As if it were a miracle and a music concert and a sporting event all rolled up into one. "Welcome!"

As she got out, she smiled back at him. "Thank you so much."

He bowed deeply and then frowned as Boone scooted across the seat and unfurled his huge shoulders and towering height out of the back.

"I would have come around to your side, sire."

"Oh, I know. Thank you, Fritz, for bringing us here."

There was a moment of consternation as if the *doggen* were still stuck on the door-open fail. But then he snapped back into the happy.

"Allow me to show you in," the butler said before walking toward a heavy steel door. "May I please get you some victuals?"

As if they would be doing him a favor to ask for something to eat.

While Boone and the butler talked, Helania glanced around. They were in some kind of underground parking area that had been built to downtown, commercial-grade standards, and the place was not empty. There was a bus with blacked-out windows parked across the way, and a couple of cars lined up, including a very fancy low-slung Audi of some description that had snow marks down its sleek sides.

Wow. She couldn't believe anyone had taken something like that out in the wintry streets. Hardcore, indeed—

"Helania?" Boone said. "Do you want anything to eat?"

"Oh, no, sorry." She shook herself back to attention. "I'm fine, thank you."

As the butler held the heavy panel open with ease, she decided he was heartier than his age suggested. And as she entered the facility, she was not prepared for what she found. When Boone had said the place was top-notch, she had assumed the training center would be sizable and kitted out well. But . . . wow. A long, long corridor stretched out to the other side of the world, as far as she could tell, and radiating off it were countless doors, some of which were open. As they walked along, she saw classrooms worthy of a major university, and what looked like interrogation rooms. In the air, she caught a very faint whiff of chlorine, which suggested they had a pool somewhere close by, and as the butler stopped at the open doorway of a professional-grade medical examination room, she could hear the clinking of weights and the bouncing of basketballs off in the distance.

"I shall go summon Doctor Jane," Fritz said with a deep bow. "And I shall await to be summoned for your return trip."

After both she and Boone thanked the butler again, and Fritz walked off with a skip in his step, they looked into the exam room. There was a patient table in the center under the medical lights, a thin sheet of paper pulled down over its padded surface, a pair of stirrups at the ready. There was also a lamp with a crane neck off to one side.

Internal exams were so much fun.

"What are they going to do to me," she said aloud.

"Not much today," came a response.

Helania pivoted and instantly recognized the female who spoke. It was the doctor she'd mistaken for an angel, and she was totally relieved that that was who'd be seeing her.

"Welcome to our humble abode," the doctor said as she came over and offered her hand. "I'm Jane. Let's get this over with quickly so you can go back to your regularly scheduled programming."

Helania shook that palm and took note of the short blond hair and dark green eyes. Yes, she remembered the kindness the doctor had shown, even if she had not been aware of many specifics.

"Thank you for being so good to me," she said to the female. "I am very grateful."

A reassuring hand came down on her shoulder. "I just wanted to help. You were really not feeling well."

The doctor greeted Boone with a hug and then indicated the way into the exam room. "All we're doing tonight is checking vitals and taking some blood to assess your hormone levels. Then you're free to go."

Eyeing those tucked-in stirrups, Helania was beyond grateful. "Terrific."

As she entered the room, she took off her parka and put it on a side chair, then hopped up onto the table. When Boone stayed out in the corridor, she frowned.

"Aren't you going to come in with me?"

◆　　◆　　◆

Boone sat and watched everything from one of the three chairs that were lined up against the wall across from the examination table. Blood pressure. Heart rate and oxygen stats. Temperature. Stethoscope to the chest. Meanwhile, the two females were talking about needlepoint the whole time. How Helania had gotten into it; how Doc Jane's mother had done it; where to get the best canvases and yarn.

It was a good thing that neither of them was looking for commentary from him on the subject. For one, he didn't know from knitting— or needlepointing, he guessed it was. Two, it was so much easier to hide the fact that he was hyperventilating if he didn't open his piehole. Oh, and three, he wasn't sure he even had a voice.

Being in this medical environment reminded him of all the risks of pregnancies, especially the ones that came at the end. Vampire birthing beds were especially dangerous for both the *mahmen* and the young. So many died, and it was just dawning on him that Helania would be subject to those terrifying mortality rates.

From an evolutionary point of view, no wonder the needing was such a thing. Without those intense cravings, he couldn't imagine females would ever be willing to volunteer for pregnancy.

"Okay," Doc Jane said, "now I have to poke you a little."

Boone swallowed hard and threw out a hand to Helania's parka, which had been placed in the chair next to his—as if that would somehow translate into him helping support her directly. But like the vitals part of things, it was so no-drama. Doc Jane brought a little rolling tray over, inspected the inside of one of Helania's elbows . . . then it was a case of wipe-down, needle insertion, and the tube's belly was filled. Doc Jane then retracted the tiny steel sword and covered the hole with a cotton ball. Crooking Helania's arm up, she took the tube and affixed a printed label on it.

"Will you . . ." Helania cleared her throat. "Will we know the results right now?"

"No. It's too early." The doctor held up the vial. "This will give us a descending baseline, however. We'll need you back in forty-eight hours. If your hormone levels go up from here, then you're pregnant. If they continue to go down, you're not."

"And what happens if I am?"

"Then we schedule you for regular monitoring. Or, if it's easier, I'll transfer the care over to Havers so you don't need to be escorted in here for your appointments."

"I don't want to inconvenience anyone—"

"She'll be treated here," Boone heard himself say.

"I'm happy to do it either way." Doc Jane smiled at Helania. "I think what's important is that you choose how you'd like to handle things. I won't be offended, I promise. The way I see it, there is so much outside of your control during pregnancy that it's important to grab the reins when you can."

"I agree with Boone. I'd rather do it here."

Boone nodded. "Good. That's decided."

"Then it would be my honor to see you through to birth if you are pregnant." Doc Jane nodded to the door. "Now, I understand Butch is waiting to see you all? You're free to go, and I'll see you about this time the night after tomorrow if that works for your schedule."

"It works. But will you call me with the result from tonight?" Helania asked.

"Sure. But again, whatever number it is won't tell us anything until we have something to compare it to."

"Okay." Helania hopped off the table and came over for her coat. "Thank you."

"I'll be in touch," the doctor said as she opened the door and waited for them with a patient smile.

Boone handed Helania's parka over, and then they were out in the corridor and he was leading the way back toward the schooling part of things. "We're going down here."

As they walked along, he wanted to put his arm around her. "Are you okay with how that went?"

"I really like Doc Jane."

"Me, too."

"It's just a waiting game now."

They fell quiet again, but he was sure they were both thinking the same thing: Holy crap, what if they had created a new life? And she had to carry it safely to term?

The implications seemed as vast as the galaxy, and it was a relief to stop in front of the door to one of the interrogation rooms.

"I think this is the right one." He knocked. "Butch?"

When someone answered on the other side, Boone opened the way in. One look to the right at the photographs that had been put on the wall and he recoiled. Behind him, Helania likewise gasped.

Over at the table, Butch looked up from a pad of notes. "Oh. Sorry. Should have given you a heads-up."

Boone went over and stood in front of the photographs from the morgue, his size guaranteeing that nothing of the images showed.

"We don't have to talk here," Butch said.

"No." Helania shook her head. "I will not ignore this or pretend any of it didn't happen."

As she approached the wall, Boone didn't budge, but she wasn't looking at what he was blocking. She was focused on the center portion that was marked with a roman numeral II. Reaching up, she touched a piece of paper with her sister's name on it.

"How you doing with Isobel's death?" Butch asked quietly. "And I'm sorry to be blunt about it."

Boone opened his mouth to stop the line of questioning, but Helania got there first. Looking over her shoulder at the Brother, she said, "I'm glad you're up front. And as for handling it? Not much better than I did when I first found out."

"I know where you're at."

"Yes, you've seen a lot of homicides, I imagine."

"I lost my sister, too."

Boone looked at the Brother sharply. "I didn't know that."

Butch leaned back in his chair, balancing on its two hind legs. Tapping a blue Bic pen on his thigh, he focused on the layout he'd made. "My sister was abducted, raped, and murdered, and I was the last one who saw her as she drove off with the boys who did it to her. I was twelve years old. She was fifteen."

Helania walked over to the table. When she tried to pull a chair out, she frowned.

"They're screwed down," Butch said as he righted himself. "I have a screwdriver—"

"No, it's okay." Helania slipped into the space between the table and the seat, her back to the photographs and notes. "Can you tell me . . . can you tell me about how you dealt with her loss?"

Butch now tapped the pen on the pad he'd been scribbling on, its 8½ by 11 inches filled with blue crosses, arrows that jumped from sentence to sentence, and doodles of . . . golf carts?

"I'll be honest, I'm still not over it. When I think about Janie, it's just what you said. Fresh as it was the instant I found out. It takes a lot of time before you don't wallow in grief every second of the day and night. More time than you want it to. I promise you, though, one evening you're going to wake up, and you'll be in front of the mirror brushing your teeth . . . and you'll realize that you actually slept through the day and you don't feel like you're in someone else's skin."

Boone went over and joined them. The experience of wedging his body into that landlocked chair wasn't half as smooth as it had been for Helania, but he made himself fit.

"All death is hard," Butch murmured to the pair of them, "but it's so much worse when you feel like you could have done something to stop it."

Boone nodded. "Amen to that."

"You truly feel responsible for your father's death?" Helania asked.

"I tried to get him to stay home that night." Boone pictured his sire clear as day in his mind, Altamere sitting at that desk in his study and glaring as Boone tried to reason with him. "But he insisted, and the thing that I worry about . . . the thing that haunts me? It's what if I . . ." Boone cleared his throat. "What if I wanted this to happen? What if I . . . wanted him to be gone, so I didn't try hard enough to keep him away from those people?"

"But you did talk to him, right?" Helania said. "You did warn him about not going."

"Maybe I could have done more."

Butch shook his head. "I was there when you came to speak to Wrath. I saw the conviction on your face when you went on about your dad. If I could play my mental tapes back to you? You'd see what I did—a good son trying to do the right thing privately and then coming to his King when he'd taken things as far as he could on the DL. And the reality is, if you hadn't told us what was going on, the Brotherhood wouldn't have been there and more people would have died that night."

"What happened?" Helania asked.

As Boone gave the details factually, he wished he could believe what the Brother said. Doubts lingered, however—and the same appeared to be true for the other two.

They had all lost a family member in a violent way, and each one of them felt responsible.

Looking around the table, Boone felt like a little club was meeting in this room, and how apropos that the mountings on that wall were about death.

After a quiet stretch, Butch looked past Helania's shoulder at what he'd put up. "You know, as someone who's walking the same path you guys are on, but who's a little further along? All I can say is that it's a process, and the only way through the worst of the pain is putting one foot in front of the other. There are stages, but the bitch of it is is that you never really get to the end. You never stop missing them. The stuff at the beginning is the worst, though. You're both going to be looking under all kinds of stones and searching for answers for a while. What you have to do is ride it through and don't self-medicate. I tried that for three decades, and drinking and using drugs didn't do shit except give me cirrhosis of the liver. It's better to do the work and get it over with than put your head in the sand and drag the shit out forever."

"I miss Isobel so much," Helania said.

Without thinking, Boone reached across and took her hand. When he realized what he'd done, he wondered if she'd prefer he not touch her. But instead, she held on to his palm hard. As their eyes met, he felt a communion with her, although it was sad the kind of territory that they had in common.

It would have been so much better if it had been . . . needlepoint, for example.

Still, he was grateful to know he wasn't alone, and that she was with him. The Brother as well.

Ducking his thumb under, Boone deliberately stroked the fine network of scars that marked Helania's palm, leftovers of her work with that shovel.

She offered him a sad smile. Then she focused on the Brother. "So do you have anything new?"

The Brother tilted back in his chair again and crossed his arms. His hazel eyes once again narrowed on the photographs, the articles, the notes on that wall.

"No," he muttered. "We're going cold at this point. But Boone said you'd reached out to some of your sister's people on social media?"

"I can give you the sign in details to Isobel's stuff so you can see for yourself?" Helania shrugged. "Unfortunately, I don't think there's anything super helpful. Maybe you'll notice something I missed, though. You're the professional."

"Something has to break," Butch said under his breath. "We just have to catch a break before someone else gets hurt."

# THIRTY-THREE

As Helania recited the sign in and password to her sister's Facebook page, she watched the Brother Butch take down the details on a fresh sheet of paper. She never would have guessed that he knew first-hand what she was going through with Isobel's killing, and the fact that they had both lost siblings made it possible for her to give him free rein with anything that might help him.

They were a kind of kin. By bloodshed.

"There's a computer in the office down here," he said. "I'll sign in on it after you all leave."

"Can I do anything to help?" she asked.

"Just let me know if you hear from anyone on a different platform. All we can do is keep digging until something turns up. It always does. Unfortunately, the revelations are on God's time, not man's, and He makes us wait."

"I don't know when I'm returning to rotation," Boone said. "But I'll go back to Pyre and keep an eye on things until then."

"We'll add you to the monitoring list, son. Beginning with midnight tonight, we're going to have brothers and fighters on-site there every hour that place is open. Just in case."

"So people will be safe," Helania said with relief.

"It's for vampires, first and foremost, although, of course, if they see something affecting a human, they'll intercede as a secondary priority."

"Good to know." Helania slid out from her chair. "I'm going there tonight."

Butch frowned as he stared up at her, and she braced herself for a load of let's-be-reasonable.

"I don't think that's necessary," the Brother said. "And it's risky, given how connected you are with the investigation."

"I've never been in danger there."

"Do you know that for sure? Someone could target you just because you called the killings in."

"But it's a confidential line."

Shaking his head, the Brother got to his feet. "I apologize for sounding paranoid, but I don't trust anyone with my witnesses. Things can go in directions nobody can guess. I want you safe, so please stay out of Pyre's Revyval."

Boone stood up as well. "We have no right to tell her what she can and can't do. She's not a suspect or a person of interest. She's a witness, you just said so."

"And that's why I'd like to keep her on the side of the living and breathing."

"How about she can go if she wants, but I'll be there with her."

The Brother looked back and forth between them. Then he picked up his pad. "Okay. That I can live with."

"I won't let anything happen to her."

Helania would have argued the self-sufficiency line again, but the Brother had a point. She wanted to help the investigation . . . as the closest representative of Isobel. But maybe there were risks at the club that she couldn't assess? And why be stupid about that. Besides . . .

As her hand went to her lower abdomen again, she knew there might be another reason she wanted to stay alive—

For some reason, it was at that moment that she realized Isobel would never know any young she might have.

With a fresh wave of sadness hitting her, Helania said, "I really hope we find whoever is doing this."

The Brother's eyes were grave as he tucked into the neck of his silk shirt and took out a heavy gold cross. "I swear on my Lord and Savior that I will *never* give up until whoever killed your sister is found and dealt with properly. This is my vow to you and your Isobel. I will not quit and I will never abandon the search—and God will show me the way. He always does."

Helania stared up at the male. And then, even though she should probably have kept things professional, she threw her arms around him and hugged him.

Pulling back a little, she looked into his surprised face. "You treat every victim like it's your sister, don't you. And every perpetrator like it's her murderer."

The pain that flared in his eyes was hard to see—because she had the same thing in her heart. "Yes," he said. "Every one of them is my sister."

"You'll find the male." She glanced at Boone. "And we'll work together with you."

The Brother gave her a hard embrace and then stepped back. "Thank you."

"For what?"

"Believing in me."

She eyed his cross. "It's all about faith, isn't it."

After Boone said goodbye to the male with a clap of the palm, Helania stepped out of the room with him and the Brother strode off down the corridor.

Boone took out his phone. "I just need to text Fritz that we're ready to go."

"No hurries."

Settling back against the cool concrete wall, she found herself wondering if she would be coming here often. For appointments. As her belly got bigger and life grew inside of her.

A quiet, tentative excitement kindled deep in her heart.

A young. Someone to love. Something to focus on other than herself and her grief over Isobel—

Down the way, just past the exam room she'd been in, a door opened and two males filed out of what had to be a weightlifting facility. They were shirtless and sweating, and they paid no attention to Helania or Boone. They just walked off in the opposite direction—

Helania straightened, her body moving before her brain told it to change positions. Flaring her nostrils, she took a stumbling step forward. And then another.

The scent of one of them was familiar, even though he was a stranger. And the connection that was made instantaneously in her mind was terrifying.

Boone snapped to attention. "Helania? What's—"

She pointed at the tall male on the left, the one with a Mohawk, and yelled, "You! It was *you*!"

✦    ✦    ✦

Butch was all up in his head as he headed down to the training center's office. Anytime Janie came up, in any situation, he always got rattled a little. But there was more to it than that. Somehow, staring into Helania's yellow eyes, as she had put her faith in him with the same trust he put in his God, had rocked him to his soul.

*You treat every victim like it's your sister, don't you. And every perpetrator like it's her murderer.*

On one level, it wasn't that tough an extrapolation. Hello. Childhood trauma affecting the adult course of life? Particularly as it motivated said individual to get what had gone wrong in their own past right in the futures of others? Not exactly Einstein material. But still, to hear Helania spell it out like that?

Wow, did it make him want a Scotch. Or fifteen.

But the urge for a drink, and not in a cocktail kind of way, was not something he was going to act on. Using alcohol as an emotional eraser was part of his old way of life, and he'd be damned if he was going to fall back into that shit for even a night—

"—it was *you!*"

Butch pulled up short and turned around. Down by the weight room, Helania was advancing on two members of the Band of Bastards, her finger pointed in accusation, her body trembling.

As Balthazar and Syn likewise pulled a pivot at the shout, Boone jumped in between them and the female, holding his arms out to prevent Helania from getting too close.

With a curse, Butch instinctively reached for the autoloader he had holstered at his hip, but he kept the gun down by his thigh as he jogged back to the drama.

"What's going on here?" he said evenly, slipping into cop-mode.

A quick glance at the two Bastards, and it appeared as if an attack from them was unlikely. Balthazar was looking confused, nothing but WTF on his face. And as for Syn?

"He killed the female! He killed my sister!"

Helania was talking fast but clearly, and that finger pointing at Syn was a lineup ID like you read about. And the Bastard's reaction was interesting—because there was none. The warrior just stared down at the female, nothing changing in his face, his eyes, his stance.

"You were with that murdered female at the club!" Helania said. "I scented you then. *You* were the one who took her down to the lower level. And when I went down there after I smelled the blood, *your* scent was in the air! It was you!"

Syn continued to play the Sphinx card, his features remaining composed, almost bored. But Balthazar? The Bastard was now looking at his comrade with anger . . . as if maybe, just maybe, he had been through this before with the guy.

Butch glanced at Boone. "Do me a favor, take her back to the room we were in? I want to talk to Syn—"

"He did it!" Helania lunged at the male, but Boone held her in place. "You bastard! You fucking bastard!"

Butch stepped up to the female, and as he got her attention, he lowered his voice. "I believe you. I believe that you saw him with the female who was killed. I believe that you tracked him down to the lower level. Right now, I need you to let me speak with him, okay? And then I want to talk more with you."

Helania was breathing heavily, her face white, her eyes wide. But to her credit, she calmed herself down.

"Don't let him go," she said harshly. "Don't you dare let him go."

"I won't. I swear. On my Janie."

Helania looked at Boone. After a tense moment, she let the male lead her away, the two of them walking off toward the interrogation room. She glared over her shoulder the entire time, and even after that door was shut, Butch could swear that he felt her accusing eyes through the fucking concrete.

Butch turned back to the Bastards. He found it curious that Balthazar had stepped in close to his comrade, like he was worried that the other male might do something stupid. But like there was anywhere to run to?

Then again, given Syn's hard stare, maybe there were other kinds of "stupid" to be worried about.

"Well, that was unexpected," Butch said to the Bastard in a relaxed tone. "You want to talk about what just went down?"

"Not in the slightest," Syn drawled. "You need to speak to her. Not me."

"I'm not sure I agree with that." Butch closed the distance between them and met those eyes square-on. "I just had a positive ID on you being with a female who was killed, on the night she was killed, in the club she was killed in. And given the way your buddy here is looking so exasperated, I have a feeling this is not the first time you've been in this kind of trouble. Am I right?"

Syn shrugged. "I got nothing to say."

"At all?"

"Are you going to play human world now? Read me some rights before you handcuff me and throw me in a cell?"

Butch didn't think it was helpful to go into the fact that there were no jails for vampires, at least not in Caldwell. Now, out West, they had options, but the Nevada desert was a long, long way away. Then again . . . maybe they could squeeze the sonofabitch into a FedEx box, poke some holes in it, and ship his ass out to the penal colony.

After Butch figured out what the fuck was going on, of course.

Balthazar glared at his comrade. "Either you start talking or I do."

"I told the guy, I got nothing to say."

There was a long silence. And then Balthazar focused on Butch. "My friend here has a little problem with dead bodies. They seem to happen a lot around him, and they're not always the ones we want."

"That human man in the alley had it coming to him," Syn muttered.

"But you didn't have to do it the way you did." Balthazar shook his head and crossed his arms over his chest. "If something happened at Pyre, you need to come clean."

Syn cocked an eyebrow and then shrugged. "Fine. I was with a female at the club, but I don't know whether or not she was the one who was killed."

Butch frowned. "Why didn't you tell me before now? I asked everyone to let me know if they'd been down there."

"I didn't think it mattered."

Butch raised his chin. "I've got a dead female on a slab getting cut up right now by Havers for her autopsy. And you didn't think it matters."

"No, I didn't."

"Well, see, here's my problem. If you'd told me beforehand, I wouldn't be thinking right now that you're hiding something."

Syn rolled his eyes and made like he was going to turn around. "This is boring me—"

Butch moved fast, grabbing the other male and shoving him back against the concrete wall. Pinning Syn at the throat with his forearm, he dropped his pad and put the muzzle of his gun at the Bastard's temple.

"You think this is a fucking joke?"

Out of the corner of his eye, Butch saw Boone and Helania watching down by the door to the interrogation room, but he couldn't worry about that. If he had to shoot the Bastard to get some answers, he would pull the trigger in a heartbeat. Losing an ear, for example, could be painful. So was getting a lead slug in the upper arm. The knee. There were plenty of nonlethal places to shoot, and pain tended to be a great opener of proverbial doors.

Syn, however, did not seem to be impressed by the show of gunmetal. His black eyes gleamed with intelligence, but absolutely no emotion at all.

"A female is dead," Butch gritted out, "and you've just been accused of killing her. And you're staying silent?"

"I have no comment, but I will do something." Syn smiled in an evil way, that black stare suddenly glowing red as a blood moon. "How about making it a two-for-one on the dead bodies?"

The male was too fast for Butch to catch him. Syn grabbed the gun and shoved its loaded muzzle into his own mouth.

In his eyes, in his red, glowing eyes, there was one and only one message: *Do it.*

# THIRTY-FOUR

Down by the interrogation room, Boone just wanted to make sure that he protected Helania from any stray lead that got to flying. But of course, that imperative became a moot fucking issue when Syn put Butch's goddamn gun in his *mouth*.

The two males were both shaking as they stood locked on the verge of a trigger pull, the naked upper torso of the Bastard carved in high relief, Butch's life-sized build that of a prizefighter's under his slick clothes. And within a split second, as if a silent alarm had gone off, Brothers flooded in from the gym, the office . . . the other clinic rooms. Moments later, the gun was out of Syn's oral cavity, the pair were separated, and Vishous was walking Butch down to the interrogation room.

As the pair went inside, Boone considered giving them some space, but Helania wasn't having it. She marched right in after the Brothers—and that meant Boone was going in, too.

Vishous wheeled around and pegged the two of them with icy eyes. "Give me a minute with him. You don't have to leave, but you both need to chill."

Boone nodded as he and Helania backed up against the far wall. Together, they watched in silence as V forced Butch down into a chair and appeared to hold him in place with a heavy hand. They spoke softly to one another, and out of respect, Boone turned away so he was less likely to overhear.

"Are you okay?" he whispered to Helania as he looked over her pale face.

She shook her head slowly and spoke in a rough, low voice. "I know it was him," she said urgently. "Oh, God . . . it was him that night. And maybe he killed Isobel, too."

As she began to tear up, he put his arms around her and she sank into his chest until he was holding her upright. It was then that the Brothers looked over.

"I'm sorry," Butch muttered. "I behaved unprofessionally. It won't happen again."

Helania lifted her head off Boone's pec. "Are you kidding me? I want to shoot him, too."

"No one's shooting anybody," Vishous cut in. Then he rolled his eyes. "And you know people be losin' their shit if I'm the one saying something like that."

"You're sure that's who it was," Butch asked Helania. "You have no doubts."

"I know what I scented. I'll take a polygraph. Or blind test me in a lineup, I will pick him out a thousand times correctly."

"Okay." Butch looked up at Vishous. "I want Syn held down here in a patient room with full guard until further notice. He should be considered a suicide risk, so strip the place of anything he can stab, cut, or hang himself with. I'm going to go search his room up at the mansion now and we need to get him to talk. Get Xcor down here. If there's anyone who can get him to open up, it's his goddamn boss. And I want that shit recorded."

Vishous nodded. "You got it."

"But first, you need to update Wrath while I confirm details here with Helania."

As the other Brother departed, Boone had no doubt that everything was going to be executed exactly as Butch wanted, and that was a relief.

Dear God, the idea that it was one of their own who was the killer? Boone couldn't believe it—and yet as he remembered those red eyes flashing in that alley and thought about what the Bastard had said to him as they'd stood over the mutilated body of that human assailant?

He didn't doubt that Syn was capable of killing for sport.

Butch looked around and cursed. "Damn it, I left my pad out in the corridor."

"Do you want me to go get it?" Boone asked, even as he went back over to block the photographs with his body.

"No, it'll be fine." The Brother focused on Helania. "Can you tell me again exactly what Syn was wearing the night you saw him with Mai in the club?"

She nodded and walked across to the table. Sitting down, she put her hands out in front of herself, and Boone got the impression it was to prove she wasn't hiding anything.

"He had a black knit hat that he'd pulled down low. Dark sunglasses. And all black clothes."

"Can you be really specific as to what kind of clothes? A cloak like you? Or—"

"Leathers. Black muscle shirt, I think. And then a leather jacket."

Boone spoke up, indicating his body. "Like mine?"

"Yes, exactly like yours."

"What kind of shoes? Or boots?" Butch asked.

"I don't know. I'm sorry." She shook her head. "And before you ask, I didn't see his face really. I've got to admit that. But his scent is unmistakable."

"You're doing great. You've given me more than enough, and way more than I thought we'd get tonight." The Brother took out his gold cross again. "See? What I say. On His time."

Helania sat back and looked over at Boone. "You know, if I hadn't come here for my check-up, I don't know how I would ever have run into him."

"It was just meant to be," Boone said.

Helania glanced at Butch again. "What happens to him now?"

"He waits down here while I search his rooms and see what I can find. If there's any trace of Mai's blood or scent on anything? Any evidence like meat hooks hanging in his frickin' closet or a piece of clothing from any victims? Then I take him to Wrath and present everything to the King, along with your testimony—just like if I were up in front of a judge with it. Wrath decides Syn's fate."

Helania's eyes narrowed. "And what is most likely to happen with that?"

The Brother was silent for a moment. "If Syn is the killer? He will not be living at the end of it. That I can promise you—"

"I want to be there. When he dies." She sat forward and grabbed a hold of the Brother's sleeve. "Do you understand. Nothing is more important to me than that. I want to see him killed. That's the only way my sister can rest in peace."

Butch rubbed his face like he had a headache. "We don't know for sure that Syn killed your sister."

Boone spoke up. "But there could be a connection there. A very likely connection."

"Yeah." Butch got to his feet. "I have a feeling there might well be."

"I want to be there," Helania insisted. "When he's killed."

"That will be up to Wrath. If we end up with a death sentence, you'll have to petition the King to be a witness and see what he says." The Brother put a hand on her shoulder. "But knowing him the way I do? He will understand completely where you're coming from."

◆    ◆    ◆

To Helania, the ride back to her apartment in the Brotherhood's fancy Mercedes seemed to take less than a breath. Okay, fine . . . maybe it was more like two deep inhales and a hiccup. But it was no longer than that.

And there was a further distortion to time as she exited the warm interior thanks to the elderly butler holding her door open: She couldn't decide whether it had been days or seconds since she and Boone had first sat in the back of the car and driven out to wherever the Brotherhood was hiding all those facilities.

While she was playing around with theories of relativity in her head, Boone got out from the rear seat, too. And just as it had been in the training center's parking area, the butler became flustered because he hadn't had time to go around and do his duty with that door.

The two males said some things, and then she was thanking Fritz and the car was driving away on the snowpack.

"I just want to see you to the door," Boone said. "I don't have to stay."

"It's okay." She shook herself. "I mean, I'd like you to come in. If you have a minute."

So much for her bid for independence, she thought, as they walked to the front entrance of her building. And yet she wanted Boone to come down to her place and not just because she didn't want to be alone. It was because she wanted to be with him—and not necessarily sexually.

She just needed to make sure all of that had actually happened, her seeing that warrior in the corridor . . . them talking to Butch about the losses of sisters and a father—

As she and Boone entered her building's outer door, they paused by the rows of mailboxes while she got the right key out.

"I never expected the killer to be connected with the Brotherhood." She put her key in the inside lock and turned. "I mean . . . he's one of them, right?"

"No, he fights with them." Boone helped her get the heavy weight open. "It's a big difference."

They were silent as they went down to the basement level, and she let them into her apartment.

"Wow," he said as he closed them in. "This place is so clean."

"I had to find something to do with myself during the day." She took off her parka and hung it by her Pyre's Revyval cloak, her hand lingering on those folds of black cloth. "It kept my mind off of things."

When she looked over at him, he had taken a seat on her sofa and had one of her needlepoint pillows in his lap. His deft fingers were traveling over the orderly lines of stitching, tracing a hyacinth.

"This must have taken a long time to do," he murmured.

"It's another excellent distraction." She came over and sat down with him. "Keeps my mind engaged just enough so my thoughts don't spin out of control."

"Maybe I should take it up." He put the pillow aside. "I could sell them and live off the proceeds."

"It helps me pay the bills."

"Well, I've given up sleeping, so I have extra time on my hands now."

They stared at each other. And when she leaned in his direction, she wasn't sure what he was going to do. Things were better than they had been right after the needing, but there were so many unknowns.

Boone stopped her by putting his forefinger on her lips. "Are you sure you want to do this?"

"I specifically asked Doc Jane if, you know . . . if I'm not pregnant, whether the fertility lasts any longer than the symptoms. She said it doesn't. So we don't have to worry." She frowned. "Unless things have changed for you."

"You mean whether I want you?" He brushed her lower lip with his thumb. "They haven't. I'm still not going to tell you no. Not now, not ever."

She could have said something to him in return, communicated with words that though their situation was complex, her feelings for him were not.

Instead, she let her mouth do the talking by sucking his finger in between her lips and rolling her tongue around it.

The purr that came out of him was what she wanted to hear. And Boone's next move was to retract his finger and replace it with his tongue as he licked his way into her. The kiss was everything she needed, and she arched against him as she wrapped her arms around his neck. When he pushed her back into the sofa, she let herself go.

Except she wanted him to know she wasn't using him as a distraction. She did not want to think, it was true. But there were so many other reasons she needed him in this moment.

"Boone . . ."

"You don't have to explain." He pulled back. "I just want to be with you and I'll take you any way I can get you."

Helania stroked his face as she scented the dark spices that she had come to associate with him. "I don't deserve you."

"Ditto."

Their mouths fused in an even deeper kiss, and they kept that up as clothes were pulled off and stripped down and thrown to the floor. When they were naked, she parted her thighs and welcomed him.

"I'll go slow," he said. "In case you're still sore."

"Okay."

She did wince a little, but then he was filling her up, deep inside, thick and hot. Yet he didn't move.

"Helania . . ." he whispered. "Take my vein."

Unbidden, her eyes shot to the thick jugular that ran up the side of his throat. It had been so long since she had fed, and the stress she had been under compounded a sudden piercing hunger.

And then there was the possibility she was pregnant.

"Are you sure?" she breathed.

"Do you want me to beg?"

Her fangs dropped down out of her upper jaw in a rush, and he groaned as her lips parted to reveal the twin points. With a quick shift, he repositioned their bodies so that she was on top of his hips, in control . . . dominant.

"Take me," he said. "Use me."

The hiss that left her was the kind of sound she had never made before, and as she struck at his throat, Boone shouted her name, his hips punching up, his arousal pushing even farther into her. His taste in her mouth and down the back of her throat was an intoxicating thrill, and as she began to drink, he began to move his pelvis.

Swallowing the nourishment only he could give her, she was filled up in her belly and in her sex as he orgasmed, the sweet pain of her bite clearly sending him over the brink. And that was all she needed. She found her release, too, the rings of pleasure radiating out from her core joining the rush of elation that went along with the strength he was giving her.

As incredible as the sensations were, as tempted as she was to keep going with his vein, she was very careful not to take too much. The fact that he was so pure of bloodline, and had also recently taken from a sacred Chosen—something Helania had never heard of anyone doing before—meant he probably could have given her so much more. But she truly cared about and for him, and she would rather go blood hungry than ever endanger his precious, precious life.

When she had taken enough to sustain herself, she licked the puncture wounds closed and then kissed his mouth. And still their bodies moved together, orgasms compounding orgasms, the sex an expression of all the things neither of them seemed to be able to put into words.

There were so many unanswered questions. So many strings yet to be gathered. So many paths diverging before them.

They had this moment, however. And she could only pray it was not their last.

# THIRTY-FIVE

Back when the Band of Bastards had moved in with the Brotherhood at the mansion, the decision had been made to open up a previously closed-off collection of bedrooms. Accessed by going out through the far wall of the second-story sitting room, the footprint of the additional suites extended over the entire kitchen/pantry/laundry wing as well as the garage.

As Butch proceeded down a very nicely appointed hall, he didn't spare a glance at any of the oil paintings of English landscapes that hung from the paneling, nor did he check out the fresh-even-in-winter flowers on the side tables, nor did he hi-how're-ya the occasional bust that sat on the ledges under the windows.

He was focused on Fritz. The butler was about three-quarters of the way down, standing in front of a closed door with a quizzical expression on his face.

"Sire?" he said as Butch approached. "The King indicated that he wished for me to unlock this door for you?"

"Yup."

"The King indicated you were going to inspect the rooms? At my Lord's direction?"

"Yup. That's the plan."

*And thank you, Wrath.*

Maybe it was the fact that Butch had been a cop in the human system for all those years. Or maybe it was because he felt like he needed to cover his ass to make sure there weren't any problems in the household. Or maybe he was simply acknowledging his cousin's position of authority over all matters under this roof—and within the race. But whatever the reason, he'd felt compelled to ask Wrath if it was okay to go through Syn's shit.

And what do you know, based on Helania's ID of the Bastard, said permission had been granted.

Butch came to a stop in front of the butler. "I want you to be my witness as I go through everything."

"Witness?"

"To attest that I didn't plant anything or otherwise mishandle Syn's belongings."

Fritz bowed low. "It is my pleasure to be of service in any way you require."

"Good deal. Thanks. Now let's open things up and see what we got."

The butler inserted a copper key that was nearly the size of his own hand in the lock, and there was a clunking sound as the old-fashioned tumblers disengaged. No creaking hinges. That would never happen in a household run by Fritz.

As the light from the hall streamed into the darkness, Butch frowned at what he saw—or, to be more accurate, what he did not see.

"What the fuck?" he muttered.

"This is the way he wishes it to be."

Butch shook his head as he entered. The room was totally bare. No carpet. No bed. No bedside table or bureaus. No writing desk or side chairs or any of the antique stuff that filled out every other single square inch of the mansion, like Darius had had a binge-shopping addiction that could only be satisfied by Christie's.

Butch looked over his shoulder. "Where did Syn put everything? The furniture, I mean."

"He requested that I get rid of it, and so I reapportioned some of the things to other suites, and the rest went into the basement. I offered to order him something more to his taste, but he informed me that, as a soldier in the Old World, he was used to sleeping in hiding-holes and outposts with nothing more than whatever he could carry on his back. Even the most rudimentary of decor made him feel cramped."

As Butch walked around the bare floorboards, the footfalls of his loafers echoed around the barren walls. "You're sure that it's looked like this since he moved in? There's no chance that in the last forty-eight or seventy-two hours that he came back and cleaned anything out?"

As Fritz's face fell and he paled, Butch realized what he'd done. Rushing back to the butler, he put his hands out—but then dropped them because he knew he'd only make things worse if he tried to touch the *doggen*.

"I'm sorry," Butch said in a rush. "I was just mumbling, you know, talking to myself. I did not mean to insinuate that you were misremembering or that you were not aware of the makeup, layout, and contents of every single room, closet, hallway, and basement in this house."

Fritz hesitated, as if he were worried that Butch was attempting to cheer him up rather than telling the truth.

"I swear on my Lord and Savior," Butch said as he took out his cross. "The only reason why I spoke that out loud is because it is vital that I see everything in these rooms exactly as it was, without anyone trying to hide their tracks by throwing out something."

"Is Syn a suspect?" Fritz asked. "For something that was stolen?"

*Yes*, Butch thought. *A life. Or two. Maybe three.*

"It's a difficult situation." Butch glanced around. "Well, I guess this is a dead end—no, wait, the bathroom and the closet. There has to be a closet in here."

Walking over, he peeked into the bathroom. The marble expanse had been stripped bare as well, all of the luxuries Butch was now used to seeing gone: No bath mats. No fluffy extra towels. No robes. There was a toothbrush and a single tube of toothpaste. Crest Original.

As if the guy didn't like fussiness anywhere near his fluoride, either.

Butch opened the drawers. Cracked the cupboards. Leaned into the toilet room.

Razor and shaving lotion were all he got.

He glanced at Fritz. "Where does he sleep?"

"I believe you will see it the now."

"The closet?"

"Yes, I believe so."

Walking over to a set of double doors, Butch opened them and blinked as the light came on overhead.

"Okay, this is a criminal waste," he said as he looked at the bare hanging rods that ran around the room-sized space at shoulder level. "I could fit at least half my wardrobe in here."

Or all of Marissa's, Jane's, and Vishous's clothes—and his golf cart.

But there was what Fritz had been talking about: In the far corner, a ring of guns and knives had been set in a semicircle, the circumference of which fit a Syn-sized body.

The clothes, such as they were, were stacked in a pile at the foot of the arrangement.

Getting out his phone, Butch stood in the open doorway and took a video of the closet. Then he entered and went over to the clothes. After taking a number of mid-distance and close-up shots, he snagged a pair of nitrile gloves out of his pocket, snapped them on, and went through the layers.

He found a black knit cap. Black sunglasses.

And two pairs of leathers that smelled like they had been places.

He glanced over at Fritz, who was standing in the doorway, his old hands churning in front of him as if he were desperate to help in some way.

"How many pairs of leathers does Syn own?" Butch asked.

"Two. I have ordered more in his precise size, but they are downstairs in the packaging in which they arrived. He has not accepted them as of yet. He is waiting until something is worn through, he told me. Only then will he replace what he has."

Butch laid out both pairs on the wall-to-wall carpeting, stretching the long legs flat. After photographing the sets separately and then together, he turned them over and did the same to the back sides. Then he repeated the process with the leather jacket before he went through its pockets.

Bullets. Switchblade. Length of chain.

Trident sugarless gum in cinnamon. Okay, so the Bastard was clearly worried about both clean breath and healthy tooth enamel.

Sitting back on his haunches, Butch cursed.

"Whatever is wrong?" Fritz asked.

He debated whether or not to press the butler on if he were certain nothing had been taken out of the closet.

Yeah, 'cuz that had gone so wicked well with the whole decor convo out there.

Refocusing on the leathers, Butch turned them back over so the fronts were showing and stared at the wear marks. The stains. The scratches. Leaning down, he breathed in through his nose, testing the scents.

Okay, right, lot of *lesser* blood. Some male blood that had to be Syn's own. Dirt. Sweat. Gunpowder. Sex.

But . . . no female blood. On either set.

Which was kind of a well, shit. Leathers were not the sort of thing that you just threw in the laundry and sent around for a ride with some Tide. They were not cleaned that easily, and going by the butler's statement, these were the only two pairs that Syn owned.

So, assuming what Fritz said was accurate, it wasn't like Syn had killed those females, ditched whatever he was wearing on his bottom half, and then thrown on a fresh pair when he got home. Unless he was ordering them himself on the sly and having the rogue leathers shipped to some place in town.

If Butch had some bank account information, he could check and see any transactions that had gone through to that effect. But something told him that that kind of hassle was probably not a big priority for someone who lived this sparsely. Although if you were trying to cover up homicide? You'd Amazon Prime the fuck out of another pair of pants.

*Wouldn't you?* he thought.

"What about muscle shirts?" Butch said. "Does he submit them for laundry regularly?"

Fritz bowed. "He does, indeed. He also has two sweatshirts that he alternates between, as well as some gym clothing."

"I want to speak with the laundress, please."

Fritz bowed again. "Right away, sire. Stay here. I shall bring her unto you."

Left alone, Butch sat back on his ass and let his blue-gloved hands dangle off his knees. Staring at the leathers, he tried to find the hole in the reasoning. Some other explanation for why the only two pairs of pants the male seemed to own did not smell like death or the blood of a female.

Maybe Syn had borrowed someone else's leathers when he'd done the killing and then dumped those. Maybe . . . Fritz had miscounted.

That last one was probably not it.

Leaning to the side, Butch looked out at the vacant bedroom. So empty. So lonely. So . . . not the private quarters of a well-adjusted guy. But the anti-hoarding didn't mean Syn was a killer.

Helania, on the other hand, had not only been totally certain that she'd seen the Bastard with the deceased, the dark glasses and knit cap she'd described were right here with the rest of Syn's clothing—

"Sire? This is Lilf." Fritz entered the closet with a uniformed female *doggen*. "She would be pleased to answer any of your questions."

As Lilf bowed low, Butch noted that her pressed gray-and-white uniform matched her gray hair.

"Sire," she said, "how may I serve you?"

"Hi, Lilf. Thanks for coming here."

Butch got up to his feet and indicated the pile of clothes: Three muscle shirts, all pressed, and three undershirts, all pressed, and one black sweatshirt. There were also six pairs of thick black socks and a jockstrap.

"Do you wash all of his clothes? Syn's?" he said.

"I wash everyone's clothes, sire."

"Good, and thank you for doing such a nice job on my own, by the way. Now, can you please tell me if, in the last five nights, you have scented vampire blood on any shirt, pant, sock, fleece—anything owned by anyone in this household? I mean, vampire blood that was not that of the owner."

"Allow me to think." Lilf's eyes traveled around the barren closet. "Well, yes. The Brother Vishous had a muscle shirt with blood, not his own, on it. Just this morning. It was female in derivation."

No doubt from when the brother had moved Mai's body. "Good. Okay. Anyone else?"

"Balthazar and Zypher had the same blood on their shirts. I could tell by the scent."

*They had helped V*, Butch thought.

There was a long period of silence. "I'm sorry, sire, I seem to be quite slow this evening."

"Take your time, Lilf. It's really important that you're one hundred percent sure."

The *doggen* crossed her arms over her chest, lowered her chin, and shut her eyes. As she seemed to fall into a trance-like state, Butch prayed that she would remember that—

"No one else," she said as she lifted her lids. "Just those three. In the last five nights."

"Out of the entire household."

"Yes, sire." She glanced at Fritz. "Have I done something wrong?"

Fritz patted her on the forearm. "Oh, no, dear. You're doing just fine—as long as you're certain."

"I am." She looked at Butch again. "I do all loads sequentially. There is a system that rotates through all the bedrooms. So I know whose laundry is whose."

"Is there any way that V, Balthazar, or Zypher's things could have gotten mixed up with someone else's?" Butch spoke very carefully, as he didn't want to offend the *doggen*. "Is it possible that you could be confused about whose muscle shirt is whose?"

Maybe V threw out his, and Syn's was the other of the three she was counting. It wouldn't explain why the Bastard's leathers were not marked with the scent of Mai's blood, but it would be something to go on.

"No," Lilf said confidently. "All loads, no matter how small, are kept separate as each person in the household prefers things cleaned in a different way. Some like fabric softener, some do not. Some like fragrances, some do not. Many have a specific preference of detergent, so as I check in the hampers—"

"You check their contents in?"

"Yes, I have a log."

Butch stared at the *doggen*. "Of every piece of clothing sent to the laundry, by owner?"

"Yes, and it has notes on stains, which is how I am sure about the blood." She tilted her head to side. "How else could I do things properly?"

Dayum. He'd hit the jackpot. "How far do the records go back?"

"Since the first load I did for the King under this roof."

*Well . . . there you go,* Butch thought.

"May I see the log?" he asked. "Not because I'm doubting you, I'm just curious how it's all done."

And because he was double-checking her.

"Oh, yes, sire. Right this way."

As Fritz and Lilf walked out of Syn's suite, Butch followed along. He was quiet as they went down a back set of stairs to the laundry facilities, but he was not on autopilot.

Quite the contrary.

He was trying to figure out how Syn had managed to slit Mai's wrists and throat, and string her up by a meat hook . . . without getting any blood on his leathers. His knit cap. His shirt—

Butch pictured Syn coming out of the workout room, covered with sweat.

"Wait!" he exclaimed.

As both *doggen* halted on the landing with a start, he waved his hand back and forth. "Sorry, I didn't mean you all. I forgot about the lockers down in the training center."

The evidence he needed would be there.

He was sure of it.

✦     ✦     ✦

Back at Helania's apartment in her bedroom, Boone was naked and on his back under the covers, his female's body tucked in tight against him. He was pretty sure she was asleep. After she had taken his vein and they had made love again in here, she had been in that post-feeding logy state, and he was happy to be her bolster as she went boneless and gave herself up to rest.

As he stared at her ceiling, he was aware they were in a holding pattern.

The door to sex was open again, and he was glad about it. But the larger issue of who they were to each other was tabled for the moment.

If she was pregnant, she was right. He was going to want to mate her and that was that. He was not going to have her and a young of his out in the world alone, no way—and it was not a case of honoring his bloodline. Hell, he wasn't even part of his own family tree anymore, was he.

Getting disinherited was a pretty clear line in that kind of sand.

But for him, taking care of her and their young, making sure any offspring of his had a stable, loving home, was a personal imperative, not one tied to the shitshow he had been born into. His sire's performance as a father was an example of everything Boone did not want to be—

"I need to find that female."

Boone lifted his head. "What?"

Helania rubbed her face up and down on his chest as if she were trying to stay awake. "The female who came to tell me about Isobel. Who helped me bury her. She deserves to know that the killer's been found, and she needs to decide if she wants to be there at the end, too."

"That makes sense." Boone frowned. "What do we have to go on?"

"The house. The house where she took me. I need to find it, will you help me? I want to try and remember where in town it is. I checked her profile on Facebook, but there's no address, obviously. No real name. No clues to her identity. Her picture is just a close-up of part of her face, for godsakes."

"Did she ever get back to you? I know you said you'd messaged her."

"Not yet, but I haven't checked since we went out to the training center." Helania propped her chin on her hand and looked at him. "I feel a responsibility to her. She was as upset as I was. Utterly heartbroken. Clearly, she was a very good friend of Isobel's."

"We'll find her." He brushed Helania's hair back and kissed her on the forehead. "And we'll start by searching that house at nightfall. And we'll just keep looking for her until you can talk to her again."

As Helania's lashes blinked quickly, he wished he could shoulder the pain for her. He would do anything to make her mourning easier, so yes, goddamn it, he was going to find that house, that female, for her if it was the last thing he did on earth.

"Thank you," she whispered. "You're always there when you're needed, aren't you."

"I try to be."

"How could your father not have been proud to have you as his son?"

Boone shrugged. "Different set of standards. Way different."

There was a pause. And then she said, "What is it?"

"Hm?"

She brushed her fingertips over his eyebrows, smoothing them. "You're frowning. What are you thinking about?"

It was probably not the best timing to go into it. But for some reason, he couldn't stop himself from speaking—probably because of the conversation they'd had with Butch in that interrogation room.

"I sometimes think my sire might have had my blood *mahmen* murdered."

Helania jerked up, her citrine eyes popping wide. "Are you serious?"

"It's okay." He soothed her shoulders with his hands. "It's all right."

"No, it's not. What happened?"

"I don't know. She wasn't sick. She wasn't old. She wasn't pregnant. Except one evening, she woke up dead." He shook his head. "I wasn't any closer to her than I was my sire, but even a stranger could tell she was woefully unhappy."

"Did she . . . commit suicide?"

"You can't get into the Fade that way. Or at least that's what they say—and I know she believed it. I overheard her talking to my aunt once, saying that the only thing that kept her going was the thought that eternity was waiting for her at the end of the suffering. Provided she didn't do anything rash."

"How did she die?"

"I never knew. I came down to First Meal, and my father informed me she had passed. That was it. Like it was an update on the weather or something. I never got the story of the how and I should have asked. Even though I probably wouldn't have gotten any kind of answer from him, I regret that I didn't even try."

"Was your father upset?"

Boone shook his head. And he was a little surprised at how hard it was to say the words. "My father was in love with someone else."

"He was cheating on her?"

"It was more than that, I think. It was a full-blown relationship."

"And he stayed with your *mahmen* because divorce doesn't exist in the *glymera*?"

"No, I think it was because it was a male. He was in love with a male. With Marquist, the one he left everything to."

Helania's jaw slowly fell open. "Did your *mahmen* know?"

"She must have. Even though aristocrats are very particular about their vices, very private about them, and that kind of relationship was not—is not—allowed, there is no way when Marquist moved in that it wasn't apparent to her. How could it not be?" He shrugged. "Besides, I doubt it was my father's first affair in that regard, and maybe that was why she cheated on him, too."

"She did?"

"I'm not even sure I'm biologically his." As Helania's eyes popped again, he laughed bitterly. "Yes, I'm afraid things only look good from the outside where I'm from. And that is precisely why, right after my *mahmen* died, my father moved another 'appropriate' female in. His second *shellan* fared no better than his first, but at least my step*mahmen* seemed better prepared to live with the situation."

"Boone . . . I had no idea you grew up like that."

"It's all right."

"No, it's not." Helania massaged the center of his chest, right over his heart. "My parents didn't have much when it came to money, but their love was the binding to my sister's and my lives. I can't imagine what it was like not to have that example to believe in, to model, to hope for for yourself."

The idea that that kind of loving relationship had existed between her parents made Boone want her for his own *shellan* even more.

"I'm so sorry," Helania whispered. "That sounds so lame, but . . . I wish—"

"It's okay," he said as he leaned up and kissed her. "It feels good to get it all out in the air to someone. I've never told anybody the real story—and as for my blood *mahmen's* death, I'm not sure which one of them did it." Boone laughed in a hard rush. "Knowing my father, he probably refused to get his hands dirty. And hey, Marquist is good with a carving knife. You should see what he can do to a roast beef— although those nights in the kitchen are long over now that he's lord of the manor."

"Can you do something about this? Maybe Butch can help?"

"It was two decades ago, and all I have are my suspicions. Besides, now I have a conflict of interest because I was disinherited in favor of Marquist. If he committed a murder tied to my *mahmen?* I think he's disqualified from getting the assets because she was my father's *shellan,* and if she had lived, she would have kept everything—and I would be her sole heir."

"But if what you think is true, Marquist could be getting away with murder and taking your inheritance."

Boone thought about it for a time. And then he focused on Helania. "Well, then that former butler can pat himself on the back and enjoy the money and the house. I'm not going backward, only forward."

As he said the words, he realized . . . he *really* wanted her to be pregnant.

He wanted to start his life over. With Helania and their young.

And he wanted to do things right, like her parents had done.

# THIRTY-SIX

As the door to the patient room opened, Syn looked up from where he was sitting on the foot of the hospital bed. When he saw who it was, he cursed and stared down at the floor. Anyone else. He would have preferred anyone else, and no doubt that was exactly why the Brothers had chosen the male.

And what do you know, Xcor, the leader of the Band of Bastards, was not alone. Vishous was behind him, and as the pair of them entered, the Brother closed the door and locked it.

"So they sent you," Syn muttered. "I should have guessed."

Xcor sat down on one of the chairs that were lined up against the wall, his enormous body filling the piece of furniture. The male had recently gotten a skull trim, and the lack of hair made his neck look even thicker, his shoulders bigger, his chest broader. As was typical of him, his face was unsmiling, that harelip distorting his mouth into what looked like a sneer, but was actually just a misalignment of the upper lip.

Or maybe the guy was pissed.

"As if I would not have come on my own," Xcor said in a low voice.

That Old World accent, so similar to Syn's own, was a reminder of how many years they had been together. Fighting, surviving . . . being angry at destiny. But Xcor had changed tracks. He was happily mated now and even had step-young.

*Never would have seen that one coming,* Syn thought as he looked into the eyes of his mentor, his leader . . . his friend.

The stare that came back at him was so level, so unemotional, it carried a punch to the gut that Syn had to resolutely ignore. As much as he hated to admit it, the two of them were on different sides of the table right now and it bothered him.

Xcor glanced up at Vishous. "Can you leave us?"

The Brother shook his head and lifted his phone. "And I'm recording."

"Such an official show all this is," Syn said.

" 'Tis official." Xcor eased back in the chair, his weight making the plastic and metal creak. "A female is dead."

"Wasn't it two?"

"Are you saying that to show off?"

"No, just to correct the record given that we're so serious." Syn nodded over at the Brother who was looming by the door like a prison guard. "And also to give his phone something to do."

There was a long silence, and the fact that his leader, and others, were operating under the belief that Syn had done the killing made absolute sense. The present was always judged on the past, and his actions spoke for themselves.

Or maybe it was more like his corpses spoke for themselves.

After a while longer, Xcor said, "It's not like you to leave the bodies behind. Usually no one finds them, at least for a while. And then they're hard to identify."

"You sound disappointed in me."

"It would have made things easier," the male muttered dryly.

Syn raised his eyebrows. "But that poor female would still be dead, wouldn't she. And the other. Boo-hoo."

"So you're admitting you did it."

"What do I get if I do?"

"You know the answer to that."

Thinking back to the Brother Butch shoving that gun up against his temple, Syn smiled. "I'm okay with that outcome. Can we do it now, or do you have to wait for nightfall so we can go out into the woods and leave less of a mess for the *doggen* to clean up."

Xcor's foot started to tap, his shitkicker's heel bouncing on the tile floor. "You're cycling really tight. Eight months ago. Six nights ago. The night before last with the human male in the alley. You're moving really quickly."

"So let's end it right now." Syn nodded at the gun holstered on V's hip. "He can do it. Or if you want to, you do it."

The Brother Vishous frowned, the tattoo at his temple distorting. "I still haven't heard you say you killed the females."

Closing his eyes, Syn thought back to that night, that club . . . the female with the wig and the bustier, the breasts and the lips. He remembered seeing her through the crowd, the push and shove, the argument she'd been in. Then she came across to him, came on to him, toyed with him, until he picked her up and took her down below. Against the door, fucking. Door falling open and them spilling into the black interior of the storage room.

His monster stirring in his skin. Prowling. Demanding to be let out.

Then him outside of the club, the cold burning his face, his body hot under his clothes, his cock still hard.

He was so tired of all this, so exhausted by his nature, his urges, this thing inside of him that had to get out. He had done his best, at least in the Old World, to choose victims who deserved it, but now . . . he just didn't give a shit anymore.

"Of course I did it," he said as he looked at the Brother. "I killed both of them and I hung them up by meat hooks in the storage rooms. And unless you take care of me properly, I'm going to do it again."

◆    ◆    ◆

Hours later, as the sun gave up on its illuminating duties and sank below the horizon, Butch was back in his evidence room at the training center, staring up at the wall, his chair on two legs. In his hands, the Bic he used to take notes, notes, and more notes was traveling in and out of the stalks of his fingers, pirouetting around the digits in an endless dance.

When the door opened, he didn't look over. No need to. By the scent of Turkish tobacco, he knew who it was.

Righting his chair, he pulled over some of the papers on the table to make a spot for Vishous if the brother wanted to park it. "How's tricks, kid?"

"You tell me."

The door closed, and his best friend went over and stared at the black-and-white photographs of Mai. Both V and he stayed silent for a very long time, and he had to admit he was glad his roommate was in the house, so to speak. V was the smartest person he'd ever met. Surely, if there was anyone who could make sense of this fruit salad of WTF, it was Vishous.

Because things just weren't adding up, and that did not make sense. It just . . . did not. Everything on the surface was pointing directly at Syn, but that was it. The evidence didn't back things up, and it was hard to fathom why somebody would cop to a killing—or two—that they did not commit. Butch had a few other angles he could explore . . . but if the way the case had been going so far was any indication, he wasn't going to get any better answers than the ones that had been coming through to him already.

"You mind if I light up?" V asked as he backed up like the close-up hadn't worked so maybe a panoramic view of things might help.

"Nope. I'm thinking of volunteering for the habit as well at this point."

Vishous went to pull back one of the chairs. When it resisted, Butch sat forward and reached for his Phillips head. "Here, let's unscrew the—"

The brother yanked the thing up, the high-pitched whine of metal reaching and surpassing its structural integrity making Butch wince. As some of the screws bounced on the hard polished floor, V turned the chair around and inspected the mangled feet.

"Didn't think that one through," he muttered.

His solution to the inevitable instability was to pound those four feet into the concrete over and over again until the thing was somewhat level on its legs.

"There," he said as he parked his ass. "Fixed it."

The fact that he was sitting off-kilter and had made holes in the floor seemed petty to point out.

"Good job," Butch said.

"I could do the other two?"

"I think we're okay. But thanks for the offer."

Vishous nodded and got out his papers and his tobacco pouch. As he rolled one up, Butch watched those strong hands, the one that was gloved and the one that wasn't.

"So what are you thinking?" the brother said as he licked down the edge of the paper and smoothed the flap in place.

Butch shook his head and refocused on the pictures of Mai. "Autopsy came back."

"Any surprises?"

"Nope." Butch rubbed his shoulder and rolled it around in its socket. "Toxicology will take a while, but what's going to come from it? That she had drugs in her system? That maybe he drugged her before he slit her throat? Even if that was the case, I've been in Syn's room. He doesn't keep anything in it other than weapons and not enough clothes to get me through an afternoon. There were no drugs or paraphernalia."

"He could have tossed it all." V exhaled away from Butch even though they were in an enclosed space. "Gotten rid of the leathers and the jacket. And any drugs."

Butch shrugged. "When it comes to his leathers, the count is right. I went to the supply closet. His backups, the ones Fritz ordered for him, match the receipt. The laundry count is also pristine. Everything is accounted for."

"There are all kinds of way to explain that. He could order the leathers himself."

"Doesn't have a credit card. I got all his bank information—or shall I say the lack of it—from Balthazar."

"Maybe he has an account we don't know of."

Butch inclined his head. "True."

V picked an errant flake of tobacco off his lower lip and pulled a half-empty mug of cold coffee over to ash in. "Syn fucking did it. He admitted it to me. You listened to the recording."

"Yeah." Butch fished into his silk shirt and took his cross in hand, rubbing the heavy gold. "I know—"

The knock on the door was sharp and a one-off.

"Come in," V muttered.

Balthazar entered and reclosed things. The Bastard was in his field clothes, but without his jacket or his weapons, and Butch had to wonder if he'd deliberately removed the latter as a measure of respect. Known for being a thief, Balthazar was nonetheless an honorable, stand-up guy—at least to the short list he considered worth being honest with. As for the rest of the world? He was liable to rock the five-finger discount and then some.

In truth, he reminded Butch of some of the Irish mafia thugs in Southie, and oddly, it made him respect the guy.

"Hey," the Bastard said. "You wanted to see me?"

Butch got to his feet and offered his palm. "What's doing. Thanks for coming down."

"Sure. Yeah."

Vishous offered his palm over his shoulder, and the other male clapped it. "You want a cigarette?"

Balthazar squeezed his muscle-loaded body into the chair on the other side. "Wow, this is a tight squeeze. And yes, please, on the nicotine."

"You want I fix your chair?" V offered.

"No," Butch said. "We're done with the redecorating. My eardrums can't take another round of that."

V shot him a buzzkill glare and then got to work rolling one for Balthazar.

Butch sat forward and linked his fingers around his pen. "I'm thinking you know why I've asked you to sit down with me."

"My cousin Syn."

"Yeah. I've kind of got issues with him."

"I know you do." The Bastard looked down at his own callused hands. "He's a tough case, and it makes me sad."

There was a quiet moment as V passed a fresh hand-rolled over as well as his lighter. While Balthazar accepted both and lit up, Butch thought about the barren rooms Syn kept himself in. "Sad" was a good word for that living space, even if you assumed he was just staying with a tradition that he felt comfortable in.

"Oh . . . this is nice tobacco," Balthazar murmured. "So smooth."

V smiled with satisfaction, like the guy had complimented his car. "Anytime you want one, I got you, true?"

" 'Ppreciate you." Balthazar exhaled in a long, slow stream and then looked back over at Butch. "So . . . Syn. How can I help?"

"Tell me about the shit in the Old World," Butch said.

Balthazar turned the hand-rolled around and stared at the glowing tip. "I love my cousin. I have a great deal of loyalty toward him. He's not a bad male, but he . . . growing up, he was in a bad situation. Back then, things were different. Young civilians were bred to work in the fields and provide food—they were farm equipment, not blessings. His sire was a drunk who needed something to hit, and Syn decided at a young age that he'd rather it be him than his *mahmen*. So he took the beatings."

Butch shook his head. "I knew households like that on the human side."

"People can be assholes, no matter the species." Balthazar shrugged and tapped his head. "One night, Syn's father took a copper pot and chased the poor kid into the pantry. He beat Syn's skull so hard it bent the fucking metal out of shape. He was never the same after that. Seizures. Blackouts. And . . . the rage came after that."

"Classic concussive trauma," V muttered.

"Even if that hadn't happened, I think Syn would have had a lot of anger, but after that . . . he was different."

"How did he get out of the situation at home?" Butch asked.

"He killed his father." Balthazar rubbed his eyes as if he were seeing things he would have preferred not to. "I was the one who found the body. It was unrecognizable. Field dressed and decapitated. I didn't know who it was until I saw the head off to the side under a goddamn bush. Syn was sitting there, next to the remains, covered in his sire's blood staring at the knife in his hand like he was surprised by what he'd done with it."

"His first taste of death," V whispered.

"I didn't blame him for that one." Balthazar shook his head and ashed into the mug. "His father had to go. But then, after his transition, there were others. A lot of others."

"Females?"

"Yeah, females, too. To his credit, he never targeted someone who didn't deserve it. The people he killed were murderers, cheats . . . thieves." The Bastard looked up and smiled remotely. "I get a free pass on that last one because I'm family to him."

"Sounds like you lucked out there," Butch said.

"Yes, indeed." Balthazar took a drag on the hand-rolled. "Things get gruesome when he goes to work and he's very creative."

"So the two females who were found down at Pyre are right up his alley."

Balthazar got to his feet and went over to the black-and-white photographs of Mai's body. "This is a little tame for him, actually."

"Well, he got depraved enough for my tastes." Butch shook his head as he looked at the wall of evidence that he'd created. "Autopsy showed he had sex with her after she was dead."

Balthazar shot a look over his shoulder. "He penetrated her, you mean."

"Not just that. It was the full bifta, as they say."

The Bastard came back over to the table with a frown on his face. "You're sure about this?"

Butch fished around the papers on the table and pulled the report out. "Yup, this just came over to me and it's right here." He turned the top page of the autopsy document back and got to the notes. "Semen was found in the vagina, and Havers was able to determine by examination of the tissue that it was after death. I'm going to ask Syn to give me a sample, and if he refuses, I'll have to force the issue. Maybe that'll finally give me the concrete evidence I need."

"Wait, you're sure. About the semen?"

Butch tapped the page. "It's in the report. And though I have a dim view of my brother-in-law in some respects, I've never had a reason to doubt his clinical findings."

"Well, because if it happened after she died, then Syn wasn't the last male with her."

Frowning, Butch put the autopsy report back down. "What makes you say that?"

Balthazar exhaled a plume of smoke. "Because he can't ejaculate. He never does. So if you're sure that the sex happened afterward, then there was another person with the victim that night."

# THIRTY-SEVEN

The following evening, Boone materialized from Helania's apartment to his father's house. As he stood in the cold, he looked at the study window that he'd broken with the garden hose and its holder. The sounds of two workmales talking inside the house were carried through the hole Boone had made, the flimsy tarp that had been temporarily hung offering scant filter of what was being said.

Chatting aside, they were making progress. The broken, jagged panes of glass had been removed, and were in the process of being replaced one by one. By dawn, he was willing to bet, it would be all fixed.

Then again, Marquist always had been efficient at getting things done, hadn't he—

Helania's springtime scent was the first announcement of her arrival, and right on its heels was her physical form as she materialized beside him. Courtesy of her having fed from him, she could track his whereabouts anywhere, so he hadn't had to give her an address.

As she looked at the mansion's formal entrance, her eyes widened. And then she took a couple of steps back in the snow and stared up, way up, at the house's refined and elegant exterior.

Her expression turned to flat-out shock. "When you said you lived in a big place . . . I had no idea."

Boone shook his head and went over to open the heavy door. "It's still just a roof and four walls at the end of the night."

Stepping inside, he held the great oak panels wide and waited for her to join him. As she approached the doorway, she was careful to stomp the snow off the treads of her boots, and when she came across the threshold, she didn't go far.

Her eyes bounced around the foyer, moving from the stairwell with its carved balustrade to the parlor where he'd had that Fade Ceremony to the open archway of his sire's study. And the entire time she surveyed the grandeur, Boone felt like he wanted to apologize for the show of wealth.

"This is not me," he heard himself say. "I am not this house."

Helania looked at him, and it was a while before she spoke. "But this is where you're from. This is the world you live in."

"Well, it's not anymore." Boone shrugged. "Come on, let's grab a car so we can start looking for that house and get out of here—"

"Where is your room?"

"Upstairs. But it's not important."

"Oh. Okay."

As he held out his hand, she came to him, and he led her through to the back of the house. Passing through the polishing room, she lost her momentum as she eyed the silver trays that were lined up and the uniformed *doggen* who was rubbing them with a pink paste that gradually turned gray.

"Oh, my Lord!" The maid dropped the sponge she was using and bowed low to Boone. "It is my honor—"

"It's okay, not to worry, it's fine—" Boone cut himself off and wished he could get the *doggen* to stand up straight again. Turning to Helania, he said, "I'd like to introduce my—"

"Friend," Helania said as she put out her hand. "I'm his friend."

The *doggen* stared at the palm that had been offered to her with utter shock. Then she glanced at Boone in confusion. "My Lord?"

Boone stepped in and discreetly lowered Helania's arm. "You're doing a wonderful job, Susette. Thank you so much. We'll just be going the now."

As he whisked Helania away into the pantry, she tugged at his sleeve. "What did I do wrong? I don't understand?"

Boone paused in the staging area with all of its counter space taken up with stacks of porcelain dishes. As he eyed the dinner plates, he wondered, given those trays that were being worked on in the other room, whether Marquist was going to try to throw himself a congratulatory party.

*Good luck with that*, Boone thought as he refocused on Helania.

"Have you ever met a *doggen* before? Apart from Fritz?" he asked. "And I don't mean to be disrespectful, I really don't."

"Um . . . no. I've never even been in a household like this."

"Okay, so, *doggen* are very old school and all they want to do is take care of their family. They don't believe they are on our level, and so for you to offer your hand, they don't know how to handle being acknowledged like that. It's unfathomable to them. I personally have never agreed with it, but they have chosen their way, and it is an argument I haven't even tried to broach out of respect for their traditions."

"Oh. I didn't know."

"It's all right. It's forgotten." He smiled darkly. "Besides, it's out of my life now, too, so we don't have to worry about it."

Pulling her into the kitchen, he figured the explanation had good timing given all the *doggen* who were cooking and preparing Last Meal. As Boone checked out the quantities, there wasn't enough to suggest other people were coming over, but he wondered how long that would last.

"Where's the master of the house?" he asked Thomat, who was over by the stove.

The chef bowed. "I believe I am looking at him, sire."

Boone wanted to roll his eyes but stopped himself. "Marquist, I mean."

"He is upstairs, being attended to by a trainer and then a masseuse. Then it is my understanding that he has a tailor coming by, followed by a cobbler."

"Getting himself all done up. Guess my father's clothes didn't go far enough for him and he's given up his nights of shining shoes, huh."

"It is an abomination."

Boone let that one lie where it landed. "I'm taking my car out—oh, and this is Helania. My friend."

As Thomat bowed in the direction of the female, she tucked her hands under her arms, and said, "Pleased to meet you."

"It is my honor." The chef straightened. "If there is aught that you require, mistress, please let me know."

"Thank you."

When Helania glanced at Boone, he gave her a subtle thumbs-up. "We'll be back in a couple of hours, Thomat. To pick up some of my things."

"Yes, my Lord."

It was on the tip of Boone's tongue to suggest the male not use that term anywhere in Marquist's earshot, but he figured that went without saying. Or perhaps the chef didn't care.

*Might be an interesting grudge match*, Boone thought. *Former butler versus current chef?*

All things being equal—and they weren't—he'd bet on Thomat.

Leading the way out into the garages, Boone flipped on the caged lights that hung over the lineup of half a dozen cars. As Helania inhaled sharply, he was reminded that he should be impressed by the display of wealth. But it was what he was used to.

"The Bentley's mine," he said, pointing down the row.

"Which one is that?"

"The gold one. Four down. It has all-wheel drive."

The Continental GT Speed was owned by him, and as he got be-hind the wheel and double-checked that the keys were still in the center console, he realized he could sell it and get some money out of the thing. It had to be worth over a hundred thousand, which was enough to put a down payment on something small on the outskirts of town.

Of course, in this fantasy, he had Helania moving her stuff in with his, and the two of them waiting out the eighteen months before their young arrived in the kind of mating bliss that books were written about.

Ah, fiction. So much better than reality.

Helania got in next to him and shut her door. "Wow."

As she ran her fingertips over the burl ash panels on the dash, he wondered why he'd never particularly paid attention to them. It was really nice wood, and it should be noted.

Instead, he'd only gotten the car 'cuz he'd needed wheels and his cousin knew a guy down in Manhattan who could get him one delivered in twenty-four hours.

The color hadn't mattered. Nor the interior. Nothing about it had seemed particularly significant . . . when in reality, it was a beautiful car, expensively made.

Rich people had a knack for ignoring the wealth that surrounded them, didn't they.

Hitting the garage door opener, Boone craned around and reversed out into the snow. "So where should we start?"

Helania stared out the window at the mansion as they K-turned in the courtyard and he headed them out to the road.

"It's just a house," he muttered. "And I don't mean that like I'm criti-cizing you for looking at it like that. It's more a case of my not liking what the place represents."

"I don't mean to be . . . agog, I think the word is. I've just never seen anything like this outside of the movies. I mean, it's way bigger than Jake Ryan's parents' place."

"Whose?"

"*Sixteen Candles*. The movie. He's the love interest."

"We need to watch that together someday."

"Yes, someday," she murmured as she bent forward to keep looking at the house.

Out on the road, he took them down to the little center of ritzy, locally owned shops where he imagined all the ladies of the houses on his street went to get their nails done, buy presents for each other, and see their decorators and hairstylists.

"Can you recall which neighborhood the house was in?" he asked.

Seeming to shake herself into focus, Helania eased back in her seat. "I wish I had paid more attention that night. But I distinctly remember us passing by Temple Beth Shalom. Do you know where that is?"

"You mean out toward the satellite municipal library? On Sheffield?"

"That's the one."

"I know exactly where that is," he said as he hit his directional signal.

◆    ◆    ◆

About an hour later, Helania looked out the car window beside her, and stopped measuring the streets, the houses, the neighborhoods, against an eight-month-old memory of hers. Instead, she assessed the snowflakes that were starting to fall.

"A storm's here," she said.

As the Bentley's wipers started moving back and forth, Boone cursed. "Is this the blizzard they were talking about?"

"Who was?"

"I don't know."

He sounded tired, but not as if he were ready to pack in the towel yet. She wasn't sure she had much more of this endless circling in her, however. As important as it was to find the house, they were just driving around, following a series of her whims, wasting gas—and now with a storm coming?

God, she wished she could make her brain work better.

The Bentley slowed to a stop on the shoulder of the road, and Boone leaned forward, squinting at a street marker. "Manchester Avenue? Ring any bells?"

Helania glanced around and didn't recognize a thing about the area they were in. "None. And these houses . . . all I recall is that it was a white house with a lot of bushes in front. Tall bushes, so you couldn't see much. I don't know. I think I've wasted our time."

"It's not a waste. Let's keep going."

Fifteen minutes later, the wipers were going back and forth much faster, and the snow falling in the headlights was slashing down.

"I think we should head back," she said. "The storm's getting worse."

"Yeah. But there's always tomorrow night."

Boone turned them around, and as the tires of the powerful car gripped the accumulation that was already inching up, she was glad about the four-wheel-drive thing. "Thank you for this."

"It was my pleasure to serve you."

The words he spoke were offhand, but they made her think about the *doggen*, that house . . . the world he had grown up in.

"Are you sure you're okay giving all of that up?" she asked. "The money, that mansion . . ."

"I've thought a lot about it in the last twenty-four hours, and I can say, hand on heart, that I am. I was never happy there anyway. It's like what you said, you didn't know any different and you're content where you are? Well, I've been on the other side, and I hated it a lot of the time, so I feel lighter and freer."

"I'm really sorry about your *mahmen*. You've had a lot of death in your life."

"No more than anyone else over time—"

As a phone started to ring all around the car's interior, she shot upright. "What the—"

"Sorry, Bluetooth." He frowned. "You mind if I take this?"

"Oh, no, please do."

Boone accepted the call and spoke into the air. "Hello, Rochelle?"

A disembodied voice flooded the cockpit. "Boone?"

"Hey," he said as he braked at a stop sign and then kept going straight ahead. "I meant to call you back last night. Things have been . . . a little hectic on my end. You okay?"

"Are you in the car?" The voice went in and out. "The connection's bad."

"Must be the storm. And yes, I am." His brows went low. "Is everything all right?"

Helania shifted in her seat. So . . . this was the female he'd almost mated. The one who had wanted to back out of the arrangement that he otherwise would have followed through on. The one who was supposedly in love with someone else.

It was hard to deny that she was preternaturally interested in hearing the voice properly. But really, being territorial made no damned sense given everything Boone had told her about the female and their relationship.

"—come see?" Rochelle was saying. "—to talk—to you."

"You want to come see me? Sure, but—"

"Come to—your . . . -se?"

"My house?"

"Yes?" was the reedy reply. "Now?"

Boone looked at the dash. "I'm half an hour away from there. See you in thirty minutes?"

"—minutes?"

"Thirty," he said loudly. "Thirty minutes."

"Yes . . . thirty."

As the call ended, he looked over. "You mind if we go back to my place? I want to fill the car up with clothes and some of my books, anyway."

"Yes, sure." She found herself putting her hand on her belly. "I'd like to meet Rochelle."

"You're really going to like her. She's a female of worth."

Helania forced a smile and then went back to measuring the swirling pixelation of the flakes in the bright headlights.

Given everything that was going on, she did not have the energy or composure necessary to get through meeting Boone's aristocratic almost-*shellan*. But she would do it just to prove to herself that she could stand on her own two feet.

She was all about independence, she reminded herself.

Time to put her money where her mouth was.

"And listen," Boone said, "I just want you to know. I don't have to go to your apartment, you know, after these fourteen nights are up. I figure I'll get some of my stuff now and keep it with me. Marquist is not going to lock me out again, not after the smackdown Wrath put on him. But you never know how things are going to go, and I might as well start the migration earlier rather than later."

Helania pictured him moving in with her, his male clothes in her closet, his big boots taken off just inside the door on her mat, two coffee cups in the sink after First Meal instead of only one.

"You're welcome to stay with me."

# THIRTY-EIGHT

As Butch got a load of Wrath stalking down the training center's corridor, he had to admit the King was still the kind of thing that could make a grown male's ass pucker. Especially given the pissed-off cloud of aggression that floated around him like an evil aura. Vishous was on one side of him, Tohr on the other, Xcor riding the six—and oh, shit.

Wrath had left the golden retriever behind.

So he was getting ready to yell a lot.

Butch straightened from his lean against the concrete wall. "What's doin'."

"Where is he?" Wrath demanded.

"Over here."

Butch led the procession of doom to the patient room they'd been keeping Syn in, like the Bastard was a wild animal with a communicable disease. Knocking on the door, Vishous popped things wide open before there was an answer.

As Wrath crashed through the bodies between him and the room, it was clear that blindness wasn't completely dispositive when it came to his spatial orientation. But there were limits.

"Someone point me in the Bastard's direction," he barked.

Tohr stepped up and pivoted the King without saying a word. And then he backed the fuck off like he didn't want to be knocked out by shrapnel.

Syn, who had been vacillating between not-giving-a-shit and fucking-everyone-and-his-mother-off, straightened on the bed and for once didn't pull the smirk routine. Not that Wrath technically would have noticed—although, given the King's ability to scent things, he might well have picked up on any disrespect. And in his current frame of mind, he was clearly inclined to bitch-slap the stoopid right out of anybody.

"Talk to me, Butch," the King snapped as he glared down at the Bastard.

Butch had been preparing for this ever since he'd pulled the trigger on getting the King down here. The case was bizarrely stalled; there weren't many more rocks to look under when it came to the Bastard, and they couldn't keep the guy down here forever if there wasn't a valid reason for the lock-and-key routine.

Syn deserved to be released or rifled in the skull. Or at least given some kind of idea as to when either of those two eventualities were going to fall on his head. It was only fair—and the kind of call only Wrath could make.

Clearing his throat, Butch kept shit efficient: Helania's accusation and ID. Syn's confession. The shit about the laundry. The count of the leathers. The fact that, contrary to what he'd assumed would be the case, the locker Syn used down here in the training center not holding anything relevant to the case. The failure to ejaculate.

The last thing that he spelled out was Balthazar's report on the past, minus the Tiny Tim details about the family situation and the traumatic brain injury.

Now, technically, that last part, about the other killings in the Old Country, as well as the brutal one three nights ago of a human assailant, were prejudicial. Evidence of previous crimes was never admissible in human courts. But this was the vampire world, so the rules were different and Wrath was so much more levelheaded than human juries—

"So did you fucking do it or not," the King snapped.

Okay. Fine. Maybe "levelheaded" wasn't exactly the right word.

"You heard Butch," Syn said.

Wrath leaned down to the Bastard, his long hair falling off his heavy shoulder and swinging loose like a shroud. "Well, I want to hear you say it."

Syn shrugged. "No reason to duplicate efforts. And he did such a good job—"

As something rushed forward, Butch caught the movement out of the corner of his eye—and had to quickly hell-no that shit. Vishous, apparently coming to the conclusion that his status as resident smart-ass was being challenged by Syn's show of attitude, had decided to bum-rush the hospital bed.

Butch lunged forward and caught his best friend before shit went total chaos.

"Not helpful," Butch hissed in V's ear as he dragged his roomie back. "You've got to chill."

"Listen to your bestie, V," Wrath muttered. "And stay out of this."

There was a long period of quiet, during which Syn refused to meet his King's blind eyes—and Butch passed the time making sure his tight hold around V's chest didn't lose tension. Knowing V, the brother was in danger of trying to beat a confession out of the Bastard.

And not only was that coercive, Butch had the sense it was what Syn wanted.

"I'm going to be perfectly clear here," Wrath said in a sharp voice. "We are not going to play suicide-by-cop with you. If you want off this planet on a technicality, that's fine, but I am not going to let my males help you do it. You're either going to have to kill yourself or wait for the Grim Reaper to serve you your walking papers. But what you are *not* going to do is use us and that situation down at Pyre to help you get into the Fade."

Syn crossed his arms over his naked chest and clenched his jaw.

"So," Wrath continued, "I'm going to ask you again. Did you kill those two females at Pyre?"

The silence that followed was so dense and so long-lasting that Butch nearly screamed. Except then Syn opened his mouth.

"Yes, I killed them. Both of them."

The King's nostrils flared, and nobody in the room moved. In fact, Butch was pretty sure everything in Caldwell stopped dead.

"Why are you lying to me," the King said grimly.

◆   ◆   ◆

Given the blizzard-like conditions, Boone made better time getting back to the house than he thought he would, although even the Bentley's all-wheel drive struggled to get them up the hill to his former neighborhood. When they pulled into the drive, he went right to the front door so that bringing his things out would be easier.

As he shut off the engine, he looked over at Helania. "We'll go out again. Tomorrow night."

She nodded. "Yes, please."

They both got out of the car, and she waited for him to come around, the heavy falling snow making a picture out of her as it collected in her beautiful hair. Stepping up to her, he captured her face in his hands and stared down into her eyes. There were things he wanted to say, but he kept them to himself, mindful of the news they were waiting to hear. Whether or not she was pregnant didn't change anything for him, and to prove that, he felt as though he had to wait until they knew one way or the other before he could tell her he loved her.

If she wasn't with his young, he would be disappointed, but it would be his best shot at reassuring her his feelings and commitment were real. And if she was?

Well, as Doc Jane had said, they'd just have to cross that bridge if they got to it.

Boone brushed his thumb over her cheek. "I want you to know that the fact you're here makes it easier for *me* to be here."

Helania linked her hands over his forearms. "I'm really glad."

Dropping his head, he kissed a snowflake off her lower lip. "Come on, it's cold."

Approaching the front door, a gust pushed at their backs and he had to catch her and help her up the steps. Entering the foyer, it was a relief to get out of the storm, but when the lights dimmed and then flickered, he shook his head.

"I think it's getting worse," he said as he muscled the heavy door closed against the wind. "If that's possible."

Helania looked down at her boots. "I'm covered in snow."

"This carpet can take it." He stomped his feet to make her feel better. "Not to worry."

She insisted on taking her footwear off, and then she was careful with her parka. "Do you have a ladies' room? And maybe a cup of tea—"

"Welcome home, my Lord." Thomat came out from the back. "Would you all care for some coffee? Hot chocolate?"

"Oh, hot cocoa, please." Helania smiled at the chef. "And I'll help you get it ready."

As the chef recoiled, she cursed. "Oh, no. I did it again. I'm not supposed to help, am I?"

Thomat smiled slowly at her. Then he glanced at Boone. "If my Lord would permit his gracious guest to aid us in preparing hot cocoa and perhaps a small plate of sandwiches for tea, we would be most welcoming of her participation. With my Lord's permission."

Boone smiled back at the chef. Then he mouthed, *You're the best.*

"Hey." Helania nudged him in the side. "I can read lips, remember."

"Yes, you can." Boone swooped in for a quick kiss. Against her mouth, he whispered, "Do you want to translate what's on my mind all of a sudden?"

As she blushed, she said, "Not in mixed company, no, I don't. But I am so ready for something warm."

Thomat hid a laugh, and then he bowed and indicated the way to the kitchen. "Follow me, mistress, and I believe you inquired after a water closet. I shall be pleased to show you to our formal one for the females."

"Wonderful. Oh, and I'll make sure we have something for Rochelle, too."

"Thank you," Boone said as a warm feeling filled him that didn't have a damn thing to do with the furnaces in the house.

Helania gave him a little wave, and then the chef in his formal white coat, and the female in her jeans and sweater, went off together through the elegant dining room.

The door knocker sounded.

Hurrying over, he opened things. "Oh, Rochelle, come in—this storm is rank."

Rochelle entered and stamped her high-heeled boots on the carpet as he shut the storm out again.

"Horrible," she said. "Just horrible—"

As the lights dimmed once more, they both looked up to the fixture overhead. Outside, the wind howled even louder.

"I think it's getting worse?" she said as she unwrapped the cashmere scarf that covered her coiffed head.

"Here, let me take your coat."

After he helped her out of a lemon yellow drape that was heavier than it looked, Rochelle removed her gloves and smoothed the chignon she had her blond hair in. Her cheeks were bright from the wind and the cold, her lipstick a perfect nude color, her makeup light and tasteful. The perfume she was wearing . . . Cristalle by Chanel, her signature scent.

Her eyes were curiously frantic.

Boone frowned as he put her coat aside and took his own off. "Come in here, sit down by the fire."

As he drew her into the parlor, she didn't go toward the cheerful flames at the marble hearth. She went to the windows that faced out into the storm—and he was reminded of that night, a year ago, when he had come down to this room and found her looking out at the darkness in just the same way.

"What's going on," he said soberly. "Talk to me."

Rochelle took a deep breath, her reflection in the glass one of almost unfathomable grief. "This is where it all started."

"I'm sorry?"

She looked over her shoulder. She was wearing winter-white slacks with a matching jacket, a citrine version of Tiffany's Bird on a Rock on the left lapel.

"Here in this room," she said. "This is where you and I met for the first time alone . . . and everything changed."

Boone inclined his head and sat on the sofa. "It is. I was just thinking that myself."

"I need to be more honest with you than I've been."

"Okay." He patted the cushion beside him. "Come over and sit, you're looking very pale."

But Rochelle didn't move toward him. She covered her face with her hands and took a deep breath. "I don't know how to do this. I've practiced and practiced. But now that I'm here with you . . ."

"Rochelle. There is nothing you can tell me that will change my opinion of you. Do you understand that? Nothing."

Dropping her hands, she approached the sofa and perched on the very edge of a cushion. After a long silence, her voice was low.

"When I came here and told you I couldn't go through with the arrangement, I misled you."

"How so?" Not that it mattered to him. "And whatever it is, it's all right."

"I told you . . . I told you I was in love with someone."

Boone reached out and put a hand on her thin shoulder. "It's all right, just tell me—"

"It wasn't a male."

"So he was a human?" Boone eased back and shrugged. "I mean, you told me he was a civilian, were you just worried about telling me he—"

"It wasn't a 'he.'"

"I don't underst—" Boone's brows popped. "Oh."

Rochelle crossed her legs and linked her hands on her knee. "Yes . . . oh. It was a female. I was in love . . . with a female."

As his surprise faded, the math that followed was quick. "No wonder you kept it a secret. The fucking *glymera*—"

"Does this change how you think of me?" Her eyes locked on the fire, as if she couldn't bear to see any disapproval on his face. "You can be honest. Please."

Boone recoiled. "Of course it doesn't. Did the fact that I fell in love with a civilian change your opinion of me?"

"Are you serious?" Rochelle frowned. "Not at all. I was just glad you were happy. Are happy, that is."

"Well, I only want *you* to be happy. As far as I'm concerned, that's all that matters."

Lowering her head back into her hands, Rochelle started to shake— and Boone stroked her shoulder, letting her have a moment of emotional release.

"She's dead," Rochelle said. "My love is dead . . ."

"Oh, God." Boone eased to the side and got out a handkerchief from the back pocket of his leathers. "She's dead?"

Sniffling, Rochelle accepted the square and pressed it to her face. "She's dead and part of me died with her. I haven't been the same since. I am never going to be the same."

"Dearest Virgin Scribe . . . Rochelle. Tell me what happened." He rubbed her back again. "From the beginning. And I can't imagine what it's like, holding this all in."

His friend took a shuddering breath. "When I came here, a year ago, to break the arrangement with you, she and I had decided to stop fighting the attraction and commit to a relationship. I was scared about my family finding anything out, but she was . . . she was my whole world. I'd never been so happy, so complete. And she didn't know about you. She didn't know about . . . all of this and everything that comes with it." Rochelle indicated the formal room with her hand. "I knew I couldn't go through with the mating with you. Not just because of what it would do to her, but because of what it would do to you. Both of you deserved more than that. And she especially deserved my respect and my love. She was no one's shameful secret."

"So you came here . . ."

"And I told you, and you called me brave." Rochelle sniffed again and patted her nose. "I'm not brave. I was trying to hold on to my family and have her at the same time. I knew my parents would never understand or accept her, and worse, I'm their only offspring. After me? There is no one left of the bloodline. I was hemming and hawing over this so-called problem . . . when . . ."

Distantly, he caught a whiff of hot chocolate and straightened. Maybe he should tell Helania to wait a moment? After all, even though he trusted Helania with everything in his life, she was a stranger to Rochelle.

"Ah . . . listen, Rochelle." He reached for her hand. "I'm just going to—"

As the contact with his friend's palm was made, Boone froze, a sense of shock and disbelief flooding through him. While Rochelle sniffed again and looked at him as if she were waiting for him to finish her sentence, he slowly turned her hand over.

There, in the center, was a network of fine scars that had been salted into place.

"What is it?" she asked him.

Boone swallowed hard as he stared at the wounds. "Where did you get these?"

"I buried my love. Out at a state park. With her sister—"

The crash of a tray shattered the quiet, and Boone jumped up. Helania was standing in the archway of the parlor, her face white, her hands shaking, the mugs of hot cocoa and plates of sandwiches in a mess at her feet.

"What are you doing here?" she croaked out to Rochelle.

# THIRTY-NINE

Helania went completely numb as she stared at the female who was sitting, composed as a matron, on Boone's formal sofa. The clothes and the jewelry were nothing familiar, nor was the makeup or the hairstyle, but the face . . . that face was unforgettable.

And the recognition was not only on Helania's side.

The female slowly stood up, her hand falling out of Boone's, her visage going pale. "It's . . . you."

Helania went to take a step forward, but when she put her foot down, it was on broken china. Falling off-balance, she caught herself on the archway's molding. When she looked up next, the female was right in front of her.

"I don't understand," Helania said.

The female stared at her for the longest time. "You look so much like her it hurts."

The next thing she knew they were embracing like family who had been separated for a generation. And in that moment, Helania did not care about anything other than the fact that this stranger, whom she'd met at a great, tragic turning point in her life, was *here*.

"They found Isobel's killer," Helania said in a rush. "We have him. I was trying to reach you to let you know."

"They do?" The female pulled back. "They found him?"

"Yes. The Brotherhood has him."

"Oh, thank God."

"I tried to contact you on Facebook to let you know. He didn't just kill Isobel. He killed another female—"

"I know." The female looked at Boone. "And that's why I asked to see you tonight."

It was at that point that Helania put two and two together more properly. "Wait . . . you were arranged to be mated with Boone. You were going to be his *shellan.*"

"Yes." There was a long pause. "I'm Rochelle."

"Rocky B. Winkle. On Facebook."

"Yes." The female looked back and forth between them. Then she stepped away. "Helania . . . how much did Isobel tell you about us?"

"She said that you were best friends? And you told me that yourself."

Rochelle took another step back. "Did she . . . tell you about her boyfriend?"

"Yes, oh my God, do you know him? Can you get in touch with him?" Helania nodded toward Boone, who was sitting with great stillness on the sofa. "He and I have been working on the investigation into Isobel's death—and also on a second killing. That's how he and I met, by the way. And we've been hoping to find that male who meant so much to Isobel." She glanced back at Boone. "See, I told you Isobel's mate wasn't the one who killed her. I knew he made her happier than I'd ever seen her before."

When no one said anything else, Helania looked to the female, but Rochelle just kept staring at Boone. Who kept staring up at Helania.

"What?" Helania said.

The other female took a deep breath and dropped to her knees. One by one, she gathered the broken china pieces and put them on the tray that Helania and Thomat had worked so hard on to kit out nicely.

"We're going to need a cloth of some kind to properly clean this up," Rochelle murmured. "Perhaps we should call a *doggen*—"

"You can tell her what you just told me," Boone said softly. "It's okay."

Rochelle froze with half a plate in her hands. Lifting her eyes, she stared upward at Helania. And then in a quiet voice, she whispered. "Your sister . . . was my one great love."

Helania opened her mouth to say something—but then she blinked. Did a double-take. Felt sure that she had not heard what she had, but rather had read the female's lips incorrectly.

"Isobel . . ." Rochelle repeated, "was my lover. We were so much more than friends."

Tears threatened in the female's lovely eyes . . . and then spilled down her cheeks, dripping off into the ruined china.

"I never knew," Helania heard herself say hoarsely. "I never guessed . . ."

*That my sister was gay*, she thought.

"I told her she couldn't tell anyone." Rochelle placed the half plate onto the tray and sat back on her high-heeled boots. "I made her promise, because of who my family was, that she wouldn't tell a soul. And that was the first of so many regrets for me after she was gone."

"I never guessed," Helania repeated. "She referred to you as her—"

"Boyfriend. I know. I told her to."

"Wait, that night." Helania lowered herself down so they could be eye to eye. "That night you came to tell me she was dead . . ."

"I knew where she lived. She'd told me your address. When we found her in that club . . . I can't even tell you what that was like. I knew she would want you to know immediately—instead of having to wonder and worry about what had happened to her when she didn't come home. So I took her body to my secret house, the one I bought on my own and my parents never go to—"

"The white house."

"On Macon Avenue. Where we prepared her for the Fade Ceremony."

Helania glanced back at Boone. "So we were close tonight." She refocused on Rochelle. "We were trying to find that house. I couldn't remember the address. I was desperate to find you."

"I live there now." Rochelle let herself fall back so she was sitting on the floor, and the fact that her pristine white slacks were getting stained with hot chocolate didn't seem to matter to her in the slightest. "That night, while you and I were preparing her, I wanted to tell you the truth. But I'm a coward—and I didn't know how you'd react, either. The last thing I wanted to do was spoil your memories of your sister. She loved you so much. She thought about you all the time. All she ever wanted was to take care of you—and the idea I might ruin that memory of her in your mind . . . I couldn't tell you because I didn't know what your thoughts on us were going to be."

Helania remembered back to the months leading up to Isobel's death. How Isobel had been so very happy, so radiant, so optimistic. Unlike anything Helania had seen before.

Reaching out with her scarred palm, she put her hand on the other female's shoulder. In a strong, certain voice, she said, "Let me tell you what my thoughts are. You were the love of her life, too, and you made her happier than I'd ever seen her."

Rochelle's eyes welled with new tears. And then the female put her scarred hand over Helania's.

"I cannot tell you," the female said roughly, "what that means to me. It's like Isobel just spoke to me from the grave."

◆    ◆    ◆

Sitting on the sidelines, Boone was both having trouble catching up and feeling very proud of the two females on the floor in front of him. Surrounded by the broken shards of the *glymera's* propriety, Rochelle and Helania were reaching across, literally and figuratively, the divide of misinformation and lifestyle and death . . . and finding solace in each other.

Even though he'd never met Isobel, he had to imagine she was staring down from the Fade, glowing with happiness that the two most important people in her life were finding a measure of peace.

After they embraced for a second time, Rochelle looked at Boone. "But there's more. And this is why I asked to see you."

Boone got up off the sofa and decided to join the not-so-tea party on the hard floor. It just felt so right to throw convention and standards away and cop a squat here in the archway, broken crap all over the place, secrets being revealed, questions being answered.

Healing beginning.

He picked up the handle of a mug and toyed with it. "Tell us."

"It goes back to before. When the arrangement was made." Rochelle frowned and shook her head. "Shortly after I met you, I started to feel as if I were being watched. Followed. I couldn't pin it down, but I would be at my parents' house and I would look out the windows . . . and I would swear that somebody was there. It was so eerie. And then one night, I met up with Isobel at Pyre, and I felt like this male was following me as I went around the club." She looked at Helania. "We used to go there because we didn't have to hide our relationship. With all those masks and cloaks, we could be free. But I remember that night—we'd gone in my car because I'd just gotten it and I felt like driving. After we arrived . . . I just had this strange sense I was being trailed."

"Fucking Syn," Boone muttered.

"It kept up for quite a while. And then . . . Isobel was killed." Rochelle closed her eyes. "I didn't go back to the club after that and it disappeared. The sense . . . went away. I didn't think about it again until . . ." She looked back and forth. "Until Mai was killed a week ago."

Boone jerked forward. "Mai? Wait, what? You know about her killing, the second one?"

"She was our friend. Isobel's and mine. She was the only person who knew about us."

"She was the other female?" Helania stammered. "That night I came to your house? But wait . . . oh, of course, I didn't recognize her when I found her because she was wearing the mask. And then in those terrible pictures after she was dead . . . I couldn't bear to look at them on that wall in the evidence room."

"Mai was the second death down there." Rochelle looked at Boone. "And I found out about it from a friend of ours the night—"

"Of my father's Fade Ceremony," Boone filled in. "That's why you were so upset."

"To lose her as well. It was almost too much."

Outside the mansion, the storm surged with a gale-force gust, the lights flickering and going out. But just as Boone was thinking about finding a candelabra, the electricity came back on.

Rochelle put her hand over her heart. "When I heard about Mai, I didn't know what to do. Who to talk to. I didn't know whether the deaths were connected, although—"

"They were," Boone said. "And it has to be the same male who was stalking you. There are too many connections."

"That's what my intuition tells me. Two deaths, in the same place, so close together? But I hesitated to come forward because I'd kept everything with Isobel a secret. I was stewing over it all when I saw the posting the Brotherhood put out on social media—and that's when I got your direct message." After she nodded to Helania, she looked again in Boone's direction. "I texted you last night to come see you so we could talk it all out and figure out what to do."

"We were at the training center. I meant to text you back, I'm so sorry."

"We're here now, it's okay. And you tell me they found out who it was?"

Boone nodded. "He's one of the fighters who works with the Brotherhood. He has a history of stalking and killing females."

"So he must have found Mai and Isobel through me? But how did he find me, and why am I important?"

"He went to Pyre. Just like you did. He must have started following you because of that."

"I guess that was the connection. So am I next?"

Before he could answer, she got a distant look on her face, and Boone frowned. "What else?"

"Well, it's about Mai." Rochelle took a deep breath and glanced at Helania. "I think she might have had contact with him. By phone."

"How so?" Boone said.

"After Isobel's death, Mai moved into my house on Macon Avenue. She said she needed a place to stay, but I think she was just worried about me, and I'd taken to spending a lot of the days there. I mean, I was crying at the drop of the hat, and I couldn't explain to my parents why, you know? They're good people, but they're totally traditional. Anyway, over the last week or two, I could hear Mai arguing with someone on the phone during the day, her voice raised. Whenever I asked her what was wrong, she wouldn't tell me. It was clear, though, that she was very upset. Maybe it was that male."

"Syn has a cell phone for sure. And with the kind of reach the Brotherhood has? He could have found her contact information through a species database or something."

"That must be how it happened." Rochelle looked at Helania. "I go out and visit Isobel at her grave. Do you?"

"Yes, absolutely." Helania frowned. "And you know, I kept all of her things. Would you like to come to my apartment and see them? Maybe you would like some?"

"You would do that?" Rochelle said in a choked voice. "Give . . . some to me?"

"Yes." Helania smiled. "I am absolutely sure that that is what she would have wanted."

"When can we go there?"

Helania glanced at Boone. "We're headed back to my apartment now. Come with us. And we can update the Brotherhood from there if you like. You'd certainly have more privacy."

Boone got to his feet and brushed off his leathers. Bending down, he picked up the tray. "We have a plan. I've just got to get a change of clothes and some books, and we're out of here."

Rochelle's expression warmed. "Are you two moving in together?"

"Ah, kind of," Boone said as Helania stayed silent.

"Well, I'm happy for you both."

"Thanks, friend." He nodded at the tray. "I'll be right back."

As he took his leave, he heard the females start talking about Isobel, and was aware of being sad he'd never meet Helania's sister . . . and Rochelle's great love.

She must have been a helluva good person, he thought.

Back in the kitchen, he dumped everything on the tray in the trash and told Thomat to have someone clean up the floor in a little bit—he wanted to give his two females a little more time to themselves. Then he went back through the pantry and paused in the open door to Marquist's former suite.

Ah, yes. Moving boxes. Just what he needed—

As his phone went off, he took it out, and as soon as he saw it was Butch, he answered. "I was just about to call you. We found Isobel's . . ." He hesitated, unsure of how much Rochelle wanted to keep quiet. Plus God only knew where Marquist was in the house. "We found the friend who helped bury Isobel, the one Helania was looking for—"

"Syn didn't do it."

Boone took his phone away from his ear and stared at the thing. Then he put it back into place. "What did you say?"

"He lied. Wrath could scent it." The Brother laughed in a harsh rush. "The great Blind King doubles as one hell of a polygraph test."

"Wait, this makes no sense. Helania saw him with Mai, with the female he killed."

"He was with Mai. But he wasn't the *last* person to be with her."

"That's not possible. Why would he lie?"

"Look, I'm not going to argue or debate why in the hell that fighter would cop to something he didn't do because I can't fathom his reasoning about anything at this point. He's really fucked in the head, to be honest. But be that as it may, he did not kill either of those females or the human one who was found first at the club."

Boone thought back to that alley, and the human male he'd castrated and tortured . . . that Syn had taken responsibility for.

Before he could bring all that up, Butch continued, "Bottom line, we've got no concrete evidence on him anyway. No bloody clothes. No meat hooks hiding under his bed, not that he has one."

Boone could only shake his head. "It doesn't make sense."

"Actually, it makes perfect sense when you remember what I told you about confirmation bias. I've been there—fuck it, I *am* there with this case. I just thought you'd want to know the updates, and Helania needs to be told, too. I think you should both come down here."

Boone looked over his shoulder. "She's here with me at my house. We've promised the friend that she could go check out some of Isobel's stuff back at the apartment. But after that we can come in, and I want to bring the friend with us. There's another angle to everything, but I can't go into it where I am now."

"Okay. Just call Fritz. He's ready to go get you, even in this storm."

As Boone ended the call, he felt like throwing his phone at the wall. What stopped him was the fact that the fucking killer was still out there somewhere and he might need the goddamn thing.

Stepping over the threshold of Marquist's former quarters, he headed toward the moving boxes—

The lights went out, this time with no flicker warning. Disoriented in the dark, Boone bumped into a chair, then kicked into something low and heavy, the whatever-it-was toppling over and scattering whatever it held.

Just as he was fumbling with his phone to get the flashlight on, the electricity came back on and he looked down.

What he'd managed to bootlick was a shoe-shine kit, the wooden box on its side, the put-your-foot-here contours of the top popped open. Metal tins of polish and a stained chamois rag, as well as a vial of little sole nails, had spilled like blood and organs from a victim, the impact of his steel-toed shitkicker spreading them out in a fan.

Of course Marquist would leave the kit here. No more shoe polishing—

Boone frowned as something caught his eye. Lowering himself down, he got a closer look at the carpet. The tiny sole nails that had come out of their container were like nettles, and he picked one up, inspecting its sliver of a body and pin-headed top.

It was just like the one that had come out of Mai's skin.

But . . . it wasn't possible there was a connection.

Rising to his feet, he looked around the sitting room with fresh eyes. Except, come on, like he expected Marquist to have a meat hook hanging on the back of the door?

Proceeding into the bedroom area, Boone checked out the bedside table, ducked under the bed skirt—another meat-hook-free zone—and opened the blanket chest in the corner.

Which had blankets in it, natch.

He was turning around toward the open closet when the heating fan came on, a barely perceptible draft of cool air the preamble to the hot stuff—provided, of course, the electricity wasn't cut again.

And that was when he caught the scent. It was so subtle, he barely noticed it.

But like sharks in ocean waters, vampires were evolutionarily adapted to find blood.

His head cranked around of its own volition, and then his body moved slowly.

Off in the distance, he heard the thump of the front door shutting, but he didn't pay any attention to the sound. Every part of his consciousness was trained on that closet.

With a feeling of utter unreality, he reached out and pulled heavy, black folds forward.

When he'd looked in here the night before, he'd made a wrong assumption. What he'd thought was a black bathrobe was, in fact . . . a black cloak. And as he put his nose to the thick fabric?

He smelled blood. Dried blood, but blood nonetheless. And it was from a female.

What the fuck?

# FORTY

In the foyer of Boone's family's mansion, Helania stood aside as Rochelle put on a lemon yellow draping coat—which was probably worth more than the truck Helania had back at her place. And yet the female had no pretension about her.

"I really need you to know," Rochelle was saying, "that I was wrong to make Isobel stay silent about us. I put her in such a terrible position, and all because of my own fear. But that's over now. I'm not hiding any longer. If all this has taught me nothing else, it's that life is short, no matter how many nights you're given, and I'm not wasting any more time. I'm going to come out to my parents and move all the way into that white house—and just so you know, you and Boone are welcome anytime."

Helania smiled a little sadly, and then murmured, "You never know what the future holds."

Putting her hand on her lower belly, she thought about duty and obligation—and people sacrificing for a greater good that meant they didn't live their full lives. She and Boone were going to have to resolve their relationship at some point, but she was afraid of the future for them. Pregnant or not . . . she wanted to believe they would be together, but she worried about that dutiful side of him.

The part that meant he sacrificed himself, no matter the cost.

Sure, the sex they had was good. But it was nothing worth compromising your future for.

As the lights went out again, she waited for them to come back on. When they did, Rochelle was looking over expectantly, as if she were hoping for a less obtuse statement of where things stood between Boone and Helania.

"It's just," Helania said, "you know, he and I—who knows what will happen."

The beautiful blond aristocrat frowned. "He's in love with you."

Helania recoiled, but at the same time, a secret place in her heart got excited. The former she didn't try to hide. The latter, she forced herself to temper.

"He can't be in love with me. I don't know if he's told you, but I went through my needing the other night. So . . . if he said we're getting mated or something, it's only because of that—"

"He didn't tell me anything about your time having come. But he did say to me that he'd fallen in love with you at his father's Fade Ceremony."

Helania did the math on the days of the week. Wait . . . that had been before her needing. "What are you talking about?"

"Right in there." The female pointed off across the foyer. "In the males' formal bathroom. He was melting down in the middle of the crowd after the ceremony, and I took him in there for a break. He told me he was in love with you. Look, you guys do what you want, but bonded males? They fall within seconds, as the saying goes. And I have to tell you, Boone's one of the very best males I—"

The blow to Helania's head came from out of nowhere. One moment, she was grappling with a total game changer; the next, she was aware of the other female rearing back in terror. Before she could ask why, a ringing pain exploded in her skull, the impact of whatever it was causing her to lurch to the side, stumble . . . fall.

As she hit the ground, her vision went fuzzy and her hearing phased out completely. But as it turned out, she was just a secondary target. Rochelle was backing up against the foyer wall, someone coming toward her with menace and a long-bladed knife.

Training all her will into her eyesight, Helania tried to carve a window of focus out of everything that was so blurry—and finally her vision cleared. It was then that she saw the attacker's face, even if she couldn't tell much about his body or his limbs.

It was a formally dressed male, with salt-and-pepper-streaked hair that was brushed back from his forehead. He had a murderous expression on what was otherwise an evenly featured face, and his lips were moving as he spoke. Helania fell back on old habits as she read them.

. . . *should have killed you instead of those other two. More efficient that way, but I thought there would be talk. My master did not deserve his bloodline to be sullied by that broken arrangement. And I know what you were doing with that female. I saw you, I watched you.*

Helania tried to lift her head, lift her arm, shift her body, cry out.

*Your friend asked for it. She dared to threaten me with exposure. Somehow she found out it was me and—*

Isobel. Mai.

This was the killer!

Adrenaline surged through Helania's body as her instincts fired and aggression flooded into her veins. Forcing her head up, she looked for a weapon. For anything. The male was crazed and dangerous—

The knife that came up over his shoulder was viciously sharp, and the light from the chandelier overhead gleamed on its polished steel blade.

Shoving herself off the floor, Helania—

Boone's leather jacket was lying on a chair right beside where she'd landed, and she remembered it back in her apartment, falling to the floor from the weight of the guns in it.

She moved faster than she had ever before in her life, some vast reserve of inner power mobilizing her body. Lunging for the jacket, she grabbed hold of the folds just as the lights went out again.

*Dagger hand*, she thought as she flipped the leather around, her hands shaking. He was right-handed—

Plunging into the deep pocket on the right side, she palmed Boone's gun and freed the safety. She knew it was loaded by the heaviness of it, and what do you know, the weapon was the same make and model she used.

When the lights came back on, she had the barrel up in position and she pulled the trigger just as the attacker started the downward arc of his stabbing motion.

The bullet went right into the head at the temple. Exactly where she had aimed.

One kill shot was all it took.

In a horrible montage she knew she was never going to forget, a fine spray of blood and splatter of brain matter hit the heavy front door in a daisy pattern and the male crumpled down to the floor.

Her whole body shook. But the gun was steady as a stone in her palms as she kept it on him.

"Get behind me Rochelle," she ordered.

The other female scrambled and tripped, coming around and taking cover as Helania kept Boone's muzzle trained on the male.

"Go get Boone now—"

"I'm here!" his voice shouted. "I'm right here."

Helania nodded as his thundering footfalls came down to the drama, his attention no doubt caught by the sound of shot. But she did not move. The attacker's body was twitching in random places, and she wasn't sure whether he was going to get back up.

Dimly, she heard Boone talking on his phone. And then, in her peripheral vision, she was aware of other people coming into the foyer, staff members, given their uniforms.

Abruptly, Boone was very close to her, standing just off to the side of her straight-out, stiff-as-a-board forearms. "Helania, you can lower the gun now—"

"I don't know if he's dead," she choked out. "How do I know he's dead."

"You got him," came his gentle voice. "You saved Rochelle's life and you got him. But I need you to put the gun down. The Brothers are on their way and we don't want anyone to get hurt."

She focused on the red stain on that door . . . and the little hole she could see in the center of it where the bullet had ended its journey through living matter inside of the wood.

"I wanted to be there when Isobel's killer died," she said hoarsely. "I needed to be there."

"Well, you did one better. You *ahvenged* your sister in the proper way. You took his life as he took hers."

That was what unlocked her. All of a sudden her hands and her arms were shaking and weak, and just as she was about to drop the gun from her hold, Boone scooped the weapon out of her palms and put the safety on.

Falling into his strong body, Helania wept for everything.

For Isobel.

For Mai.

For what would have happened if, God forbid . . . she had missed.

◆    ◆    ◆

As Boone held Helania against his body, his brain tried to catch up with reality: Marquist was slumped on the floor, part of his brain and a splash of his blood on the front door. Rochelle was collapsed onto a chair, her hands to her face as if she were holding in a scream. Thomat and the *doggen* had rushed in from the kitchen, their bodies together in a clutch as they held on to each other.

Outside the house, the winter storm raged, winds rattling the shutters, snow lashing at the windows. But that was nothing compared to the frozen chaos inside the silent, still foyer.

Rochelle lifted terrified eyes. "He tried to kill me. Helania . . . saved me . . ."

"Why?" Boone asked. "What the hell was he thinking—"

"He said it was for his master." The female looked at the body, which had finally stopped twitching. "He said . . . he refused to let shame come unto this household."

"So he was the one stalking you?" Boone repositioned Helania against him. "He must have found out—"

"About Isobel," Rochelle finished. "But you and I had already ended the arrangement and she was killed after that. Why did he have to take her if it was already done?"

Boone could only shake his head. "He told me he would do anything to protect this house and my sire. He must have worried that if you were seen with Isobel, the truth would come out and the shame wouldn't have been solely on you."

Helania lifted her head off his chest. "He killed my sister for social propriety?"

"And Mai," Rochelle added. "He said that Mai had been threatening to come forward with details about the killing, details that would prove he was the one who did it. She had been determined to discover who was trailing me and had found him through the coat check girl. Somehow, that human knew him from a self-defense training course they had taken together. He told me he thought that was ironic . . . he was babbling incoherently."

"Poor Mai," Helania said. "She was really good to my sister."

"She was my dear friend." Rochelle shook her head. "She knew that ever since Isobel died, I've been utterly heartbroken. Part of that was not knowing who had killed her and why. Clearly, Mai was trying to solve the mystery and get me answers."

"I wish she'd asked for help," Boone said sadly.

"There are too many secrets in the *glymera*," Rochelle gritted out. "Too many things that our class refuses to talk about. And silence is deadly—"

The banging on the door was loud.

"Do not come in yet!" Boone shouted. "Hold on!"

Looking down at Helania, he smoothed her hair back. "Are you okay to stand."

"Yes," she replied. "I have my own two feet to hold me up. And they will do the job."

After dropping a quick kiss on her mouth, Boone went into the study. The workmales who had been fixing the damage there earlier had mostly finished with the window, but they hadn't completely sealed up the hole before they'd clearly gone home due to the storm. The piece of bright blue plastic tarping had been secured against the panes, and he ripped it free.

"Over here—come in here!" he called through the vacancy in the panes.

Not that the Brothers couldn't have just materialized in anywhere— but if Butch had taught him one thing during the investigation, it was that crime scenes needed to be protected and he knew it was safer for the Brothers, however many were coming, to gather in his sire's study first.

And sure enough, one by one, they appeared: V was first. Then Tohr and Phury. Last was Qhuinn. Butch entered from one of the parlor's French doors when V went over and opened it up for him.

The former cop looked through into the foyer. "What the *hell* happened here?"

Boone glanced back at Rochelle. When she nodded, he went through it all: Their broken arrangement. Her relationship with Isobel. The stalking. The killing of Isobel to keep the secret. Then Mai's threatening Marquist and him murdering the female and desecrating her in a fury.

As he spoke, Butch and the Brothers walked over and took a look at the body.

"And then Marquist tried to attack Rochelle," Boone said. "But Helania . . . took care of the problem."

Helania looked up from where she'd taken a seat on the floor next to Rochelle. Her face was pale, and she was still shaking, but oh, she had been so brave. So strong. So . . . sure . . . when the moment had really counted.

He had never been so impressed with anyone in his life. And all he wanted to do was hold her and make sure she was still alive. Even though he could see reality right in front of him, his heart was so terrified at the prospect of ever losing her that he kept worrying that somehow the ending had been different and he just refused to see the truth.

"Helania shot him once," he concluded. "Exactly where she needed to."

Butch glanced over at the females. "Are you both okay?"

Helania put her hand to the back of her head. "He hit me with something."

"It was the butt of the knife." Rochelle reached out. "Are you all right? I should have stopped him, but I didn't know what to do."

"We'll get you checked out right away," Butch said as he leaned down over the body. "Doc Jane should be here any second."

As the Brother dropped on his haunches and examined the gunshot wound, Vishous shook his head and lit up a hand-rolled.

"Holy fuck," the Brother announced, "the *butler* did it?"

# FORTY-ONE

Confirmation bias was one thing, Butch thought as he reemerged from a walk-in freezer the size of a garage.

"But evidence is evidence," he murmured as he looked down at the meat hook in his hand.

Glancing back into the cold storage, he shook his head at the two sides of beef that were hanging in the center of the room-sized freezer unit, ready to be thawed and hacked. The hooks were exactly like the one Mai had been strung up with.

"Did you find what you required, sire?" the household chef asked.

Butch nodded. "Yeah. I did."

The *doggen* bowed. "Is there anywhere else I may show you?"

Thomat had been great: Taking him into a suite of rooms just down the hall, showing him the closet out of which Butch had carefully taken a bloodstained cloak. It had been in the butler's office area that he'd retrieved a small vial of cobbler's nails. He also had the knife from the front foyer and then the firsthand accounts of Helania and Rochelle, Boone's former intended.

"I think I'm good," Butch said as they walked back out into the kitchen proper. "Thanks for the paper bags."

"My pleasure, sire. May I open another up for you?"

"Yeah, that'd be great. Thanks."

The chef flapped one free of its folds and Butch put the meat hook in there. Then he grabbed the two that had the cloak and the knife and headed back to the foyer. Rhage had come late and was making up for his delay by doing the duty with his camera phone, taking pictures of the body and the door.

But like the stuff in the Hannaford bags, all of that was kind of belt-and-suspenders irrelevant. The explanation had been provided, the faith in God's powers of revelation rewarded, the this-then-that-then-the-other-thing finally spelled out. Still, habits of a professional lifetime and all that malarkey.

Setting the bags down, Butch went into the parlor, where Boone was sitting with the two females and Helania was getting checked out by Doc Jane.

"You've got a heck of a knot back here," the doctor was saying. "And you probably have a concussion of sorts, although I can't do any diagnostic imaging to prove that. The good news is your pupils are equal and reactive, and you passed your neurological exam just fine, so I think you'll be right as rain. Just let me know if you see double, feel nauseous, or can't seem to stay awake, okay? And no . . . you don't have to worry about any effects on anything else that may be going on."

"Thank you," Helania said as her hand found her lower abdomen. "I'm grateful."

As the doc gave all three a hug and then took off, Butch shook his head. "I know you guys have got to be in shock."

"That's an understatement," Boone murmured as he stroked Helania's back.

"Listen," Butch said, "I've got a good idea of how things went down tonight, but just so we can close the case, I'll have to ask that you all come into the training center for something official. But we can wait. Tomorrow is fine for that."

"Thank you," Rochelle said. "I'm not thinking straight right now."

"I don't blame you. This is tough stuff. Do you have someone who can come and get you?"

Rochelle frowned. "I really can't bear the thought of going home—"

"You can stay," Boone said. "With us."

"Yes," Helania added. "Please. In fact . . . can we all just stay here for the day? The storm is terrible and my apartment is small."

"Sure," Boone offered. "Doesn't matter to me where we are, as long as we're together."

"Thank you." Rochelle lifted her hands and started pulling pins out of her hair one by one. "That would be . . . thank you."

As she shook her chignon out, took her high-heeled boots off, and repositioned herself with her stocking feet tucked under her, Butch smiled. Nothing like letting your hair down with family who happened to be friends, he thought.

He'd learned that one firsthand.

"Okay," he said. "We're going to remove the body now. I want you guys to stay here, if you don't mind."

"No problem," Boone said as the females nodded.

"And listen, I'm going to get in touch with Mai's parents before the end of tonight. I'll go to their house in person. They're going to want to know what happened."

"Of course," Rochelle said. "That's very good of you. And please feel free to be completely honest. I have nothing to hide, not anymore."

"You got it." Butch then hesitated as he looked at Boone. "You know this house is yours now, right?"

"What?" the male said in surprise.

"Marquist is dead. You're your sire's living next of kin. It's all yours. I know it's not the time to think about it right now, but the law is the law. It is what it is." Butch waved a dismissive hand in the air. "But like I said, that's nothing to think about right now. Don't even know why I felt the need to say something about it."

That last one was bullshit, of course. The bottom line was the kid had been never been anything but perfectly loyal and an all-around stand-up male. And meanwhile, he'd been royally screwed over by his sire and by that butler—and sometimes, fuck it.

You just wanted the good guy to win in the end.

"Call me if you need me," Butch said to them.

Pivoting away, he was striding out of the room when something caught his arm. As he turned around, it was Helania.

"Your sister is really proud of you right now," she whispered. "You've helped give yet another group of people a measure of comfort and the kind of resolution they need to move on."

Butch's breath caught. And he didn't know what to say in return.

But that didn't matter. Helania wrapped him up in a hard hug, and sometimes that communicated everything, didn't it.

As he lowered his head and embraced her in return, he felt, deep inside his chest, the lingering pain he always carried with him . . . lift a little more.

*This one was for you, Janie,* he thought to himself.

Then again, every killer he'd ever found had always been for her.

◆    ◆    ◆

As Boone watched Helania and Butch hug, he was reeling from what the Brother had said about the will. But he supposed Butch was right. With Marquist dead and no other beneficiary named . . . he was the next of kin.

Getting to his feet, he made like he'd gone vertical just to stretch his back, but that wasn't why he'd stood up. He was looking around the parlor with new eyes and had the sense that he was trying on for size the idea of staying put.

Except that was crazy. He didn't want any part of this *glymera* bullshit. He hadn't been a fan of it before, but after what Rochelle and Helania had been through? He was so not interested—

Through the archway, he saw the staff of the house still clustered together in the foyer, Thomat and the dozen or so *doggen* standing in that clutch they'd formed. And they were all looking at him. They had clearly heard what Butch had said.

Because there was hope in their faces.

Loyalty . . . for Boone . . . in their eyes.

"I think they want you to stay," Rochelle said softly.

As Helania came over to him, he opened his arms, and she eased right up against him. They stayed there as Marquist's remains were removed, the big front door opening, the storm's gusts sweeping in and replacing the warmth with cold. But then the Brothers said goodbye, and Boone watched through the parlor window as the surgical van pulled away and proceeded out the drive.

In the wake of the departure, there was the strangest silence in the house, an emptiness that was at once shocking . . . and liberating.

"How'd you like to have something to eat?" Helania asked him. "That's what I was trying to do before . . ."

"Everything went off the rails?" he murmured.

"Yup."

Rochelle stood up. "I think we should try the whole hot-cocoa thing over again."

"Maybe it's bad luck?" Boone offered. "We could give something else a shot."

"Nah, I'm not superstitious," his friend said as the three of them started to walk out of the parlor.

In the foyer, Boone paused and looked at the staff. "Thomat, I think everyone needs a good meal. Some food. Some drink. And by that, I mean . . . the whole household. Together."

As he met the chef's eyes straight on, he was aware that he was laying down a rule. A new operating system. A fresh way of conducting things in the house.

And if the chef didn't agree? Then Boone realized with total clarity that he would walk away. Sell the house and the stuff. Cut a clean break with the sick, twisted, toxic legacy he'd been born into.

Thomat looked around at the other staff. There was some whispering. And then the chef bowed deeply.

"My Lord, we would find that most agreeable. Perhaps we shall adjourn to the kitchen and communally decide upon a menu?"

Boone smiled slowly and put his arm around Helania's shoulders. "Good deal. That's . . . that's just the way I'd like it to be."

Falling into a loose group, everyone headed through the dining room and out into the polishing room and the pantry. As he passed by the opened door of the butler's suite, he leaned in and closed it firmly.

An hour later, they were all seated around the dining room table, passing silver trays and porcelain bowels around, the eclectic meal of leftovers and easy-make sides created by all hands, everyone served by each other, all plates filled with the same food.

Boone sat at the head of the table, with Helania not at the far end, but right beside him. Rochelle was down in the middle, sitting between Thomat and one of the maids. Everybody was talking, and there were occasional laughs, although Boone was aware that they were all still recovering from the extraordinary turn of events.

Helping himself to more mashed potatoes, he looked at Helania.

And found himself wondering whether she was with his young.

That was the only way he would feel better about things. If they had a—

Frowning, he stopped that thought by remembering what she'd said about them getting mated. Talk about a no-win situation. He was in love with her. He had realized that in so many different ways and so many different situations, but he was trapped by the prospect of the pregnancy. If he told her he loved her now? If he asked her to mate him? She'd already made it clear she'd just see it as him meeting a duty. And the problem was . . . even though she might not have noticed herself, he could sense a very subtle change in her springtime scent.

He had a feeling . . . that she was with his young.

"Are you okay?" she asked as she reached out and took his hand.

"Yeah, I'm fine." He forced a smile. "These potatoes are great."

"They're how we made them in my family. The cream cheese makes all the difference."

"You don't say," he murmured, rubbing the hollow pit behind his sternum. "Cream cheese. Who'd have thought."

◆    ◆    ◆

As Helania followed Boone down a long, formally decorated hallway, she looked at all the closed doors and lost count at sixteen.

Incredible, how big the house was.

Finally, he stopped. "So this is my bedroom."

"I'm excited to see it."

"It's nothing fancy." He caught himself and then laughed a little. "I mean, it's not like—oh, whatever, let's just do this."

As he opened the door, she stepped inside to—"Wait, is this a living room?"

"It's the sitting area of the suite."

"Oh." She shook her head ruefully. "Wow. Okay—"

She stopped talking as she looked through an archway on the far wall. Called by what she saw, she walked forward into a dream bedroom. The bed was Boone-sized, for real, a huge king that was draped in monogrammed sheets and covered by a duvet that had some kind of a seal on it in the center. But none of that was what had gotten her attention.

It was the books.

Lining the walls, set into shelving, there were hundreds of books, some modern, some old, some bound with leather, some with cloth. As she stepped up to read the spines, she smiled to herself. Her solution to being quiet had been movies. His clearly was reading.

And she loved that they had introversion in common.

"This is amazing," she breathed as she glanced over her shoulder. "I had no idea you . . ."

She let the sentence drift as she took in his somber expression—

and his sad eyes. Without having to ask, she knew where he'd gone in his mind, and she thought about what Rochelle had told her by the door, right before things had gotten really crazy.

With so much answered tonight, there was still one very open issue. And it was a big one for the both of them.

But she also knew the solution. Had known it . . . pretty much all along, even though she'd been afraid to admit it.

Crossing over to him, she took Boone's hand and led him to his own bed. As they sat down together, he stroked his thumb on the inside of her wrist . . . but he would not look her in the eye. And that sadness of his was a heartbreaker.

Helania swallowed hard. "I'm so glad I met you."

He made a noncommittal noise in the back of his throat.

"And I'm grateful for everything you've done for me in these last couple of . . ." Nights? God, it felt like years. ". . . you know, since I met you. About Isobel. And the case."

Her words were failing her. Her brain wasn't working right.

But her heart knew exactly where she stood.

Shifting over in front of him, she got down on one knee and captured both his hands in her own. Staring up into his surprised eyes, she smiled—and suddenly found every syllable she needed.

"Do you remember when I told you I didn't want you to ask me to mate you?"

He closed his eyes and stiffened. "Yes."

"I said that I would never be sure whether it was out of duty and obligation."

"You did."

"I said that I wanted to be chosen."

He exhaled and popped his lids. "No offense, but we don't need to rehash it all. That was a painful conversation I will not forget anytime soon—"

"Well, I've decided something."

He put his hand out to stop her. "We don't know if you're pregnant. So there's nothing to decide. But I want you to know, if you are, then I am—"

"I love you, and I want to know if you'll be my *hellren.*"

Boone blinked. Then jerked back in surprise. "What? Wait, what did you—"

Helania smiled. "I'm asking you. See, it's different this way. No obligation on your part, as we don't know for sure if I'm pregnant, and I'm doing the choosing. I'm *choosing* you. I'm telling you that I love you and I want you and—"

That was as far as she got.

"I love you, too," Boone said in a rush as he came down onto the carpet and kissed her. "Oh, God . . . yes, please, I will mate you. I don't care if you're pregnant—" He yanked back. "I mean, I do care. I really want you to be."

Helania blinked back tears as she took his dagger hand and placed his big palm on her belly. "I really want to be, too."

"What's changed?" he breathed.

As she thought about everything the last couple of nights had brought, and then remembered her sure shot as she had protected her sister's one true love from a madman, she shrugged.

"Like I told you when you asked me if I could stand on my own downstairs"—she stared into his beautiful eyes—"I've found my two feet. I don't need to be Wonder Woman, and I don't have to always get it right . . . but when you know who you are and that you can take care of yourself, then you're free to love whoever you want honestly and completely. Whether they're a male or a female . . . or a young you birthed of your own body."

Boone's smile was a sunrise that illuminated not just his face, but clearly his soul, too.

"Well," he whispered against her mouth. "If that isn't a blood truth . . . I don't know what is."

# EPILOGUE

Boone traveled through the winter air in a scatter of molecules, tracing the trail Helania left for him by virtue of their having fed from each other. As he re-formed, he found himself in a snow-covered, wooded glen, the forest of pine trees thick until they parted for some explicable reason to create a perfectly circular clearing.

Helania was standing off to one side, her red and blond hair free and teased by a soft breeze, her face somber, her eyes trained on the ground.

When she noticed him, she smiled, the haunted look leaving her stare. "Hi."

"Hi."

Walking through the snow, his boots packed a pattern of prints into the pristine fall of tiny flakes, and as he came up behind his female, she settled back against his body. With his arms wrapped around her, and his eyes on the same spot as hers, he was content to wait until she spoke.

"This is where we buried Isobel," she said after a moment. Then she laughed a little. "In case you haven't figured that out."

Boone kissed the top of his love's head. "Thank you for bringing me here."

"I wish you had known her."

"Me, too. I think I would have loved her."

"Oh, I guarantee you would have."

The wind that traveled through the clearing was gentle and not as frigid as it had been, as if it had warmed itself and slowed down out of respect for the dead.

"I want to believe she's in the Fade," Helania said, " and not just . . . you know, under the earth."

Boone found himself looking up to the sky and measuring the stars that twinkled in the great black expanse overhead. As he considered the chances of him and Helania finding each other, and of Rochelle being who she turned out to be?

"It's like Isobel found one last way of taking care of me," Helania murmured.

"What?"

"I don't know. It's just pretty remarkable, the whole story. You ending up in my life as you did. Rochelle—"

"Being who she is in it all," he finished. "I was just thinking the same thing."

Helania leaned to the side and smiled at him. "I love when we do that."

"Me, too."

She straightened again and refocused on the ground. "And yes, I kind of think my big sister had a hand in all this."

From out of nowhere, a waft of fine French perfume entered the forest, and there she was, Rochelle appearing in the snow. She was in a raspberry coat and heavy, fur-trimmed boots, and as she tromped over, she, too, stared at that spot in the middle of the clearing.

As the female came up to them, Helania reached out and took her hand. "Hello, friend."

"Hello, friend." Then Rochelle sighed sadly. "I'm sorry. It's hard to come here."

"I feel the same way." Helania went back to looking at the ground. "But it's an important night."

"We have some news to share," Boone said. "And we want you to be the first to know."

Rochelle craned around, her eyes lighting up. "No. Are you serious? You're serious?!"

"We're pregnant," Helania said. "We just found out—"

As Rochelle let out a triumphant shout, the happy sound flushed an owl from its perch. "You're pregnant!"

Rochelle all but tackled Helania in a hug, and then the female was squeezing the breath out of Boone. "I'm so happy for you guys! Oh, my God! The two of you are with young."

"Thanks." Boone stepped back. "But listen, there's no 'we' here, okay? Helania's the one who's doing all the work. The whole 'we' thing is nuts. I'm the luckiest male on the planet, and she is carrying my young, but it's her body that's going through it, not mine."

Rochelle threw her head back and laughed. "Laying down the law, I see. Fine. And I like your attitude, Boone."

Helania linked her arm in his. "Yup, me, too. What can I say, he's a keeper."

"We're going to name her Isobel," he said. "If she's a girl. And either way, we want you to hop on a human train with us. They do this thing—"

"It's called godparents," Helania finished. "We want you to be the godmother, no matter what kind we get."

Rochelle's gloved hands went to her cheeks. "You are making me cry right now."

"Please?" Helania said. "You're the closest tie I have to my sister, and I want you in our young's life as an official member of the family."

"Not that you aren't already one," Boone tacked on.

"Amen to that." Helania glanced over at the clearing. "It's why I wanted to tell you here. It's like . . . Isobel's with all of us, you know? Because if she were alive, we would have told the two of you at the same time. So what do you say?"

Rochelle's answer was a group hug.

And really, that was the best affirmative there could be.

As Boone wrapped his arms around the two females who were laughing and crying at the same time, and as he thought about how he was making his own family, something above, in the night sky, got his attention.

Way up in the heavens, a brilliant shooting star was traveling in an arc . . . that made a perfect smile formation directly above them.

Lifting a hand, Boone waved to it as its trail faded and mouthed, *Nice to meet you, Isobel.*

Something told him it would not be the last time, and he was relieved by that. After all, death was not stronger than love, and the signs of angels were all around.

You just had to look for them . . . and know that big sisters always did their duty, even if it was from the Fade.

# ACKNOWLEDGMENTS

With so many thanks to the readers of the Black Dagger Brotherhood books! This has been a long, marvelous, exciting journey, and I can't wait to see what happens next in this world we all love. I'd also like to thank Meg Ruley, Rebecca Scherer, and everyone at JRA, and Lauren McKenna, Jennifer Bergstrom, and the entire family at Gallery Books and Simon & Schuster.

To Team Waud, I love you all. Truly. And as always, everything I do is with love to, and adoration for, both my family of origin and of adoption.

Oh, and thank you to Naamah, my Writer Dog II, who works as hard as I do on my books!

Do you love fiction with a supernatural twist?

Want the chance to hear news about your favourite authors (and the chance to win free books)?

Keri Arthur
Kristen Callihan
P.C. Cast
Christine Feehan
Jacquelyn Frank
Larissa Ione
Darynda Jones
Sherrilyn Kenyon
Jayne Ann Krentz and Jayne Castle
Lucy March
Martin Millar
Tim O'Rourke
Lindsey Piper
Christopher Rice
J.R. Ward
Laura Wright

**Then visit the Piatkus website**
www.piatkus.co.uk

**And follow us on Facebook and Twitter**
www.facebook.com/piatkusfiction | @piatkusbooks

piatkus